PATERNITY

A HAZARD AND SOMERSET MYSTERY

GREGORY ASHE

This book is a work of fiction. Names, characters, places, and incidents either are products of the author's imagination or are used fictitiously. Any resemblance to actual events or locales or persons, living or dead, is entirely coincidental.

Copyright 2018 Gregory Ashe
All Rights Reserved

ISBN #:9781720031895

CHAPTER ONE

DECEMBER 22
FRIDAY
6:47 PM

"Stop yanking on my collar."

"It doesn't look right."

"Your face isn't going to look right if you keep it up."

"You're just—there. See? It's fine. No, wait. Hold on."

"Somers, if you touch me again, I'm going to break your hand."

That threat, at least, brought an impasse. Emery Hazard gave his partner—and roommate—a furious look and, just to be safe, stepped out of reach. John-Henry Somerset, who went by Somers, crossed his arms.

"If you'd just let me—"

"Drop it, all right?"

Somers let out a defeated sigh and held his hands palm out in surrender. He sank back a step, positioning himself near the sofa. Their apartment, with only two bedrooms and a combined living area and kitchen, didn't offer much space for retreat. Somers gave a shake of his head and turned in a circle, his gaze flitting from object to object, as though the apartment's clean, contemporary furnishings had suddenly absorbed his interest.

"What the hell's gotten into you?" Hazard said. He studied his partner. Somers had the slender, toned musculature of a swimmer, and the blond good looks of a swimmer who could sell a hell of a lot of Speedos. Normally, he skated by on those looks; his clothing was frequently rumpled, his hair mussed, his general appearance making Hazard want to shake him—or at least run an iron over his shirt.

Tonight, though, Somers had tried for something more: a blue gingham shirt, a navy sports coat with brass buttons, and dark corduroys that hugged his butt and made it occasionally difficult for Hazard to breathe. The look, however, wasn't quite working: the gingham shirt was creased across the chest, and the buttons were done up wrong, and the hem of his pants was coming out. Somers seemed oblivious to his own condition, however; he fiddled with the buttons on his sports coat, and then a flicker of apprehension crossed his face, and he took a step towards Hazard.

"You don't normally wear your hair like that—"

Hazard planted a hand on Somers's chest and shoved the blond man towards the sofa. "Sit."

"You're being ridiculous."

"I'm being ridiculous?" Hazard didn't bother to wait for a reply, but he did—when he thought Somers wasn't looking—check himself in the mirror. Somers was a damn fool. His hair always looked like that.

"What's Nico wearing?"

"Sweet Christ," Hazard muttered. Then, in a louder voice, he added, "It's one dinner."

"I know what it is, Hazard. I asked you what Nico's wearing."

"I don't know what my boyfriend is wearing, Somers. I haven't seen him today. I've been busy working. You remember work, right?"

"You're just mad because I took a personal day." Somers glanced at the door, thumbing the brass buttons on his sleeve so that they ticked against each other. "Seriously, though: is he wearing a suit?"

Hazard shrugged into his jacket, grabbed his keys and his wallet, and started for the door. Either he left now or he might very well kill Somers, and that wouldn't look good on their quarterly evaluation. Before Hazard could open the door, though, someone knocked. Hazard pulled it open and found Nico standing in the hall, holding flowers.

Nico Flores, with his shaggy black hair and his caramel skin, straddled the threshold between boy and man. He was twenty-five, but a very young twenty-five, and his height and slender build made him look lanky when he loafed around in his ratty clothes.

Tonight, though, there was nothing ratty about Nico—and nothing lanky either. Dressed in a stylish gray suit with a white shirt open at the throat, Nico looked exactly like what he was: a model. True, Nico was more than that—he was a theology grad student and a very smart young man. But he was, at that moment, hot enough to start a fire just by dragging his feet.

"These are for you," Nico said, passing over the flowers.

Hazard kissed him, accepted the bouquet, and said, "I was going to pick you up."

"I know. I wanted to surprise you."

Hazard led Nico into the apartment, passing into the kitchen to find a vase where he could display the flowers. Somers, when he saw them, collapsed back into the chair.

"He's wearing a suit."

Nico glanced at Somers and then at Hazard. "What's he talking about?"

"Forget it."

"A goddamn suit."

Nico glanced down at his clothes. "I thought we were going to—"

"We are. Just ignore him."

It was, however, surprisingly difficult to ignore Somers. He lurched upright and stabbed an accusing finger at the two of them. "It's going to be hard enough with just one of you there. You get that, right? But both of you? And he's wearing a goddamn suit?"

Nico's cheeks colored, and in a whisper he asked, "He doesn't want to go to dinner with a gay couple? Why'd he invite us?"

"He's not homophobic," Hazard answered. Then, in a louder voice, he added, "He's just an insecure asshole."

"I heard that," Somers called.

"Will somebody tell me what's going on?" Nico asked.

"What's going on," Somers said, stalking towards the kitchen and stabbing another finger at them, "is that I'm trying to impress someone tonight, but you show up," he jabbed a finger at Nico, "in a goddamn suit, and you," a finger darted at Hazard, "are doing something stupid with your hair."

Nico cocked a quizzical eyebrow at Hazard.

"I don't know."

"Your hair does look different."

"I told you!" Somer shouted. "I knew it!"

"Jesus Christ. Would you please not encourage him?"

Nico's refined features twisted into a mask of complicated emotions. He didn't like Somers—oh, he'd never said those words, but his feelings were obvious. He was convinced, for some reason, that Somers was infatuated with Hazard. It didn't matter what Hazard said to convince him otherwise. But right then, something was warring with Nico's dislike, and it took Hazard a moment to realize what it was: compassion.

"I don't get it," Nico finally said, still directing his words to Hazard, even though his gaze never left Somers. "He knows he's hot, right?"

Somers, who had begun pacing, paused. His chest puffed out a little.

"I asked you not to encourage him," Hazard said with a sigh.

"Well, he is. And what is this? A date? I mean, she's not going to be looking at either of us. We're gay, right? It's not like we pose any kind of threat."

"Try telling him that."

"Did you at least offer to help him?" Nico asked.

"No," Somers said. "He didn't."

Hazard threw up his hands. "The damn fool was worried about my collar. And my hair." Nico opened his mouth, and Hazard hurried to add, "Which looks the exact same as it always does."

Nico, with an exaggerated roll of his eyes, left the kitchen. Taking Somers by the arm, he steered him to the center of the room. Nico released him, examined him with a critical eye, and said, "Pants off."

"Really?" Hazard asked.

"You could have helped him."

Somers gave Hazard an indignant look. "He's right. You could have helped me."

"Nobody can help you."

In response, Somers whipped off his pants, standing there in a pair of boxer-briefs patterned with hearts. The underwear left almost nothing to the imagination, and Hazard felt his throat dry up.

"You can leave those on for now," Nico said dryly. "I'll fix your hem. Emery, will you please iron his shirt?"

"Hell no."

"Emery Hazard."

"He's a grown man. He can iron his own damn shirt."

"I don't know how to iron my shirt," Somers confided quietly to Nico.

"That's the most pathetic thing I've ever heard," Hazard said. Shaking his head, he crossed the room and waited while Somers slipped out of his jacket and shirt. Underneath, he wore a white tank top that exposed smooth muscle and the dark ink of curling tattoos that ran to his wrists. At the sight of so much bare skin, Hazard felt a squeak growing in his throat. He ripped the shirt out of Somers's hand and went to find the goddamn ironing board.

It really didn't take that long. Nico was back with the pants in a flash, and as he handed them to Somers, Somers said, "How'd you learn that?"

"On the runway," Nico said with a shrug. "You've always got to be ready in case something falls apart at the last minute. Emery, are you done with the shirt?"

"Yes. I'm done with the goddamn shirt."

Nico took it without comment and, after Somers's failed third attempt to button it, began to do up the buttons himself.

"Will you stop looking so goddamned pleased with yourself?" Hazard demanded.

Somers had the decency to try to look abashed, but he didn't get very far.

"There," Nico said, patting Somers on the chest. "You look good."

"Yeah?"

"Jesus, he's a glutton for compliments."

"Really good," Nico said, ignoring Hazard. "Hot stuff. She's going to fall for you hard."

Somers was beaming; it was infectious, which only made Hazard more irritated, and he grabbed Nico by the arm and hustled him towards the door.

"Thanks," Somers called after them.

"Do not answer him."

Once again, Nico ignored Hazard. "See you there."

Only when they were riding down in the elevator did Nico ask, "So who's the girl? I've never seen him so nervous."

It was stupid. It was stupid and selfish and petty. Somers could date whoever he wanted. He could date anyone in the whole world, as far as Hazard was concerned. He could date a serial killer. He could date a fish-woman. He could date the woman who had broken his heart and kept him in limbo for years. Hazard tried to shove the thoughts away, and he didn't like the surge of vicious satisfaction he felt as he answered.

"His wife."

CHAPTER TWO

**DECEMBER 22
FRIDAY
7:00 PM**

WAHREDUA WAS A MIDWESTERN college town, and like so many Midwestern college towns, it had experienced a genuine boom of culture and prosperity at the beginning of the twenty-first century. Moulin Vert was one sign of that prosperity: Wahredua's finest French restaurant, with real candles and real crystal and real snooty waiters, as though they'd been shipped over special. At the door, Hazard helped Nico out of his coat and passed their garments to the coat check.

As one of the black-uniformed staff led Hazard and Nico across the dining room, most of Moulin Vert's patrons stopped to stare. In part, Hazard knew, they were interested in the appearance of a gay couple at one of Wahredua's more conservative establishments. In part, too, they were interested in Emery Hazard, the only gay cop on the force, a local boy who had come home and made a name for himself by solving two sets of brutal and bizarre murders. A lot of it, though, had to do with the fact that Nico was just so pretty; straight or gay, every eye in the room paused and did a little private lusting over the Argentine boy.

Their table stood at the back, with four seats and four places. As they sat, Nico said, "So they're divorced, but they're getting back together again?"

"What does it matter?"

"It doesn't."

"All right."

"So if it doesn't matter, why won't you talk about it?"

Hazard growled, barely managing to swallow the noise. "She never divorced him."

"You don't like her."

"I haven't seen her in fifteen years."

"You hate her."

"I don't have any feelings for her one way or the other."

"That's a lie." Nico smiled to soften the words, and his hand slipped into Hazard's. "What was she like in high school?"

"Popular."

Nico's smile broadened, and he squeezed Hazard's hand.

"I don't know. She was . . . she had a difficult life. We never interacted much. She was very pretty and very popular. I was—" Hazard paused and shrugged.

Nico squeezed his hand again. "You were the only gay boy in town."

Hazard touched the stem of his glass; the crystal was cold, and the cold ran straight up his arm, and it made him think of how cold it was outside, of how he didn't want to be here, in this goddamn restaurant, and how he could drive home and tear that very expensive suit off of Nico piece by piece and spend the rest of the night making his boyfriend forget he'd ever heard of John-Henry Somerset.

"She came from a bad family," Hazard heard himself saying. "Her father was in prison for most of her life. Her mother, well, the rumor was that her mother worked as a prostitute."

"Did she?"

"How the hell should I know? Kids are stupid. They'll say anything, and they'll say it twice as fast if it's mean and if it hurts someone who's better looking or more popular."

"They also say things that are true." Nico wrinkled his nose, and his eyes roamed across Hazard's face. "Your hair is longer."

"God damn it. It's the exact same as always."

"No. It's definitely longer."

At that moment, Somers came across the restaurant towards them with a woman on his arm. She was tall—not quite as tall as Somers, but tall enough that she probably wore flats more often than not. Her hair had changed since Hazard had last seen her; it was short and artfully curled, and it accented the delicate features of her face. Seen from a distance, there was something ethereal about her, in the pallor of her skin against the dark hair and dark dress, as though she were a spirit out of the past. Out of Hazard's past, more precisely. One thing, though, hadn't changed: Cora Malsho Somerset was still beautiful in a way that devastated Hazard. That beauty went through him like a bulldozer. Who in the hell could compete with that kind of beauty? Not Emery Hazard. Not that he wanted to. Not even a little.

They all stood up and shook hands and murmured polite greetings, and then they sat, and silence took over. Hazard knew that once he started looking at Somers, he would have a hard time stopping. Instead he focused on a middle space between Cora and his partner. The silence stretched out. And out. And out.

"God, I could use some wine," Somers said.

Cora looked away, as though embarrassed by the comment. No doubt she was; Somers had gone through a phase of serious drinking after she had kicked him out of the house. Even now, when their fights grew too serious, Somers plunged into a bottle as fast and as deep as he could. Hazard's face heated. And a drunk Somers, it turned out, often had far too few inhibitions.

Nico was the one who broke the tension with a laugh. "We could all use a drink." He raised a hand, signaling their waiter, and glanced at Hazard.

"Whatever you want," Hazard said.

"Emery pretends he doesn't care," Nico said, flashing a smile at Cora. Then he paused. "I know you."

"What?" Somers said.

"What?" Hazard said.

Cora's refined features eased into a smile; it was like watching an iceberg melt. "We've never—"

"No, I know you. You were at Fashion Week. At the Frenzy."

Cora gave a helpless shrug, glancing at, of all people, Hazard. "I was."

"You were amazing. I still can't believe how you handled that old man." Nico burst into a genuine laugh; his heart-stoppingly handsome face brightened. "God, weren't you at Maggie Grober's brunch?"

A blush suffused Cora's face. "Please don't tell me you remember."

Nico, bursting into fresh laughter, elbowed Hazard. "She threw wine in Stefan's face."

Cora held her napkin in front of her face.

"Who the hell is Stefan?" Hazard asked.

"Oh, you know. I was telling you about him and his partner, the ones with the two little dogs. Remember? How they walk them in that park we always drive by? God, you never listen. Anyway, Cora threw wine in his face."

Cora dropped the napkin; her face was flaming now. "He grabbed my—" She cast an embarrassed glance at, again, of all people, Hazard. "He grabbed me, and he was making this awful joke about filling out a dress. I wasn't going to let him get away with that." She laughed, and the sound wasn't anything like what Hazard remembered from high school. This laugh was full-bodied, genuine, and it only made her blush deepen. Wiping her eyes, she said, "I never thought you'd remember me. I know who you are, of course. Everybody knows. But I never thought—I mean, I'm just there to help out."

Leaning in, Nico added in a mock whisper, "And to teach Stefan a lesson."

Again, Cora burst into laughter. As she wiped at her eyes, she spoke to Hazard for the first time in fifteen years. "Everyone knows Nico Flores. When John-Henry told me we were going on a double date, he mentioned Nico's first name, but I never would have put it together."

"Everyone knows him, huh?" Hazard raised an eyebrow at his boyfriend.

Elbowing Hazard again, Nico turned his attention to Cora. "You're friends with Moody, aren't you? The two of you are always together. She's vicious, isn't she? I mean, very funny, but she cuts like a knife."

"You should have heard her when she saw Stefan at the Trustees' Gala," Cora said, muffling giggles with her napkin.

At this point, Hazard leaned back in his chair. Somers, who was seated across from him, let out a breath. Nico and Cora didn't notice; they were too wrapped up in their own conversation. From the sound of it, they shared a surprisingly wide circle of friends—most of whom Hazard would have sworn he had never heard of.

"Do you think we can still get that wine?" Somers asked in a low voice.

Hazard grunted.

"It's going pretty well, right?"

Hazard grunted again.

"Did you know they . . ."

"Yeah, Somers. Of course I knew. I had magically figured out that they were best friends, I just decided not to tell you."

A moment passed, and Somers asked, "Who's Moody?"

"How the hell should I know?"

"You need some wine."

That was starting to sound better and better. Hazard motioned over the waiter again and this time ordered a bottle. The candlelight flashed against the bandage on Hazard's hand, a shining reminder of Hazard's most recent case. Together with Somers, he had been trapped at an estate just outside Wahredua. One murder had spiraled into a series of deaths; Hazard had come close to dying himself after a brutal, physical confrontation. The worst of the bruises had healed, but the deep cut on his hand was still a painful scab.

"How is it?" Somers asked, nodding at the bandage.

"What did I tell you?"

"You said that if I asked you about your hand one more time, you'd shove it down my throat." Somers grinned. "But we're at a very fancy dinner, and even a thug like you has some manners."

Hazard opened his mouth to tell Somers exactly what he could do with his manners, but Nico and Cora's conversation caught his ear. Cora was speaking, her voice low, her hands wrapped together on the table, her eyes studying her hands.

"—didn't know Emery very well, of course, but that's what—" She paused, as though suddenly aware of Hazard's attention. Her eyes, dark and gleaming like polished obsidian, glanced towards him and then away. "I'm sorry. I—this is very awkward for me."

"Why?" Hazard asked. Then he grunted, biting back a swear as Somers kicked him in the shin. Hard. Somers jerked his head angrily, and Hazard forced his voice to a slightly warmer tone. Very slightly. "I mean, I don't know why you should feel awkward."

Cora laughed, and this time it had none of its former humor. "That's very kind of you, Emery. But you don't have to pretend that I wasn't an absolute bitch in high school."

Hazard stared at her. Everyone was waiting for him to respond; he could feel the anticipation. Nico leaned back in his seat, and his hand dropped under the table, his fingers lightly squeezing Hazard's.

"You weren't a bitch," Hazard finally said. "You were a teenager. We all were." His voice turned dry. "Nobody should be held accountable for what they do between fourteen and twenty-one."

With another cold laugh, Cora sipped at her wine. When she spoke, her eyes were still locked on her pale hands. "The things I said about you, Emery—I'd understand if you never wanted to speak to me again. I told John-Henry this wasn't a good idea." She made as if to rise.

Somers latched onto her arm, and he said, "Cora, you don't know Emery. He's not that kind of person. The things I did to him, the things I allowed to happen, Emery should have killed me." A trace of Somers's normal, shit-eating grin appeared. "Most days, he still wants to kill me, although maybe for different reasons. What I'm trying to say is that he's a good man. The best man I know. And I want you to know him too."

Something flashed in Cora's face. Hazard wasn't particularly good at reading other people's emotions, but he thought he recognized this one: hope. The realization left him unnerved, as though he'd lost his footing in the conversation. Why the hell did she look like Somers had just tossed her a lifeline? Because she'd made a few nasty comments about Hazard in high school? Was she really the kind of person who carried that kind of guilt for fifteen years?

They were waiting for Hazard to speak, he realized. His jaw felt rusty as he opened his mouth, and the words bounced off his teeth with tinny, hollow sounds. "I'm not a good man, but Somers is right about one thing: I'm done with that part of my life. Let's leave the past in the past." Hazard paused, fighting the selfish part of himself, the part that wanted Somers all to himself, the part that wanted him to snap at Cora with every cruel thought he'd ever had. Then, forcing the words out, he added, "I hope you'll do the same."

Cora glanced at Somers and then at Hazard. She nodded slowly.

Nico squeezed Hazard's fingers fiercely. Then, as though that weren't enough, he bent over and kissed Hazard's cheek.

"You are amazing," he whispered. The fresh stubble on his cheek scraped Hazard as he pulled away.

No one seemed to know what to say next. Somers and Cora both drank deeply of their wine. Nico leaned against Hazard, the tips of his fingers playing against Hazard's. A low thrum interrupted the silence, and Somers pulled out his mobile phone. His eyes widened, and he glanced at Hazard and then Cora.

"It's my father."

"Go on," Cora said.

Somers nodded, as though barely hearing her. He punched something on the screen, put the phone to his ear, and lurched away from the table. The glasses rattled as Somers caught one of the table's legs with his heel. "Father," he said as he walked towards the door. "What's wrong?"

Nico's dark, deep eyes rested on Hazard. "Is his father ill?"

Hazard shook his head.

"He seemed upset."

Yes, Hazard thought. Yes, Somers was probably upset. In fact, scratch that: Somers was definitely upset. Hazard only knew the outline of Somers's relationship with his father, and much of that was guess-work, but certain elements seemed clear. For one, Somers never spoke with his parents. For another, Glennworth Somerset, his father, seemed like just about the coldest asshole this side of Antarctica. And there were other things, things that Somers had hinted at when he'd drunk too much.

Hazard realized that Cora was studying him with her dark, glittering eyes. Hazard was speaking before he realized it. "You know better than I do."

Cora shrugged. "I'm not sure that I do. John-Henry's parents all but disowned him when we got married. They softened a little when we had Evie, and they all but welcomed John-Henry back into the viper's nest when we separated. His father called me a few times. He's an attorney, not that he's ever done much besides draw up a few contracts and cash a lot of checks. But he called a few times, threatening to sue me, threatening to sue for custody of Evie, threatening to sue for the house. I thought John-Henry had put him up to it. That was when things were at their worst between us.

"Then, one day, I ran into them at the store. I don't even remember which one. It was a clothing store, I think. Probably the Nordstrom's. You'd think I would remember. I don't know what I was thinking, but I walked right up to John-Henry and I told him that he could sue me, he could take everything I had, but that he'd never get Evie. I turned around, ready to march out of that store and never look back, but I stopped because I heard—" She paused, tracing the rim of the wine glass with a slack finger. "When I turned around, Glennworth Somers had a bloody lip, and John-Henry was shaking his hand. I didn't know what to do. I couldn't believe what had happened. I ran; it was like I'd done something wrong, like I'd been the one who punched him. I never—I've never talked to John-Henry about that. Never. But I knew that he wasn't the one making those threats."

Somers reappeared in the doorway, and Nico's eyes narrowed. "He's much more complicated than he seems, isn't he?" Nico said. "I mean, he's so . . . he acts like a frat boy sometimes, and the way he talks, the way he stands. But he's not what I thought. Tonight, for example."

"Tonight?" Cora said. "What about tonight?"

Nico shook his head, and before Cora could ask again, Somers had reached their table. He crooked a finger at Hazard.

"We've got a call."

"We're off rotation tonight."

"Well, we caught one."

"What happened?"

"Will you come on already?"

Hazard studied his partner. "What the hell could have happened? Are Lender and Swinney already on another call? All the patrol guys—"

"Will you get off your fucking ass," Somers shouted, and then he broke off, reining in his voice. In a harsh whisper, he continued, "Will you get off your ass and come with me? We've got a call. What else do I have to say?"

The Moulin Vert had gone silent; everyone, from the stuffy waiters to the even stuffier guests, paused and stared at Hazard's table. Somers seemed to notice the attention; his face colored, and he rolled his shoulders. Swearing under his breath, he stalked towards the door. Conversation began to resume, voices breaking into low, excited murmurs.

Fishing the keys out of his pocket, Hazard said, "Can you take her home?"

"You're going with him?" Nico asked, a mixture of shock and anger tightening his face. "After he talked to you like that?"

"I can take a cab," Cora said.

"I'm going with him because we have a call. Can you take her home?"

"I'll take an Uber."

"Well?" Hazard dropped the keys into Nico's hand.

"Yes, fine," Nico said. "I'll take her."

Planting a kiss on Nico's cheek, Hazard squeezed his hand and trotted towards the door. Part of him was aware of the stares that followed him. The town faggot had gotten in a fight with his cop partner. The town faggot had kissed his boyfriend in public. The town faggot—Christ, that was never going to stop. He'd be dead and buried and they'd probably put up a sign marking the town faggot.

But most of his mind had already raced ahead, towards Somers. In their time together as partners, Hazard and Somers had passed through some difficult and dangerous times. Nothing had ever made Somers act this way. Hazard wasn't given to premonition; he wasn't particularly good at reading the emotions of the men and women around him. Even he could tell, though, that something had deeply upset Somers, and Hazard wondered what it could possibly be.

CHAPTER THREE

DECEMBER 22
FRIDAY
7:27 PM

SOMERS SLAMMED DOWN THE ACCELERATOR, and the Ford Interceptor leaped forward. It was a new car, purchased by the department to replace the Impala that Somers had destroyed by driving it—albeit unintentionally—into a flooded river. Under other circumstances, an act like that might have cost Somers his job; at the least, it should have planted him firmly behind a desk. Instead, Somers had cracked a string of grisly murders, and in addition to winning him public acclaim, it had diverted the worst of the administration's anger.

The Interceptor, a black SUV with buttery leather seats and the lingering aroma of new car, plowed through Wahredua's snow-choked streets without a problem. Thank God for that; Somers was driving like a madman, and as he took the corners of the cramped riverside streets, only the Interceptor's excellent tires kept them from skidding into the cars parked along the side of the road. Without taking his eyes from the road, Somers punched at the radio, cranking the dial. Static pounded through the car, along with squelched bursts of country music, until Somers settled on a station. Heavy metallic music rattled the windows; Hazard's head rang from the noise.

With a flick of his hand, Hazard silenced the stereo. "What's going on?"

"I was listening to that."

"No, you were trying to blow out your eardrums. And mine too. What happened?"

"You turned off my fucking music. That's what happened."

"Was it something with Cora? Did I say something? Did Nico—"

"Don't be an idiot."

"Somers, either tell me what's going on or stop the car."

In answer, Somers dropped his foot on the accelerator. Gray snow sailed up on either side of the car, the slush hissing and slapping at the Interceptor's frame.

This was unusual. No, beyond unusual: it was out of this world strange. Somers never acted like this. Somers was always the cheerful one, the optimistic one, the positive one. He was always, definitely, the kind one. And here he was, acting like a prime cut of asshole, which meant that something had gone topsy-turvy in Hazard's world.

Hazard, to his own surprise, found himself reaching out to lay a hand on Somers's shoulder. "Hey. What's going on? Is someone hurt? Is it your dad? Your mom?"

Somers barked a laugh, but some of the iron had left his voice when he spoke. "I know I'm acting like an asshole. I want to be an asshole right now. Can you give me five minutes? Five minutes that I get to be an asshole."

"Yeah," Hazard said, dropping his hand. "Five minutes."

"Nico's a little bitch."

"Whoa."

"Who the hell does he think he is, sneaking into that dinner, nosing around Cora like he—like he knows her. Talking to her like that. I brought Cora there so she'd talk to you, not to the overgrown baby that you're dating. And instead, what does she do? She spends a fucking half hour talking to Nico like whatever he does is the most interesting thing in the whole goddamn universe. You know what he is? He's not a baby. A baby is something you care about. He's—he's irrelevant. He's totally irrelevant to you. You think that's who you're supposed to be with? A horny grad student who can't pick up his own dirty socks? Come on, Ree. I'm sick of you dicking around like this."

"When your five minutes are up," Hazard said, cracking his knuckles, "we're going to talk about this."

"And you: why won't you admit that your hair is different? What the hell is going on with you? Tonight, what was that about? You haven't seen Cora in, how long? Twenty years? Twenty years, and you can't do more than say hello, shake her hand like it's a dead fish, and then pretend like she's not there the rest of the evening?"

Hazard dropped back into his seat, watching the dashboard clock. The Interceptor launched out of Wahredua, rattled across the old MP tracks, and plunged into the darkness beyond. At this time of year, when darkness came early, Warhedua looked like the last place of light and warmth in a burned-out world. Ahead of them, the sodium lights dropped away until the only thing illuminating the asphalt was the Interceptor's headlights, bluish-white, the color of fresh snow if it had somehow transformed into light.

"You know," Somers continued, his voice still biting and low, "I thought maybe things had changed. I thought my life was going to be different. All this press from the Windsor case. Cora. But then my father calls, and it's like the world stopped turning twenty years ago, like I'm just this kid who won't take out the trash or do my homework. Like he's going to say jump, and I better damn well jump high enough to impress him, and that's a joke because he's never been impressed in his whole life. Not by me, anyway."

"Your time's up. Either apologize about Nico or get ready for a broken jaw."

Somers blinked rapidly into the blue luminescence from the dash. The muscles along his jaw tightened, relaxed, tightened, relaxed. He probably could have bitten through an engine block like it was cream cheese.

"I shouldn't have said that about you. You were really kind to Cora. She was so sure that you were going to—"

"I don't give a fuck about that. Apologize about Nico."

The muscles in Somers's jaw flexed and released, again and again. His fingers fanned out along the steering wheel. "Look, I'm pissed about my dad, and I took it out on you. I hate feeling like this, you know? And I hate the way I just acted. I hate that I said those things—"

"Somers, you better goddamn apologize about Nico right now, or you won't be able to apologize until they unwire your teeth in about six months."

For a moment—a long moment, maybe thirty seconds—Hazard was sure that Somers wouldn't apologize. There was so much anger in his face, so much tension. Then he braced the heels of his hands on the steering wheel, forcing himself back into the seat as though bracing for a collision. He sucked in a breath, shook his head, and said, "I'm sorry I said that he was—"

"No. Don't qualify it."

"I'm sorry."

"Don't do that again."

"What I said about you—"

"Jesus, Somers. Don't you get it? I don't care. I have never given so much as a goddamn second to caring what you say about me, what you think about me, any of it. Drop it and tell me what's going on."

"But you care what I say about Nico?"

"What the hell is going on?"

"I don't know. All right? That's the thing that pisses me off. I don't know what's going on. Here's what I know: I haven't talked to my father in six months. And you know how I know that it's been six months? Because that was the last time my father got pulled over for speeding, and he just about ripped out Miranda Carmichael's throat when she pulled him over. I had to dance like a cat with its tail on fire to keep her from dragging him to jail. You know Miranda; she's a rock, and she wasn't going to put up with that behavior.

"And when I've finally got it all sorted out, when I've promised Cravens that I'll pull doubles and when I've promised Carmichael a month of lunches and when I've finally put the whole damn mess to bed, what happens? I'll tell you what: nothing. Nada. Silence. My father might as well be on the moon. Until tonight, that is. He calls me up. He tells me to get over to the house. 'We have a disturbance.' Those were his words. And then he told me, again, to get over to the house. I said he should call the police. He said—" Somers broke off, taking a shuddering breath.

"He said what?"

"Never mind. The important part is that he's got me by the balls. Again. And here I am, running across town to put out one of my father's little fires. I don't know what the problem is, but here I go."

"Here we go," Hazard amended.

"Yeah," Somers said, his voice softening. "Thanks."

"Why didn't he call the police?"

"Because as usual, my father prefers to handle things like a gentleman, which means not involving the authorities."

"You don't count?"

"I'm family. I'm expected to keep my mouth shut and make problems disappear. Another cop wouldn't do that. And don't give me that look. I'm not crooked, Hazard. But I sure as hell have pulled every string I can pull. I've pulled them until they've just about snapped off in my hands. Tonight's just going to be one more time."

"You don't want to do this," Hazard said, "so let's not do this. Let's go back to the restaurant. I'll call Nico. They might still be there; God knows they were having enough fun without either of us."

Somers shook his head. The anger in his face had dissipated. His eyes, a deep blue, like tide pools, looked darker than ever, like the water at the bottom of the ocean, where blue became black. Those eyes looked bruised. Haunted.

"Somers, what did he—"

"I'm sorry I was such an asshole."

Hazard tried to think of the best response to this. For all his openness and cheer, Somers still had boundaries—narrower than most, perhaps, but still strong. Finally Hazard settled for a copy of the smirk he normally saw on Somers's face. "You got your five minutes. Now how do you explain the rest of your life?"

A very small grin cracked the corners of Somers's mouth.

They turned off the state highway and onto a private drive. It carried them around a low hill, and then the Somerset home appeared. In darkness, after all these years, the place was nothing like what Hazard remembered. He had never been invited to Somers's house; the school's golden boy and the town faggot had crossed paths only—

—in the locker room, with Hazard's skin prickling under Somers's caress—

—when Somers and his friends had decided to make Hazard's life hell. But Hazard had seen the house: an impressive, sprawling brick construction that, in hindsight he realized, had been meant to look Victorian. That memory of ruddy brick and black shutters could not have prepared him for the blaze of light that awaited on the other side of the hill. The Somerset home glowed like a fallen star: white tinged with blue and green and red, the bulbs pulsing and flickering in time to some unheard music. Somehow, though, it managed to remain tasteful; anyone else, Hazard guessed, would have ended up with something that looked like glowing Yuletide vomit.

Expensive cars lined the circular drive, a series of darkly-colored BMWs and Mercedes that wore snow like ermine, the cars of rich old men who had gathered to enjoy the company of other rich old men. Somers slammed the brakes as they got to the middle of the drive, directly in front of the house, and he swung the Interceptor at an angle across the slush-covered asphalt.

"Do you want me to handle this?" Hazard asked.

"No thanks."

Somers had already come around the Interceptor by the time Hazard got his feet on the ground. Even outside the house, the air was full of the smells of pine and cinnamon and rum. Hazard hurried to catch up to Somers; his footsteps made squelching noises in the softening snow, and the sound made an odd counterpoint to the muffled music that came from inside the house. By the time Hazard had reached the porch, though, Somers had stopped.

He had stopped dead, in fact, and his face had hardened. Then Hazard saw what had made his partner stop.

The door was open, and shouts echoed inside.

CHAPTER FOUR

**DECEMBER 22
FRIDAY
7:45 PM**

HAZARD PULLED HIS .38 SPECIAL from the shoulder holster where he kept it, while Somers reached to the small of his back and retrieved his Glock .40 caliber. The crackling tension between them dropped away; the familiar, unspoken precision of their movements took over. Extraneous details became muffled: the holiday jazz, the scent of pine boughs, the creak of the porch as Hazard shifted his weight. What came into focus were the .38 in his hand and the door.

Hazard kicked the door, and Somers rushed past him. Hazard entered at a diagonal to Somers's path, taking the opposite corner. As he entered the foyer, screams filled the air. Hazard found himself scanning a pair of older women in glittering evening gowns, both frozen with terror, and an older man who was howling like he'd had his balls shot off. The shouting that Hazard had heard from outside continued, although now Hazard could tell that it came from deeper inside the house.

"What the hell is going on?" Somers snapped, easing out of a shooting stance and lowering his gun.

Hazard continued studying the foyer, not quite ready to relax. Rooms opened in three directions, and a staircase led up to an open landing. One doorway led into a large room with sofas, a fireplace, and a Christmas tree surrounded by brightly wrapped presents. The room opposite it seemed to be a formal dining room. Ahead of

Hazard, towards the back of the house, the foyer opened onto a much larger space with an even larger Christmas tree and more sofas and chairs. Pine garlands ribboned down the staircase, filling the air with their fragrance, and the syrupy sweetness of rum threatened to drown the house.

"What the hell?" another man's voice called, growing louder as the shouting died. "This is absolutely ridiculous—oh. It's you."

The man who stood opposite Somers did not really look like him, but Hazard still recognized Glennworth Somerset. He shared something of Somers's chin and eyes, but otherwise he was quite different. Hazard remembered Glenn as a stout, dark-haired man who wore too-tight polos and too-shiny loafers. Over the last fifteen years, Glenn Somerset had grown even stouter, with the heavy stomach and thin arms and legs of a man who had eaten himself out of proportion. His dark hair had gone gray, and a second chin wobbled as his gaze settled on Somers. Yes, those ocean blue eyes were definitely Somerset eyes: once or twice, Hazard had seen the same cold, superior rage in Somers's eyes that he now saw in Glenn's.

"It took you long enough, didn't it?" Glenn snapped. "Shut the door. You weren't raised in a barn." And then, without waiting for a response, he turned to the other man, whose screeching had finally stopped, and added, "For heaven's sake, Rudy, have some dignity." With that comment, Glenn marched deeper into the house.

Hazard hooked the door with his heel and shut it. More men and women began to drift to the doorways, observing the tail end of the scene that had just played out, and as the stragglers appeared, Hazard holstered his gun. There had to have been at least fifty people—some had even appeared on the upstairs landing, staring down in confusion—and they buzzed with low, excited conversation.

"Come on," Somers said, holstering the Glock and heading deeper into the house.

As they passed through the building, Hazard found his initial impression of the Somerset home reinforced but also deepened: the sweetness of the rum was tempered by cinnamon and nutmeg and clove, by the smell of sweat and cashmere and silk; a woman's deep voice swung on the stereo, rasping out Christmas songs; and sweat prickled on Hazard's back in a mixture of warmth and adrenaline. Beyond the enormous Christmas tree, french doors looked out on an illuminated patio. Outside, electric heaters glowed cherry-red against the night, warming an expanse of winter where a few of the bolder party guests stood, their glasses glittering like stars in the darkness.

Through the next door lay a kitchen full of gleaming marble counters and appliances big enough to feed a few dozen people, and Somers passed through the kitchen and into another large room with yet more sofas and yet another Christmas tree.

Here, a smaller group had gathered—three men, all roughly the same age, all dressed in tuxedos and wearing the look of men who'd been serving up shit for everybody else to eat for the last forty years and made a real killing at it. Glenn Somerset was one of them, and the second man looked familiar, and the third, with a shock of snowy hair and liver spots along his jawline, was Sherman Newton, Wahredua's current mayor and, Hazard was fairly certain, a man who had killed for profit at least once and who had also tried to kill both Somers and Hazard. All of the men were staring at a naked Santa Claus.

Glenn's eyes flicked at Hazard and Somers for a moment before returning to their object of contemplation. Seated in a straight-backed chair, naked except for the traditional red-and-white cap, sat a middle-aged man whose paunch spilled over his bare thighs. Several days' growth of beard covered the man's cheeks and jowls with graying stubble, and he reeked, a peppery, oniony smell that made Hazard's eyes water. Twitching and muttering to himself, the man shifted on the chair, his dilated eyes roving around the room without seeming to see anything.

"I didn't realize it was this kind of party," Somers said.

"Don't act like a fool," Glenn said, his eyes flicking to Somers for a moment before resting on the naked Santa again. "Will you get him out of here? Use the back door. I've been humiliated twice tonight; I don't need a third time."

"What happened?" Hazard said.

Glenn turned towards Hazard. His eyes were the same ocean blue as Somers's, but hard, like the ocean had frozen solid. Those eyes stared at Hazard for several rapid heartbeats before moving away in silent, utter dismissal, as though Hazard weren't even there. An uncomfortable silence filled the room.

"I asked you—"

Somers put a hand on Hazard's chest. "What happened?"

"John-Henry," the mayor rumbled. He had a deep, patrician voice like he'd spent most of his life at Yale or God only knew where, and he used it to good effect. "Just look at him, son. What do you think happened? He's high on who knows what, and he broke in here acting like a lunatic. Your father and Sheriff Bingham had to wrestle him to the ground."

The sheriff. Hazard knew he'd recognized the third man, but it wasn't until now that the realization clicked. Sheriff Bingham was a tall man. Thin. He'd been sheriff for thirty years, maybe, and he'd been tall and thin for all of them, a kind of whipcord, rawhide thin, like a millstone had ground any traces of joy and life from his bones. In the months since Hazard had returned to Wahredua, he'd seen the sheriff once or twice, but for the most part the city police and the county sheriff's department kept their distance from each other. Now it was something of a shock as the sheriff spoke up. "He had a gun, John-Henry. What were we supposed to do?"

"No one said anything about what you were supposed to do," Hazard said, but Somers was already shaking his head.

"Please ask . . . him," Glenn said, "to wait in the car. It's bad enough that you brought him here."

"If you have something to say—" Hazard began.

To his surprise, Somers cocked his head at the kitchen. "Let me talk to you for a minute."

Hazard followed, and when they had left that damn room with its third goddamn Christmas tree, Hazard planted himself against the goddamn marble counter and crossed his arms. "Did you hear what he just said?"

"Can you let me handle this?"

"He wants me to wait in the car. Like I'm what, your dog?"

"Ree, it's not that simple, I—"

"It's really simple. Either I'm your partner, or I'm a damn dog. Which is it?"

Neither man spoke for a moment, and then Somers threw up his hands. "Christ, you're my partner. Do I really have to say that?"

"That's not what it looks like in there."

"This is complicated, all right? My dad—"

"How about I make it abso-fucking-lutely uncomplicated? Give me your keys."

Somers sighed.

"Give me the damn keys."

"Can you just wait here while I talk to my dad?"

"You aren't going to give me the keys?"

"I'll find out what happened, we'll take naked Santa to the station, and this will be over."

"Fine. I'll stand in the snow."

"Don't be like this, Ree"

Hazard ignored him, marching towards the front of the house. In the largest room, with a Christmas tree that looked like it had been yanked straight off a mountain, Hazard stopped. Two large tables lined one wall, and food covered both tables: turkey, ham, sweet potatoes, potatoes au gratin, rolls, and on and on. More food than even the industrial Somerset kitchen could have produced. Hazard's stomach grumbled; he hadn't had dinner because of this damn interruption, but he sure as hell wasn't going to eat Somerset food. He took another firm step towards the door. He was going to stand out in the snow until his feet froze off, and if Somers didn't like it, he could—

Pie. Hazard forgot where he was going. He forgot to keep walking. He had missed a third table. Pies upon pies upon pies. Enough pies to keep a clown college practicing their throws for a solid week. Before he realized it, Hazard found himself loading a plate with ham and potatoes and dressing, and then he loaded a second plate with pie: apple, pecan, chocolate cream. In one corner of the room, near a darkened hallway, an empty armchair stood by itself. Hazard settled himself in the armchair, grateful that the enormous Christmas tree provided something of a screen, and began to eat. It was Somers's fault that Hazard had missed dinner; this made up for some of it. As Hazard chewed a bite of honey-baked ham, though, a finger found his shoulder. It traced the length of his collarbone and then outlined the swell of his bicep.

"And who is this drink of tall, dark, and handsome?"

CHAPTER FIVE

**DECEMBER 22
FRIDAY
7:53 PM**

SOMERS WATCHED HAZARD STORM OUT of the kitchen. The big man was always so careful with his movements, but right then, he looked like a hurricane on a bad day; Somers was half-surprised Hazard didn't tear down the house on his way out. Swallowing a sigh, Somers turned back to face his father. Better that Hazard be angry than that Hazard learn what Glenn Somerset believed about him. Even Hazard in hurricane-mode was better than that.

As Somers returned to the TV room, as it was called in the Somerset house, he forced himself to take a deep breath. And then another. It didn't do a thing. Not a damn thing. But he did it anyway, hoping to ease the strain in his chest, where he felt as if someone had wrapped rebar around his ribcage and was clamping it tighter and tighter. Yeah, right, a deep breath. What the hell was that?

Somers's father still stood with Sheriff Bingham and Mayor Newton, forming a triangle around the naked Santa. Santa was high; that much was obvious. He was also, to judge by his condition, either unstable or mentally ill. He seemed to have no idea where he was, and he also seemed untroubled by his current situation. Somers approached the man, lowered himself to eye level, and asked, "My name is Detective Somerset. Can you tell me your name?"

The naked Santa smacked his lips and rolled his head on his neck.

"Hey," Somers said, raising his voice, "your name. Who are you?"

"For heaven's sake," Glenn said. "Can't you do this at the station? You know how important this party is, John-Henry. You know the kind of work that goes into it—not that you ever troubled to help, but still, you know what your mother goes through trying to put this together. I'd think the least you could do is get this thing out of here so that we can try to salvage the rest of the night."

"Now, Glenn," Mayor Newton said in his thousand-dollar voice, "take it easy on the boy. It's not his fault this happened."

As though in response, Santa smacked his lips again.

"Take care of this," Glenn said. "Morris. Sherman. I'm not standing here a moment longer. My son," he laid special emphasis on the word, "can handle things from here."

The sheriff eyed Somers as he followed Glenn out of the room. Mayor Sherman, however, lingered. As always, the mayor wore a genial expression, as though he were an elderly uncle with a soft spot for rascals. Somers had seen that expression for most of his life—the mayor was an old family friend—and Somers had known, for most of that time, that the mayor's good-natured appearance was just that: an appearance. Mayor Sherman Newton might look like he spent his days puttering around his office, handing out gumballs to small children and kissing babies, but the reality, Somers knew, was that Sherman Newton had cut plenty of throats to get where he was. And he'd likely cut plenty more if he felt it necessary.

Somers's most recent case, carried out while he and Hazard had been trapped at a vacation property known as Windsor, had touched one strand in Mayor Newton's web: the murder of a wealthy real estate investor had led to Mayor Newton's own development firm gaining control of valuable intellectual property. Someone—Somers and Hazard were unable to prove who—had sent a hired killer to eliminate everyone at Windsor, as a way of erasing any possible witnesses. And this man, standing in front of Somers in a two-thousand-dollar suit and shoes that had been hand-made in Italy, was most likely the one who had sent that killer.

As though sensing Somers's train of thought, Newton gave a quavering smile, produced a cough drop from one pocket, and unwrapped it. He popped it between his lips, and his jaw closed with a crack. Then, without a word, Newton nodded at Somers and sauntered out of the room.

Somers, alone with Santa Claus, stared after the trio of old men. Then he turned to Santa Claus. The naked man was picking at scabbed sores, muttering to himself as his head jerked up and around, trying to catch sight of something invisible to Somers.

What now? Take this poor guy into the station, lock him up in the drunk tank, and keep him until Christmas rolled past? Somers blew out a frustrated breath. Glenn Somerset probably would have preferred for Somers to take Santa out back and put a bullet between his eyes. Less mess, that's what his father would have said. And where the hell had Hazard gone?

Casting a last glance around the TV room—God, what a pretentious name—Somers gave Santa a conspiratorial grin. "Hang out here for a minute, all right?" Then he snapped a cuff around one of Santa's wrists and fastened the other end to the chair.

Santa didn't seem to notice. Instead, he gave a triumphant cry, plucked something from his thigh, and held it up to the light. It looked like an ingrown hair.

CHAPTER SIX

DECEMBER 22
FRIDAY
7:57 PM

SOMERS MADE HIS WAY through the kitchen and back into the family room, which was big enough for a family of about two hundred. The Christmas tree was twenty feet tall. Maybe taller. It was hard to tell, and Somers couldn't bear the thought of asking his father. Glenn Somerset wouldn't lie about something like that. Glenn Somerset might not lie about anything. That was the whole goddamn problem.

From the looks of it, most of the party had drifted into the family room, mingling in clusters around the tree, the buffet, the fireplace—complete with a real fire—and, of course, the bar. The normal congregants made up tonight's celebration: middle-aged men and women of a certain social standing and a certain degree of prosperity, universally white, with the exception of Jeremiah Walker. Walker, a professor of economics at Wroxall, was one of the few people of color who had penetrated the inner circle of Wahredua's elite. He'd had a son, an illegitimate child with a white co-ed, and the mother and child had hung around Wahredua. The boy had even gone to school with Somers. Hollace Walker. Hollace, who had bought the coke that one night, all those years ago.

There was Hazard. And there was Somers's mother, running her finger down Hazard's arm like she wouldn't mind eating him up in two bites. Perfect. Tonight was just going perfectly. Somers shot across the room, ignoring those who called his name or tried to catch his attention.

Grace Elaine Somerset was pretty, but Somers had grown up under the impression that she was beautiful: there were so many pictures of her, so many goddamn mirrors, so many pots and creams and powders and pencils, so many versions of Grace Elaine. There was the doting mother, the doting wife, the philanthropist, the church lady, the PTO president—on and on. A different Grace Elaine for every day of the week, plus two on Sundays. And Grace Elaine had aged with the same purposefulness and planning that marked everything she did. Now, with perfectly ashen hair and surgically smooth skin, she looked like she inhabited some middle ground between thirty and fifty—like a butterfly, impossible to pin down without killing the effect.

By the time Somers reached them, Hazard had gotten to his feet. He was holding what looked like two plates and an ungodly amount of pie, which he juggled as he tried to shake Grace Elaine's hand. Grace Elaine, for her part, studied Hazard with chilly rigor. When Hazard tried to let go of her hand, Grace Elaine's fingers tightened.

"Detective Hazard," she said in a kitty-cat voice. "You've really been a very naughty boy, you know. When John-Henry told us that you'd come back and that you were partners, we expected at least a courtesy call. After all, we're such very old friends."

Hazard's natural pallor gave way easily to a flush. "Hello, Mrs. Somerset. We've never met before."

"Don't be silly. You went to high school with John-Henry. I've seen you hundreds of times. At school. Around town." She paused, and the kitty claws came out. "At John-Henry's football games."

"That's enough, Mother."

"John-Henry, darling. I didn't think you were coming."

"I wasn't coming. Father pitched a fit."

"You really shouldn't say those kinds of things about your father." Grace Elaine still hadn't released Hazard's hand. She leaned towards Hazard now. The cut of her ashen hair swept across her shoulders. "Detective, you won't listen to all the horrible things John-Henry says about us, will you?"

Hazard risked a glance at Somers, and Somers was surprised to see panic in his partner's eyes. "Somers—I mean, John-Henry—"

With a ringing laugh, Grace Elaine cut him off. "Oh, dear. I know what you call him, Detective. There's no need to change on my account."

"Mother, leave him alone."

"Leave him alone? A guest in my home, who doesn't know anyone? That's not very hospitable, John-Henry."

"Leave him alone."

"We were just talking about old times."

"Drop it, Mother."

"You know. About your football games. Emery—I may call you Emery?—Emery just adored those football games, didn't you?"

"That's enough," Somers snapped. He seized his mother by the wrist and hauled her away from Hazard. When they were a safe distance away, Somers said, "I expected this from Father, but not from you."

Massaging her wrist, Grace Elaine pulled free from Somers's grip. Her smile could have blasted a hole in a steel plate. "Darling, you're acting sensationally. He's an old friend. We're just catching up."

"You don't have any friends, and even if you did, Hazard wouldn't be one of them. You're playing with him, Mother. I don't know what you're planning, but I know you've got something that will hurt him. You wouldn't be talking to him if you didn't."

Grace Elaine didn't answer, but the corners of her smile sharpened.

"I'm telling you right now: stay away from my partner."

"John-Henry, you never could tell me what to do. I owe the pretty detective a debt. Don't you remember? It's been such a long time, but I do plan on paying him back." The smile sharpened even further. "With interest."

Before Somers could respond to the threat, Grace Elaine waved at Walker and drifted towards him, and they passed together through the kitchen door. Somers stood there, unwilling to stare after her, unwilling even to look at her. That goddamn party. He rubbed at his eyes. Why had he let everything go to shit at that goddamn party? And why had he let Emery take the fall for it? Bing had been such an asshole about the whole thing, and—

"You want to tell me what all that was about?" Hazard asked, his low, rumbling voice breaking through Somers's thoughts.

Somers scrubbed at his eyes once more and then opened them. "How much pie did you eat?"

Hazard, his eyes flashing to the half-eaten meal, lowered the plate. "Your mom looked like she wanted to eat me for dinner. Or carve off my skin. Maybe both. What the hell was that?"

That? Somers wanted to laugh. That was a nice family evening at the Somerset home. That was nothing. It was the icing on a cake the size of the Eiffel Tower. "Nothing," he finally said. "It was a misunderstanding."

"Sure. She looked like she was just about to misunderstand me out of my clothes."

"Jesus, man. That's my mom."

"I'm gay. What the hell are you worried about?"

"Nothing. It's just. I don't know, just shut up, will you?"

"Where's the coked-out Santa?"

Somers jerked a thumb over his shoulder. "I left him in the TV room."

"The what?"

"It's just a name."

"You call that enormous space at the back of the house the TV room?"

"Can we please talk about this another time?"

To Somers's relief, Hazard obliged him by falling silent. Around them, the party had picked up momentum: another Ella Fitzgerald song was rolling over the stereo, and several couples had taken to dancing at the center of the family room. Laughter punctuated bright bubbles of conversation. Somers realized that his initial impression of the party had been somewhat skewed: yes, much of the crowd was the traditional set that appeared at all of his parents' dinners and parties, but there were a few younger people. Three of them, in fact, looked strangely out of place this evening. And one of them—

"That girl is touching your dad a lot," Hazard muttered as he shoveled another piece of pie into his mouth. He chewed, swallowed, and pointed with his fork. "A hell of a lot."

Somers ground his teeth, but Hazard was right. The girl—and sweet God, she really was a girl, not more than eighteen—was practically wrapped around Glenn Somerset. Glenn had penned the girl between the Christmas tree and the picture window, but it didn't look like the girl needed much penning. She seemed pleased—eager, even—to have his attention. He spoke; she laughed. He spoke; she cocked her head with earnest interest. He spoke; she beamed like someone had flipped a switch on sunrise. Her hands, as Hazard had noticed, rarely left Somers's father. His arms, his chest, his cheek, his shoulder, his hands. Over and over again, his hands. They might as well have been playing patty-cake.

"They might as well be playing patty-cake," Hazard said, in a dangerous echo of Somers's thoughts.

As though someone had called out a cue, two teenage boys moved across the room, hooked the girl, and escorted her into the kitchen. She struggled for a moment, but not enough to draw attention. What was that about, Somers wondered. Trying to rescue her? Or trying to stake their territory? Somers didn't have much time to decide. The boys moved quickly, trying to look natural and instead looking so pissed off they were both in danger of popping an artery.

"Shut up, all right?" Somers said. "Just shut up." Somers ran a glance around the room, praying, but he knew it was vain: Grace Elaine stood in the Christmas tree's shadow, a champagne flute in one hand, carrying on a conversation with Jeremiah Walker; they had come back from the kitchen. It was perfectly obvious that she could see what was happening between Glenn and the girl. It was also perfectly obvious, to Somers at least, that his mother was in a killing mood.

"Who is she?"

"I don't know. Some skank that my father dragged out of the closest sorority. Can we not talk about that little—"

"Careful there," a man's voice interrupted, the sound deep but breathless. "That's my daughter you're talking about."

Somers turned around. He'd read once—more than once—about how much blood the body held. A lot of blood, that was what he recalled. He had the vague thought that it could fill a kiddie pool, something like that, something gratuitous and horrifying like that. And right then, as his eyes came to rest on a face he hadn't seen since—

—that night—

—senior year of high school, Somers felt like an artery had been slashed, all the blood pouring out of him, leaving him cold, like a red flood rushing out of him, taking his thoughts and his words and the possibility of movement. It was like that. It was exactly like that.

"Aren't you going to say hi to an old friend?"

Hazard was the one who spoke, and his voice was full of dislike. No, worse than dislike. Hate.

"Bing."

CHAPTER SEVEN

DECEMBER 22
FRIDAY
8:14 PM

HAZARD WAITED FOR A RESPONSE, but the newcomer—who wasn't really that new—ignored him, his gaze fixed on Somers. Somers, for his part, seemed to have lost the power of speech. After a moment, Hazard spoke again. "What do you want, Bing?"

Morris Jeffrey Bingham, junior, looked like a much younger version of his father, the sheriff. On Bing, the patrician nose, the tight lines of the jaw, and the dark curls all melded into the features of a hunk hitting middle adulthood. Snow dusted his coat and hair. Hazard remembered Bing, but only like a man in a desert remembers water: his throat tight, and everything shimmering like a mirage. Back then, Bing had been the sizzling kind of hot, the kind that was dangerous to look at for too long. That had changed only slightly in the passing years.

Bing, four years older than Hazard and Somers, had already graduated high school by the time Hazard was a freshman. The older boy had stuck around, however, attending Wroxall College and coaching the high school football team. Hazard tried to conjure up disdain for the man. He remembered that Bing had picked up a class at the high school—teaching woods? Metals? Shop, definitely teaching some kind of shop class—just so he could coach, and wasn't that pathetic. But the scorn felt shadowy and insubstantial. Back then, Hazard remembered, it had been impossible to live in Wahredua and not know who Bing was; it would have been like living on earth and never quite catching a glimpse of the sun—in this case, a particularly deadly sun, since Bing had never missed an opportunity to make Hazard's life hell.

Jesus, Hazard thought, aware that he was staring at Bing. Staring at him just like that day at the lake. What had it cost him that time? Bruises on his arms, bloody knees, and a hell of a lot of humiliation.

Bing still hadn't responded to Hazard. He hadn't, for that matter, so much as looked Hazard. After another pause, he gave Somers a friendly shove. "Come on, you're going to catch a fly, Somers. What the hell? Are you having a stroke? Do I need to get a doctor?"

"Holy shit," Somers said. He shoved back at Bing, a wild grin spreading across his face. "Holy shit," he repeated, drawing out the words. "What are you doing here? Did you come to spike the punch and joyride in one of my father's cars again?"

Bing shoved Somers again, a little harder this time. "That's what you remember? Don't tell me you forgot about the best part of that night." He hesitated, as though daring Somers to answer.

At the same time, both men said, "Jessica Riner." They burst into laughter, and Somers clapped Bing on the shoulder.

"Somers," Hazard said. "We need to go."

"In a minute."

"We've got a—"

"I know what we've got, Hazard. I'm just talking to my buddy for a minute. Where the hell have you been? Last I heard, you were in Chicago working for some big consulting firm. Are you back for the holidays?"

"No, man," Bing said. "Back for good. Brought the whole family, set up house, all of it."

"And you didn't tell me!"

"It's been a crazy couple of months." Bing rubbed at one cheek, and Hazard noticed, for the first time, that Bing's eyes had bags, that his color was sallow. Rode hard and put away wet, that's what Hazard's mother would have said. "I've been meaning to give you a call, but one thing led to another. Anyway, here we are now."

"Months? You son of a bitch. What kept you so busy for the last couple of months?"

"Buy me a beer sometime and I'll tell you."

"Somers," Hazard said.

"I already said in a minute."

"Sorry to interrupt the frat boy reunion. I know you two probably want to do a keg stand and smoke a joint and bang some hot babes, but we've got a job to do."

"What's your damn problem—" Somers began, but before he could finish, Bing stepped forward, interposing himself between Somers and Hazard.

"Hold on, Somers. I've got something to say to you, Emery." The name sounded forced, unnatural in Bing's mouth. For the first time, his eyes fixed on Hazard. "What I did to you was really shitty. I knew it back then, and I was too big of a coward to do any different."

No one spoke for a moment; around them the hub of voices and music continued to rise and fall. A stray current of air brought the thick, cloying smell of eggnog.

"Well?" Somers said. "He apologized to you. Aren't you going to say something?"

"He didn't apologize," Hazard said. "He made a statement. It happened to be a true statement, but that's all."

"Jesus, Hazard—"

"No." Bing shook his head and stuck out a hand. "He's right. I didn't say it, so here goes: I'm sorry."

"Fine," Hazard said, ignoring the hand. "Somers, can we go—"

Ugly red blotched Somers's cheeks, and he was shaking his head. "Give me five minutes. Or is that too damn much?" Hazard didn't bother to reply, but as he walked away, he heard Somers behind him saying, "Sorry, I don't know why he's being such an asshole."

Bing said something in reply, but the noise of the party swallowed the words, and the next thing Hazard heard was Somers laughing. After crossing the room and putting as much distance between himself and the newly-reunited frat boys as possible, Hazard took up position near one of the doors. At that moment, his phone buzzed, and he took it out to find a message from Nico.

Everything ok?
Yeah. Somers's an asshole.
No joke. Where are you?
Long story, the whole thing's a shit-fest, got to go.
Tonight?

Hazard hesitated, knowing what Nico was asking but unsure of what he wanted. *My place.*

Nico answered with a heart emoji, and Hazard dropped the phone back into his pocket. As Hazard raised his head, he found himself facing Grace Elaine again. Somers's mother had returned with Jeremiah Walker, and it was clear from the frigid glances that she was shooting at her husband that she hadn't missed any of the interaction between Glenn Somerset and the girl who had been, minutes earlier, trying to pin herself to his lapel.

When Grace Elaine had approached Hazard earlier, her aggressive approach—running a finger over him like she meant to strip him out of his clothes—had thrown Hazard into confusion. Now, with space between them, he could study her more carefully. It was clear that John-Henry's good looks had come from Grace Elaine, and it was equally clear that the features that in Grace Elaine appeared pretty were more dynamic, more magnetic in John-Henry. Still, there was no denying that Grace Elaine was a very attractive woman, and judging by the way she held herself as she spoke to Jeremiah—as though she were the only thing in the universe except maybe that goddamn Christmas tree—Hazard guessed that she knew it too.

What Hazard didn't understand was why Grace Elaine had reacted to him the way that she had. Her sexual aggression had masked something else, and while Hazard didn't have the same interpersonal intuition that Somers did, he had a good guess what Grace Elaine was hiding. She hated him. Like her husband, Grace Elaine Somerset held some sort of—

—the locker room, with the steam curling up around Somers's slender, golden perfection, with his touch raising goosebumps on Hazard's skin, and the heat of his lips like a match on a strike strip, was that it, did she know?—

—grudge against Hazard. What? And why?

Lost in thought, Hazard only noticed Somers when his partner had almost reached him. Before Hazard could speak, Somers held up both hands. "I know you want to punch my teeth into the next solar system or something like that, but will you just listen to me for a minute?"

"Why don't you talk to Bing? He seemed happy to listen to you."

Somers cocked his head, as though thinking, and then his eyes widened slightly and he gave a half-nod.

"Don't do that," Hazard said.

"I didn't do anything."

"Yes, you did. You think I'm jealous of Bing."

"Ree, that's—look, he and I are just friends. It's been a long time since I've seen him."

"Just friends? What's that supposed to mean, Somers? You're my partner, not my boyfriend. Remember?"

Somers didn't say what he was thinking, but it was obvious, even to Emery Hazard.

"My point," Somers said, still holding up his hands, "is that I came over here to explain why I acted like a dick."

Hazard shrugged, looking past Somers's shoulder to scan the far side of the room. The two boys—the ones who had escorted Bing's daughter out of the room a few minutes earlier—had returned. Bing's daughter was squeezed up against Glenn Somerset again, but now Hazard's attention went to the boys. They were in their late teens, juniors or seniors in high school. Hazard hadn't noticed them before because they had been on the opposite side of the Christmas tree, and the massive, confettied monstrosity had hidden them from view. Both boys had dark hair, and their formalwear was slightly disheveled: collars undone, ties loosened, shirt cuffs hanging open. One of the boys was staring at Glenn Somerset and the teenage girl with a look of undisguised fury. The other boy—and this was where it got interesting—was sitting in his lap and running fingers through his hair.

"What's that about?" Hazard asked.

"Can I explain this first?"

"Those boys: they're together, right?"

Somers cast a glance over his shoulder, immediately dismissing the boys and turning back to Hazard. "Look, things got weird between me and Bing at the end, before I went to college. I never really got my footing back, and it threw me off to see him."

"They're definitely together. They're kissing, but the bigger one looks ready to bite out the other boy's tongue he's so mad."

"Are you even goddamn listening to me? I acted like a huge dickplug."

"Yeah. You did. I don't care. Something's not right."

"Something's not right." Somers flapped his arms. "Great, now he finally clues in to the fact that something's not right. Yeah, I know something's not right. I screwed up. That's what I'm trying to say. I . . . I saw Bing, and all of the sudden it was high school all over again, and I just—"

"I already told you," Hazard said, pushing past Somers, "I don't care if you reverted to preschool." Hazard's attention had already moved past the conversation and towards the scene unfolding across the room. The bigger boy had stood up, dumping the other boy onto the ground, and he was marching towards Glenn. A fight was about to take place—or, perhaps more accurately, a brutal ass-whipping. Glenn still hadn't noticed, but the girl had. She latched onto Glenn even more tightly, hissing something at the boy who was marching towards them. He shouted something back at her. He looked like he had big plans for breaking every bone in Glenn Somerset that he could reach.

As Hazard stepped forward to intervene, movement to his left distracted him. Santa, naked except for his trademark cap, barreled into the family room. He was holding a gun, a compact revolver, and he swung it in a wide arc. Hazard was already drawing his weapon when Santa fired the first time. A Christmas ornament, strung high overhead, exploded, and shards of glass rained down into the party. The screaming began just as the lights went out.

Screaming. Everyone screaming. The darkness was full of people jostling, fighting their way to the door in a blind, mad panic. Hazard fought against the crowd, but it was like fighting against the tide. He managed to free the .38, but now people pressed against him, and Hazard didn't dare bring the gun up for fear of hurting someone. He fought back against the crowd, using his size and muscle to force a path diagonal to the current.

A second shot rang out. The muzzle flash painted a starburst and then the blackness rushed in again. Again, the screaming rose in pitch, and a seemingly endless number of people pressed against Hazard, insane with their need to reach the exit. Hands clawed at his face and throat and collar. Stiletto heels stabbed at his feet. Rank sweat and boozy, panicked breaths made it hard for Hazard to pull air into his lungs.

A third shot. And then a fourth.

Hazard broke free from the crowd. He launched himself at the blank space where he had seen the most recent muzzle flash. For a long moment, he had the sensation of falling, robbed of his sense of space by the darkness. Then Hazard hit something—someone. Someone big and flabby and surprisingly solid. Hazard's size, though, and his momentum were enough to carry both men to the ground.

Blind in the darkness, Hazard struggled to hold onto his own gun while grappling with the man. A fifth shot. A sixth. Was that an arm? Christ, where was his arm? Hazard brought his elbow down hard and heard something crack, and a wheezing scream. Another shot. And then Hazard had hold of an arm, and he followed it up to a wrist. He slammed the wrist and hand against the floor, and something heavy and metallic clattered across the floor.

No more shots. The screaming had grown more distant, and Hazard guessed that most of the people had made their way out of the Somerset home. The man under him struggled, and Hazard dropped another elbow. He was rewarded by another pained explosion of breath.

Then a bluish-white light shone across the floor, and Hazard had his first glimpse of his captive: naked, bloody Santa Claus, his nose broken, his lips split. Hazard flipped Santa onto his belly, found his cuffs, and snapped them around Santa's wrists.

"It's all right," Hazard said, shouting because the noise of the gunfire had blown out his hearing. "His gun went that way."

Somers, his own face streaked with blood—his nose looked suspiciously swollen—pivoted, sending the weak gleam from his mobile phone spilling across the enormous room.

At the edge of the light, two bodies lay in a twisted pile, their clothing soaked with blood: Glennworth Somerset and the girl.

CHAPTER EIGHT

DECEMBER 22
FRIDAY
8:45 PM

SOMERS KNELT OVER HIS FATHER, trying to stop the bleeding. Santa Claus had shot Glenn Somerset in the stomach at least once, maybe twice. It was hard to tell because the lights were out and because there was blood. So much blood. Somers barely remembered crossing the room to where his father lay. He remembered glancing at the girl—Bing's daughter—and knowing she was dead; a bullet had punched through her back, and she wasn't breathing. He didn't remember where he got the fabric that he now wadded up and held against his father's stomach. All his attention now focused on this makeshift attempt to stop the bleeding. In the tips of his fingers, Somers felt a pulse. His own? Or was that his father's heart pumping blood out of the gaping wound?

Somers could hear it—a soft, squelching noise as blood soaked through the improvised bandage. That was crazy. That was batshit. There was no way that Somers could hear, actually hear, blood pumping out. But he could. He could hear that squelching. His Great-aunt Elaine had a red rubber hot water bottle that she would put in her bed in the winter, and when she would carry the bottle to the sink and empty it, it sounded like this: fingers compressing the rubber until it squeaked against itself. God, this was insane, the whole thing was insane, and if his father—

—died—

—no, that wasn't even a legitimate thought, that wasn't something he could allow himself to consider.

It was with something like surprise that Somers realized the lights had come back on. In the warm, yellow light, his fingers were so many colors: crimson, purple, blue, black. Somers forced his gaze up, towards his father's face. The flesh was puffy, creamy except where the day's growth of stubble gave everything an aquamarine cast. His eyes were closed, but he was breathing. Pretty strong breaths. Yes. Good breathing. The lungs hadn't been damaged, thank God. Over the years, Glenn Somerset had put on weight, but he looked very small now laid out on the floor. It was like gravity had stretched him, stretched him like taffy, and Somers thought that liquids had constant volume but no definite shape. Like all that blood, spilling out thinly across Somers's knuckles. Someone was talking to him, Somers realized, but he didn't care. His father was oozing out across the floor, all that blood, what a joke, what a goddamn joke.

"—and if you touch him I'll break your nose." That part managed to penetrate Somers's fog, and he realized it was Hazard speaking. He was using that low, deadly voice that made the hair on the back of Somers's neck stand up, the voice like he'd do everything he said and it wouldn't bother him a bit.

"We've got a job to do," a snippy young man's voice answered.

"Open your mouth again," Hazard said. "Go ahead."

If the snippy young man had more to say, he didn't voice it.

A moment later, Hazard's face swam into Somers's line of sight. "Somers, the paramedics are here. You've got to get out of their way."

Somers blinked. The words washed over him, past him, away.

"Come on," Hazard said. His big hands, surprisingly delicate, prized Somers's fingers off the makeshift bandage, and Hazard helped Somers to his feet.

"No," Somers said, shaking his head and stretching back towards his father. "I've got to—"

"They're going to take him to the hospital," Hazard said, steering Somers a safe distance away. "That's the only chance your father has."

Somers stared as the paramedics went to work. Their movements were precise, efficient, and controlled. One was the young man that Somers had heard objecting; the other was a much older woman with leathery skin. The young man's hands trembled, but he kept working. The woman—her hands looked like they could have held an ocean and not spilled a drop. Liquid—

—blood—

—had a constant volume but no definite shape.

Faster than Somers would have believed, they transferred his father to a gurney and wheeled him from the house. Somers glimpsed Sheriff Bingham embracing his son, both of them paralyzed by the death of Bing's daughter. And Somers noticed his mother trailing after him, her movements stiff, as though she hadn't walked in years. She glanced around, her blind gaze moving over Somers as though he weren't even there, before settling on Jeremiah Walker. He crossed the room as though summoned by that gaze, settling an arm around Grace Elaine's shoulders and urging her after the gurney.

"You need to go," Hazard said, turning Somers towards the door. "Your mom is going to need you. We'll take care of everything here."

Everything here. Two words. Everything here meant bullet casing. It meant blood. It meant the gunpowder smell that had replaced everything else. It meant talking to drunken socialites. It meant facing a murderer. It meant a dead girl. Somers felt as though he were rising from deep waters—slow at first, and then faster and faster as the pressure shot him towards the surface. He saw, now, that Wahredua's finest were already here. How much time had passed? Somers cast a quick glance. Where was Santa?

"Let's go," Hazard said, giving another push. "You can ride in the ambulance. I'll meet you there as soon as I can."

Somers shook his head.

"Your mother—"

"Fuck no." Somers lifted his hands, intending to press on his pounding head, but he saw the blood again. Already it had dried, turning sticky and crusty as it did. "I just—I need a minute—"

"You need to get your ass out of here." Martha Cravens, Wahredua's Chief of Police, marched towards them.

Cravens was a big woman with an hourglass shape; large without being fat, her hair stylishly gray, she somehow managed to give off the air of being someone's grandmother. The reality was very different. Cravens had toughed it out as one of the only women on a small-town police force, and she had earned respect and trust while doing so. She had been talking, Somers noticed, with Mayor Newton, who was one of Cravens's strongest supporters. The mayor folded his arms and studied Somers from across the room; there was something in the old man's face that made Somers's skin crawl.

"That's what I've been telling him," Hazard said. "Look, I'll drive you there."

"No way." Somers raised his hands again, saw the blood again, stopped again. "No."

"I know what you're thinking," Cravens said. Her face was hard—lined with sympathy, yes, but still hard enough to crack a goddamn Rolex so it wouldn't ever tick again. "You think you're going to take matters into your own hands. You think I might be stupid enough to let you within ten miles of this business because it's personal, because you're a good detective, because you've put in your time."

"Chief," Somers said, his voice thick, so thick it barely escaped his throat. "You're out of your goddamn mind if you think I'm not handling this."

"What's there to handle, Detective? Everybody saw the shooter come into the room with a gun. We don't need to do a goddamn thing except wait. We'll take statements, pick up the casings, and we'll run ballistics, just to be sure, but that's just to keep lawyers from crawling down our throats. There's no case to work. This thing was shut almost before it opened." Cravens's face softened, the lines around her eyes and mouth deepening. "John-Henry, the best thing you can do is help your family right now."

Somers shook his shoulders, as though trying to throw off an invisible hand.

"Come on," Hazard said in a quiet voice. When Somers didn't respond, he said, "John-Henry."

The sound of that name on Hazard's lips, a name Hazard hadn't used since—

—the locker room, Somers's heart thudding as he saw the desire in Hazard's eyes—

—high school, made Somers blink. He nodded. Cravens grasped his hand, and Somers let Hazard hustle him out into the night. It was cold, much colder than Somers remembered. His breath misted, but it was so goddamn cold that the mist should have crystallized, fallen to the earth, and shattered. Spindrift glistened in the headlights of a dozen police cruisers. Pebbly snow chittered against the metal shells. Overhead, the stars looked close enough that Somers thought he could reach up and shove them around a little.

The stars. Somers shouldn't have been able to see the stars. His father had lit up the house like the Bellagio, and the lights had blotted out the sky. But the exterior lights, the decorative lights, had not come back on.

"Keys," Hazard said, still guiding Somers towards the Interceptor.

Somers fished them out of his pocket and pressed them into Hazard's hand: the skin warm, callused, strong.

Why hadn't the exterior lights come back on?

Hazard wasn't acting like Hazard either. He was shivering, and for the first time, Somers noticed that Hazard wasn't wearing his jacket. He also noticed that Hazard was holding the door open for him, waiting for Somers to climb into the car.

"Where's your jacket?"

Shaking with the cold, Hazard jerked his head at the car. "Will you get in?"

"Did you leave it inside?"

"Yeah, sure. Before I freeze my fingers off if you don't mind."

Somers climbed into the seat, Hazard shut the door, and a moment later he climbed behind the steering wheel. The SUV roared to life, and warmth fluttered out of the vents.

"That was your jacket. I was using it to—my father's stomach, the blood—" Somers cut off, unable to finish the statement.

Hazard shrugged.

"Jesus, if I'd just taken him to the station like my father asked." Somers rocked forward. He lifted his hands to cover his face, but again the sight of blood stopped him. Scrubbing at his shirt, Somers tried to clean the tacky mess from his hands, but all he succeeded in doing was spread a rust-colored stain across the cloth. He scrubbed harder; the friction brought heat to his hands. If the goddamn blood would just come off—

Hazard's hands closed around his wrists. "Breathe."

Somers couldn't breathe. He rocked forward again. "I should have just taken him to the fucking station. But I had to be an ass. I had to make a point. I had to—"

The sound of paper ripping filled the car, and Somers glanced over. Hazard had a packet of alcohol-cleanser towelettes, and he was working one of the cloths free. Without speaking, Hazard gripped Somers's hand and began cleaning the dried blood from his fingers. Somers knew he should say something. Stop. That would be the smartest thing. Or, let me. Anything would be better than silence. Even crying, even sobbing would be better than the sick feeling in his stomach and the tightness in his throat.

But Somers didn't say anything because right then, Hazard's touch felt like the only thing keeping him from flying apart. Hazard cleaned with strong, firm movements, but again he showed that surprising gentleness as he manipulated Somers's hands. When he had finished—and, in the process, used all of the towelettes—Hazard grabbed Somers's chin. This grip was not gentle; it was painful, and it hurt more as Hazard forced Somers's head so that their eyes met.

"You say one more time that you should have taken him into the station, and you'll be shitting out your own teeth for the next year."

Somers started to laugh. He wasn't sure where the laughter came from—the sick feeling inside was still there, just pushed to the back a little—but the laughter felt real. He laughed until a hint of a smile cracked Hazard's stern expression and Hazard's fingers dropped away. Still laughing, Somers leaned back against the glass. Cold soaked through his jacket and shirt, and it felt clean against all that sickness inside him.

"That's your idea of being comforting?" Somers said as his laughter faded. The tightness in his throat had eased. He still felt like shit, but he felt like shit with his eyes open.

"That's my idea of keeping you from being an even bigger horse's ass."

"Can we—I mean, would you take me to the hospital?" Somers paused. "I can ask one of the uniforms to drive me if you need to get home."

Hazard growled something under his throat and shifted the Interceptor into gear. Their tires stirred up tiny cyclones of snow as they pulled away from the Somerset home and headed into the city.

"What was that?"

"I said you really are a dipshit."

"Hazard?"

Hazard didn't respond.

"Ree?"

He grunted.

"Who turned the lights back on?"

"I don't know. Somebody."

"What happened?"

"The breakers tripped. All of them."

"And somebody reset them?"

"Sure, somebody."

"All of them?"

"Christ's sake. Yes."

So why hadn't the outside lights come back on?

Before Somers could voice the question, Hazard's phone buzzed. The dark-haired man answered, speaking in a low tone—grim monosyllabics punctured by a single, violent, "What?" After listening for another minute, Hazard threw the phone skidding across the dash.

"What?" Somers said. "Is it my—"

"No. Nothing about your dad, not yet. He's still in surgery."

"Then what?" Somers tried to think, but his reactions were dulled by emotion and exhaustion. "Nico?"

"Santa Claus is dead."

Somers stared at Hazard. "That's a joke."

"He was shot while trying to escape arrest."

CHAPTER NINE

**DECEMBER 22
FRIDAY
9:30 PM**

HAZARD FLOORED IT, and the Interceptor shot through Wahredua's slush-choked streets. His hands tightened around the wheel, and the still-healing cut throbbed. It didn't matter. It hurt like hell, but it didn't matter. He couldn't loosen his grip.

When Wahredua Regional came into sight, only a single pair of red-and-blue lights pulsed in the parking lot. There should have been more. The whole place should have been lit up. Instead, Hazard realized as he pulled the Interceptor into the lot and towards the red-and-blue, he and Somers were the first to arrive.

"They're all at my parents' house," Somers said, with his maddening habit of answering Hazard's thoughts.

Hazard's partner looked better. Not great; John-Henry Somerset usually looked great, and this was about forty percent of that. The icy blue of the dash lights washed his face, sank deep into the new hollows under his eyes, highlighted lines of fatigue and worry that Hazard had never seen before. His nose was still swollen, with blood crusting the nostrils. But Somers's eyes were alert. He was talking. And most important, he wasn't talking about blaming himself for what had happened. God only knew what he was thinking.

When they reached the gray sedan, Lender and Swinney stood silently in the rushing wind and snow. Swinney looked smaller than ever. Wahredua's only female detective wasn't, by nature, a retiring woman; she had her reddish-blond hair cut short except for the bangs, and her personality tended to match the fiery color. Tonight, though, she was a huddled figure, her back to the gale.

Albert Lender, her partner, looked like he would have been more at home with a slide rule or a protractor or anything but the revolver he held in one hand. Short and squirrely, he wore enormous eyeglasses with thick frames of yellow plastic. From behind snowmelt-covered lenses, he blinked at Somers and Hazard. More snow glazed his bushy mustache. He didn't look like a traitor. He didn't look like a dirty cop. But that hadn't stopped him from helping Mayor Newton try to kill Hazard and Somers.

The only problem was that Hazard didn't have any proof. The jagged cut across Hazard's palm, which he had inflicted on himself by driving a shard of glass into another man's neck, throbbed in time with Hazard's pulse. That fight—that brutal, insane fight in a darkened basement, that fight that Hazard had been sure would be his last—that had been because of Lender.

Somers had already moved to a patch of trampled snow. So many tracks crossed here—tracks from different tires and different shoes—that it seemed impossible to pick anything out. Hazard hunkered next to his partner, and Somers pointed. Black snow. Black now, but when Hazard dug a penlight out of his pocket, the congealing slush changed to a dark maroon. Blood.

"You all right?" Somers asked.

Lender was shaking. In the rushing cold, the movement might have been mistaken for shivering. For all Hazard knew, it might have been genuine shivering. But it didn't look like it. Lender's face was corpse-pale, almost green in the ambient light, and he looked ready to toss up everything he'd eaten since the Sunday before last.

"Fine," Swinney said. She unfolded herself slightly, and her hand drifted to her hip where she wore a holstered gun.

"Lender?" Somers asked.

"Fine."

"You want to tell us what the hell happened?" Hazard said. "How'd you manage to get our prime suspect killed?"

"He tried to escape," Lender said. The words sounded rote. Mechanical. He was still holding the gun at his side.

"He was cuffed," Somers said. A tremor ran through his voice. It was small, that tremor, but seismic shifts were happening. Small now, but something big was about to blow. "And naked. Did he get out of the cuffs again? How the hell did he get out of the cuffs?"

"He didn't." Lender swallowed. His index finger, resting along the barrel of his gun, twitched. "He knocked me off my feet."

Another twitch.

The world suddenly seemed very stark: great pools of starchy light from the sodium lamps, and everything else darkness. Everything except for that revolver and Lender's nervous finger.

Somers's hand drifted along his hip, moving for the .40 caliber holstered at the small of his back. Hazard's hand began to rise. The cut across his palm buzzed like a power saw. His thoughts came in clipped observations: Lender would try to shoot first; that much was obvious. Normally, Hazard would have put his money on Somers—or on himself. But Somers was half-crazed with grief, and Hazard's injured hand would slow him. And what about Swinney? She looked so small, just a crumpled black coat and a damp blur of red. What was she going to do?

Swinney spoke. "He went for my weapon."

Lender's finger twitched one last time and went still.

"What?" Hazard said.

"My service weapon. He knocked Lender onto his fat ass. Santa has his back to me, and he got his hand on my service weapon." Her fingers brushed the leather holster again. "Couldn't get the damn thing out, though. Couldn't undo the snap. Lender saw him go for it—"

Too loudly, too abruptly, Lender repeated, "I saw him go for it."

Something flickered across Swinney's face, gone almost before Hazard noticed it. Her hands rested on her belt, clutching so that her knuckles shone white. The wind shrieked, piling snow against Hazard's legs.

"Where is he?" Hazard asked.

"They took him inside to see if they could—" Lender stopped. The snowmelt on his glasses ran like a river. He swallowed. Then he flexed his hand, and the revolver clattered onto the white-dusted asphalt. "Maybe it's a good thing. No trial."

None of the others had anything to say. Hazard shook his head. "Let's go."

"We've got to close this down," Lender said. "Officer-involved shooting."

Sirens sang out farther back along the road, and Hazard shook his head again. "Looks like the two of you have everything closed down already. Come on, Somers."

They walked towards the hospital. A spot at the center of Hazard's back itched. That's where he would have put the bullet if he were in Lender's shoes, and damn, it itched bad.

Snow, with its limestone taste, layered the inside of Hazard's mouth when he spoke. "Did you see his glasses? There was no way he could see Santa going for Swinney's gun. What the hell kind of story was that?"

Somers's voice came out low, still shaking with that seismic upheaval. "He's a murdering bastard."

"Why?"

"Because he's in Newton's pocket, that's why."

"But why would someone want that guy dead?"

"Because Newton paid him to kill my father. Because he's covering his tracks."

A sudden pressure came off of Hazard's chest. He sucked in a lungful of air. Snow, like he had run his tongue through bone dust, the slickness of its melt. "You can't say that again. Not anywhere we can be heard."

"I'm not an idiot."

Hazard grabbed his shoulder. "You can't say it again."

Somers glared at him and shook off Hazard's hand.

"What about Swinney?"

This time, Somers hesitated. "She was scared."

"Of us?"

"I don't know."

"Was she lying?"

Somers considered this for a moment. "She was backed into a corner. I don't know."

"Would she have shot?"

"Christ." Somers scrubbed at his face and spread his hands.

They made it inside the hospital without another word. In the emergency room lobby, a lone man with his arm in a homemade sling occupied one of the vinyl-covered chairs. Deeper in the hospital, voices mixed with the sound of squeaking metal, doors closing, and footsteps. The clean freshness of the snow was gone, replaced by a sterile, metallic odor.

The woman behind the desk glanced once at Hazard and then looked at Somers. "Detective," she said. She didn't look like she practiced smiling, but she looked like she'd give it a try for John-Henry Somerset. "Your father is still in surgery. The waiting room—"

Now, the tremor had gone out of Somer's voice. It was eerily calm, and Hazard had a vision of the quiet in the last instant before a volcano erupted. "The man who was shot in the parking lot. Where is he?"

"He's—" the woman paused. "Your father, don't you—"

"Where is he?" Hazard said.

"They couldn't do anything for him," she said, her back stiffening.

"He got nicked in the parking lot." Hazard layered scorn in his voice. "What? Was there traffic?"

"Nicked? You call being shot in the chest five times a nick? Dr. Osthoff did everything he could. You can't—"

"Where is he?"

"In the morgue."

Hazard let out a breath. "I'm going down there. Right now. You stay up here until you hear something about your dad."

"You can't go to the morgue—" the nurse began.

Before she could finish, Cravens tromped into the waiting room. Her bun of gray hair sagged, heavy with snow, but her steps carried their familiar, determined energy. Crossing to the desk, she fixed Hazard and Somers with an irritated look.

"I told you two to get over here and take care of Detective Somerset's mother. What are you doing?"

Hazard opened his mouth, but the bristling nurse spoke first. "They're trying to get a body out of the morgue."

"That's not what I said," Hazard said.

Cravens gave him a withering look. "Do what I told you, Detective. I'll take care of this."

"Detectives Lender and Swinney are involved in this shooting, Chief. They can't be involved in investigating it."

"Detective Hazard, do you think I need you to tell me to do my job?"

"No, Chief. But if you'll let me explain—"

"Unless you'd like to spend the next six months working nights and weekends on our safe parks initiative, you'd better do what I asked you to do, Detective. You'd better do it right now."

"You're not listening to me," Hazard began.

To Hazard's surprise, Somers gripped his arm and shoved him towards the nearest hallway. Cravens watched them, her face hard and illegible until Somers had steered Hazard out of sight.

"You can't just shut your mouth," Somers muttered. "You can't just do what you're told."

"Do you want Lender and Swinney on that case?"

"No, dumbass. But neither does Cravens. If you had kept your mouth shut, you would have figured that out." Hazard opened his mouth, but he shut it again when Somers squeezed his eyes shut. "I can't do this right now, Ree. I just can't."

He sounded more like the normal Somers. Those tremors had vanished, and his voice had smoothed out. But he didn't look like Somers. He looked like a man hanging by a frayed rope.

When they reached the waiting room—a glass box with chairs and a humming TV and magazines from six months ago—Grace Elaine Somerset took one look at Hazard and shook her head.

"No."

"Fine," Somers said, nudging Hazard back into the hallway.

When the door swung shut, Hazard watched through the glass as Somers spoke to his mother. The two exchanged a flurry of words—furious words, to judge by their expressions, but muted by the closed door—and then Somers shook his head. When he opened the door again, he dragged two chairs out into the hall and collapsed into one of them. Hazard studied Grace Elaine through the glass. If looks could kill, Hazard would have been dead, with a smoking bullet hole right through the heart.

"Will you sit?" Somers said. "She'll beat you in a staring contest, anyway."

So Hazard sat. And as the adrenaline seeped out of his body, as exhaustion took over, as the lines of grief on Somers's face deepened and spread, Hazard felt lost. Polar explorers, he thought he had read somewhere, would have their ships get stuck in the ice. They'd be in the exact same place, trapped, but they'd be lost. And that's how this felt. Somers's hand rested on the arm of the chair, brushing Hazard's. That's what this was: being lost and being stuck in the same goddamn place. Because right then, they were touching, but they might as well have been at the ends of the earth because Emery Hazard was too much of a coward to hold Somers's hand. Somers was hurting. He needed something. Someone. Anyone. And that was what decided it: Hazard shifted, ready to take Somers's fingers in his own.

Somers leaned forward, his hand moving away from Hazard and into a pocket. "I should have called Cora. She's going to kill me. I'll be right back—"

A doctor—a surgeon, still dressed in scrubs, a mask hanging loose around his neck, came up the hallway towards them. Hazard had the brief impression of silvery hair and almond-shaped eyes before the man had reached them. Somers had shifted to the edge of his seat, and Grace Elaine stood in the doorway. Her manicured nails gripped the frame as though it were the only solid thing on earth.

"He's stable."

There was more, but Hazard didn't hear it because Somers had turned, burying his face in Hazard's chest. What Hazard remembered, though, even more than the feel of his arms around

Somers, even more than the shaking in Somers's shoulders, was the unadulterated fury in Grace Elaine's face.

CHAPTER TEN

DECEMBER 23
SATURDAY
6:42 AM

SOMERS DIDN'T SLEEP. He sat outside the door to his father's room, the .40 caliber Glock on his lap, his hand on the gun's butt. At some point in the gray hours—hours that hummed with the constant pulse of machinery inside the hospital—the world slipped into a dreamlike quality. The walls and hallways stretched into vast distances. The brushed-nickel handrails shimmered like ice in sunlight. Above Somers, the flickers in the fluorescent lights became pauses of darkness.

But he didn't sleep, not exactly. Another day, another case, his mind would have been racing: collating suspects, cordoning off possibilities, drawing up a plan. This night, though, he just sat with his hand on his gun. The gun, the door, the man inside that room: the three coordinates that mattered now. More than once, in those humming hours—God, that noise at the back of his head—he thought he saw Lender at the end of those long, distended hallways, and then Somers would flex his fingers on the Glock and ready himself to shoot.

A hand on his shoulder brought Somers upright in the tubular chair. A second hand caught his wrist.

"It's me. Hey. Dummy."

Somers blinked. Hazard stood over him. The big man was, as always, groomed to an irritating degree. His long, dark hair—too long for regulation, even combed and parted, but it looked so damn good—shone in the fluorescent lights.

"I should have known. Cravens promised she wouldn't let you stay all night."

"She didn't." Somers cracked his jaw and settled back into the seat. "But she put Orear on the door. I wasn't going to leave my father with Orear on the goddamn door."

"You bullied Orear into going home."

"I told him I'd take care of it."

"You forced him."

"I told him he could either walk out or go with my foot up his ass. He decided to walk."

Hazard's face betrayed nothing. The smooth skin, so pale that it was almost blue, was a taut, blank canvas. "Go wash up," Hazard finally said, releasing Somers's hand. "You look like hell."

"They've got showers," Somers said, stretching expansively. "Big enough for two."

As usual, the comment did what Somers intended: it kindled sparks in Hazard's cheeks, and Hazard flipped the bird.

Instead of a shower, though, Somers settled for splashing water on his face and running a wet paper towel around his neck and under his arms. His nose was still tender. Nothing for it now, though—and at least it wasn't broken.

By the time Somers got back to his father's room, Hazard was speaking in a low voice with Cravens. The chief looked like she had spent the night working: her hair had worked its way free from its bun, and her shirt and jacket were rumpled. Coffee stained one cuff. Her jaw, however, was set in resolve. She looked like she'd still rather put her head through a brick wall than walk around it.

"Moraes and Foley—" she was saying.

"Moraes and Foley couldn't find their asses in a paper bag," Hazard hissed. "Not even if you were holding their hands while they did it." Hazard glanced over his shoulder—a furtive look, as though he had done this before, checking to see if Somers were approaching. When he saw Somers, he straightened and fell silent.

"What's going on?" Somers asked.

"Nothing," Cravens said. "I just wanted to see how things were going. It looks like Orear didn't stay the night."

"It's personal, Chief. You know how it is."

"I also know that I gave you an order to go home and get some rest." She waved a hand when Somers tried to speak. "I just stopped by to see how your father's doing."

"He's alive. Five shots, and he's alive. That's more than the killer wanted."

"Detective Somerset, what happened last night was a tragedy. More than a tragedy. And I know that for you—and for many people in Wahredua—it was personal."

"Excuse me? What are you trying to say?"

Cravens's shoulders sagged. "Nothing."

"That didn't sound like nothing."

"She's saying," Hazard broke in, "that this wasn't anything but an accident."

Somers looked from Hazard to Cravens. "That's crazy. That guy shot my father. He shot that girl. He tried to shoot other people. If Detective Hazard hadn't stopped him, he would have killed other people."

"I know, Detective. I know perfectly well what happened."

"It sure as hell doesn't sound like it." The words sounded strange in Somers's mouth. Normally, moments like this—tense, high-pressure moments—were when he was able to shine. Normally he knew what to say and how to say it. Right then, though, the words just poured out of him. A quiet part at the back of his brain observed, disappointedly, that he was sounding an awful lot like Hazard. Somers couldn't keep the words from flowing out, though. "It sounds like you have no fucking idea what happened last night. That's what it sounds like. I had him cuffed, and he got loose. How do you explain that? I'll tell you how: somebody with keys unlocked him. Now that means you've either got a crooked sheriff or a crooked cop or both."

"I understand that you're upset, Detective. I understand that this has been a terrible twenty-four hours for you. I understand that you're speaking out of distress and grief. But don't think for a moment that my patience is unlimited. Here's what happened last night: a man with a history of mental illness approached your parents' home. He entered their home."

"Armed with a fucking gun."

"Yes, with a firearm. He entered their home. He was detained by your father and some of the other guests. Your father called you for help. Then, for God only knows what reason, you decided to handle the matter on your own, without following proper protocol. Those are grounds for serious charges, Detective."

Somers stared at Cravens. She was threatening him. Using a calm tone, using soft words, but she was still threatening him. And the worst part was that she was right.

Before Somers could regain his voice, Hazard spoke, the words so rough and jagged that Somers could barely understand them. "If you think you can—"

Cravens's calm shattered. In a seething whisper, she said, "Will you listen to me for Christ's sake? You're in hot water. Both of you. Right now, nobody is looking at you. Everyone's too upset about the shooting. But if you keep sticking your noses into this, they will start asking questions. Don't look at me like that, Hazard. This isn't a threat. It's a warning."

"That man shot my father," Somers said.

"And he's dead, Detective. He was killed while escaping. That's a tragedy too; that man should have stood trial and been held accountable for what he did. Not just for shooting your father but for killing that sweet, young girl. She—"

Hazard's voice sliced through the next words. "She's dead?"

"Yes." Cravens balled her fists. She took several long, deep breaths, and then she said, "As I was saying to Detective Hazard, at this point, there's no need for further investigation into what happened at the Somerset home. The shooter has been identified by multiple people. He is now dead. There is no case; there will be no trial. That is the beginning and end of the story, gentlemen."

"And the killer? The one who got himself shot so conveniently?" The words tumbled out of Somers; God damn, he really did sound like Hazard. "What about him? What about an investigation into his death? What about the cuffs?"

"You should be very careful about how you phrase that question, Detective. No handcuffs were recovered at the scene. No one saw you put him in handcuffs."

"You're saying I'm lying."

"I'm saying that you've been through incredible trauma over the last twelve hours. You're not thinking clearly. As with all officer-involved shootings, the department will investigate. I told Detective Hazard, and I'll tell you the same thing: you and Detective Hazard have a conflict of interest in this case, and so Officers Foley and Moraes will be looking into Detective Lender's shooting." She sighed. "I know this isn't ideal, but all of my detectives have their feet in this mess, and it's the best I can do."

Somers turned, feeling strangely helpless, like a child facing someone much larger and much stronger, and he was half-surprised—only half—to find himself looking to Hazard. Fury darkened Hazard's expression.

"It's not good enough," Hazard said. "If Somers say he put him in cuffs, he did. Somehow he got loose. That shooting wasn't just an accident. And that man's death wasn't an accident. There's no chance in hell he was trying to escape, not the way Swinney and Lender are telling it, and even if I'm the only one who—"

"That's enough, Detective." Cravens was breathing rapidly now, her face pink and almost gnomish in its tightly controlled anger. "You aren't thinking clearly. You're not in your right mind—you're not in your goddamn head, that's what. You need to take a few days of leave. Both of you."

"Chief," Somers began.

She cut off his words with a slicing gesture. "Enough, Detectives. Enough from both of you. Consider this mandatory leave. Get some rest. Get out of town if you need to. But get your heads back on straight because if I ever hear you suggest what I think you were just suggesting, I'll have you out the door so fast you'll be spinning in the snow. Do I make myself clear?"

Somers managed to say, "Yes." Hazard didn't speak; he gave a single jerk of his head.

Shoulders sagging again, Cravens reached out a hand as though to pat Somers's shoulder. Then she dropped her hand. "I am sorry about your father, Detective. We're all thinking about you. Please let me know if there's anything we can do to help."

Somers wanted to tell her what she could do to help. She could let him investigate the shooting and the too-convenient death of the shooter. But instead, he worked up a smile and nodded. It felt about as real as paste and paper, but Cravens smiled back and trudged up the hallway.

"Jesus," Somers said when she was gone.

"About time you said something worth saying," Hazard said.

"Are you kidding? I sounded like you. I sounded worse than you, and that's almost impossible. I sounded like a lunatic."

"You sounded like you were finally making sense."

"Jesus," Somers muttered. "Just Jesus Christ. Great, that's what I need, for you to think I'm making sense."

"Come on," Hazard said, starting towards the service stairs.

"Where are you going?"

"To find out who tried to kill your father."

"You—" Somers called after him, but by then, Hazard had already disappeared down the stairs. Swearing, Somers trotted after him.

"Just Jesus Christ, this is what I need."

CHAPTER ELEVEN

**DECEMBER 23
SATURDAY
7:12 AM**

HAZARD DROVE A CHERRY-RED VW Jetta that was, if Somers were being fair, more of a faded pink than cherry-red and that had a significant amount of rust eating at the wheel wells. It was about a cubic meter too small for Emery Hazard; when he sat behind the wheel, he looked like he'd been vacuum-packed inside a Matchbox car.

"This is a joke," Somers said.

"The Interceptor has official plates," Hazard said. "Everybody will spot it from a mile away."

"Everybody will spot this from a mile away. A clown car? What are we supposed to do when we get out? Blow balloon animals."

Hazard responded with a vicious—and lengthy—description of what Somers could blow. The only way to shut him up was for Somers to get into the car. They drove across town in the VW, and sardines in a can was too spacious a metaphor. Somers's shoulder rubbed Hazard's as the car bounced along. Hazard's hand brushed Somers's leg when he shifted gears. The VW made a soft, whining noise, like metal that had almost, but not quite, been worn smooth. It was so small that Somers could smell Hazard's deodorant. He could feel the heat pouring off the bigger man. And his hand. His goddamn hand. How many times did he have to shift gears? It was going to make Somers's head explode.

"What's wrong with you?" Hazard said. "Your face is red."

"Can't this thing go any faster?"

"Are you too hot?" Hazard stretched across Somers, his big, ropy muscles pressed against Somers's chest as he fumbled with the window. "You need some air."

"Just get off me." Somers shoved Hazard back into his seat and took a deep breath. That damn pomade, too.

"What the hell is your deal?"

"If you shift one more time, I'm going to—I don't know what I'm going to do."

Hazard frowned, but he drove them the rest of the way in second, and they coasted through two stop signs. He parked in front of the Newton Mortuary, a red brick building with a steeply pitched roof. Inside, Hazard led Somers to the medical examiner's office at the back of the building. He punched in the code to the door—a masterpiece of cryptography, 1-2-3-4-5—and they stepped into the dingy, black-and-white room.

Little had changed in the months since Hazard had arrived in Wahredua. The octagonal tiles that ran across the floor and up the walls still looked like they needed a wheelbarrow of Ajax—even a wheelbarrow might not be enough. The autopsy table with its chipped enamel was still slowly rusting away, the reddish-brown stain flaking away from the metal to fall and bloody the tile. Inside one of the cadaver drawers, a row of vodka bottles stood at attention, each with varying amounts of hooch still inside. Last of all, completing the picture, was the homemade desk—nothing more than a piece of plywood laid across two sawhorses—covered with papers, files, empty bottles, black and blue pens, a pair of crystal apples, and what looked like a zipper detached from someone's jeans.

Also on top of the desk lay a completely naked man. Although to be fair, Dr. Kamp, Wahredua's medical examiner, was neither completely naked nor completely lying down. He looked like he had fallen asleep while kneeling; at one end, his mass of frizzy white hair rested on the desktop, while at the other end, his bare ass stuck up into the air, escaping the white lab coat he had pulled around his shoulders. Even from a distance, the doctor reeked of stale vomit and cigarette smoke. He was either unconscious or dead, and Hazard didn't think he was lucky enough for Dr. Kamp to be dead.

"See if he's got a file started," Hazard said, starting towards the drawers.

"No, no, no." Somers snagged Hazard's sleeve and jerked his head at the desk. "You see if he's got a file started."

Hazard's eyes narrowed. "It's your turn."

"My father's the one who got shot."

"We're supposed to take turns."

"I'm the victim of a personal tragedy."

"You're a manipulative little asshole." But Hazard altered his course towards the desk and the reeking doctor.

"Thanks, Ree."

"Shut up."

While Somers crossed towards the cadaver drawers, Hazard paused and studied the tableau in front of him. Even with only a soiled lab coat tugged around his shoulders, Dr. Kamp seemed untroubled by the mortuary's chill or by the obvious discomfort of his position. From what Somers had told Hazard, Kamp was a retired brain surgeon—a once-brilliant, once-successful man. It was hard to reconcile that account with the expanse of sagging flesh and bristly white hairs that confronted Hazard.

Breathing through his mouth, Hazard rifled through the papers on the desk. It didn't take him long to find the file that Kamp had started last night—at some point between the transfer of Santa Claus's body to the ME's office and Kamp's eventual, alcohol-induced blackout. Paperclipped to the inside of the folder was a picture of Santa Claus, stripped now of his hat.

In death, Santa Claus looked like a different man. Gone were the manic energy, the jittery movements, the dilated, empty eyes. Flesh sagged, exposing purple veins and gray stubble, as though Santa were a balloon that had lost all its air.

"Found him," Somers announced, sliding out a tray.

"So did I." Hazard joined his partner and displayed the folder. "Wayne Stillwell."

"What do we know about Mr. Stillwell?"

Hazard glanced at the folder. The ME's file contained a printout of Stillwell's information. "Fifty-seven years old, revoked driver's license, approximately six feet tall, two-hundred-and-seventy pounds."

"Big boy."

Hazard glanced down; graying, rubbery paunch spilled over Stillwell's hips. "He moved fast. And he fought."

"Kamp hasn't started the autopsy yet," Somers said, his finger hovering over Stillwell's chest. Instead of the Y incision that would have marked the ME's work, the flesh was torn and broken by multiple bullet wounds. "The nurse said five shots."

"Hard to tell; he might as well be ground beef up here."

"Meth?"

Hazard shifted his weight and thumbed the single page. "No tox screen. They won't bother."

"I'm not asking about the file. I'm asking you."

"He was on something."

"High enough to try to fight his way free of the cops?"

"Maybe."

"High enough that, even in handcuffs, it would take five shots to stop him?"

Hazard snorted. "I was with you last night, Somers. I saw Lender. Who are you trying to convince?"

"I'm not trying to convince anyone. I'm just trying to figure this out. He was cranked up. He showed up at my parents' house. My father stopped him and took away his gun. My father called us. We arrived. We talked. We decided to stay a few minutes."

"If you start that again, you'll be chewing your own teeth."

"I'm not blaming myself. I'm just laying out the facts."

"Bullshit."

"Anyway, at some point, Stillwell gets free, recovers his gun, and runs into the family room. He shoots high, destroys that ornament, and then starts shooting at my father."

"The lights go out."

"The lights go out." Somers let his hand hover over Stillwell's body again, as though he might sense some truth that lay inside the corpse—nestled alongside the bullets that had killed him, perhaps. "Someone planned this."

Hazard said nothing.

"Someone inside the house helped Stillwell. Someone made sure the lights went out. And someone paid Lender to kill Stillwell before the truth could come out. It's got to be the mayor."

"It doesn't have to be." Somers looked at Hazard, and the expression was so dead, so hostile, that Hazard rolled one shoulder. "I'm not saying it wasn't him. I'm just saying it's not necessarily him." Again, in Hazard's mind came the memory of Grace Elaine Somerset's face when she heard her husband was still alive. Fury. Fury like a woman who might start breathing fire.

"Who else would want my father dead?"

"That's a good question. Why would Mayor Newton want him dead?"

"Because Newton's crooked. He's corrupt. He's greedy. Because he's already tried to kill us." Somers swore and turned in a circle. "Will you stop looking at me like that? Fine, I don't know why he would do that. He and my father were friends. Are friends. God, I don't know."

"The only reason to suspect Newton is because Lender conveniently shot Stillwell. Let's suppose, for a moment, that Lender is open to bribes. Any number of people might have paid him to take care of Stillwell."

"Great. So anybody with a few thousand dollars could be our suspect."

"Not necessarily. It has to be someone who was at that party. Or who had a connection at that party."

Somers scrubbed the back of his hand across his chin; blond stubble rasped. "All right. So we start with Stillwell and move backward. We see who contacted him, when, why. We see if he has priors."

Nodding, Hazard said, "There are two other things that bother me."

"The lights."

Another nod. "Why turn out the lights right when Stillwell started shooting? Wouldn't that throw off his aim?"

"It did. That's probably the only reason my father is still alive. Whoever planned this was trying to cover his tracks, but it backfired."

Hazard wasn't sure about that, but he didn't have a better theory, and he let it drop. "The other problem is Stillwell himself."

"What about him? He was cranked up and crazy. It probably didn't take much to convince him to try to kill my father."

"Possibly. But why did Stillwell wait? Why didn't he shoot your father when he got to the party?"

Somers grimaced. "He was crazy. Maybe he didn't know who my father was. Maybe he was just too high. Maybe he was supposed to wait for the lights to go off. Christ, Hazard, I don't know."

Again, Hazard let the matter drop—not out of any sensibility to Somers's feelings but because Hazard didn't have an answer himself. The question prickled at him, though, and he didn't like that.

"The girl," Somers said abruptly. "Bing's daughter. What was her name?"

Hazard shook his head.

"Is she here?"

She was. Her body lay in the drawer next to Stillwell's, and Hazard recovered her file from under Dr. Kamp's head. He scanned the single page and looked at the girl.

Hadley Jessica Bingham, eighteen years old, looked much smaller than her age. On the metal tray, emptied of life, stripped of a future, she might have been twelve or ten—a child. It was hard to reconcile this frail shell with the provocatively dressed young woman clinging to Glennworth Somerset. It was harder still to imagine her as Bing's daughter.

"My father's such a fucking prick," Somers said, and he kicked the wall of drawers.

"He didn't do this."

"She's dead because he liked the attention. She's dead because he encouraged her, for God's sake."

"She's dead because Wayne Stillwell shot her."

"Let's go," Somers said. "I'm going to—I don't know what I'm going to do. Let's just go."

Hazard moved to slide the drawer back, and then he stopped. In a plastic bag next to Hadley's body, Kamp had stored her possessions: a black clutch, a pearl necklace, a mobile phone. There would be no investigation into Hadley's death. These paltry belongings would be returned to her family.

"What are you doing?" Somers asked as Hazard retrieved plastic gloves from Kamp's desk. "Hazard—Ree—you can't—" Somers fell silent as Hazard opened the plastic bag and removed the phone.

Without speaking, Hazard found an unused bag, carefully wrapped the phone, and stored it in his pocket.

"We can't take that."

"We aren't. I am."

"Ree, if someone finds out—"

Hazard stripped off the gloves and threw them in the wastebasket. "We're on leave, Somers. Forced leave. If anybody finds out about any of this, we'll be out of a job. Don't pretend this is something else."

Somers was silent as they returned to Hazard's cramped VW. Hazard handed over Stillwell's address, taken from Kamp's file, and Somers plugged it into his phone. They drove across Wahredua, towards Smithfield and its warrens of abandoned buildings, drug dens, prostitution, and crime. As they drove, a smile tugged at the corners of Somers's mouth.

"What?" Hazard finally snapped.

"You know what I realized? Taking that phone? I bet that's the closest you've ever come to getting a girl's phone number."

The crack of Somers's head against the window was immensely satisfying.

CHAPTER TWELVE

DECEMBER 23
SATURDAY
8:00 AM

ASIDE FROM THE ACHE IN HIS SKULL—Hazard still didn't know how to take a joke—Somers felt surprisingly good. Oh, sure, he hadn't slept. His body had a strangely heavy weightlessness, like an anvil that had been let loose in outer space. His thoughts, disjointed and fragmented, floated between anger and determination.

But overall, he felt good. He had the shooter's name and address. He had a possible suspect in Mayor Newton. And most of all, he had Emery Hazard. Hazard, with his eerily cold, analytical way of seeing the world. That dispassionate reasoning was worth a hell of a lot. Even if Hazard couldn't take a damn joke.

The address for Stillwell's last official place of residence was deep in Smithfield. Smithfield, situated on the northwest side of Wahredua, where the old Missouri Pacific lines ran and the newer—and already downtrodden—trailer park stood, was the dark side of town. It was a place where people tried as hard as they could to look the other way. It was a place where nobody wanted to know your name. It was the place where John-Henry Somerset, a recruit fresh out of the academy, had cut his teeth. These streets were still his streets, and today, he was going to prove that.

As they pulled up in front of a block of apartments, the winter sunlight slashed out from the horizon. At this hour, the light ran parallel to the snow, so that the long, ruffled blankets glowed. Beer cans and broken bottles, poking out of that white radiance, ruined the effect somewhat. The building itself looked like this winter, maybe even this day, might be its last. The bricks crumbled along the corners, revealing the lighter-colored, powdery innards, and even with snow covering the roof, it was clear that swaths of shingles had been ripped away and never replaced. Somers had seen buildings implode on TV, controlled demolitions where cement and steel and glass folded inwards, and he half-expected this apartment building to do the same: shrivel up, fall, and exhale one last, dusty breath.

"You know this place?"

Somers shook his head.

When they reached the front door, though, Somers saw the brass lettering under the cramped porch: The Haverford. "Shit."

Hazard paused with his hand on the buzzer. "What?"

"This place is trouble."

"You said you didn't know this place."

"I didn't." The wind whistled down Somers's collar, and he shivered as he gestured at the nameplate. "You don't remember that name?"

Hazard shook his head.

"The Haverford? Hollace Walker? Senior year?"

"I said I don't remember."

"You were friends with Hollace, weren't you? Didn't he tell you—"

"I wasn't friends with anyone, Somers. Did you hit your head too hard?"

"He was trying to impress some of the guys. He came here to buy some coke."

"It's freezing out here; do I really need a history lesson?"

"Three cops have been shot inside the Haverford. How's that for a history lesson? Don't ring that damn buzzer, Hazard. We're not going in this way. Not unless we're wearing Kevlar."

Without waiting for a response, Somers abandoned the cramped porch and strode down the block. Hazard came after him, his huge feet compacting the snow, crunch-crunch-crunch. The wind picked up again, blowing snow crystals in Somers's eyes, and he blinked them clear; the sunlight made the beaded melt iridescent. On the next block, a bulky figure hauled a shopping cart by its front, using both hands two drag frozen wheels through the snow. Somers watched the man—the woman?—with the shopping cart and thought Smithfield never changed. He could be gone a hundred years and he'd come back and it would be the same. Shittier, but the same, if those two things could be true at the same time.

"Three cops got shot? And Cravens didn't blow this thing down?"

"Three cops didn't get shot at the same time. I said three cops have been shot inside the Haverford." Somers turned the corner, following the south side of the massive brick apartment building towards a fire door. "Murray got shot here in seventy-nine. He survived. Shot in the ass by a grandmother. The woman didn't even get out of her lawn chair, just lined up a shot through the door and got Murray in the right cheek. Murray says those were different times. He even went back on the streets when he could walk again."

"In the ass?"

"Ask him about it sometime."

"No thanks."

"The other two, they were different. About ten years ago. Maybe twelve. I was still at college, so I only heard about it when I moved back. But everybody was still talking about it a few years later when I got the Smithfield beat. Everybody wanted to make sure I knew what had happened." He paused outside the metal fire door. The snow along the frame had been knocked free, and in the snowfall, footprints beat a path in and out of the doorway. A quarter-inch of the door protruded past the lip of the frame, and Somers pinched that thin length of metal and pulled. Scattering snow, the door swung open.

"They were trying to scare you."

"Some of them." Inside, they stood in the shaft of a stairwell. The steps were barely wide enough for a grown man, and Somers knew that if he stretched, he could touch both walls at the same time. A slurry of half-frozen snow and dirt and spilled tobacco covered the steps, and Somers picked his way through the mess. "My father, he was trying to scare me. He made that happen, you know."

"Smithfield?"

Without looking back, Somers could imagine the skepticism on Hazard's face. "Yes, Smithfield. He pulled some strings, had Cravens stick me out here."

"Who told you?"

"Nobody had to tell me. Glenn Somerset isn't particularly subtle. The day I got the posting, my father called. He took me out to dinner. Just the men, you see. A conversation between men. And he told me his own version of what had happened in the Haverford, and he said if I wanted to get my head blown off, I had the perfect opportunity. Then he called over the waiter and asked for the dessert menu. He ordered a fucking cherry cobbler."

The memory of that night clung to Somers: it had been a bistro, a pop-up restaurant that had barely lasted long enough to get the menus printed, but Somers still remembered the smell of rosemary, the waxiness of the cheap linens, the pop and creak of new vinyl upholstery. And he remembered his father leaning back, a forkful of cherry cobbler levitating at eye level, and the message in his father's face.

"So he was trying to warn you. Why would he get you posted there and then warn you about it?"

"Because that's what my father does." Somers glanced up. Stillwell's apartment was in the four hundreds, and that meant there were still two more flights to go. Dull circlets of sunlight, penetrating a single row of glass blocks in the wall, did little to alleviate the darkness in the stairwell, but they gave enough light to reveal the vapor of Somers's breath. "That's what Glenn Somerset is best at. Hammer and tongs. Or hammer and anvil, I guess. Rock and a hard place. Frying pan and fire. Once he's got you where he wants you, he hits as hard as he can and expects you to pop."

"You're saying he—what? He got you that posting in Smithfield because he wanted to make you quit?"

"He wanted to make me go to law school."

Hazard snorted. "You?"

Somers paused; his shoe squelched into the slush covering the steps. "Yeah, me. Is that so hard to believe?"

"No."

"Well, why'd you say it like that?"

"Are you going to tell me what happened with the other two cops? Or am I going to freeze my balls off in this stairwell?"

"I got good grades, Hazard."

"Fine. Whatever. Can we go?"

"I took the LSAT."

"Yeah, sure."

"You're an asshole, you know that?"

"Either start moving, or I'll plant you on your asshole. Understand?"

Somers pushed himself up to the next step, careful to slide his shoe backward—forcefully—along the step. Slush splattered wetly, and Hazard swore.

"Nico just got this suit cleaned."

"You want to hear about those two detectives?"

"Did you hear what I said? He's going to kill me." Hazard paused. "You didn't say they were detectives."

"Partners. At the Haverford on some sort of drug-related investigation."

"Jesus Christ. We don't do drugs. Lender and Swinney do drugs."

For a moment, the only answer was the slap of their soles on the wet cement. Then Somers spoke. "They were both shot. One in the head—dead instantly, of course. The other in the gut, in the chest, in the legs. Hard to say, but I doubt those happened all at once. I'm guessing whoever did that shooting, he did it slow and purposeful. I bet he really took his time. Made sure that detective enjoyed every minute of it."

"Why the hell are you telling me this?"

"Because there's so many damn stairs and because I feel like it. You know what my father told me?"

Again Somers pictured that bistro—Le Gourmand Toulousain? Was that the name? His fingers curled inwards, as though still clutching that too-slick tablecloth. The smell of cherry cobbler, acidic, stung his mouth.

"Do you know?" Somers asked the dark, hulking silence behind him.

"Fuck me if I know. You're going to tell me anyway."

"He said the one who was shot in the head, that bullet was a .38 Special."

They climbed another full flight of stairs before Hazard said, "So what? He was saying that the cops turned on each other?"

"No." Somers stopped at the fourth-floor landing, put his hand on the access door, and paused. "He was saying one cop turned on the other. Killed his partner. Shot him in the head. The way I always imagined it, it was a plan that went wrong. This detective, the dirty one, he must have been taking orders from someone. They showed up at the Haverford. Maybe it was the wrong place. Maybe it was the wrong time. The dirty cop shoots his partner. And then—" Somers shrugged.

"And then whoever is paying him shoots him."

"Takes his goddamn time doing it too."

"What's to say your dad didn't make up that detail? Did you ever check?"

"Did I ever investigate a dirty cop who'd been gunned down and lionized? No, Hazard. I wanted to keep my job."

"You should—"

"My father doesn't lie, anyway. At least, not unless he absolutely has to. He usually finds a way to make the truth much more devastating. You know what makes this whole thing the biggest bitch of all, though?"

For the first time since they had started up the stairs, Somers glanced at his partner. Hazard's pale complexion was heightened by the darkness; the shadows pooled under his eyes, leaving only those glittering, straw-colored irises staring back.

"What really pisses me off about this, what makes the whole thing unbearable, is that my father was right. There's a dirty cop on the force. Odds are, there are a lot more than Lender who are dirty. I could shoot Lender just for that, just for proving my father right."

When Hazard spoke, his voice had become low, rasping like scree sliding down a mountain. "What about Hollace?"

And then, there it was again: that night, that last night with Bing at the party. Somers wanted to squeeze his eyes shut; memories rolled through him like a film on a reel, twenty-four frames per second, and if he squeezed his eyes shut, he'd have to see them in living color. The coke, and the party, and the bedroom, and the photograph. God damn Hollace Walker. But even that wasn't really fair, because Somers had unrolled the fuse a long time before that night, and the coke was just the spark that got everything going.

"Nothing," Somers managed to say, his eyes still open, fixed on the empty dark of the stairwell. "Not a damn thing happened to Hollace Walker."

CHAPTER THIRTEEN

DECEMBER 23
SATURDAY
8:09 AM

THE DOOR TO APARTMENT 423 was locked, but Somers slid a credit card through the loose frame, and a moment later the door swung open. Inside, the apartment looked even worse than the crumbling building that surrounded it. Once the high-pile carpet had been a fluffy oatmeal color; now, after God only knew how many years, it had been flattened into a hard, polyester shine the color of dirty socks. Cheap particle paneling covered the walls, and over the years tenants had knocked various holes and gouges and divots into the boards, exposing the compacted sawdust within.

Wayne Stillwell's contribution to the apartment, it seemed, was garbage: heaping, contractor bags of garbage filled much of the space, while more garbage overflowed onto the other available surfaces. Crushed plastic cups, empty pizza boxes, microwave dinner trays, shredded t-shirts, a pair of hot pants wrapped around a vaguely vaginal ceramic lamp, wads of cotton batting that had, at some point, been shat upon, and three-quarters of a taxidermied dachshund—fortunately, in Somers's opinion, it was the front three-quarters, although to judge by the little dog's eternal grimace, it didn't seem too pleased with its afterlife.

And everywhere, everywhere, Santa Claus with children. A pair of shelves peeled back from the wall, rusty teeth slipping from the plaster. Crowding those shelves were sculptures of Santa, snow globes with Santa, hand-painted wooden tablets with Santa, even a Santa diorama made of toothpicks and marshmallows and a scrap of red flannel no bigger than Somers's thumbnail. In all of the representations, children crowded around Santa. In one of the snow globes, children gathered at Santa's knee, as though listening to a bedtime story. One of the sculptures showed them tearing open presents while Santa looked on with a smile. No, not a smile. A leer. A grotesque twisting of a mouth made fat, caked with crimson lipstick. The marshmallow Santa held a whip made of Red Vines, his arm back, ready to flail the marshmallow children lashed to his sleigh.

"This is disgusting," Hazard said, prodding a pizza box with the toe of his shoe.

"This is insane. Genuinely, certifiably insane." Somers moved deeper into the apartment. More Santa decorations covered the walls: cheap four-color prints torn out of magazines, flattened Coca-Cola cans, a pair of stuffed dolls. Stillwell had even hammered decorative ceramic plates to the walls; one of the nails went right through Santa's crotch. "What was he? A pedophile?"

Hazard only grunted; he still stood near the door, studying the apartment. He looked like he thought he might catch something if he moved any closer.

"He liked Santa," Somers reported as he ducked his head around the corner: a kitchen, the linoleum rubbed away in spots to reveal plywood, a microwave the size of a small car, and more Santas. Some of Stillwell's collection was homemade—or at least, modified. One of the kitchen Santas held a metal skewer; on the end of it, Stillwell had impaled thumb-sized baby dolls. "But he did not like children."

Hazard had stripped off his jacket and was now rolling up his sleeves. From one pocket he produced a pair of disposable gloves.

"Hey," Somers said. "What about me?"

Wordlessly, Hazard pulled out a second pair of gloves and flung them at Somers.

As Hazard waded into the garbage, Somers moved towards the back of the apartment. He passed through the kitchen, glanced into a bathroom with chipped tile and a blackened bathtub—it looked as though a grease fire had charred the enamel—and found the bedroom.

The hoarding was worse here; black contractor bags mounted to the ceiling, filling the air with the stale, decaying smell of aged, yellowed paper and body odor and the slightly sweet, slightly gassy smell of fermentation. A path led through the bags, and Somers had to turn sideways to squeeze between the walls of garbage. How had Stillwell, with his sagging gut, managed to fit through here?

The path crooked once, and at the end of it Somers found the bed. One side of the queen mattress was covered with old newspapers; Somers handled one, and the edge of the paper crumbled. The date was June 7, 1987, and when he set the paper back down, some of the ink transferred to his glove, leaving a smeared inversion of the print. The bedsheets were matted, and a brownish stain outlined where Stillwell had slept. How long would it take to stain sheets like that? Five years of never changing them? Ten? Once, Cora had asked Somers to change their bedding, and he had forgotten. She'd come home that night, come home from whatever it was she'd been doing—tap? Had she been going to tap classes? Or had it been a benefit dinner, even back then?—and she'd been furious. Two weeks. The sheets had been on there two weeks, and she'd ripped the sheets off the bed and washed them herself, and Somers had spent that night, the next night, and a lot more after that on the couch. Christ, and that had just been two weeks.

Somers turned to rejoin Hazard at the front of the apartment, but a click and a soft whir of air made him pause. He leaned over the bed, and the noise continued—the sound of a small fan that had almost blown out, its spinning interrupted by squeaks and stumbles and lurches. Grimacing, Somers climbed onto the bed, towards the noise.

And then he saw it, tucked into a cramped alcove in the garbage at the foot of the bed: a computer. A hefty old Apple desktop, with an honest-to-God dial-up modem. The screen had a slight greenish tinge, and the keyboard shone with a grimy patina. Grateful for the disposable gloves, Somers shuttled the mouse back and forth.

The greenish tinge on the screen flickered, and then a desktop appeared. Somers stared at the monitor, at the clunky icons, at the pixelated rendering of the images. Jerkily, the mouse icon followed his movements, and he clicked on the Safari icon. In fits and starts, the browser's white box filled the screen, followed by blocky text. Somers scanned the text.

It was a Craigslist ad, he realized. The posting was simple and straightforward: *Wanted: Santa Claus to appear at a very adult Christmas party. No kiddies here, just a few lovely ladies looking to be satisfied. $200 cash on arrival. Men only; no little boys needed.* Someone named ur_gurl_wants_it99 had posted the ad in the personals section under Casual Encounters.

"Casual sounds right," Somers said, scrolling down. That was all the information on the page, though, and so he eased himself off the bed—cringing as he passed over the sweat-stained sheets—and hurried back to the front of the apartment.

Hazard knelt, a pile of burrito wrappers on one side and what looked like it might have originally been a toilet bowl, sans tank, on the other. Someone, presumably Stillwell, had glued two urinal cakes to the outer rim of the tank.

"What the hell have you been doing?" Hazard gestured at the toilet. "I'm one bag in and this is already the worst idea you've ever had."

"Is that a face?"

Hazard's eyes narrowed; he was fighting the urge to glance at the toilet, Somers could tell, and it made Somers struggle to hide a smile. "Will you get over here and help?" Hazard demanded.

"I'm serious. I think he made a toilet face. A toilet friend."

"I don't care. Get over here. I'm not doing this by myself."

"Was there anything in the mouth? The bowl, I mean. Did it have a tongue?"

"I don't give a damn if it's a face or if it's a spaceship or if it's the pope's goddamn chalice. Quit dicking around."

"Craigslist."

For a moment, Somers had to fight a burst of laughter. Hazard was staring at him, a mixture of bafflement and fury growing on his face. A lock of his long, dark hair—really, it was so long it was obvious that Hazard was growing it out, even if he denied it—had fallen across his forehead, curling in a way that made Somers want to brush it back.

"What are you—"

"There's all sorts of interesting things on Craigslist."

"So what?"

"People post ads for all sorts of things."

Hazard's eyes narrowed to slits.

"I was just thinking that if you wanted some extra money before Christmas—"

"If you tell me that you were thinking we could sell this toilet on Craigslist, or these Santas, or anything in this goddamn apartment, I'm going to rip your head off and leave it in this fucking abomination of a toilet."

"Toilet face," Somers corrected.

Anger blotched Hazard's cheeks, and he was making a choking noise like he might have swallowed his tongue.

"Anyway, that's not what I was going to tell you. I was going to tell you that I just found an ad on Craigslist. An ad you might be very interested to see."

The choking noises grew, if possible, even more furious.

"An ad asking for a Santa to appear at a Christmas party."

Hazard went silent. Somehow, it was much more terrible than the red in his face and the growling. He got to his knees. Then to his feet. His movements were stiff, hostile, like a man about to take a really wide swing and hope he hit as hard as he could.

As Hazard shoved past Somers, Somers called, "If you're thinking about answering, though, it's too late."

Hazard shouted something back that was mostly incoherent—and about as foul as anything Somers had ever heard. He let a smile crack his face and trotted after Hazard.

He found his partner in the bedroom, his huge form awkwardly crouched on the bed as he examined the computer. Without turning his head, Hazard said, "You're an idiot."

"Who do you think ur_gurl_wants_it99 is?"

"You're annoying. And immature."

"But I'm not the one that had to discover the toilet face."

Hazard flicked him the finger, still studying the screen.

"Seriously," Somers said. "Who do you think could have posted it?"

"Anyone could have posted it. That's how Craigslist works. There are no filters—nothing serious, anyway. Unless someone complains, you can post just about whatever you want and get away with it."

"How'd you learn that?"

Hazard grunted and scrolled.

"Were you trying to buy something? A black velvet Elvis? New red pumps?"

"That's about the stupidest thing you've ever said."

"Gay sex? Were you trolling for sex on Craigslist?"

"Never mind, that's definitely the stupidest."

"I hooked up with a guy off Craigslist once."

Hazard's face shot towards Somers, as fast as though someone had cracked him across the cheek. And then, blushing, he turned back to the computer.

"I did," Somers said.

"I don't care."

"You don't want to talk about it?"

"I literally cannot think of anything I want to talk about less."

"Turned out to be my roommate. Isn't that weird? I don't know if I would have gone through with it if it had been a stranger." Somers paused. "Of course, if he had looked anything like you, he could have been from Mars and I probably would have—"

"What the hell has gotten into you?" Hazard leaned back from the computer, his weight dimpling the mattress. "Your dad got shot. Why are you acting like this?"

"Acting like what? I'm joking around, Hazard. Yeah, someone shot my father. But we're on the case. We're going to find the bastard behind this. So I'm excited. So I'm a little wired. So I'm joking."

"A joke? Don't bullshit me. You want to get a rise out of me. How? By talking about sex? You want to talk about—what? Me? Us? Here's an update on us: we were on a fucking double date last night, Somers. You were with your wife." He let the last word hang in the air. Then he sliced one big hand through the space between them as if he could pare away what he'd just said. "Look, I know you've been through a lot. This is, what, some kind of compensation? You're reacting to the stress, fine. You want to give me shit, fine. But don't do this. We've already done this, and it doesn't ever end well." Hazard paused again. "For either of us."

For the last twelve hours, give or take, Somers's emotions had run wild. Hate, fear, grief, self-loathing, guilt, despair. And, mixed in with all of that, underlying all of it, a magnetic current of something else: the need to fuck something up. And here he was. He'd done it. He'd done it again with Hazard. This wasn't the first time in his life. He'd done it before, with Cora. When things got hard, when the stress mounted, when it looked like he might fail at something important, something he cared about—boom, there was an easy way out. Don't fail; just fuck things up on purpose.

He should apologize. He should open his mouth, say those two simple words: I'm sorry. That's all. Hazard had proven willing to forgive in the past. Beyond all possible expectations, beyond reason, Hazard had been willing to overlook Somers's shitty behavior from their youth. So here it was, easy, just say it. Say those two words.

Instead, though, Somers fixed a crooked smile on his face and said, "Who do you think could have posted that?"

For a long moment, Hazard didn't answer. He shook his head slowly and turned back to the screen. Somers waited, and the silence stretched out. It was broken when Hazard typed something. Then he clicked the mouse. He typed something again. His jaw was so tight that Somers was surprised he couldn't hear teeth snapping.

This was it, Somers knew. He'd finally pushed Hazard too far. And why? Because John-Henry Somerset was feeling shitty? Because he—

—loved—

—because he liked to see how far he could push? Especially how far he could push Hazard? And, deep down, because part of him knew that what he had said was true, and that he'd wanted to say it: that he'd spent the second half of high school wanting to have sex with Emery Hazard, and he'd spent the first half of college trying to make up for the fact that he'd never gotten to do it. And now, when Somers had a chance to apologize and set things straight between them, what did he do? He opened his mouth and said something that he knew would push Hazard just a little further. This time, he'd gone too far. This time, Hazard wouldn't let it slide. This time, Hazard would—

"Take a look at this," Hazard said.

Somers craned his neck, trying to catch a glimpse of the screen, but the stacks of garbage blocked it from view. Easing his weight onto the soiled mattress, Somers crawled towards the computer. Hazard, with shoulders like a goddamn gorilla, took up most of the space, and Somers had to crowd next to him to see the monitor. Their shoulders brushed, and Hazard's movement was swift, mechanical, passionless: he scooted away from Somers as though he'd touched a hot plate.

"His email," Hazard said. "That's how Craigslist works. You have to contact the poster through an email address, usually one that Craigslist provides. That way it's anonymous, or close to it, but the website isn't handling all the messaging." Hazard scrolled and clicked. "Here. Here's the messages back and forth about the Santa job."

Somers scanned them. There were half a dozen messages, and the styles of each sender marked them: misspellings, randomly capitalized letters, and a tendency towards unsubtle sexual advances marked Stillwell's emails; the other emails, in contrast, were compact, carefully formatted, and filled with dense lines of instructions and requirements.

"That's my address," Somers said.

"That's your parents' address."

"That's what I mean. Look—she says that she wants him to show up with only a Santa hat at seven o'clock."

"Either he was late or your dad waited to call us."

Somers ignored the comment. He scanned through the messages again. Ur_gurl_wants_it99 had made the event sound sexual, as though Stillwell would be arriving at a bachelorette party—or at an orgy. Stillwell's replies made it clear that Stillwell, at least, thought he was up for the job. Aside from those facts, though, there was relatively little to glean.

"What's missing?" Hazard said.

"There's nothing in there about a gun. Or about killing somebody."

"Exactly. So why did your dad tell us Stillwell arrived with a gun? And if your dad was telling the truth, why did Stillwell take a weapon?"

"If my father was telling the truth?"

"You know what I mean."

"If my father was telling the truth, then Stillwell did it because he's a goddamn lunatic. He was probably planning on raping ur_gurl_wants_it99 and whoever else was at the party. Maybe he was planning on killing them when he was done. He was sick in the head, Hazard. Take a look around you."

"Yeah. Take a look around."

"What?"

"Take a look around. What do you see?"

"Garbage. A lot of garbage. And my partner who's wasting my time."

As Somers scrambled off the bed, Hazard followed him, hounding him with questions. "And what did you notice about Stillwell last night? What was he like? What doesn't fit?"

Twisting through the narrow space between the stacked garbage, Somers shook his head. "I don't know."

Hazard's fingers gripped his elbow. "God damn it, Somers, will you use your head?"

Somers knocked Hazard's hand away. Turning in a circle, he ran his fingers through his short blond hair. What was Stillwell like? Who the hell cared? Somers didn't want to think about what Stillwell was like. He wanted to go straight to Cravens and demand that she come look at the emails. He wanted to sock Hazard in the face. But he didn't want to think about Wayne Stillwell, naked and coked up, his belly overflowing his thighs.

"Dammit." Somers dragged his fingers through his hair again. "He was high, all right? And I know what you're going to say. You're going to point at that goddamn Christmas plate he hammered to the wall, or to that Santa that's fucking his reindeer, or some other damn thing, and you're going to say that an addict doesn't hold on to stuff like that. An addict sells his stuff so he can get dope."

Hazard folded huge arms across his chest.

"So what?" Somers continued. "All that means is that he wasn't an addict. That doesn't mean he didn't get high every once in a while. It doesn't mean that he didn't want to get amped before his big night with all those lovely ladies."

The stitches in Hazard's jacket creaked as he flexed his shoulders.

"It doesn't mean a goddamn thing, Hazard. Stop it."

"But it's worth thinking about."

Somers shook his head and started for the door.

"Where are you going?"

Somers took the stairs two at a time. Slush splashed underfoot; his leather soles threatened to slide out, but Somers just gripped the handrail and plunged down the cement well.

"You're out of your damn mind," Hazard said.

Somers kicked open the fire door, trampling snow as he made his way up the block. The day had brightened. The angle of the sun had changed. The early morning light spilled down like an anvil, turning everything gritty and flat.

When Somers reached Hazard's cherry-colored VW—the color was even more ridiculous against the grimy snow—he reached for the door. Hazard's enormous paw flattened against the glass and forced the door shut again.

"You're being rash."

"I'm being rash. That's great." Somers tried to drive his elbow into Hazard's stomach. "You sound like a Hallmark special."

"Somers," Hazard said, in that low voice that thrummed inside Somers's chest. That big paw came up and grabbed Somers by the shoulder. "You want to tell Cravens. You want her to see the emails. You think she'll change her mind and open the case."

"You're goddamn right. Now get off me before I break your hand."

"Breakfast."

The word was so unexpected that Somers stopped struggling. "What?"

"Eat breakfast. Let's talk about this. Then, if you're determined to tell Cravens, I'll back you up."

Hazard's scarecrow eyes glittered in the sunlight. His big mitt was surprisingly gentle. Wind teased the long lock of dark hair that curled across Hazard's forehead, and Somers could hear himself back in Stillwell's apartment, could hear the snide, childish tone, *Of course, if he had looked anything like you—*

Letting out a breath, Somers nodded.

CHAPTER FOURTEEN

DECEMBER 23
SATURDAY
8:57 AM

HAZARD DIDN'T TRUST HIMSELF to speak as they drove across Wahredua. There were too many things to say—and too many things to say wrong. Too many emotions. That was the real problem. Why couldn't things be simple?

Around them, Wahredua drifted past like the backdrop for a forgotten 80s movie. The town was much older than the 80s, of course, but this part—safely away from Smithfield, and yet not participating in the trendy revival on Wahredua's southwest side—looked like something out of a John Hughes film: ranch homes with carports, with blocky wood siding in creams and tans and browns; expansive, snow-covered yards; and an adobe-colored strip mall. The strip mall itself was nothing remarkable. The plaster was crumbling. The neon sign near the street flashed HERRY CHISTM S. The parking lot snow had a distinctly yellow color, as though every dog in ten miles had decided to combine efforts here. But the strip mall did have one thing that nobody else in Wahredua had: Big Biscuit.

Big Biscuit was a diner. That was the short of it. The long of it was a tangle of memories, smells, tastes, and, for Hazard, a knot in his gut. Big Biscuit meant high school. It meant popular kids, kids like John-Henry Somerset. It meant danger—brighter, flashier, even more impossible to miss than the strip mall sign. The old thoughts ran through his head: watch out; they'll see you; keep quiet; don't move.

Once, and only once, Hazard had gone to Big Biscuit. He had made Jeff go with him. They had been dating then—if you could call it dating when nobody knew, when you didn't hold hands in public, when you didn't kiss except in the basement with the door closed, if you could call that anything but a joke—and Hazard had insisted. He was tired of feeling ashamed. He was tired of feeling like an outsider. Everyone went to Big Biscuit. John-Henry Somerset went to Big Biscuit. And Hazard wasn't afraid—he remembered telling Jeff that, repeating it, insisting on it until Jeff's shoulders had rolled forward and he'd nodded and squeezed his hands together until his knuckles popped. And right then, with the VW bouncing over the broken asphalt in the parking lot, Hazard suddenly felt tired. What a joke. The whole thing had been such a joke.

"You know this place?" Somers asked. He still didn't sound like Somers. He still had that edge in his voice.

"I grew up here, didn't I?"

"Yeah, but you never came here. I mean, I never saw you here." Somers slackened, his head drooping against the glass as he stared at Big Biscuit's stained walls and drooping canopy. "I was here all the time in high school. It was cool, you know? Eating at a diner was cool. God, we were so stupid."

Stupid. And the thought of Jeff's knuckles popping.

"Did you come here?" Somers asked as they got out of the VW. Snow crunched underfoot. Yellow snow.

"Why the hell do you care?"

"It's just a question."

It's just a question, Hazard thought. The sound of Jeff's knuckles popping, that sound, that goddamn sound, and he says it's just a question.

"Well?"

"Yes."

"I never saw you here."

"Oh well," Hazard said, but inside he was thinking, three o'clock, we came here at three o'clock in the afternoon because we were scared, because I was scared and because I was too stubborn to listen to Jeff. Three o'clock. And at three o'clock in the afternoon, when Big Biscuit had the fewest customers, Mikey Grames had been there. Like he'd been waiting. Like the whole thing was a setup. And Mikey Grames had cut his initials into Hazard's chest. Three o'clock in the afternoon, and all for a damn biscuit.

No. More than a biscuit. It had meant a lot more than that, and Jeff understood that. But who the hell cared anymore?

Inside, the air still smelled like sausage—the fat, greasy patties, their edges blackened on the griddle. The decor had remained the same: red vinyl, chrome fogged by fingerprints, and vinyl squares that looked like they had disintegrated rather than simply wearing away. Once they were inside, Somers took charge, navigating towards a booth at the back. Their waitress, who looked young enough that she might need a booster seat when she sat behind the wheel of a car, dropped two glasses of water on the table and whipped out a pad of paper.

"Big Biscuit Breakfast," Somers rattled the words off without looking at the girl. He sipped his water and added, "Coffee, too. Cream and sugar."

The girl—the child—stared at Hazard.

"Could I see a menu?"

Somers choked on his water; he fumbled the glass trying to set it down. The girl, in contrast, grew icily still. She put the point of her pencil between her teeth.

"What the hell do you need a menu for?" Somers said in a low voice. "Just order what you usually order."

"I'm not hungry for that." Hazard stretched up out of the booth, glancing around the diner for a glimpse of the food that might be available. The other patrons congregated in a tight bracket: white men over sixty in denim overalls and work boots, all of them.

"Hazard, just order something," Somers hissed.

"Cantaloupe."

Eyes widening, the girl bit down on her pencil. The tip of a pink tongue poked out between her teeth, and the pencil lead clattered onto the tabletop.

"For the love of God," Somers muttered, wiping at his eyes. To the girl, more loudly, he added, "He'll have the same thing. Eggs over easy."

"No, I'll have them—"

"Eggs over easy," Somers repeated.

The girl stared at each of them in turn before dropping the pencil to the page. She seemed to have forgotten that the lead had broken, and she scribbled at the page with the useless pencil and walked away.

Somers dropped back in his seat, eyeing Hazard with disgust. "You said you'd been here before."

"I have."

"It's not the Moulin Vert."

Hazard didn't respond.

"What'd you think they were going to have on the menu?"

"Drop it, Somers."

"Who'd you come here with?"

It sounded like an honest question. A few months ago, though, it would have triggered Hazard's defenses because it was a question that touched, however tangentially, on Jeff. Now, Hazard knew, that wasn't Somers's way. Somers never beat around the bush; he'd come straight out and say whatever he was thinking. Unfortunately.

But even though the question was honest, Hazard found himself drawing out packets of Sweet 'n Low and Splenda and shuffling them like he was doing a card trick.

"Oh," Somers said. "Really? With him?"

"Why shouldn't we?" Hazard said, cramming the sweeteners back into their cardboard tray. "Because we were faggots?"

"Ree."

"What? That's what you thought."

"You don't know what I thought. You've never asked me."

"What does it matter, Somers?"

"It matters because of this." Somers gestured at the space between them, as though the thumbprints swarming the tabletop held some sort of secret. "That's why it matters."

"The day I came here," Hazard said, "Mikey Grames was sitting right over there. Third stool from the left. He had on those Ralph Lauren jeans he was so proud of, and they were halfway to his knees. He looked like a damn idiot. I sat in the booth near the window. With Jeff. I had — Christ, I don't even know. Coffee. An egg. Honest to God, I don't remember because all I could think about was Mikey Grames. He noticed us. He was staring. And all I could think was that this was my fault because it had been my stupid idea. Jeff never would have come here."

"Ree, you were right. You had every right to come here. Mikey —"

"He left. We were halfway through eating, and he left, and that was worse because of the way he looked at us. On the way out, he stared at us like he wanted to kill us. And I remember having something in my throat, some food that I didn't remember chewing, and I didn't choke, but it was there, suffocating me because I couldn't swallow. He was going to kill us. We were on opposite sides of the booth, Jeff and I. We weren't touching or kissing. We weren't dressed like faggots, but we might as well have had on silk shirts and leather chaps as far as Mikey was concerned. And you know what? I couldn't do it. I couldn't eat any more. We paid — Jeff paid — and we left. Jeff went home. I was sick. I wanted to throw up, but I couldn't. I started walking home."

Hazard paused. He wanted to say the rest of it. He wanted to tell Somers the end of the story: Mikey and John-Henry and Hugo catching him a few blocks off Market Street, fencing him into the alley, while Mikey pulled out a pocket knife and carved the first three lines of a G into Hazard's chest.

But what was the point in telling it? What was the point in bringing that up? To make Somers feel guilty? There might be some satisfaction in that, but it would be a petty, vicious kind of satisfaction, and Hazard had had enough of that for one life.

"What?" Somers said.

"That's it. I walked home."

"That can't be it. You said you started walking home. Something else happened. Did Mikey come back?"

At that moment, the waitress returned. She set down four plates, two for each man: pancakes, eggs, bacon, sausage, and the eponymous big biscuit. A sticky-looking syrup container followed, along with pads of real butter. Then, planting her hands on her hips, the waitress studied the table, nodded, and left them. Customer service, Big Biscuit-style.

"What'd you like about this place?" Hazard said, spearing a sausage patty. "You heard me bitch, now tell me your side of it."

"Ree, what happened?"

"It's history. Tell me what the cool kids did." Hazard surprised himself with a smile. Part of that was the sausage; it was damn good.

For a moment, Somers said nothing. His face was far off, as though he were trying to find the ending to Hazard's story. He stirred his eggs with his fork, piercing one and spilling yolk across the sausage and bacon. "It was a lot of things, I guess. Good food." He ate a sausage for emphasis. "That goes a long way, especially for teenage guys. You know: carbs and protein, and you can eat all you want because you're seventeen and you'll burn it off without getting out of bed."

"This was the only place that served pancakes and bacon?"

"Not the only place," Somers said, spreading butter on his pancakes and drowning them in syrup. He carved a slice out of the fluffy mound and shoveled it into his mouth. "The best place."

"Come on."

"I don't know. It's not like something special happened. It just . . . happened."

"You can do better than that." Hazard followed his partner's example; the first bites of pancake melted in his mouth.

"Well, some of it was football. The guys liked to come here. It was a varsity thing, no freshmen or JV allowed, and that made it really attractive. It was a big deal when you got to go to Big Biscuit. We'd go before games, after games. Sometimes both. We'd go on the weekends. Bing—" He paused. "Damn, I hadn't thought about that. Bing used to come here. He was so young, you know. Just a few years older than the rest of us, even if he did teach metals and coach varsity.

It seemed so cool, hanging out with him. He was in college, and he was our coach, but he was also just cool."

Hazard noticed that, at some point, their waitress had returned with their coffee. Big Biscuit service again—usually the coffee came first. He sipped at the drink, barely noticing its heat because he was thinking about what Somers had said. Thinking about Bing.

Back then, nobody had been cooler than Bing. He'd had it all: good looks, athletics, brains, money. In a town like Warhedua, that had made Bing magnetic. No, not magnetic. It had been more like gravity. Things had revolved around Bing; they always had. Even Emery Hazard, on the edge of Wahredua's solar system, had felt that pull. Until that day at the lake, when Hazard had been walking along the beach, and Bing had stood there, framed by the sun and the water, stripping away shirt and shorts and kicking them into the sand, Hazard drooling enough to raise the water level a few inches.

"Anyway," Somers said, breaking Hazard's train of thought, "that was it. Some of the girls knew we came here, so they would come too. I never really thought about the fact that you didn't come here." His face screwed up. "I should have invited you. I mean, it's a diner, right? Everybody should have come here. It's just a place."

Hazard shrugged, but he knew Somers was wrong—and he knew that Somers's knew too. Somers might not phrase it in the same words, but both men knew that the question wasn't about place but about power. And one way of showing power was to be different, to do things that other people couldn't do. A little tick ran through Hazard and he felt a thought come into alignment. Yes, power was about doing things that other people couldn't do—and, often, doing them in conspicuous ways.

"Your dad," Hazard said.

"What?"

"He's a lawyer, right?"

"I guess so. He's a partner in his firm, but I don't think he does much besides play golf. What? Are we done talking about Big Biscuit?" Somers flashed an easy smile, but those blue-green eyes, like the oceans in a beer commercial, were troubled. "I still want to hear about what happened to you."

"Who would your father want to impress?"

"What are you talking about?"

"Law firms need clients, right? That's a big part of their business. So who did he want to impress?"

"I have no idea. I don't talk—" Somers paused. He ripped a piece of bacon in half, chewed, swallowed, and then said, "My father and I don't talk about that kind of stuff. He's still angry I didn't go to law school, and the whole thing's boring as hell anyway."

"What about the mayor? What about the sheriff?"

"Who did they want to impress?"

"No. Did your father do business with them?"

"Christ, Hazard, I don't know. What's your point?"

"Your dad was showing off."

"What?"

"Last night, at the party. He was showing off when he called you."

Somers's blond eyebrows drew together. "He's called me plenty of times—"

"But he called you last night when Stillwell had a gun. And think about it: there were lots of younger men at that party, so why were your father, Mayor Newton, and Sheriff Bingham the ones keeping an eye on Stillwell? Because that's who your father was trying to impress. One of them. Maybe both. He wanted them to see that he had a cop in his pocket. Think about it: why didn't the sheriff handle things?"

"Mayor Newton appoints the police chief. He's got the whole department in his pocket."

"But this is different. This is private, on-demand, and there's loyalty: a family bond."

"You don't know much about my family, I guess."

"You went, didn't you? Your dad called and you went to help him—"

"Look, Hazard, I see what you're getting at, but it doesn't make any sense. I've been doing this kind of stuff for my dad for years. Last night wasn't any different. Let's drop it and focus on what we know."

Hazard sheared through a sausage link and ate it in two bites, his teeth clicking together as he chewed. It wasn't the same. Last night was different.

"Here's what we know," Somers said. "Someone contacted Stillwell, hiring him to show up at the party under false pretenses. A lot of false pretenses. Stillwell showed up at the party with a gun. Stillwell shot my father. And Stillwell was killed while in police custody." Through another mouthful of pancakes, Somers said, "It's Newton."

Hazard grunted.

"Don't make that noise," Somers said, spearing a fork towards Hazard. "You know it was him. You know it."

Batting the fork away, Hazard said, "You're leaving stuff out. Important stuff. Nobody mentioned a gun in those emails. Nobody hired Stillwell to do a hit. And I agree Stillwell's death is suspicious, but if Lender's dirty, then he might be dirty for a lot of people."

"But we know he's dirty for Newton. We know that much."

"Christ, keep your voice down, will you? Look, I'm not saying it wasn't Newton, but I'm saying we don't have anything to base it on. If we go to the chief and tell her that we believe Stillwell was hired to kill your father, she's going to ask us why. What do we have to offer her? Nothing."

"Somebody hired Stillwell to go to my parents' house. It's not nothing."

"No, it's not. But it's also not enough to convince the chief that this is murder for hire. She wants it buried; you heard her. All four of her detectives smell like shit around this case, and the faster it's closed, the better. You know her better than I do. What's she going to do if she even suspects we're nosing around Newton for this?"

Conflict twisted Somers's face. "She'll—"

"Be honest."

The conflict in his face folded into despair. "Jesus, man. Somebody tried to kill my father. You want me to just shut up about it? Go back to work? Pretend it didn't happen?"

Hazard lanced his eggs; yolk poured out, mixing with the sausage crumbs. He mopped at the mess with his biscuit.

"That's it? We're just going to sit on this because you're scared?"

"Don't do that bullshit," Hazard said, not bothering to look up from sopping up the yolk on his plate. "You know that's not what I said."

"So what are you saying?"

"I'm saying get your head out of your ass and work this case like a real detective. You're the best one I know when you're not dicking around feeling sorry for yourself."

The silence that followed was so deep, Hazard felt a moment of vertigo as if he could have fallen into that silence and kept on falling. It made him dizzy, and he finally looked up, not able to bear it any longer. Pink brightened Somers's cheeks; he was biting his lower lip. His tousled blond hair looked like he'd just gotten out of bed—and he hadn't been sleeping.

"What?" Hazard said.

For a moment, it looked like Somers would say something. Then he shoved back his plate and glanced at Hazard's half-eaten pancakes. "You going to finish those?"

Hazard curled an arm around the plate protectively.

"Work the case like a real detective, huh?"

"It'd be a nice change."

"I'm the best one you know."

"Oh God."

"No, you said it. You can't take it back."

"Fuck me."

"I'm the best."

Hazard shook his head and turned his attention to the pancakes. "Ree?"

"Just drop it, all right? I'm never going to say it again."

Somers laughed, and it was the closest he'd sounded to normal in the last twelve hours. "Let's work the shit out of this case."

With a grunt, Hazard worked his fork against the pancakes. "In about fifteen minutes."

CHAPTER FIFTEEN

DECEMBER 23
SATURDAY
9:40 AM

HAZARD FINISHED HIS PANCAKES. The last bite had been as good as the first: tender, fluffy, bathed in butter and syrup. Eying the empty plate, Hazard wondered if he had overestimated his own abilities; his stomach was dangerously full.

The time spent eating had diluted the atmosphere, and for that, Hazard was grateful. Somers's anger he could understand. Somers's frustration, Somers's rage, Somers's frenzy to act—all of these things, he could process, parcel out, and deal with. But this other side, this dangerous proximity to—

—intimacy—

—Somers's soft side made Hazard uncomfortable. Uncomfortable? That was mild. Hazard would have jumped head-first through Big Biscuit's plate glass window to avoid that kind of conversation because it was during that kind of conversation that Somers's blue-green eyes got soft, that he leaned a little closer, that the smell of his aftershave rolled over Hazard, the smell of sea-salt drying on skin and crushed amber, that Somers's turned his elbows in, looking awkward and coltish. It was during those kinds of conversations, Hazard had discovered over the last few months, that he was most in danger of—

—falling in love—

—making a mistake. Better to eat in silence, better to chew slowly and sip lots of coffee, better to let time defuse the bomb that was ticking down between them than to take that kind of risk.

What about Nico? The thought rang clear as a bell in Hazard's head. Why didn't Hazard fear those kinds of risks with Nico?

"You're making that face again," Somers said.

"It's the coffee."

"The coffee's fine. What's wrong?"

"We can't focus on Newton."

"Because of Cravens." Hazard nodded, but to his surprise, Somers continued, "And because everyone at the party is a suspect. Don't look so surprised. It's insulting."

"I'm not surprised."

"If your eyes got any wider, Ree, they'd drop out of your head. I get it; I've been focused on Newton for the last twelve hours, ever since Stillwell was shot. And I still think Newton is behind all of this. But the fact is that it could have been anyone at the party. Someone had to free Stillwell. Someone had to give him the gun. And someone had to blow the power. How am I doing?"

"Someone at the party was involved, although they might have been working for someone else."

"And?"

"And the killer couldn't have been just anyone at the party. We actually have a fairly limited group of suspects." Hazard cleared the center of the table, shook open a clean napkin, and sketched a diagram of the Somerset home. "Stillwell was back here, in the TV room. We were in here."

"The family room."

"Whoever untied Stillwell and gave him the gun had to pass through the family room and kitchen to get to the TV room. Unless there's another door?"

"There is. In the kitchen. It leads out to the garage. And one that goes to the back porch."

"Damn it. Were they locked?"

"I don't know."

"Damn it." Hazard studied his sketch and, after a moment, added the door. "That opens up the possibilities. We'll have to consider that. But for now, we can start our list with the people we know had access to Stillwell."

"Mayor Newton," Somers said, holding up a hand before Hazard could speak. "And Sheriff Bingham. They both were in that room at some point during the evening."

"After you handcuffed Stillwell?"

Somers screwed up his face as though trying to remember. "Yes. Bing and his father went into the kitchen after I finished talking to Bing. Mayor Newton followed them in there."

"I didn't see that."

"Probably because you were too busy sulking."

Hazard decided not to respond to that comment. Instead, he said, "The two boys—the ones who dragged the girl off your father—they went in there. And right before Stillwell started shooting, one of the boys looked like he was going to attack your dad."

"Six suspects: Mayor Newton, Sheriff Bingham, Bing, the two boys, and the girl."

"The girl's dead."

"That doesn't mean she didn't do it."

Hazard shrugged. "There are two more people. You're not going to like this."

"My mother. I know she didn't make a good impression on you last night, but she's not the killer." Somers held up a hand again. "I'm not arguing with you; we'll look at her just like anyone else. I know the spouse is statistically likely. But I'm telling you it wasn't her."

Nodding, Hazard said, "And Jeremiah Walker."

"Eight. Eight people who had access to Stillwell. But eight people who would want to kill my father? Eight people with a motive? That's not likely."

Hazard peeled off a twenty and threw it down on the table. As he got to his feet, he gave Big Biscuit a long glance. He was a grown man now, not a scared, marginalized boy. He had fought hard, he had found a place in this world, he had made himself strong. No.

More than strong. He had made himself invulnerable to the old hurts. And here was the proof: all these years later, eating in Big Biscuit.

So why were the shadows of his thoughts about Mikey Grames, about the knife, about the scar still shiny on the flat skin of his belly? Why was he thinking about Bing, and his torn knees, and the lake? Why did it feel like nothing had changed in fifteen years and nothing would change in fifty?

"Well," Hazard said, forcing himself into motion, away from this place, away from the shadows of the past. "Let's find out who might have wanted him dead."

CHAPTER SIXTEEN

DECEMBER 23
SATURDAY
10:25 AM

HAZARD DROVE SLOWLY through Wahredua, angling the VW towards the outskirts of town and the quiet stretch of country where the Somerset home stood. Overhead, the sun had intensified, but the temperature continued to drop. Trickles of melt from the blackened piles of snow froze almost immediately against the asphalt, turning Wahredua's roads into sheets of ice. The VW slid over the frozen asphalt like a soap bubble; Hazard was half-certain that he weighed almost as much as the car, and on days like today, he hoped that extra weight would provide much-needed traction.

When they reached the Somerset home, the pseudo-Victorian brick structure looked as it always had: a sprawling display of wealth and power, its black shutters and red brick a violent contrast to the blankets of snow. In the daylight, the lights strung along the brick and slate and the iron fence looked dull and tiny. Hazard slowed as they approached the gate, which was shut; today, the Somerset home was not receiving visitors.

"Nine-five-four-six-eight," Somers said, but his eyes hadn't left the fence.

Hazard keyed in the code at the gate security box, but he hesitated before accelerating. "What are you looking at?"

"The fence. The lights are off."

"It's daytime."

"Yeah, I know. They were off last night, though. After the power went out."

Hazard studied the fences and its strands of blank, blind bulbs. "What do you think happened?"

Somers shook his head. "I don't know. But someone wanted the power to go off at a certain time."

After another moment, Hazard eased the VW forward, its tires throwing up chunks of re-frozen snow. They parked, and Somers led Hazard into the house. Hazard paused in the entry hall. Then he swore and hammered the door shut behind him.

The house was clean. Not just clean. Spotless. No crime scene tape marking off the area where Glennworth Somerset had been shot. No evidence markers. Even the goddamn punch bowl was clean and sparkling. The only sign of the violence and death that has visited the Somerset home was the careful rearrangement of the family room: someone—certainly not Grace Elaine herself, although she had just as certainly given the instructions—had moved the enormous Christmas tree so that it sat directly on the spot where Glenn had been shot and where Bing's daughter Hadley had died. Although it was hidden now by the crimson tree skirt and the metallic shimmer of the wrapping paper, blood stained the wooden floor.

"What the fuck happened?" Hazard said.

"Hello? Who's there?" Heels clicked in the hallway, and a moment later, Grace Elaine appeared on the landing above them. Head cocked, she was putting in an earring as she looked down. "Oh."

"Mother," Somers said. "What is going on?"

Grace Elaine didn't look like she was going to the hospital. She didn't look like she'd spent the night grieving and worrying. She looked like she was headed to a charity luncheon or a ladies' society or a very elegant house of prostitution: black pumps, a grey wool dress with seed pearls and amethyst stones, and enough silver around her neck to sink the Titanic. What she was wearing, just what she was wearing, had doubtless cost more than everything Hazard's own mother had ever spent on clothes in a lifetime. His own mother, who had worked away her life at a sewing machine, growing smaller, growing more hunched, growing more furrowed and squinting by the year.

"What are you doing here, John-Henry? I have to run out. The arts conservancy has their Christmas luncheon in twenty minutes, and I wasted half my morning trying to find that bluebell brooch that Emilie made." She paused at the bottom of the stairs, fixing the second earring, and then kissed the air near Somers's cheek. "You look tired, darling." Then her gaze shifted to Hazard, and her voice took on its kitty-cat tone. "Detective, if I'd known you were coming I would have made plans to entertain you. I could just tie you up for hours."

In spite of himself, Hazard felt a blush growing. Somers spoke first, though, his voice quaking with that same seismic anger Hazard had heard earlier. "I look tired."

"Yes, dear. You look horrid. Cora won't have you back if you can't bother to brush your hair. And I won't blame her, John-Henry, I really won't." She paused, tugging the silver collars into place. "Is that blood? Oh, John-Henry."

"Yes, Mother. It's blood. It's Father's blood. And Hadley Bingham's blood. She's dead, you know. And Father's in the hospital, in case you hadn't heard."

"Don't be sensational. You know perfectly well that I went to the hospital last night."

"Really? That's strange because I sat with Father all night, and I didn't see you there."

"You did?" Grace Elaine blinked. "Why?"

"Because he almost died, Mother. Because he still might die."

"Yes, dear. I know." From a closet on the side of the entry hall, she retrieved a heavy wool coat, which she held out to Hazard. "Help me with this, won't you?"

Hazard's fingertips tingled as he held open the coat for her. This is what a mouse feels like, he thought. Right before the trap clicks. Right before that wire snaps his back. This is what it feels, not quite knowing, but knowing.

But no wire snapped his back. Grace Elaine shrugged into the coat, buttoned it, and turned to face Hazard. She smiled at him—a cat, Hazard thought, a kitty cat with a mouse's tail between its teeth—and ran a finger down the curve of his arm. Then she turned to Somers, kissed the air above his cheek, and drifted towards the kitchen and, beyond that, the garage.

"And don't make a mess, John-Henry," she called back to them. "That woman, the deputy, she said I could straighten up, and it took poor Margarita all night to get things looking even halfway decent. I swear, if you track mud on her floors, you'll have to deal with her. You really will. Now I'm off. Wish me luck, Emilie's going to kill me for not wearing that brooch. Much love, darling. Bye."

And without another word, she was gone.

"A deputy told her she could clean up the place?" Somers said, as though not quite believing his own words. He turned slowly in a circle, examining the rooms around him as though seeing them for the first time.

"The sheriff must have taken possession of the scene," Hazard said. "Otherwise, Cravens would have left somebody to make sure the place wasn't disturbed. She wouldn't have released it. Not even with Stillwell dead. She wouldn't have done something like that."

"You know why Cravens did. You know why she went along with it, I mean. The mayor. He's got his wingtips on her neck, and so she smiled and nodded and handed everything over to the sheriff. And he just destroyed our crime scene."

Hazard shrugged, but he didn't answer. He could feel that tingling again, that sense that he had crawled too close to the cheese and that the next movement, the next breath would be the end. Snap. Just like that. He wasn't normally given to flights of fancy, and he blamed it on this house, on these people, on the whole damn mess.

"Let's see if they left anything for us to work with," Hazard said.

The family room—that enormous, echoing space with a Christmas tree two feet taller than the Empire State Building—offered no answers, however. In fact, it offered few questions, aside from the most obvious one: why had Cravens withdrawn her officers and allowed the Somerset family to clean up the crime scene? Hazard didn't know, but he didn't think he'd find answers in the room. He shifted furniture, combed the bookshelves and the mantle, adjusted pewter knickknacks that showed no trace of dust, and he found nothing. He crawled under the enormous Christmas tree, scooting along his belly so that the crimson tree skirt bunched up as he went, and he found only a purplish stain on the wood. Did it feel wet still? No, that was more imagination—imagination that, until recently, had never troubled Hazard. Under the tree, the air smelled like pine and like the stale, greenish water that had stood in its basin for too long, and the air was warm, too warm, so warm that sweat dampened a triangle on Hazard's back as he wriggled out from under the branches.

"What did they do?" Somers muttered, pacing a circle. "Have Margarita run a vacuum and mop? Where's the broken glass? Where are the bullet casings? Where is the damn gun?"

"Let's ask Margarita."

Somers called his mother, but she didn't answer. "I don't have Margarita's number. I don't even know her, not really."

Hazard stepped into the hallway, giving himself the widest possible view of the family room. It wasn't just clean; it was sparkling, like someone had spent extra money for that Pine-Sol glow. Was that just good housekeeping? Or was this a cover-up?

"We could call some cleaning services," Somers was saying, running a hand through his blond spikes. "See if they know a Margarita. See if maybe they referred her to my parents."

"You leave the dishes in the sink."

"What?"

"At home, you leave the dishes in the sink."

"I don't—well, just until I'm ready to load the dishwasher."

"And you don't take out the trash. The first time I went to the apartment, you'd left a bag of trash in the front room."

"Yeah, Ree. I was in a bad spot back then."

"No, you still do it."

"I do not."

"How many times have you taken out the trash since I moved in?"

"I don't think—"

"How many times have you washed the dishes?"

"Last Sunday. I washed everything last Sunday."

A smile cracked the corners of Hazard's mouth, and he walked towards the kitchen. "Nico spent about six hours making dinner. Milanesa. That cabbage salad. The bread pudding."

"I did the dishes, Ree." Somers trailed after him. "Listen, if you're pissed about how things are going at home, fine. We'll make a chore chart."

"A chore chart?"

Somers flushed. "Or whatever. But this isn't really the—what are you doing?"

Hazard moved down the length of the kitchen, pulling open the lower cabinets and drawers. Somers followed, sliding them shut, twin slashes of red showing on his cheekbones.

"You grew up with a maid."

"She came once a week to clean," Somers said, the red lines darkening. "I wouldn't call that a maid. Will you—Hazard, stop it. What's going on?"

Under the sink, Hazard found the trash can. He didn't bother with niceties; he was too angry. He was angry about Grace Elaine's casual disregard for the crime that had been committed under her roof, angry about the neglect, the criminally closed eyes that Cravens had turned away from the case, and, truth be told, Hazard was angry about the damn dishes back at the apartment. He toppled the trash can with his foot, upending it and strewing garbage across the floor. Dust, an empty can of sweet corn, the plastic shrink wrap from a tray of gourmet cookies, what looked like the thighbone from a chicken—ordinary trash. The kind of trash, Hazard thought glumly, that Somers never bothered to take to the Dumpster.

"You honestly think someone would just toss incriminating evidence in the kitchen trash?" Somers leaned back, arms folded across his chest, a skeptical gaze moving from Hazard to the trash can.

"It seemed like a possibility."

"You were thinking that because I occasionally don't take out the trash—"

"Is once a year occasional?"

"—that my family might be the same? That—what? My mother might have picked up the murder weapon and tossed it in with last night's leftovers."

"It was a possibility, Somers." It didn't sound quite as good, Hazard had to admit, when Somers said it out loud.

For a moment, the skeptical look lingered on Somers's face. Then it vanished, and a grin snapped into its place. "You know what my mother did with her old bras? And with the *Fit / Fitness / Fight* magazines that she used to buy? You know the ones I'm talking about? They always had a bunch of pictures of shirtless guys."

Hazard shook his head.

"You're a damn liar. You used to keep some in your locker at school."

"How did you—" Hazard cut himself off, but it was too late.

Somers's grin had magnified. "She had one with Josh Hartnett. Like, 2001 Josh Hartnett. I know because I, uh, borrowed it."

"Jesus. Somebody kill me, please. Right now."

"Anyway, you know what she did with it? You know, so my father wouldn't see it?"

"I don't know, Somers. Please drop it. I don't want to talk about your mom's old bras."

"She wrapped it up in an old newspaper and shoved it to the bottom of the outside trash can. You know, the one you put at the curb."

It took a moment for the words to sink in. "How do you know this?"

"Well, I wasn't going to let Josh go that easily. He and I had become too close."

"You're sick."

"I was seventeen. I had my hands full. Kind of literally."

"You're sick. You're definitely messed up."

Hazard didn't wait for Somers to say any more and started towards the garage. He wasn't sure if he could stand more of Somers's innuendo—or his more blatant sexual commentary. It was one thing for Hazard to work and live with Somers: to see him, to smell him, to talk to him, and somehow to pretend for sixteen hours a day that he hadn't been crushing on him since they'd hit puberty. It was quite another thing to hear about—

—Josh Hartnett, 2001, shirtless, Jesus, I think I owned that copy of *Fit / Fitness / Fight*—

—Somers's raunchier activities.

In the garage, a big blue rolling trash can sat near the door. Hazard swung open the lid and was met by stacked black garbage bags.

"Usually over here," Somers said, squeezing up next to Hazard, the tightly corded muscles along his side flexing as he plunged one arm into the trash can. "Mother's very intelligent, but she tends to repeat her—ha. See?"

He dragged out another black trash bag. Unlike the others, though, this one was not stuffed full; it was almost empty, and when Somers lifted it clear of the bin, metal and glass chimed inside the plastic. Without a word, Somers opened the bag and tipped it out onto the concrete pad. At first, a silvery dust streamed out onto the slab, followed by slivers of glass—the ornament, Hazard realized, the ornament that Stillwell had shot before the lights went out. More glass followed, larger chunks, and then the flow of debris began to slow. Somers's firmed up his mouth, gave the plastic bag a final shake, and something small and shiny clinked against the concrete.

Hazard moved instinctively, planting his shoe so that the brass casing stopped against it. One of the casings. The only one, as far as they knew, that the police hadn't bagged and, it was very possible, destroyed.

"Oh," Somers said, as though offering an afterthought, "you're going to clean this up, right?"

CHAPTER SEVENTEEN

DECEMBER 23
SATURDAY
10:42 AM

Do WE TAKE IT to Dr. Kamp?" Somers asked, studying the casing.

Hazard collected the brass with the tip of a pen and deposited their find in an evidence bag. He hesitated before shoving the bag in his pocket. "Not yet."

"Because you think Cravens will shut us down?"

Hazard shook his head. "I'd like to know if they have the other casings. If they held onto them. If they did, then we can have Kamp look at those when the time comes. If they didn't—"

"Then we've got a secret weapon."

With a nod, Hazard set to work sweeping up the broken glass and returning it to the garbage bin. At some point, Somers must have gotten tired of watching because he went back inside. The silence gave Hazard time to think. What Somers had said was the truth: having the casing was an advantage, a piece of evidence that the real killer might assume had been lost or destroyed. But things in this case were much more complicated than that. Ballistics normally helped identify the shooter; in this case, they already knew that Wayne Stillwell had done the shooting. The real killer, whoever he was, hadn't touched the gun in Stillwell's hands—not unless he was very stupid.

No, the casing provided another advantage that Hazard wasn't ready to admit to his partner. For some reason, Grace Elaine had hidden a piece of evidence. Why? Because she had hired Stillwell to shoot her husband? Maybe. Hazard wasn't sure. He knew one thing, though: he was going to hold onto the casing.

When he returned to the kitchen, Hazard was surprised to find that Somers had cleaned up the spilled trash and was now lounging against the counter, drinking some sort of bottled water that looked inordinately expensive. The way Somers's lips hugged the mouth of the bottle—Jesus, the man could drive a nun crazy. As though hearing Hazard's thoughts, Somers pulled the bottle away and wiped his mouth with the back of his hand.

"You think I should talk to Bing?"

"We need to talk to him eventually."

"No, I mean, should I talk to him? Not we. I."

"So you can throw back a couple of beers, turn on the game, chat about Jessica Riner and how she gave great head."

"Huh?"

"You know: football buddies, tossing the pigskin, run a few plays, get wasted and scream at each other about how the coach doesn't know his ass from an anthill."

Slowly, Somers set down the bottled water. A smile as bright as the moon curved his upper lip.

"Get that damn smile off your face," Hazard snapped.

Somers just shook his head.

"I'm not kidding."

"Ree, come on. You know—"

"Yeah, why don't you go talk to Bing? That's a good idea."

Somers's smile faded. "You have some kind of beef with him? What happened?"

"Nothing."

"No, it's not nothing. You do. Last night, I thought it was just—well, you know. All the old shit. But it's more than that."

"It's not more than that. And you don't know anything about that old shit, as you call it."

"I know something about it." That was all. All the humor had vanished from Somers's face, and in its place was a gravity, like the weight of the past was strong enough to drag everything back towards it, even this moment, like a black hole, so much gravity even light couldn't get away.

"You and Mikey and Hugo, you think that was it? Jesus, Somers, what? Do you think your asshole is the center of the universe too?"

"I'm not saying we were the only ones. I'm just saying I know how bad it could get. And I know that people change."

Hazard swallowed his frustrated reply. Instead, he said, "You go talk to Bing. I'll look around here a little longer."

For a moment longer, the gravity in Somers's face seemed to grow stronger, deeper, as though the past could suck them both back across the years. Then he smiled, and he was just Somers again, just a guy you could kick back and watch the game with, just so fucking perfect he could break Hazard's heart a million times before the first commercial break.

"And let my mother find you here alone? Not a chance. Let's finish up. Then we'll both check on Bing." Somers took a step forward, until he was barely a foot away from Hazard, and the smell of powdered amber, the smell of salt and sun-warmed skin stung Hazard's nostrils. Somers raised a hand, laid it carefully on Hazard's shoulder, like he was afraid the other man would break, and Jesus, Hazard thought, he felt like breaking, like that goddamn ornament Stillwell had shot, that was how close he felt to breaking. "Ree, whatever it was, you can tell me—"

"Whoever planned this must have had a way to turn off the lights," Hazard said, his voice too loud and too harsh as he pushed past Somers and headed into the family room. "Where is the circuit breaker panel?"

"The basement," Somers said, trailing behind him. "It's back this way, though."

Hazard paused, spun, and marched in the other direction.

He found the door to the basement on his third try—bathroom, pantry, then basement, and what kind of kitchen had so many doors?—and the lights came on when he brushed the switch. Like the rest of the house, the basement was impeccably overdone. It had been finished in wood, slate, dark earth tones, with a massive television taking up one wall and a wet bar taking up the other, and the air smelled like stale cigar smoke and rum. There were enough bottles lining the wall to give Saint Taffy's, the local cop bar, a run, and Hazard had a brief flash of what high school must have been like, with Somers and—

—Bing—

—his buddies sneaking down here, filching booze from Mr. Somerset, of parties with the music thudding over the built-in speakers and with half the school population grinding against each other in drunken, frenzied lust.

"Back there," Somers said. "That door past the pool table."

The room beyond that door was unfinished, with exposed cement and a single, metallic pole that must have been a structural support. The air smelled like heat-dried cardboard and dust. On one wall, the circuit breaker box hung with its door closed. Hazard approached and then, suddenly wary, pulled his hand back before touching the door.

"You think it's booby-trapped?" Somers wasn't smiling. He didn't sound like he was joking. That was the worst part of the whole thing, how earnest he was, as though everything that had passed between them—

—for the last twenty years—

—upstairs had never happened, and they were just working, just partners. "Somebody turned the lights back on," Somers added. "I don't think anything happened to them."

It was a good point, but Hazard wasn't going to say so. Instead, he reached out and popped open the panel. Inside, two rows of breakers controlled all the electricity to the Somerset house. The back of the door held a sheet of paper with labels scratched in blue ink. "Exterior one? Exterior two? Which one controls the lights?"

"Exterior two. Look, it's still flipped."

Hazard shook his head. "Why?" He ran a hand down the breakers, not testing them, just thinking. His hand came back up, levitating above the main breaker and then drifting back to the switch marked exterior two. Somers was right; it was still off, which explained why the Christmas lights had never come back on. Hazard pulled the breaker back into place. Nothing happened.

"Want me to run upstairs and see if the lights are back on?"

Hazard grunted, shaking his head. They stood there for a moment in silence. Hazard studied the panel, still thinking. He could feel Somers's eyes on him.

"If somebody wanted all the power to go off," Somers said, "they could have knocked out a transformer."

"Too widespread. Our killer wanted the lights to go off at a specific place at a specific moment."

"He could have found a way to blow the transformer. A remote-detonated explosion. He could have controlled the moment."

"Maybe the transformer is in a public space. Maybe it's too exposed. Maybe he doesn't know how to work with explosives."

"He could have knocked out the power lines to the house," Somers said. Again, not arguing. Not pushing. Just that same annoying earnestness like a goddamn Boy Scout.

Hazard grunted again. "What did he do to the lights?"

"He made them go out." This time, Somers's voice slanted into amusement.

"But the power is still on. Everything's still on. So why not reset the outside lights last night?"

Somers didn't answer; there didn't seem to be an answer. The closest thing to an answer was the unmistakable fact that the whole house still had power. Whatever the killer had done, however he had managed to make the lights go out, the answer didn't seem to be here.

Leaving the basement, Hazard climbed the steps two at a time. Somers trotted behind him. From the family room windows, Hazard could see that even in the morning sun, the exterior lights were on again. He left through the front door. The wind had settled, and the day was calm. The sun was warm on his back, and the snow seemed to double the sunlight, as though the light were radiating from opposite directions. It made everything seem disconnected, directionless, suspended. There wasn't a shadow for a mile in every direction, and it made Hazard's eyes hurt.

He followed the Somersets' wrought-iron fence. Snow, gathering on his eyelashes, melting on his lips, tasted like rust. Somers tromped through the drifts behind Hazard, whistling. It sounded familiar. The tune was clear, fast-paced, simple. Hazard stifled a groan when he recognized it.

Somers burst out laughing. "Took you long enough."

Not answering, Hazard knelt, examining the lights. He'd chosen this spot out of convenience, as a way of avoiding Somers. There was nothing to see; the lights looked like any other strand of outdoor lighting. No evidence of frayed wires. No evidence of tampering of any kind.

As Hazard straightened and continued along the fence, Somers came alongside him. "Well?"

"What?"

"Don't you feel it?"

"For God's sake, Somers. What?"

"That's our fight song," he said, slugging Hazard in the shoulder. "And don't try to pretend you don't remember. I know you were at our games."

"Bullshit."

"You sat top center. On the south side of the press box. Every. Damn. Time." He slugged Hazard to punctuate the last three words.

"If you hit me again, you're going to lose that hand."

"Dude, even my mother knows you were at my games—"

Hazard whirled on Somers, catching a fistful of the smaller man's jacket. "First of all, they weren't your games. They were high school football games. Second, who gives a damn if I was there? And third, what the hell has gotten into you? You're acting insane. Again. I get it; this is some kind of coping mechanism. But it's still bat-shit crazy."

A smile trembled on Somers's lips with manic glee. He poked Hazard in the gut, his smile spreading into a grin. "You were there, big boy."

Growling, Hazard loosed Somers's jacket and proceeded along the fence. Somers tagged along, humming the fight song again.

As they turned the corner, following the fence towards the back of the Somerset house, Somers broke off his humming long enough to say, "You know what? For my birthday, I know what I want."

Hazard said nothing.

"I want you to sing the fight song."

"Grow up, Somers."

"It's my birthday."

"Drop it."

"Ree, I'm just saying it's my birthday and I want you to sing the fight song. On my birthday."

"I will swallow a bullet before I sing that song."

"That's a little extreme. It's just a—"

"How did you know?" Hazard spun towards his partner again. Somers was still grinning. The sun bounced off his blond hair, his golden skin. It made the blue of his eyes infinitely deep. Twenty thousand leagues were nothing. You could dive for a hundred years, a thousand years, and never hit the bottom of that blue.

"I was just thinking I've never heard you sing and—"

"No. You knew where I sat. How did you know?"

"So you were at my games."

"I was at the high school games, Somers. How did you know where I sat?"

Some of the brassiness seemed to fade from Somers. Some of the glee rubbed off, tarnished. His smile became pained—still a smile, but very close to a grimace—and he rolled one shoulder. "Come on, Ree."

"Come on what?"

"It was you. I always knew where you were."

Hazard waited for the rest of it, for the smart-assed remark, for the sizzling sexual innuendo, even for the simple recitation of the past: of Mikey Grames and Hugo Perry and how they had tormented Hazard. Anything to explain Somers's remark, to make it safe, to take away the threatening undercurrent. But it didn't come. Somers stood there, as though waiting for something, and then he rolled one shoulder again and kicked at the snow and marched ahead without looking back.

And what the hell, Hazard wondered, had just happened?

He bent his attention to the lights and found nothing, and Somers stayed ahead of him, his gaze fixed on something distant, scanning something impossibly simple or incredibly complex, a

129

degree of attention that disconcerted Hazard. By the time Hazard had reached the back of the Somerset house, his back ached from bending to check the lights, and his head ached from the glare of the sun on the snow, and his hands ached from balling them up and not shaking an answer, any answer, out of Somers.

He paused, stretched his back, and studied the rear of the Somerset home. Sunlight turned the windows into opaque, white squares, and the same sunlight gleamed on the snow-covered trellis, on the lawn furniture, and on a row of four compact metal boxes. Somers stood at the center of the porch. His feet had trampled an oblong circle in the snow, and he was staring at his snow-covered shoes. He looked like he'd gotten lost a few miles back and was in danger of giving up. It took a hell of a lot of willpower, but Hazard ignored him.

Instead, he made his way to the metal boxes. They were, as he had suspected, electrical heaters. The coils were dark, but as Hazard approached, the air warmed. Soft, puddling snow confirmed that, until recently, the heaters had been active.

"Did you turn these off?"

Somers blinked. The sun filled the hollows of his eyes, making his expression impossible to read. His voice, though, sounded normal. "What? No. Why?"

"They were on. They were putting out a decent amount of heat, I'd guess. But they're off."

"My mother—" Somers began. Then he shook his head, canceling his own suggestion. He moved towards the house.

"The extension cord is over here," Hazard said.

Somers just shook his head. He disappeared around one of the sections of the house that protruded, and he emerged a moment later with something in his hand. As he came towards Hazard, he tossed it through the air. Hazard caught it, turning it over and studying it. It was a plastic timer, the kind that people used to turn a Christmas tree on or off on a schedule. Or, in this case, a bank of electric heaters.

"My father does that at parties," Somers said. "He doesn't want to come out in the cold and turn the heaters off, so he puts them on a timer."

"They weren't plugged into the timer, though."

"Exactly."

Just to be sure, Hazard followed the heaters' extension cord and found where it was plugged into the house. There was no timer. The Christmas lights were plugged into the other socket.

"So, what? The killer unplugged the heaters and plugged them in here. Why?"

"To trip the circuit breaker. The load from the heaters plus the load from the Christmas lights would definitely have been enough."

"And this?" Hazard displayed the timer.

"He forgot. He didn't notice. He didn't care. Take your pick."

"But overloading that one breaker shouldn't have affected the whole house."

Somers didn't answer, but he nodded at the enormous window that looked in on the family room. Through the mullioned glass, the Christmas tree was dark. No lights, no sparkles, no glitter. Just dark strands of lights against the dark fir.

"What the hell?" Hazard muttered. He started for the house, but Somers's voice caught him.

"Those are a man's prints." Somers directed a finger at a line of tracks that led through the crisp snow. "There's another set going to the plug where I got the timer."

"So either a man or a woman who had time to put on a man's shoes." Hazard didn't say anything, but he guessed Somers would reach the same conclusion: Grace Elaine would have had easy access to men's shoes—all the shoes in her husband's closet. No one would have noticed her slipping in and out of her bedroom or, for that matter, in and out of the garage.

Hazard followed the line of prints back to the heaters, but at that point they became so muddled with the melting snow and with other sets of prints that it was impossible to tell anything else. Somers was right, though; an identical set of prints led to the side of the house where the heaters had originally been plugged in.

Hands on hips, Hazard studied the porch. "So the killer came out here at some point during the party, and while he was here, he unplugged the heaters and switched them to the other plug. Not too long before Stillwell started shooting—we've been out here, what? Half an hour?"

"Maybe forty minutes."

"And that was long enough for the circuit to trip and for the house to go dark. The killer would have had to be very precise. Or very lucky."

"This wasn't luck." Somers paused, as though about to add something else, and then he stooped. He raked his fingers through the softened, trampled snow, and when he stood, something glittered across his palm. Wordlessly, he stepped towards Hazard and held out his hand.

Laced between his fingers, a silver chain blazed like fire in the sunlight. At its end, flat in the center of Somers's palm, was a broken piece of a heart.

CHAPTER EIGHTEEN

DECEMBER 23
SATURDAY
11:12 AM

OF THE SILVER HEART AND CHAIN, Hazard could make nothing. It bore no insignia or initials, and it was hard to tell if the break in the heart had been manufactured or accidental. Together with Somers, he scoured the patio for any other sign of who had been out here the night before, but they found nothing.

Inside, the power was still off, and Hazard used his phone as a flashlight to navigate downstairs to the circuit breaker panel. He studied the breakers in the silvery light. The main breaker had tripped, but so had the one marked exterior two.

"It doesn't make sense," Somers said. "Overloading that circuit should have tripped the breaker, but it shouldn't have knocked out the power to the whole house. That's the whole purpose of having different circuits."

Hazard nodded. He raised a hand and touched the main breaker. "It's warm."

"What?"

Hazard shifted out of the way, and Somers touched the box.

"Jesus, what the hell does that mean?" Somers didn't wait for an answer; his hand moved to the switch marked exterior two. "This one too."

Without thinking, Hazard reached out to see for himself. His thumb brushed the back of Somers's hand, and goosebumps prickled

Hazard's neck. He pushed the feeling aside. Somers was right; exterior two was also warm. That meant something, Hazard was sure of it, but it was very hard to focus. Somers still hadn't moved his hand away from Hazard's touch.

"Look," Somers said. "Exterior two is the top switch on the right. It's under the main breaker. The killer either knew that overloading exterior two would trip the main breaker, or he tampered with the panel so that it would work that way." He was silent for another moment. "That means the killer was also the one who turned on the power. He left the exterior lights off. If he'd turned them back on again, the power would have gone out when the heaters tripped the exterior two breaker. By leaving the exterior lights off, he delayed that. If we hadn't decided to investigate, it might have been a long time before someone came down here to see why the Christmas lights weren't turning on."

Hazard nodded. Somers still hadn't moved his hand. What the hell did that mean?

"Should we take the panel off?" Somers was asking. "See if the wiring is messed up?"

"Do you know what to look for?" Damn it; Hazard's voice sounded like old shoe leather.

"No." Somers flashed a grin and, seemingly without noticing, shifted his weight so that he was leaning against Hazard, both of them still facing the circuit breakers. "I picked up a few things doing odd jobs around the house, but mostly because Cora made me. What about you?"

The smell. The smell of his sweat mixing with that sun and salt smell. And the heat of his body like a line branded on Hazard's shoulder. He barely heard Somers's words. "What?"

"You. Do you know anything about electrical work?"

"What? No. I mean, a little. From doing things around the house. You know. When—" His mind went blank. "When—"

"Billy?"

"Yeah. When Billy needed me to do something."

"Like me."

"Huh?"

"Where's your head, Ree?" Somers pulled away, practically peeled himself away, and Hazard drew in a breath. "I guess I'll call an electrician and have him look at this."

Hazard nodded, still trying to collect himself. It wasn't until they were halfway up the stairs that his thoughts began turning again. "The killer knew that overloading the circuit would turn off the power in the house. That's not how a breaker box usually works, so either he's spent time at this house, or he managed to get access to the breakers recently. Either way, that might help narrow our list."

"And it has to be someone who knows more than average about electrical work. I doubt our killer would be stupid enough to hire an electrician for something like this. That narrows it even further."

When they reached the kitchen, Hazard retrieved a lime-flavored water from the fridge. He twisted off the top and slumped over the counter, elbows on the granite, trying to think.

Somers found a stool and perched opposite him, a bottled water in hand. "Well?"

Hazard took a long pull of the water; it was better than most of the flavored ones he had tried, and doubtless it was God-awful expensive. "The same three things as always."

"Opportunity, we already know: eight people had access to the kitchen and to Stillwell."

"Means is a little more complicated. Where'd that gun come from? We need to find out if that was the same gun that Stillwell arrived with, where your father stored it, and who could have retrieved it to give it to Stillwell. We also need to figure out who ur_gurl_wants_it99 is."

For a moment, neither of them spoke. Somers ran his index finger around the mouth of his bottle. The golden skin gleamed with collected water. His eyes were looking at something he didn't much like, and he was looking at it like someone watching a car shooting down a highway: small, but getting bigger, a hell of a lot bigger, getting bigger fast.

"All right," Somers finally said. "Motive. That's always the bitch, right? That's when all the dirty laundry comes out. You start looking and you realize, Christ's sake, everybody had a good reason to kill this guy, you realize the motherfucker deserved to be shot. That's how it always is, right? That's just the job."

"Not always."

"That's how it always is." Somers was silent again. His finger glided so quickly around the rim of the bottle that it produced a faint fluting sound, like somebody playing the water glasses. "He's my father, Ree. He's a bastard. I know he's a bastard. If you'd asked me yesterday, if you'd asked me at dinner, I would have said he's a bastard. For a million different things. Last night, just take last night for an example, the way he talked to you. The way he's always treated you. I'm not an idiot; I know he's a bastard. But—" He drew in a breath and let it out; his shoulders looked like they fell about halfway to China.

"You don't have to do this. I'll keep looking. I'll keep digging. You're right: he's your father. You shouldn't have to deal with this. It's a—"

"If you say it's a conflict of interest, or some bullshit like that, I'll—I don't know. I'll tell Nico you want a collection of Adam Sandler films for Christmas."

"You wouldn't."

"Damn right I would. I'm not saying I can't handle this. I'm just saying—" Another pause. "I'm just saying it's going to be shitty."

There was nothing to say to that, nothing at all, and so Hazard just nodded.

Tilting back his head, Somers pounded down the last of the water and flipped the bottle into the sink. "All right. Motive. Let's talk about motive. Who would want to kill my dad?" A wavy grin parted his lips. "Besides you. And me. And half the city."

Hazard hesitated.

"Ree, just say it. I'm a big boy."

"Your mother. Bing. Mayor Newton."

Somers said nothing.

"You want my opinion, those three are the ones to look at. Starting with your mother. I'm sorry, Somers, but that's what I think."

"Because she's the spouse?"

"Because she was looking at him last night like she wanted to cut his throat. Slowly. Because today she's going to a charity luncheon. Because she—" He paused, barely fighting back a shiver. *Because she scares me.* That was what Hazard had been about to say. Something about Grace Elaine frightened him. Something tied up in the way she looked at him and in the past and in the Hazard's own tangled feelings for Somers, as though Grace Elaine could see through the fog, as though some part of her understood, with laser insight, Hazard's ancient, hopeless love.

But he couldn't say that. Parts of it he couldn't even say to himself, not fully. So he trailed off, letting the words fall into silence.

"She didn't do it, Ree."

"You wanted me to tell you what I think."

For a time, maybe a full minute, Somers said nothing. He just looked at Hazard with those ocean-deep eyes, and then he shrugged and said, "Let's see if there's anything in my father's study that could give us an idea."

Glenn Somerset's study was located in a portion of the house Hazard hadn't visited. Seated at the front of the house, with mullioned windows opening two walls onto a winterscape of stark blue and radiant white, the study looked like something off the set of a movie: bookshelves built into the walls, leather club chairs, a fireplace, and a desk the size of a Central American dictatorship. The smell of cigars that Hazard had noticed downstairs was stronger here but softened by the aroma of cedar. Hazard moved to the desk, which was covered in papers—Somers apparently shared his sense of organization with his father—but Somers ignored the desk and crossed to the sideboard that stood behind it.

"He wouldn't leave anything valuable out," Somers said in answer to Hazard's questioning look. Somers knelt, opened the sideboard's double doors, and tapped the safe that sat inside. The sound was dull and impressively solid. "He always kept anything really important here."

"Not in a safe-deposit box?"

Without answering, Somers thumbed back a sliding cover and revealed a digital interface for the lock. He pressed his index finger to the reader, and a moment later a green light flashed. A motor spun inside the safe, and there was a heavy clunk as the lock released. Somers gripped the door and swung it open. Papers filled the safe, neatly organized in folders, as well as a collection of CDs and flash drives.

"He programmed the safe to recognize you? Why?"

"I'm his son. Why wouldn't he?"

Hazard didn't answer.

Shaking his head, Somers said, "He's a bastard, Ree, but we're family. That's always been the bottom line." Somers paused, and he closed the safe door a few inches. "Ree, I don't want to sound like an ass, but my father wouldn't want you to see what he has in here."

"This is a murder investigation."

"But it's not an official one, and we don't have a warrant. You don't have a warrant. The stuff he has in here, it's private."

"You want to try that again?"

Ruddy heat leached into Somers's cheeks, but his gaze didn't waver. "I trust you, Ree. A hundred percent. But this—this isn't mine, and I don't have that right."

"And what kind of help am I supposed to be?"

"If I find something in here that's important, I'll share it with you. If not, no harm done."

"Unless you miss something."

The heat in Somers's cheeks darkened to crimson. He let a beat pass, and then, in a firm voice, said, "Why don't you go look around the rest of the house? See if there's anything we've missed."

"Or I could go sit in the car. Like your dog."

This time, Somers didn't answer. He shook his head, but he didn't say a word, not a damn word, and finally Hazard turned on his heel and marched out of the study. His footsteps were too loud as he followed the hallway. His shoes rang out against the wood. Someone else might have said he was stomping, but that would have been stupid, a joke, totally off base. He was just walking. Just walking like he wanted to put a hole through the goddamn floor.

Halfway down the hall, though, Hazard realized he had an opportunity. Somers was fixated on Mayor Newton as the killer, and while Hazard knew better than anyone how dangerous Newton was, he wasn't convinced that the mayor was involved in this—at least, not involved as deeply as Somers suspected. No, this felt like a crime of passion. There was planning, yes. But there was too much that was strange—and whenever things started to seem strange to Emery Hazard, he suspected emotion. Emotion, he'd learned early on, made people—

—stomp like a child at the age of thirty-four—

—do stupid things. Strange things. Like a public murder poorly disguised as a random shooting. Strange things like that.

Upstairs, Hazard found the master bedroom. Like the rest of the house, it was tastefully finished: an enormous bed with the ivory canopy drawn back, sheer curtains filtering the stark brilliance of the winter day, furniture that looked like it had been handmade—and, more importantly, like it had cost a hell of a lot. Like the rest of the house, the only signs of life were incidental. The high-pile carpet had captured a dainty footprint. Perfume, something like gardenia only sweeter, lingered in the air. A ghostly sheen brightened the vanity's mirror. People lived here; Hazard knew people lived here. But looking at this room, looking at the house, it was still hard to believe it.

He moved through the space carefully, opening drawers, sliding his hands between folded clothing, doing his best to disturb nothing while searching everywhere. In this way, at least, he found himself doing a familiar part of his job in an uncomfortably familiar way. Once before he had searched a house not very different from this one, a house that was too big, a house full of everything money could buy, a house that was painfully, obviously empty in every important way.

Christ, that seemed like a long time ago. How long had it been? Six months? Seven? Seven months since he'd stood in a house like this doing—what had Jonas called it? R and R? Reconnaissance and recovery. Yes, that had been it. And Jonas had stood there, Jonas Cassidy, the captain's son, grinning like a goddamn idiot. He'd been grinning the whole time, ever since he'd been put with Hazard. He wasn't a cute kid, not really, but something about that grin, something about the way he said R and R and then spelled it out, like it was the best joke in the world, well, that made up for a lot that was missing in the looks. And when they'd gotten to the garage of that enormous, empty house, when they'd pulled back the shelving, when the smell of cat litter and clay and motor oil overflowed the mid-day shadows, when they'd seen the cache behind the shelves, Jonas had grinned like he'd pulled Jesus Christ out of the hole in the drywall instead of the first kilo of heroin.

A voice spoke from the doorway. "What are you doing?"

Hazard didn't jump. He didn't spin around. His hands—buried in Grace Elaine's panties—twitched, and his knuckles rapped against the inside of the dresser, but he kept his composure. It had been a woman's voice. Adrenaline was pounding through him, a mixture painful and exhilarating, and his brain had kicked into high gear. Not Grace Elaine's voice. The maid, Margarita? Or—

"For fuck's sake," Hazard said when he turned.

"Nice to see you too." Cora stood there, one arm across her chest, the other hand raised to her mouth as though covering a smile. Her voice didn't sound like she was within a half mile of a smile, though. "Are you stealing her underwear?"

Hazard didn't bother to answer. He went back to his search.

The silence behind him was almost as prickly as the adrenaline still stinging his veins. Cora's footsteps were soft and padded as she crossed the room. "Emery, I was just joking. What's going on?"

He was making a mess of things. That's what was going on. His hands had changed. He'd lost his normal, rigid control. Shaking, trembling, his hands knocked panties askew, spilling towers of red and black and nude cloth. Five minutes ago, five seconds ago, he'd been like a ghost. Now, he thought, well now just take a damn look.

"Is everything all right?"

"Somers is downstairs."

"Are you looking for something?" A strange note entered her voice. Amusement, Hazard guessed. Nico would have been able to tell. Somers would have known. Hazard had to settle for a guess, and he guessed she was hiding laughter. "Did you need something?"

"He's in the study."

She didn't move though. He could see her out of the corner of his eye, and she didn't budge, didn't shift, didn't turn towards the door. She stood there, that one arm still folded across her chest, the other hand still covering her mouth. She was different from the night before—different, but still the same. Different clothes. The sleek, dark dress had been replaced by a man's corduroy shirt, black work pants, and rugged winter boots. Different hair. It was still short, but instead of the artful curls, it curved naturally along the planes of her face. The rest, though—that beauty like something out of a children's book, out of a fairy tale, like someone had been spinning starlight—that hadn't changed. That was Somers's shirt, Hazard realized, and somehow that made everything worse. The next thought was half-buried, almost hidden from his conscious mind, but it was as fierce and furious as anything: can't she just leave us alone?

"I was stopping to see if Grace Elaine needed anything." Cora shivered, tucking the heavy, too-large shirt around her. "She wasn't at the hospital, and neither was John-Henry."

With a grunt, Hazard slid the drawer shut; he'd never be able to straighten everything, not with Cora in the room. He turned. He'd go—

—Somers—

—outside for a while. Get some air. Clear his head.

Except he couldn't. Cora stood in his path. She was tall, but not as tall as Hazard. Not even as tall as Somers. And she looked like she weighed less than a wet cat. But she might as well have been the Statue of Liberty planted in Hazard's way. He couldn't get around her.

"We didn't really get a chance to talk last night," Cora said. She shifted position, sliding both hands into her armpits, as though trying to keep warm. "I wanted to—"

Hazard was already shaking his head. "You don't need to."

He tried to slip around her, but Cora shifted, less than an inch, a fraction of an inch, but enough that the way was blocked. "I do. I wanted to thank you. For saving John-Henry's life, I mean."

"He saved mine too."

Cora shook her head, as though he'd said the wrong thing. She was chewing her lip, and she looked like she hadn't chewed her lip ever, maybe not in her whole life, until she was face to face with Hazard. "I know things haven't been good between me and John-Henry." The words exploded out of her. "I don't know what people told you. I don't know what he told you."

Hazard glanced around the bedroom. Glass doors opened onto a juliet balcony. He could jump into the snow. He'd break a leg, maybe both legs, but he'd get out of here. And if the doors were locked? He could throw himself through the glass. He'd survive. Maybe.

"Nobody's perfect," Cora said, her words faltering as she spoke into the chasm of silence that had opened up in the room. "I get that. I do." There was blood on her lip now. Blood on her white teeth. "You probably hate me. Does John-Henry hate me? No. Don't answer that. I shouldn't have—I don't know." She took a breath, her hands burrowing deeper under her arms, and then she laughed. "I'm doing a terrible job, aren't I? Here's the truth. I want you to be a friend. A family friend. And now I'm sure you think I'm crazy, but there it is."

Hazard wasn't thinking about the juliet balcony. He wasn't thinking about the glass doors, or counting the stitches he'd probably need, or wondering if Nico would break up with him over a pair of broken legs. He was hearing that word, over and over again. It was ballooning inside him, swelling so that it took up all the space and air.

Family friend.

Family.

Somers's family. Not his mother and father. His family. His wife. His daughter.

Jesus. His wife. This woman was his wife.

Hazard had known, of course, but somehow it was real now, so real and so big.

"Anyway, enough of that," Cora said with another laugh. "What are you doing up here anyway? Investigating your chief suspect?"

Hazard barely heard the question. His wife. Somers had a wife, and it was Cora Malsho, who had been—what? Homecoming queen?

Prom queen? Head cheerleader? She was right here, she was real, she was—

—never going away—

—waiting, Hazard realized, for him to say something.

But he had taken too long, and now shock and realization sparkled in her face, glittering and then gone. "You are. You really think she did it."

"I'm not going to—"

"You do." Cora tugged at the corduroy shirt, ran a hand through her short, dark hair, and swiveled left then right, as though re-examining the room. "Well? What did you find?"

"I can't talk about this with you." Hazard shook his head. "I mean there's nothing to talk about."

Cora stepped past him, ignoring his feeble denials. She circled the canopied bed, adjusting the pillows, pulling back the quilt, sliding her hand between the mattress and the springs.

"What are you doing?"

She straightened the bedding and marched to the dresser, working open the drawer that Hazard had been examining when she came into the room. When she saw the disarray that Hazard had left, she sighed and shook her head and began straightening Grace Elaine's underwear.

"I'm going to get Somers."

"Do you know what Grace Elaine said when John-Henry and I got engaged?"

Hazard paused at the door. He didn't want to hear. He didn't want to know their past. He didn't want to acknowledge that there was a past, that—

—Somers's wife—

—Cora had a history with Somers that had no room for him. But something in her voice stopped him: a mixture of pain and amusement, like bitters in the best cocktails.

"We were at dinner. John-Henry and I had come back from Mizzou for the weekend. He had proposed on Saturday night. And the next night, Sunday night, we stayed and went to dinner with his parents so that John-Henry could make the announcement. So that it was official. That's how it is with this family, you know. Everything is about announcements and procedures and spectacle and propriety. Everything is—" Her hands stopped rummaging, palms turning up, fingers curling in, as though trying to protect herself. "Everything is so damn staged. Like the announcement. Grace Elaine knew we were engaged. Glenn knew we were engaged. John-Henry had talked to them about it, and they didn't approve, and so they were going to pretend that it hadn't happened until we shoved their noses in it."

Slowly, one by one, her fingers extended, and she shook her head and went back to sorting the underwear.

Hazard waited. The edge of the story trailed between them like a frayed thread.

"Well?" he finally asked.

"We were sitting there at Tyrone's, you know, that steakhouse that's out Route 17, and—you've been there?"

Hazard shook his head. He'd heard of it, of course. Everyone within fifty miles of Tyrone's had heard of it, but he'd never been because his parents couldn't afford it, because it was a planet in a completely different galaxy.

"It's rustic, that's their word. There are animal heads all along the walls, and the timbers are exposed. You don't notice the timbers, though, not really, because of all those heads. At the back, right in the middle, there's a doe. I didn't even think you were supposed to shoot a doe, but there she is, tacked up on the wall. I asked what they used for her eyes once, and they told me they used lead. Most taxidermists use glass, whole stores of glass eyes if you can imagine that. But not that doe. They used lead. And it's—" Cora shivered. "I was sitting there. I had the edge of the tablecloth in my hands. I remember being excited, but it's like someone else's memory. Now, looking back, I know I was stupid. I can see all the signs. But I remember feeling excited. John-Henry told them. You know how he is."

Charming, Hazard wanted to say. Warm. Genuine. Open. Beautiful. That last word was half buried, planted in the same uneasy grave as all his other, truest thoughts about Somers. But yes. Yes, he knew exactly how Somers would have told his parents. He knew what Somers's face would have looked like. He knew how his mouth would have curved, the crinkle of pleasure around his eyes. Yes, Hazard knew, and his heart thumped so hard he thought it might explode.

"And?"

"And Glenn did what he always does when something unpleasant happens: he shot his mouth off. He told John-Henry he was ruining his life, throwing it away, he was too young, he had to think about law school—" Cora barked a mocking laugh. "John-Henry still hadn't told him about that, of course. Glenn went on and on. Loud. Everybody on Route 17 probably heard him, and they were probably glad when they hit the turn-off for 54. It hurt, but as it went on, I started to feel numb, you know, like jumping into cold water. It's bad, but it's not the end of the world. I was looking up, looking at that doe, at those lead eyes, thinking it's not so bad, it could always be worse, that could be me up there." Her hands twisted into claws again, tenting a pair of rose-colored panties, threatening to rip the fabric. "And when Glenn had finished, when he'd gone back to his burgundy and his ribeye, when it was Grace Elaine's turn, she looked at John-Henry, and she said, 'I think I won't have the creme brulee this time. It was so dry.' That was it. And it's been like that for, God, eight years. Something like that. Every once in a while she'll speak to me, but most of the time it's like I'm a ghost, and the best way to deal with me is to ignore me and hope I'll go away." Cora turned her head, and the winter sunlight spilled into her eyes, turning them into smears of dull light, like dark metal that refused to catch, like lead.

Hazard said nothing. He could hear his own heartbeat, massive, an enormous stomping sound, like his angry footsteps earlier. He could hear it, and he'd be damned, he'd be damned to hell if Cora couldn't hear it too. It was that loud. It had moved beyond sound and into space, shaking his body with each beat. He could see it all. He could see Somers taking her hand. Somers leading her home. Somers telling her it didn't matter. Somers defying his parents. Somers making it work. Jesus, Jesus, Jesus, Hazard thought. It'd be easier if someone would just rip out his heart all at once then let it go on beating like this.

"You probably think I'm telling you this to make you feel sorry for me," Cora said. With what looked like great effort, she uncurled her fingers and unfurled the pair of panties on the top of the dresser. "That's not why, though. Not entirely. I'm telling you this because I want you to know why I'm going to help you."

"What?"

"I'm going to help you. You think Grace Elaine might have had something to do with what happened last night." She paused. Then the sun shifted, and the pools of opaque light dropped away from her eyes, and she looked straight at Hazard. "I don't know if I would have ever admitted it to myself, not if I hadn't spoken to you, but I've wondered for a long time what Grace Elaine would do—or wouldn't do—if it came to that. Kill? I don't know. Honestly, I don't. But that says something, don't you think? Most people, you should be able to say no. But I can't, not for Grace Elaine."

"What are you talking about?"

"She's been having an affair. That's not really anything new; she's had them on and off for years. Glenn, too. But things have been different lately. I don't know if it has anything to do with John-Henry and I separating, but Glenn has started being . . . open about his relationships. Too open."

Hazard thought back to the night before, to the seventeen-year-old girl pressed up against Glennworth Somerset's paunch.

"New underwear," Cora said, patting the pair of panties. "New clothes. New diets. And a new fragrance." She sniffed once, as though for emphasis, and again Hazard noted the sweetened aroma of gardenias. "That's not what she wears for Glenn. She must have been going to meet her—well, the other man."

"She said she was going to a charity luncheon."

Cora's lips quirked in a smile. "Do you always believe what your suspects tell you?"

Heat rushed into Hazard's face. "Do you know who she's seeing?"

"Yes. Everyone knows. At least, everyone except Glenn. And, I suppose, John-Henry. Although it's very hard to be sure. John-Henry—he hides things, sometimes. He's not a liar. That's not what

I mean. But when he doesn't want to deal with things, he locks them away. I'm not even sure he knows he's doing it."

The locker room. The steam curling up from Somers's shoulders—more slender then, but already starting to broaden. And the shallow line between his pectorals. The scattering of blond hairs at his navel. The tips of his fingers brushing Hazard's collarbone, and the sudden, certain knowledge that Hazard's whole world had turned to fire, that nothing would ever come close to that feeling again, except maybe the kiss, the brush of Somers's dry lips. And then the door had opened, and Somers had vanished. And what had happened after that? Nothing. No, worse than nothing. Somers had pushed Hazard down the stairs. That's what fags get. And then silence. Silence for fifteen years.

He locks things away, Hazard thought. Boy, hell, does he.

"Who is it?"

"Jeremiah Walker."

"They were talking together at the party last night. I thought maybe—" Hazard stopped, shrugged. He wasn't sure exactly what he'd thought. But he'd sensed, even then, Grace Elaine's fury towards her husband.

"Emery," Cora said, folding the underwear and tucking it back into the drawer, as though she had proven her point and there was no longer need for the evidence. Her hands worked against each other restlessly, almost frantically. "There's something I need to ask you. About you and John-Henry."

Before she could continue, before the sky could finish crashing down, Somers came into the room. He paused after his second step, like a man who senses a lightning strike and can't tell where to run. "What's going on?" he asked, his gaze moving from one to the other.

Silence.

"Cora, is everything ok? Why are you here?"

More silence. Silence everywhere except Hazard's thundering heart.

"Hazard?"

And there it was, Hazard thought, and with one last, painful hammer, his heart settled back to its normal pace. That was it.

Hazard. Not Ree. Not when Cora was around, at least. That settled it.

"We were talking," Hazard said.

"I wanted to check on your mother," Cora said. She smiled, and God, Hazard thought, she really was beautiful. She crossed the room and, with an almost adolescent nervousness, kissed Somers's cheek. "And on you."

Somers squeezed her arm, and he was smiling, but he said, "And somehow you both ended up in my parents' bedroom?"

"Your mother's having an affair with Jeremiah Walker," Hazard said, wishing he didn't feel a surge of satisfaction at the way the words hit Somers. "That's motive, Somers. Two of our suspects, in fact, now have a serious reason to want your dad dead."

Somers had gone pale, the golden hue draining from his skin everywhere except the red in his cheeks, but he shook his head and held up a small electronic device. "No," he said, shaking his head again, more firmly. "No, I found it."

"What?"

"Why Sherman Newton tried to kill my father."

CHAPTER NINETEEN

DECEMBER 23
SATURDAY
11:45 AM

SOMERS STOOD THERE, the electronic recorder extended towards Hazard, but the sense of victory was draining out of him. The last few minutes had held a series of—

—unpleasant—

—unexpected realizations: Hazard and Cora had been alone, upstairs, talking for God only knew how long; Hazard had been searching his parents' bedroom; and Hazard had just claimed that Somers's mother was having an affair.

And something was wrong in that room. It wasn't the room itself; Somers's parents had lived in that room for most of their married life, and while the furniture changed regularly, the essential feeling of the room itself had stayed the same. No, the weirdness in the air came from Hazard. Or Cora. Or both. The hair on the back of Somers's neck stood up like he was about to bite down on a battery. Probably a D-cell. What had they been talking about?

Me, a darkly satisfied part of him thought. They'd been talking about John-Henry Somerset. And at the same time that the thought stroked his ego, it also left him distinctly terrified.

What—

—did Cora know—

—had they said?

"You think my mother's having an affair?" Somers finally said.

"It would explain a lot."

"Yeah? What would it explain?"

"Why she didn't go near your father last night, but she spent half the evening with Jeremiah Walker."

"She didn't go near my father because he's an asshole on general principle, and twice as much when he's had something to drink. She and Jeremiah are friends. They've been friends for years."

"They're more than friends."

Somers managed a dry laugh. "No offense, Hazard, but you're not really the expert on this."

As soon as the words had left Somers's mouth, he knew they'd been a mistake. They'd come from a place of fear, vulnerability, and hurt. They'd been meant to hurt. He wanted to catch them, reel them back, swallow them. But it was too late. Could Cora see it? Could she tell that the fresh tightness in Hazard's jaw, the sudden flatness of his scarecrow eyes, the slight flexion of his shoulders, that they weren't signs of anger—not just anger, anyway? Maybe, Somers thought. Maybe she could. Cora saw too much sometimes.

How much? How much could she see, exactly? That was a dangerous question, and he brushed it away.

"I'm not an expert on what, Somers?"

"I didn't mean it like that."

"Sure you did."

"Ree—Hazard, look, I didn't mean anything. I'm pissed off. I shot my mouth off. It was a stupid thing to say."

"What was a stupid thing to say? That I don't know anything about straight relationships? That I wouldn't recognize straight people flirting because I'm just the town faggot?"

"Jesus," Somers said. His shoulders had curled under the weight of Hazard's assault. He needed to sit down. He needed a drink. He needed to learn how to keep his mouth shut. "You know me. You know that's not what I meant."

Behind those straw-colored eyes, Hazard was a million miles away. Maybe two million. He glanced at Cora, as though the two of them had a secret, and he said, "Why don't you explain? You're credible, I suppose. You are straight, after all."

"You're being really shitty about this."

Cora glanced at Hazard and then at Somers. Somers knew that look. He knew the way she tucked her lower lip under her teeth, the way her back stiffened, the way a flush dappled her neck. Then he blinked. Was she wearing his old shirt?

"You don't need to talk to him like that," she said to Hazard. Her voice was very quiet, but quiet like the air after a nuclear blast. With two steps, she crossed the space between Hazard and Somers and placed herself at Somers's side. She didn't touch him, and briefly, Somers wondered if they weren't there yet, if she still couldn't bring herself to touch him, and he wondered how long, how long until she could, and maybe the answer was never. "John-Henry, Emery's right. I know it must hurt to hear it, but I think your mother is having an affair."

They'd never liked each other, his mother and Cora. Grace Elaine had never spoken about it, would never speak about it, but Somers knew. The night they'd announced their engagement, Somers's mother had ignored the good news. She'd said something vapid and meaningless—about a dessert, maybe?—and she'd done what she did best: she'd pretended that everything in her life was perfect. Problems, in Grace Elaine's world, were to be ignored. The way she had ignored the first time Somers had hurt another child. First grade. The pencil machine. Forest Robinson had a quarter, had been standing in line to buy a pencil, and Somers didn't have a quarter. Somers had wanted to buy one. It had been as simple as that. Forest got a bloody nose, and Somers got a pencil. Even when Miss Gosa, who'd seemed old at the time but who had probably been in her late twenties—she was still teaching, the last time Somers had checked— had sent Somers to the office, Grace Elaine had resolutely refused to acknowledge that anything had been wrong. It had been a misunderstanding.

How many misunderstandings had there been? Misunderstandings had been the backbone of Somers's life through elementary and middle school. Misunderstandings had explained all the shit Somers had done. Misunderstandings and the occasional acknowledgment that boys would be boys. Misunderstandings had explained everything up until the night that Somers told his parents he'd never play football again. There had been fights. There had been screaming. And in the end, Somers had offered up Hazard as a sacrificial lamb. Hazard didn't even know it, but Somers had done it: he'd made Emery Hazard into a scapegoat. That had been the end of his parents' screaming. After that, only silence. They had gone back to pretending everything was all right. Only now, with Hazard returned to Wahredua, that illusion could be broken.

For a long moment, Somers thought about Grace Elaine and those misunderstandings. At some point in high school, Somers had realized that he was doing something wrong. At some point, his mother's explanations had lost their magical ability to soothe his conscience, to wipe away guilt and shame. What had changed? Somers knew, but he knew in a restless, dream-shadowed way—in a way that he refused to examine head-on. He knew, though, that it was only luck or God or fortune that had saved him from the path his mother had worked so hard to hoe and hack and clear, a path to narcissism and sociopathy. Only luck or God or—

"Hazard, I'm sorry." He forced the words out, and they sounded dry and creaky. "It was just a shock, hearing that. It's not something anybody would want to hear."

Hazard didn't nod. He didn't shrug. He didn't move. For all Somers could tell, he wasn't even breathing. He was just those two flat scarecrow eyes.

"You're going to think I'm still in denial," Somers continued, "but I don't believe she did it. Because of this." He spun the recorder in his hand.

"What's on it?" Cora said.

"Bad news," Somers said. He took her hand and squeezed it. "Cora, we're going to take it from here."

"Police business," Cora said. She stretched the corduroy sleeves over her palms and smiled. "Just like the good old days."

"I'm sorry."

"No, nothing to be sorry about. I remember, John-Henry. I haven't forgotten. The late nights. The phone calls. The secrets."

"They're not secrets. It's official business. Police business. It's not you; I can't tell anyone."

She was still smiling, and Somers knew that smile like he knew how to dodge an iron flying across the living room. "Like I said: police business. Nothing really changes, does it?"

"Cora."

"I'll leave you boys to take care of business. Bye, Emery. Bye, John-Henry."

"Call you tonight."

"I may be out," she said as she walked towards the door.

Somers thought about calling after her, trying to find a new way through an old, thorny argument, and then the moment was past, and she was gone.

"She's not going out," Somers said.

No response from Hazard, but the big man's arms shifted slightly.

"She's saying that to piss me off."

"Play the recording."

Shaking his head, Somers thumbed the play button, and the recording sprang to life. A man was in the middle of a sentence. His patrician, twenty-thousand-dollar inflections were unmistakable.

"Newton," Somers whispered.

"Shut up and let me listen."

On the recording, Newton continued, "—halfway here already. Kansas. Did I say that already? In twelve hours, the problem will be resolved."

"You don't need to say Kansas." The second voice belonged to Glennworth Somerset. "Anybody with an eye left in his head could tell you he was coming from Kansas. He might as well be marching on Atlanta and burning a trail across two states. What kind of idiot have you hired?"

Newton's voice, when he spoke again, held an annoyed burr. "He's highly recommended. Excellent at what he does. And don't pretend that we don't need him."

"It's not my fault that the financing—"

"It's no one's fault. It's everyone's fault. We failed to consider this possibility, and that's the end of it. The bitch has us over a barrel, though, and we know it, and she knows it. You've seen the emails. You've seen the terms—" Newton broke off into a bitter laugh. "What she's calling terms. They'll have the land, and we'll be lucky if we can get out of the whole mess just scraping even."

"My son—"

"Your son will be fine. This is a problem. We take care of the problem the way we always have."

"I want you to promise that—"

Before Somers's father could finish whatever he might have demanded, something sounded in the background—a door opening, Somers guessed—and the voices cut off, mixed with the scramble of chairs sliding back and wood creaking. Then the recording ended. Somers slid the device into his pocket and studied Hazard's face.

The best part about working with Hazard was that he was smart. Already on the pale, hard lines of his face, his fierce intelligence showed itself as his mind turned over the significance of the conversation Somers had just played. Somers waited.

"Strong, Matley, Gross," Hazard said.

Somers nodded. Strong, Matley, Gross was the name of the investment firm that had figured so prominently in their last case. Thomas Strong, the CEO, had been murdered by one of his staff. At the same time, another employee had been working to undermine the firm while solidifying a land deal with InnovateMidwest—the real estate development company of which Mayor Sherman Newton was a major shareholder.

"We knew," Hazard said, "that Newton was involved in what happened at Windsor. He hired Frerichs to try to kill everyone there."

"That's what he's talking about. He's talking about Windsor. He's talking about the land deal that Columbia tried to set up. He's talking about us, Ree. He's talking about killing us."

"Your father—"

"My father was recording that conversation for a reason, Hazard. He said what he said because he had a reason. He does everything for a reason; that's who he is."

"Why do you think he recorded the conversation?"

"To blackmail Newton."

Hazard's straw-colored eyes held steady on Somers.

"What? It's obvious."

"He said some incriminating things himself."

"Trust me," Somers said. "If it ever came down to it, my father would squeal like a weasel. He'd barter for immunity before he handed over the recording, and then it wouldn't matter what he said."

Hazard nodded slowly, but the shadow of doubt lingered on his face. "And you think this is why Stillwell shot your father? Because of the recording?"

"Don't play dumb. My father has evidence that Newton tried to kill half a dozen people, including two police officers. Somehow Newton must have figured it out. He's tough. He wouldn't sit around and wait for the inevitable."

Already shaking his head, Hazard said, "That's a leap. We know your father had the recording. We don't know that Newton knew about it. There's no reason to think he did."

"Those bullets in my father say otherwise."

"Somers—"

"Ree, I need you to back me on this. I need you to go with me to Cravens. At least let her listen to the evidence. We'll get those emails, the ones from Columbia, that show how Strong, Matley, Gross was tied up with InnovateMidwest. If Cravens still won't let us go after Newton, then I'll listen to what you've been saying."

Hazard shook his head again, more emphatically. "You can lie to yourself, Somers. Lie all you want. But don't lie to me. You've got this in your head. You're like a dog with a bone. And it's making you blind."

"I'm not lying. And I'm not blind. You told me to work this case like a real detective. That's what I'm doing. My gut tells me this is the way to go, and now we've got evidence." By the end of the short, sharp speech, Somers felt like gasping for breath. All the air had been vacuumed from his lungs.

After a long, silent moment, Hazard nodded, but there was a flicker of something on his face. Not the usual emotions that Somers associated with Hazard: annoyance, frustration, anger, pain; not even the deep, underlying loneliness that Hazard thought he hid from the whole world. No, this was something else. Something that shook Somers as cleanly as if someone had taken a bat to his ankles and shoved him in a pair of roller skates. Pity. Emery Hazard felt pity for him, and it hit harder than anything else Somers could have seen.

Somers opened his mouth to tell Hazard where he could shove his pity, but before he had a chance, Hazard's phone rang. Hazard answered and spoke quietly into the phone. The pauses grew longer between his responses. His face tightened. Everything about him tightened until he looked like a guitar string ready to snap. After punching a button on the screen to end the call, Hazard stood silent for a moment.

"Well?"

"That was Mayor Newton. He wants to see me in his office. He says we need to talk."

CHAPTER TWENTY

DECEMBER 23
SATURDAY
11:57 AM

HAZARD FOCUSED ON DRIVING the VW, but it was harder than he would have liked. Even with the sun out and the sky blue and glassy, the ice on the roads was thick, resisting the day's best efforts to melt it. When Hazard took corners, the VW liked to skid, and the ice was turning those skids into long, sliding swoops.

Somers hadn't stopped talking since they left the house. "He wants to see you?" That was the third time. Maybe the fourth. "He wants to see you, but not me." It was definitely the fourth.

"That's all he said."

"But why? Why would he want to see you? My father was the one who was shot. I'm the one he knows. I'm the one he should be talking to."

"I don't know," Hazard said through gritted teeth. "That's all he said."

"Do you think he knows?"

"Knows what?"

"That we know about him. About everything at Windsor. About the recording." Somers absently touched his pocket where he had stashed the recorder. Then he threw himself back in the seat, his arms exploding out to fill the remaining space in the VW. "I don't know, Ree. I don't even know what he could know."

"You need to calm down."

"Calm down? Sherman Newton hires someone to kill my father. We're about fifteen minutes away from proving it, and all of the sudden he wants to talk to you. That's not a coincidence. No way."

Ahead, a cluster of government buildings occupied several of the city's grassy blocks. Most of the buildings had been built in the sixties and seventies, and they looked like it: they were plain, almost severe in their absence of decoration, and instead of carvings or adornments they stood out because of the bleak lines that framed them. From a distance, the composite stone facings looked yellowed with age. Even the windows looked yellow, cheap stuff, not glass but the kind of material you might see in a boarded-up storefront.

In contrast to those stark, squat structures, Wahredua's city hall was a masterpiece of craftsmanship. Built of limestone, it had lost most of its glimmering sheen over the last hundred years—the stone was dove-colored, and in some places, it had darkened to gray. But the city hall had been built in an age when quality was valued even at cost, and it had been built by men who had been determined to do their best. A rotunda topped the sculpted stone, and brass—still polished, thanks to years of careful maintenance—sparked at the top of the dome. A few blocks away, Hazard knew, the Wahredua police department was still housed in the old Catholic school, with most of its angels and most of its devils chipped away, and a few of each lingering within the walls. Inside city hall, he knew, plenty of devils had also found a home.

"I'm just going to say it," Somers said. Hazard found a spot and parked the car. "I'm going to walk right up to him, look him straight in the eye, and I'm going to tell him."

"Tell him what?"

"Tell him I know he tried to kill my father. I want to see how he looks. I want to be the one." Somers lunged for the door handle.

Before Somers could reach it, though, Hazard snagged his coat and hauled him backward. "That's a stupid idea."

"He called us over here," Somers said, squirming away from Hazard's grip. "Why? So he can gloat? So he can rub it in my face? I'm not going to let him shit down my throat and call it dinner, Ree. I'm going to tell him—"

Growling, Hazard shook Somers hard. Hard enough that Somers's teeth clicked together and his head snapped forward. "Will you listen to yourself? You're being stupid."

Dark crimson lines stained Somers's cheekbones. "Don't do that again."

"Then don't act stupid." Hazard held onto Somers's coat for a moment longer, sighed, and released him. "You know we don't have a case. Not yet. And you know—" He tapped Somers's skull. "—that if you say something to Newton, it'll give him a chance to cover his tracks. You're being stupid, and you're not normally stupid, so stop it."

Somers said nothing. A minute passed, a full minute, and it felt like it might have been twenty. Then, flattening his hair where Hazard had touched him, Somers shook his head. "You don't even believe he did it. You're trying to—I don't know."

"Is this how it's going to be with you? One minute you're laughing and joking, the next you're running off thinking with— Christ, I don't know what you're thinking with. Your gun? Your dick? What is it with you?"

"You think my mother set this up. You just want to keep me from embarrassing you."

"I'm a cop. I haven't made up my mind, and that's something you'd be smart to do too. Until we have hard proof, that's the only thing we can do." Then Hazard snorted. "And I stopped caring about what you think, what anybody thinks, a long time ago."

For a moment, the fury in Somers's face disappeared, and something—

—knowing—

—dangerous moved in the troubled blue of his eyes. Then it was gone, but it left Hazard feeling unsettled.

"So are you going to stay here?" Hazard said. "Or are you going to keep quiet when we go in there?"

"He wanted to talk to you."

"And you're my partner, so you're going too. Unless you're too much of an asshat, that is."

Somers didn't have a response to that. A few minutes later, they walked into city hall together. Its interior matched the outside: granite floors worn smooth by generations of concerned citizens; wood framing that glowed with polish and use; textured glass, the gold-leaf lettering flaking off; and a single, faded mural of steamboats paddling the Grand Rivere. It didn't take them long to find the mayor's office, but his secretary—an aging man who looked older, even, than Newton—left them sitting on an unpadded bench for twenty minutes.

"So much for right now," Somers muttered.

"It's a power play."

Neither of them spoke after that. At some unseen signal, the ancient secretary rose on creaky knees and ushered them into the office. The carpet was blue but flattened from age and use, and the furniture—a desk, a table shoved under the far window, and a handful of chairs—looked like it had come straight out of the fifties. The only thing new seemed to be the model of Wahredua that stood on the table. Styrofoam trees, charily spraypainted green, and a translucent plastic river, and hundreds of buildings that represented, as far as Hazard could tell, a fairly accurate version of Wahredua. A white sheet covered a portion of the model, and that, Hazard guessed, was not as accurate—not yet. Although the sheet hid the details from view, Hazard could tell that several of the draped buildings were much taller than anything currently standing in Wahredua. He was looking, he guessed, at Sherman Newton's development plan for the city, and he wondered how much blood would stain the streets by the time Newton finished.

Newton was rising, shuffling around the desk, his shock of white hair bobbing as he greeted them. The liver spots on his jawline looked darker than ever. Seated in the chairs in front of the desk were Sheriff Bingham, his khaki uniform taut over the slight bulge of his belly, and Bing. Of the three men, only Bing looked human, and only because his grief was so evident: sweat plastered his normally curly hair to his scalp, and grief had stripped him down to the bone: he looked gaunt, as though tragedy had taken great bites out of him in the last twenty hours. Hazard shook hands with Newton and with the sheriff, but his gaze lingered on Bing. Hazard had forgotten, had chosen to forget, that Bing had lost a child in last night's shooting. Glennworth Somerset had survived impossible odds, but Hadley Bingham had died, and her father mourned her loss.

For a moment, though, Hazard was a boy himself, barely sixteen, kneeling on the rocky beach, the stones cutting into his knees. Bing's hand was tangled in his hair, and Hazard was too young, too small, too weak to fight off the older boy, the stronger boy, Wahredua's golden sun. For a moment, Hazard felt himself helpless and Bing dragged him across the rocks. For a moment, polyester burned his cheeks. Brass stuttered across his lips, filling his mouth with its taste.

And then the memory was past, and Hazard faced Bing. The old helplessness was there. The old hate. Hazard wrestled with it and knew he was losing. He always lost.

Except with Somers.

"Sit down," Mayor Newton was saying, gesturing at two empty chairs. "Sit, sit."

"You said this was important," Hazard said. "We're very busy—"

"Investigating last night's shooting?"

Hazard didn't answer. Somers shifted in his seat, but a look from Hazard made him subside.

Sheriff Bingham snorted. The sound was as dry and hard and thin as the rest of him. "That's what you get with city cops. They finish on the shitter and can't tell their heads from their asses."

Newton made a clucking noise and batted a hand at the sheriff. "Detective Hazard, I want to thank you for everything you've done since returning to our town. It's a pleasure, no, it's an honor to have you with us. Not just because of what you've done here. No, sir. You have a reputation. What you did in St. Louis, well, word gets around. We've heard the kind of man you are. Let me just say it's not often a local boy makes good and comes back." For a moment, Newton hesitated, as though he'd lost his train of thought. Then a smile flashed full force on his face, and in his patrician accent, he added, "Although I have before me living examples to the contrary. Three fine young men. Three, and they've all come home."

Anger had started a slow burn inside Hazard. The mayor's words, spoken with that expensive Yale accent, hadn't hidden the poison inside. So, they knew about St. Louis? Of course they did. Cravens would have known. What had happened between Hazard and Jonas Cassidy had never made it into any reports, but Cravens would know. Cassidy was the captain's son, and the captain had made sure there was nothing in writing. But—how had the mayor phrased it? Word got around. Especially among cops, word got around. Cravens must have passed it along to the mayor. Hazard fought the urge to grab the scrawny old chicken neck and squeeze until the mayor's liver spots popped.

Sheriff Bingham shifted, agitated, in his seat. He took the cattleman hat off his knee, raised it as though to fan himself, and then gave it a disgusted look.

"Detective Hazard," Newton said into his own silence, "I asked you to come alone today. I did that for propriety's sake. I didn't feel right asking you to come, John-Henry. If you need to be with your father, I understand."

"I need to be here." The words sounded normal, but Hazard could hear the fissures behind them. The strain on Somers, which had begun to manifest in his erratic behavior, went deep. Dangerously deep, Hazard was starting to realize. And when all those massive, tectonic forces really started shifting inside Somers, hell would come boiling up. Hazard was starting to hope he wasn't around when it happened.

"Right," Newton said. "That's right, and I'll say I commend you for it. What son wouldn't go out and try to find his father's killer?"

"My father wasn't killed."

"No, of course not. But you understand what I mean."

"Frankly, Mr. Mayor, I don't understand what you mean." The stress cracks in Somers's voice deepened. "I don't understand any of this. The man who shot my father is dead. Chief Cravens told me that there's nothing more to do here."

The sheriff snorted again, the sound like a whip crack, and raised and settled his cattleman again. "That hasn't stopped you boys, has it?"

"What's that mean?" Hazard asked.

Sheriff Bingham shifted in his seat, his head coming up, his eyes dangerous, but before the thin man could speak, Mayor Newton said, "This is a complicated situation. Very complicated. I hope that everyone here can understand that."

It seemed like a question, and Newton stared at each of them in turn, waiting for a sign of agreement. Bing nodded, dropping his head into his hands. Somers nodded. Hazard locked eyes with Newton, and those eyes were like pennies, but the kind of pennies that have sat in a parking lot all summer and are black with old chewing gum. Hazard nodded. The sheriff, pinching the brim of his cattleman, didn't nod, but he did twirl the hat once, and it seemed enough to satisfy Newton.

"I don't want to speak behind my chief's back. I don't want to put you boys in a position of having to choose between the chief and the mayor." Newton paused, folded his hands on the desk, and continued, "But I feel that this situation isn't being handled properly. I've already voiced my concerns to the chief. She understands. In fact, she told me that everything on her end is settled. She told me she spoke with her detectives and they understand that they're not working this case. As far as they're concerned, there isn't a case to work. That's what she said to me."

Sheriff Bingham clutched the hat with both hands now. His jaw was set in a furious frown.

"But word gets around, boys," Newton continued. "Word does get around. Especially in a small town like ours. I hope you understand that. And before you get ruffled, I want you to know that we're not trying to sweep anything under the rug. This case is personal for you, Detective Somerset. John-Henry. This case means a lot to you, and it should. That's only right. But it means a lot to the sheriff, too. You can understand that, can't you?"

Sheriff Bingham was obviously furious—understandably so since his granddaughter had been shot and killed—but the mayor's words didn't sit well with Hazard. It sounded like the mayor was suggesting that Bingham was working the case himself, but that didn't seem to be what was happening. The crime scene at the

Somerset household, for example, had been released much too early. So what was going on?

"From what Chief Cravens has told me," Newton said, "she believes that Detective Somerset should recuse himself from this case because of a conflict of interest. It's a rather poor choice of words, since I don't think there's any conflict at all, but I understand that she's worried you may be too personally attached to this case."

"I thought there was no case. There's nothing to be attached to. My father was shot, and the shooter is dead."

"Yes," Newton said. "Dead in the Wahredua Regional Hospital parking lot. Shot trying to escape. And that shooting means that Wahredua's other two detectives are unable to investigate since they also have a personal connection."

"What's your point?" Hazard said. "We know all of this."

"We weren't born yesterday," Sheriff Bingham said. "Not the day before either. That's our point. The two of you haven't let this drop. You're out there skulking, driving around in a private vehicle, hoofing around Smithfield like nobody will notice two white boys in expensive clothes."

"You're following us? What the hell is this about?"

"The point I'm trying to make," Newton said, smoothing the air with his hands, "is that I've asked the sheriff to handle this investigation. Now, your chief has talked to you and told you to let this go. I'm telling you, as your mayor and as a family friend, to let this go. It's in good hands. The sheriff, he wants justice as much as the rest of you. And he's going to see that we have it."

Somers's face had gone red, and his hands were balled into tight fists, the skin bleached by the pressure he was exerting. He opened his mouth, but Hazard kicked his leg. For a moment, it seemed that Somers would speak anyway. Then he shoved a fist against his mouth and let out a muffled swear.

"All right," Hazard said. "What's your angle?"

"Our angle?" Sheriff Bingham. "My granddaughter is dead. That's my angle. No, Sherman. I'm going to say my piece. That little girl—my little girl—got shot." Bingham tapped his chest. "Right here. That's what my angle is. That's—"

At this last statement, Bing let out a groan that was only partially muffled by the hands covering his face. He lurched out of his seat, took a staggering step towards the door, and then spun back towards the desk. Snagging the metal wastebasket next to the desk, Bing sprinted to the door. He made it another yard before he bent, wastebasket between his knees, and emptied his stomach. When he'd finished, he clutched the wastebasket in white-tipped fingers and stumbled out of the room.

Hazard took the opportunity to study the remaining two men. Mayor Newton looked more or less the same: the liver spots danced on his trembling jaw, and his snowy hair wavered in time with his head. The sheriff, however, was almost purple with rage. He threw out one hand, pointing at the door through which his son had disappeared, as though about to utter some final statement. He looked like something out of an old painting, an allegory for justice denied. Then his fingers curled inwards, and he sank back into his seat, hands like rocks on top of his knees.

After a moment, the sheriff gained control of himself and looked at Somers. "You're Glenn Somerset's son. That counts for a lot with me. And Bing's always had a good word about you. He liked you when you played for him, he liked you when he had you in shop, hell, he liked you even after you quit the team. He put his neck on the line for you, and you threw it back in his face, and he still liked you. If you've got any of your own family loyalty, if you've got any loyalty to me and mine, I expect you to nod your head and say, 'Yes, sir,' and for this to be the end of the talk."

Somers reddened, and to Hazard's surprise, he fell silent.

Hazard waited a moment for Somers's response—honestly, the man had an answer for everything, so why had he gone quiet now?—and then said, "What you want us to do, turning our backs on an investigation—"

Sheriff Bingham didn't look at Hazard as he spoke, and his voice stayed low, hard, and fast, like a bullet in the dark. "This is the one chance you get to speak to me, and after this, if you ever open your mouth when I'm in earshot, I'll pick your teeth out one by one with my .22. I know your kind. Something squirming along on its belly.

Slime under a rock. I heard all about you when you were a boy here, and I knew then what you were. Not a decent person in a hundred miles would believe it of Frank and Aileen's boy, but there you were. No shame, not a scrap of it. And I know what you did in Saint Louis. I know about the boy up there, what you did to him. So I'll tell you two things: you don't speak to me again, ever; and you don't let so much as your shadow get close to this case. You do those two things, and I'll keep my mouth shut, and maybe you'll hold onto your job. God knows you don't deserve it."

The words hit like a punch right on the tip of the chin. The sheriff knew. He knew about Cassidy. They all knew. The rest of it, all the hateful speech about Hazard's youth, that rolled off Hazard like rainwater. But the part about Cassidy, that had hit hard.

"This is a complicated situation," Newton repeated. "Very complicated. We can all understand that. We can all appreciate that. Some of us have spoken hastily, and I regret that." Newton looked at Hazard. "But what Sheriff Bingham has said is, unfortunately, true. You need to walk away from this investigation. We're a small town, and every one of us has a long memory. This is a chance for you to redeem yourself."

The mayor kept speaking, but Hazard barely heard him. He was hearing what the sheriff had said, the implications about Jonas Cassidy. And he was hearing everything behind it, all those years, all the hateful things—

—Frank and Aileen's boy—

—since he'd been a child. He was thinking about Jeff Langham, who had been seventeen and beautiful, who had loved to lure sparrows with bread crumbs, who had loved to run track and try to beat impossible records, who had loved Emery Hazard, and who, in the end, had put a shotgun in his mouth after being raped and tortured by the boys in town.

And these two old men, sitting in their positions of power and privilege, these men wanted to slip a noose around Hazard's throat and pull it tight. They'd make him dance, and when they got bored, they'd snap his neck. His fingers had gone numb, his palms had gone numb, but even inside that numbness, there was a crazy, prickly energy, as though he'd caught up handfuls of thistles and crushed them in his hands. At the edge of that pain, he realized that he was standing, that Somers was tugging on his sleeve, trying to drag him back into his seat. Hazard realized he was speaking, and the words sounded like they were coming from somewhere far off.

"I'll find who did this. Whoever he is. No matter how high he sits. No matter how much of this town he owns. And I'll put a bullet in the back of his head and that'll be the end of it. That's what I'm going to do, and I want you to remember I told you because the next time I see you, I'll have a gun in my hand."

CHAPTER TWENTY-ONE

DECEMBER 23
SATURDAY
1:01 PM

HAZARD DIDN'T REMEMBER the walk to the car. The next thing he knew, he was standing in the cold, with the enormity of the blue sky paneled in the VW's glass, and a headache ringing all the way through his head. In one hand, he held the keys, but he was shaking too much to get them in the lock.

"What the hell was that?" Somers asked. The blond man had come around the VW to the driver's side, and now he shoved Hazard against the car. "What the hell was that?" Somers shoved him again. "Are you out of your mind? You're going to put a bullet in his head, in the mayor's head? That's your idea of keeping quiet, playing it close the chest, being safe? Jesus Christ, Hazard. You just told him we think he's the one who did all this. Even if he didn't do it, he'll find a way to ruin us." Somers touched fingertips to his forehead, then threw his hands down and started walking up the snowy street.

Hands still shaking, Hazard left the VW and trudged after Somers. It took him almost half a block to catch up, and by then the sun was in his eyes and snow had slipped inside his shoes and melted into a freezing liner for his feet. This part of the city was old, almost as old as the riverfront where the city had been born. Jefferson Street held city hall and the sheriff's offices and a dozen other government buildings, various shapes and sizes crammed to fit on available property. Perhaps because of the presence of so many bureaucrats,

Jefferson Street had thrived. It had the Wahredua Savings and Loan, Schreiber's Real Estate, the antique store run by Lorene Berger, and a three-story building with a stone facade—office space for the defunct Missouri Pacific, subdivided now among Sandamon Trucking, the Wahredua Arts Conservancy, and the local chapter of the AFL-CIO. When Hazard had returned to Wahredua, he had been unsurprised that Jefferson Street looked exactly the same, even after fifteen years. That much power didn't change easily.

But Hazard was glad that one thing hadn't changed: Jefferson Street grub. Sandwich shops, salad bars, diners, cafes, The Real Beef—a Wahredua steakhouse famous for stuffing their potatoes with burnt brisket ends—and on and on. A restaurant for each and every one of the bureaucrats. Hazard's stomach grumbled as the air brought the smell of prime rib from the steakhouse. It hadn't been that long since breakfast at Big Biscuit, but—

Somers spoke low, but the tones were agitated, the words clipped. "You want to tell me what that was about?" He stopped at the next corner, chafing his hands while he waited for the light to change.

"Not out here."

"Speak up."

"I'll tell you. Just not out here."

Making a disgusted noise, Somers turned his head, as though scanning the street. Then he backtracked to The Real Beef, and as he put his shoulder to the door, he said, "You're buying."

It was the lunch rush, but The Real Beef had been designed for dinner crowds, and a waiter seated them at a table near the window. Hazard shrugged out of his jacket. Some of the feeling in his fingers had come back, but that awful weight still pressed down on him. It wasn't a heart attack, but it felt like its dumpy cousin.

"Beer," Somers said when the waiter drew near. The man started to retreat, but Somers shook his head and called, "No. Tequila. Cuervo, if you've got it."

"Somers—"

"Don't. Just shut your mouth, all right? When I'm ready to talk to you, we'll talk."

The waiter returned with two shots of tequila; Somers took both of them and pounded them back. He waved the waiter away for more. By this point, the waiter—young, probably not past twenty-five, but still with a waxed mustache on his face like it was required for the job—was giving them a look that said he was already thinking about his tip. A few older men came by, shook Somers's hand, and quietly asked about his father. Other than that, though, nobody bothered them until the waiter returned. After Somers had downed two more shots, he ordered the waiter back for more.

"No," Hazard said. "That's enough. Bring us a couple of hamburgers. Fries. Whatever you've got."

The waiter sniffed. He honest-to-God sniffed. His ass had a little swish to it as he walked away, and it dawned on Hazard that the boy might be gay, that he was close to Nico's age. Might even know Nico. Go to school with him. And here Hazard was, getting drunk with his partner in the middle of the day. Jesus Christ, that would send Nico up in flames.

"I wasn't done," Somers said, sinking lower in his seat. He stared at Hazard, the deep blue of his eyes hooded. "You planning on ruining every fucking thing you can? Is that the goal?"

"You want to get shit-faced, do it on your own time."

"This is my own time. All I've got is my own time. We don't have a case, remember?" Somers paused, ran his arm under his red nose, and shook his head. "Did you fuck your last partner? Is that your game? It gets you hot or something?"

"You say something like that again—"

"That's what they were talking about, right? Back in St. Louis, whatever they're trying to blackmail you with. You fucked some twink cop. That's what it was. He freaked out, and you had to split. And now you're here." Somers leaned forward, elbows on the table. "So what? Same thing with me? Is that the plan?"

"You're a miserable drunk. No. Not miserable. You're a gaping asshole."

"We had a chance. We had a goddamn chance at getting him, and you had to blow everything. Why?"

Hazard shook his head.

"What? Now you aren't going to talk? You had plenty to say back at city hall. Hell, you had plenty to say when we came in here. Now you're just going to shake your head at me. That's perfect. That's typical Hazard, right there."

The waiter sauntered up to them. "Uh oh," he said in a lilting voice, setting glasses of water in front of them. "You two sound like you're having a bit of a spat. Should I come back?" He tilted his head, eyes locked on Hazard until Hazard shifted uncomfortably.

"We're fine," Hazard said.

"I want another shot. A few more shots."

"We're fine. Just bring us the burgers."

Toying with one end of the waxed mustache, the waiter paused, head still cocked, as though waiting for something. Hazard was starting to think he'd seen the young man before. Where? At the local gay club, The Pretty Pretty? Once or twice Hazard had allowed Nico to drag him there, but every time they went, boys—and men—swarmed Hazard. Their interest was fueled mostly by the fact that Hazard was a gay cop who had solved the murder of a young gay man. It had made him, in local gay culture, something of a celebrity—a trait that Nico enjoyed.

"My name's Marcus," the waiter said, cocking his hips. "If you need anything." He sashayed back towards the kitchen.

"You want him to take off his pants?" Somers asked. "You could fuck him too, I bet. Before we even get our burgers, if you're fast enough."

"You're being a—" Hazard fumbled for words. "A jerk. I know I screwed up back in Newton's office. I'm not stupid. I'm sorry. You love apologies. You think an apology fixes everything. So there it is: my apology. I'm sorry."

To Hazard's surprise, Somers turned away. Sunlight through the window gleamed on his cheeks, outlining the tracks of tears. With one arm, Somers dashed at his eyes, and then he shook his head and cleared his throat. It wasn't enough; he dashed at his eyes again, and then again.

"Somers," Hazard said, rising halfway.

"Just sit down, all right? Sit the hell down." Somers wiped at his face again. "If you move, I swear to God I'll shoot you. You hear me? Just sit your ass down."

Hazard sank back into the seat. Somers was always happy. Somers was always cheerful. Even at the worst of their fighting, Somers never got more than angry—nothing like this. The trickle of tears, though, and the silent shudders that ran through Somers, were worse than any amount of yelling, any amount of swearing, any threats of physical violence.

"Somers. John-Henry. I'm sorry."

"I know you're sorry, you big dumb piece of muscle. I didn't sleep last night. My head's screwed on backward, and I'm pissed that the whole case just turned to shit, and now I'm drunk. Thanks a lot for that." Somers wiped his face again, and this time, his cheeks stayed dry. He looked so much younger in the winter light. Not—

—that boy in the locker room—

—a child, but a young man. The gold in his hair turned to fire as the light skimmed it. "All right."

"What?"

"All right. I know you didn't mean to do that, shout at Newton like that. So all right."

Hazard knew this was the moment to tell him about Jonas Cassidy. He knew it was time to clear the air between them, to tell his partner what had led to his return to Wahredua. He owed Somers that much. Somers had been open, more than open, about his own failings. It was one of the qualities that had made it possible for Hazard to put behind him their terrible history. But when Hazard opened his mouth, the words wouldn't come. Because when he did tell Somers, when Somers finally knew the truth, he wouldn't look at Hazard the same way. And some days, that look from Somers was the only thing Hazard had.

The moment passed, and Somers picked up his glass of water. His fingers cut prints into the condensation as he drank half the glass, and when he set it down, he seemed a little steadier. Some of the pressure that had been building up in him over the last day had been released; a little emotional steam had vented. Only a little, though—

not enough, Hazard suspected. And it would keep building until Somers found who had tried to kill his father, making Somers more and more unpredictable as time went on.

The waiter returned with the burgers, each plate loaded with french fries and toppings—lettuce, white onion that stung Hazard's eyes, tomato, pickle slices. Again, the waiter—Marcus—lingered, his gaze so sharp that Hazard felt himself shift under it.

"We're fine, thanks," Hazard finally said.

With an audible sniff, Marcus left.

"The thing with Newton and the sheriff—" Somers began, his face turned towards his plate as he layered tomatoes and onion and lettuce on the patty.

"Look, I'll make it right, somehow. If he tries to get Cravens to fire us, I'll—I'll take the heat, do something, I don't know. I'll figure it out."

"We'll figure it out, dumbass. And that's not what I was going to say. I was going to say that it changes the case."

"We're not stopping because of Newton. I don't care if he thinks he can put the screws to me. End of story."

"Maybe we've been looking at the wrong guy."

A sliced tomato dripped onto Hazard's fingers, dangling over the burger. "Excuse me?"

Letting out a sigh, Somers said, "I'm not giving up on that theory. But let's think about it: if Newton really had tried to kill my dad, why would he push the sheriff's investigation? The last thing that he'd want would be an investigation."

"It wouldn't be the first time a murderer tried to help the police with his killing. Remember, somebody had keys to those cuffs. Odds are good it was somebody in law enforcement, and the only one there was the sheriff. The mayor and the sheriff might be in this together. Anyway, people who kill get crazy. They do all kinds of stupid things. Some of them get off on it, being so close to the investigation. They all trip up, though."

"That doesn't sound like Newton."

"Even if Newton's too cagey to make a mistake like that, he might have felt pressured by the sheriff. You can tell Bingham's furious; I don't blame him. His granddaughter was killed in front of him. He leaned on Newton, got him to pull some strings."

"Maybe," Somers said. "I'm just saying, this changes things. I know I found that recording in the safe, but that's the thing: it was in the safe. Newton might not even know about it. If he doesn't, then what reason would he have to go after my father?"

"Like we said at the beginning, Newton always has a reason. Just because we don't know what it is doesn't mean that he doesn't have one."

A grin sparkled on Somers's face, and it looked surprisingly genuine after his recent storm of emotions. "So we've traded sides? Now you think he did it, and I'm saying he didn't."

"I'm not saying he did it. I'm saying that we shouldn't stop considering him a suspect."

"You still think it was my mother. Or—"

"Or Jeremiah. Yes. I do."

Somers nodded. Burger juices stained his hands and had trickled down to his wrists. He took another bite, chewed thoughtfully, and nodded again. "All right."

"All right what?"

"We need to start talking to our witnesses. This case, the thing I thought we had, it's not as open-and-shut as I'd hoped. I was blind. I was pushing too hard because I wanted it to be Newton. I wanted a quick close. But we need to go back and do it right. We've looked at Stillwell's stuff, and we know someone hired him to be there. Someone planned this. Let's start talking to the people who were in the room when the shooting happened. Let's see what they noticed."

Hazard opened his mouth to respond, but at that moment, his phone buzzed. It was a single word from Nico: *hey*. Dismissing the text message, Hazard started to return the phone to his pocket. Then he stopped. Marcus, the waiter, was watching from the doorway. Not watching Hazard, not specifically, but watching. A nervous trickle ran down Hazard's spine.

Pulling the phone back into his lap, he sent back: *Hey.*
You busy?
Still trying to figure out what happened last night.

The next message came twenty seconds later. Too long. *Right now, are you busy?*

It felt like a trap, and that made Hazard angry because he didn't know why it should feel like a trap. He was having lunch with Somers. They had lunch every day. They worked together. They lived together. They practically breathed together. It was nothing, the sensible part of Hazard's brain said. He was reading too much into the text. Nico was just bored or lonely and looking for a chance to chat. That was all.

But the dark, buried part of Hazard's brain remembered the month before, when Hazard had been in the hospital. Nico had been insistent that Hazard move out of the apartment. Nico had been furious with Somers for not calling, for not telling him what had happened to Hazard. That was all it had been: anger at Somers's forgetfulness. And even that was a lie, a lie that registered only in the deepest part of himself, where Hazard was still unwilling to admit what Somers had pointed out gleefully: that Nico was jealous of Somers.

And now this text, with Marcus watching from the doorway, with the too-long pause, with the repeated question: *are you busy?*

Somers was disconnecting from a call, and Hazard realized he had missed the conversation. "The electrician," Somers said. "Somebody messed with the breakers just like we thought. Once the external breaker overloads, it trips the circuit for the whole house. Presto, absolute darkness. Hey, did you fall asleep? If so, I'm going to have a bite of your burger. I don't know what it is. Big Biscuit this morning, but I'm still starved." He reached for Hazard's plate.

Without looking up, Hazard seized a steak knife and pricked the back of Somers's hand with it.

"God damn it. You could have said no."

Hazard ignored him. He had waited too long. The text sat there, unanswered. Grimly, Hazard typed in his response: *Yeah, busy. What's up?*

No answer. Ten seconds ticked into twenty. Twenty ticked into forty-five. Then a full minute had passed, and the screen flashed and went dark. Auto-lock. Jesus Christ. Hazard glanced up. Marcus was still in the kitchen doorway, head down, hands cupped, as though looking at a phone.

"Come on," Somers said, displaying the red mark left by the knife. "You going to eat that, or are you just being mean?"

Hazard took another bite, but it was like chewing airplane paste. Shaking his head, he shoved the plate towards Somers, who demolished the remaining burger in a few bites.

"Kind of like kissing."

"What?"

Somers gestured at the empty plate. "You took a bite. I took a bite."

"You're idiotic, you know that? And you're having the world's biggest mood swings. It's getting annoying."

"Annoying? Oh man. I better watch out. Annoying."

Hazard paid for the drinks and the burgers—although most of the bill was the drinks. When Hazard took back his card and his receipt, Marcus waggled his eyebrows and smirked. "Nico says hi."

Hazard grabbed his jacket, thrust his arms into it, and tried to ignore the boy with the waxed mustache who was, at that moment, so fucking pleased with himself he was about ready to pop.

"You know him?" Somers asked.

"No."

"We're acquainted," Marcus said.

"No, we're not."

"Distantly."

Hazard growled, at a loss for words, and charged for the door. Marcus moved in his way in some sort of half-assed attempt to block him, and Hazard shoved past him and out of The Real Beef. Somers came after him, laughing. And Somers kept laughing for half a block as they walked towards the VW.

"It's not funny," Hazard snapped.

"You didn't see the way that kid was looking at you. You're lucky he didn't cut the pants off you right in the booth."

"Are you kidding me? He's some jerk-off who's trying to rat me out to Nico."

"Are you simple? You know, like, touched in the head? Or just blind? You've got to be one or the other."

"You really are an asshole sometimes."

Scooping up snow, Somers tossed it at Hazard, who swatted it out of the air.

"Nope," Somers said, his grin threatening to shatter his cheekbones. "Not blind. I bet you could have gotten his number too. Just think about it. Two numbers in one day." Somers made a face. "Shame one of them was a girl's."

As Hazard unlocked the VW's door, he touched his jacket pocket. The small, hard shape was still there: Hadley's mobile phone, stolen from the morgue. Again, Hazard saw in his mind the two boys who had been making out in the darkest corner of the Somerset family room. He remembered the furious look on one's face and the way he had walked towards Glenn and Hadley, the way his hand had dipped inside his jacket.

"What are you thinking about?" Somers said.

"Huh?"

"I've been freezing my ass for about two minutes while you stared off into space. What's up?"

"Hadley. And those boys, the ones who were watching her."

"Those boys are jailbait. Anyway, don't you have enough guys trying to catch you as it is?"

"I'm saying what about them. The one boy, he was furious. About to start something with your dad."

"You think a teenage boy hired a Craigslist hitman on my dad?"

"I think there was something weird about them."

Somers sighed. "Well, they're on our list of people to visit. Where do we start?"

"Jeremiah Walker."

Somers scrunched up his nose and nodded. "Oh, Hazard?"

"What?"

"That guy, Marcus. The one I said likes you."

Hazard started to growl.

"You know, the one that wanted to flip you out of your pants and have you make hot, angry, beefsteak sex to him on the closest table."

"Leave off."

"I'm just asking if you remember him. Remember how you made a big deal of how he doesn't like you. How you told me I was wrong."

"Will you fucking drop it, Somers?"

"Yeah, sure. Just one thing." Somers plucked a scrap of paper from the front pocket on Hazard's jacket. "Here's his number."

CHAPTER TWENTY-TWO

DECEMBER 23
SATURDAY
1:48 PM

JEREMIAH WALKER LIVED in a swanky apartment in downtown Wahredua, just a couple blocks off the riverfront. Somers normally didn't use the word swanky, but he was feeling—
—loaded—
—good, especially after that thing with the phone number. Jesus, Hazard's face had gone red. He was so pale; the red looked about ten times redder than it did on anyone else. And the way he shifted his shoulders when he was embarrassed. And the way his eyes moved like he was trapped. And the sudden, overwhelming rush to comfort him—and that, Somers thought, pulling his mind back to a safer zone, was the kind of thinking that was going to land him in a lot of hot water. It would have been one thing if Hazard had liked Somers in return. Liked liked, not just this casual thing that passed for friendship. But Somers had tried. Somers had thrown himself at Hazard—drunken, yes, and saying things he shouldn't have said. But still, he'd done it. And Emery Hazard had shoved him aside and left the room.

The message didn't get much clearer than that: Hazard might have forgiven Somers for the past, but he wasn't interested in anything more. And, truth be told, Somers wasn't sure that he was either. But the tequila made it easier to think. It seemed to lift everything up, put it within an easy reach. Some of it, too, was the grief and the shock: Somers's nerves were raw, his emotions strung so tight that he could have plucked any one of them and it would have sounded like castrati on a bad day. Grief, panic, amusement, hilarity. Most of all, though, what Somers felt was a building pressure, like something inside him would explode if he didn't— what? Cry? Scream? Neither of those appealed to him.

Instead, he'd done what he always did: he got drunk. And inside the boozy, amber light of the tequila, dangerous thoughts were swimming. Some of those dangerous thoughts were about Cora. About what he was supposed to do with a wife who wouldn't divorce him, wouldn't let him touch her, wouldn't even look him in the eye some days. And even more dangerous thoughts about Emery Hazard, and the feel of his skin all those years ago in the locker room, and the drunken kisses in their apartment, and the feel of Hazard's nails grazing Somers's nipple at Windsor, and—

"Are you getting out of the car?" Hazard asked as he jammed down the emergency brake.

"Yeah." Somers choked on the word. "Yep. Right now."

That ass, though, Somers thought as Hazard walked towards the apartment building. God had done some damn fine work on that ass. Chiseled like a goddamn Mount Rushmore, that ass.

"Now," Hazard shouted back.

Somers scrambled out of the car and towards the apartment building. The booze was making him sloppy. The booze was making him think dangerous things. The booze was making him horny, but the honest-to-God truth, the truth Somers wouldn't bother denying, was that it felt better to be drunk and horny than the chaos, the confusion, the shock and the pain of the last day. And distantly, Somers wondered why he wasn't fantasizing about Cora, or about that girl Kaylee, or about any of the other girls he'd slept with. The answer swam towards him, and he shoved it away.

"He won't be home," Somers said. "He's a busy man."

Hazard ignored him and pressed the button.

To Somers's surprise, Jeremiah buzzed them up. They rode the elevator to the top, and instead of opening onto a hallway, it opened onto the apartment itself: a loft with exposed brick, an industrial ceiling of painted metal ductwork, and furniture that looked like it had been shipped straight from Finland or Sweden—somewhere cold, somewhere Norse, somewhere that cost a hell of a lot.

Waiting at the elevator door was Jeremiah Walker. He was tall, taller even than Hazard, but thin. Stoop-shouldered, he looked older than he was, even with his honey-colored skin unmarked by wrinkles. He offered two glasses of Scotch.

"Cold outside, Detectives."

Hazard waved one away. Somers, though—Somers was itching. The drinks at The Real Beef had been—

—a mistake—

—nice, but they weren't enough. Not for this. Not for looking into the eyes of a family friend, someone that had been at birthday parties and holiday dinners and picnics in Rogers Park, someone who might be—

—sleeping with his mother—

—a murderer.

"We're fine," Hazard said, shaking his head as Somers reached for the glass.

"Just a small one," Somers said, although the drink that Jeremiah had poured was anything but small.

"Not when we're on duty."

"We're not on duty, though. Remember?" Somers took a sip of the Scotch. It was peaty. It burned. It hit like a jackhammer, and that was everything he needed. "This is more of an unofficial visit, Jeremiah."

"I know. Come in. Would you like something to eat?"

"We're fine," Somers said.

"Let me just check on your mother," Jeremiah said. "Please, sit down."

The shock of the words made Somers half-afraid he'd drop the glass of Scotch. His fingers tightened around it reflexively. In spite of the Scotch's fire, the glass was cold, cold enough to slide right through his grip and shatter. He tilted his head back and slammed the drink down.

Jeremiah didn't notice; he moved deeper into the loft, calling Grace Elaine's name.

"You're back to this kind of shit?" Hazard said, drawing the glass out of Somers's hand and shoving his partner towards a sofa draped with an African-print throw. "What, one thing goes wrong and you're going to drink yourself sick?" Another shove. "You're going to pound booze when we're trying to interview a suspect." Another shove. Somers's knees hit the back of the sofa, and he stretched back a hand out of reflex, his fingers brushing the coarse fibers of the throw. "A potential murderer." No shove. This time, Hazard stepped in, until they were nose to nose. The smell of Hazard, clean, lingering soap, masculine sweat, overpowered Somers. God, the drink was starting a fire, a real fire, and Somers felt his legs shake. "I thought you had this under control."

"I do."

"I mean being a goddamn alcoholic."

"I'm not an—I'm fine. I just had a couple of drinks. My father got shot last night. I've got a right to loosen up, all right?"

"Loosen up on your own time, when it's not going to get me killed."

"You're so full of shit."

"I'm full of shit? You're the one who's been talking big about solving this case, and now all of the sudden you're getting plastered."

"You're full of shit because you always act like you're so much better than me. You're full of shit because you just screwed up this investigation worse than I ever could. And you're full of shit because you can't stand that you got canned and now you're here. Which one of us can hold down a job? Which one of us hasn't been fired for—" Somers stopped, but it was too late.

Hazard had gone even paler than usual, except for two sullen red spots in the hollows of his cheeks. Without a word, he stepped around Somers—hitting him with his shoulder as he did—and dropped onto the sofa.

"Look, Ree, I didn't mean—

"For the last time, Somers, don't call me that. Please."

And it was that please that hit the hardest. Please. Since when had Emery Hazard ever said please? Not since high school, maybe. No, not even then. Jesus Christ, please. What had Somers just done?

Jeremiah returned with Grace Elaine on his arm, and Somers took an unsteady step and planted himself on the sofa next to Hazard. His mother looked . . . happy. She was smiling, and it wasn't the cocktail party smile, it wasn't the PTA smile, it wasn't even Methodist Ladies' Quilt and Supper Circle smile. It was a real, silver-dollar smile, and Somers felt it ring true even across the room. It was one of the worst things he'd ever seen.

Somers had suspected, while growing up, that his parents were different from other people. Now, older, he knew that most children experienced something similar: the normal mixture of household disillusionment and teen angst. That suspicion had evolved, however, into a certainty after Somers had left home. His parents were cold, distant, unattached. An only child, he had grown up assuming—no, that wasn't true—pretending that his loneliness was normal. And when he'd gotten to college, when he'd visited the families of friends, when he'd spent time with Cora, just the two of them, starting their lives together, he'd realized that there had been something wrong in his home, something he'd never been able to articulate. Seeing that smile, though, shook all the supports, all the bridgework, all the efforts Somers had made to explain away that childhood. Seeing that smile made Somers distinctly aware of the possibility that his mother was perfectly capable of happiness.

Just not with him.

The realization sloshed against the slow fire of the Scotch, steaming up, clouding Somers's vision. He didn't realize he'd missed something until Hazard elbowed him. What had Jeremiah been saying? Something about being willing to help.

"Thank you," Somers said, taking a gamble.

His mother rolled her eyes. She and Jeremiah sat in matching, tubular chairs, their clasped hands suspended in the space between them. No sign of shame on his mother's surgically smooth cheeks. No hint of red.

"He's drunk," she said to Jeremiah. "This really isn't a good idea."

"What isn't a good idea, Mother?"

But Grace Elaine didn't answer. It was Jeremiah who did, speaking softly, his eyes locked on the woman next to him. "I've thought you should know for a long time, John-Henry. About your mother and me. I didn't like hiding this."

"From me? You were worried about what I thought?" Hazard elbowed him again, but Somers ignored him. "But you weren't worried about my father. You weren't worried about what he thought. That, that didn't bother you at all."

"Cool it," Hazard hissed.

"This is what I was talking about," Grace Elaine said, rising and freeing her hand from Jeremiah's. "He's completely irrational. It's always been like this: pouting, tantrums." Her cool blue eyes drifted over Somers, as though she were seeing him underwater. "He's an absolute child about anything that disturbs his perfect world."

"I'm a child?" Somers didn't remember getting to his feet, but he was standing now, an accusing finger lancing towards his mother. "I'm irrational? I'm the one with a perfect world? What about you, Mother? What about the time I kept missing at tee ball? You wouldn't let me sit down. I had to stand up there for twenty minutes, sobbing, until the coach finally just called the game."

"You would have quit. I didn't raise a quitter."

"And the time I broke the Chretien vase? You know, the one in the front hall? And the Newtons were about to come over, but you couldn't have that, so I got sent to a reform school for the summer when I was eight years old, and you called off dinner and said you had a headache."

Grace Elaine's mouth thinned. "And look at you now. God only knows how you would have turned out if I hadn't taken steps."

"And then you and father cut me out of your lives—"

"Don't be dramatic, John-Henry."

"You stopped talking to me. You stopped looking at me. I was seventeen years old, and I might as well have been a ghost in my own house because you were angry that I wasn't going to go out for football at Mizzou."

"Because of him. Because this—this moral degenerate, he got into your head, and you weren't strong enough or smart enough to do any better. We had options. We had choices. Your father had already talked to Jim Abeilhe at the Tegula plant. He spoke with the sheriff, and Bing was going to take care of things at school. For heaven's sake, John-Henry, he even drove into town one night and found that Grames boy, offered him—" Grace Elaine stopped. The pink in her cheeks seeped out, leaving her pale and waxy.

"He what?"

Grace Elaine's mouth tightened.

"What did he do, Mother? He went to Mikey Grames and did what?"

"It doesn't matter. Nothing we ever did for you mattered. You made sure of that, didn't you?" To Somers's surprise, he realized his mother was crying. She raised one hand, and it shook slightly as she did so, and she held it gently under one eye—not wiping, just holding it there. "Excuse me," she said. She walked deeper into the loft, her head high, her hand still held against her cheek until she disappeared into a room at the back.

"For fuck's sake," Somers muttered, taking a step. But the Scotch had made him unsteady, and his anger—and the sudden, sickening pit that had opened inside him—blinded him. He crashed into the coffee table, spilled forwards, and probably would have put his face through the glass if Hazard hadn't caught him. Hands hard and steady, Hazard straightened Somers.

Somers couldn't look at him. Couldn't bear to know what Hazard was thinking, what he suspected, what he might know. All of it had come rushing out, all the worst shit, and now Somers learned that there was more. That his father had paid off Mikey Grames to—what? Make Hazard's life miserable? Worse? Hurt him? Kill him? Somers tried to pull away, but Hazard held him.

"We should go," Hazard said.

"No," Somers said, the word sounding bubbly and loose.

"No," Jeremiah said, shaking his head as he rose. "Give me a moment. We need to talk." He moved towards the room where Grace Elaine had gone.

Somers waited for the explosion, for the accusations, for the threats. He waited for the worst of it: the hatred he would see in Hazard's eyes. The betrayal. And Hazard would be right to feel that way. He'd be right to hate Somers because the truth was, Somers was a piece of shit. Somers knew that. And he knew, now, that he could never make up for the past. He could never outrun it. Maybe some people could, but not Somers. It would always be there, like quicksand, dragging him down—and the harder he fought against it, the faster he sank.

But all Hazard said was, "Why don't you get some air?" And he gave Somers a gentle push towards the loft's floor-to-ceiling windows.

Somers didn't want air. He didn't want anything except a shallow hole in the ground where he could close his eyes and make everything stop spinning for once in thirty-three fucking years. But he made his way to the window.

It gave out over the city and the riverfront. As the sun slanted across the sky, the blue of the sky had softened, losing its brittle clarity and fuzzing into a robin's egg blue. Steam from boilers and furnaces feathered up from Wahredua's brick buildings. The river sheared off one side of town, and its brown waters looked still. Somers leaned closer. Even shut, the window leaked cold into the air, and that helped a little. It helped with all that fire and steam inside Somers. It helped a little with the sickening emptiness. It helped a little, but only a little. And out on the river, chunks of ice bobbed. Somers put his forehead against the glass—Jesus, cold—and observed. Just chunks of ice, bobbing against each other as they drifted. In Somers's vision, it looked like they were only moving a few fractions of an inch. In reality, he knew, they were racing along. And that was what all this had been like, he realized: from the outside, for a while, life had been slow and sedate. And now he was in the middle of it, right in the middle, and it was like somebody had tossed him into a flooding river.

Jeremiah's shoes clicked on the floor as the older man returned. He looked even more tired now, and his hands—very old hands, Somers thought—clasped in front of him. "She's upset, but she'll be fine." His dark eyes found Somers. "She does love you, you know."

Somers meant to scoff, but the sound came out more like a sob.

Jeremiah's clasped hands wriggled and strained, but all he said was, "She's a complicated woman."

"I'll say." Hazard's words, spoken in his usual voice—low, cold, unyielding—splintered the strange tension. "What I'd like to know is if she's the kind of complicated that would murder her own husband?"

Jeremiah nodded, as though he'd been expecting the question. "Are you asking that because we're involved in a relationship?"

"I'm asking because someone tried to kill Glennworth Somerset last night, and I'd like to know who."

"And the spouse is always the first person to look at. Yes, I understand. As you must already know, Detective Hazard, Grace Elaine is a passionate woman. She feels deeply and strongly. She is not the type, however, to hire a man to shoot her husband."

"Not even when it would make her a rich woman?"

"If that is the motive, then you must believe I am a suspect too. Is that correct?"

"I'd like to know what you saw at the party last night. And what you did."

"Yes," Jeremiah said. He paced across the room to the liquor cabinet, poured himself a Scotch, and took a sip. "Yes, I'm Grace Elaine's romantic interest. I would make an excellent suspect. I have motive. I have means—in the sense, at least, that I could have the financial resources to hire someone to kill Glenn. But did I have opportunity?"

"Tell me about what happened at the party, Mr. Walker."

"I must have had opportunity, otherwise you wouldn't be taking this so seriously." Jeremiah turned, his eyes half-closed as if in recollection, as the Scotch floated towards his lips again. After another drink, he nodded. "When we went into the kitchen. That's what you believe. Either Grace Elaine or I freed that lunatic."

"Just tell him what you saw at the goddamn party," Somers said, peeling his frozen forehead from the glass. It felt as though it had ripped off a layer of skin. "From the minute Wayne Stillwell appeared to the minute the lights went out."

If Somers's tone bothered Jeremiah, he didn't show it. He just nodded and sipped at his Scotch. "Stillwell came in through the front door. I was in the family room, but I heard him singing."

"Singing?" Somers said. "I thought he was acting crazy. Waving a gun around."

"No, he was singing. 'Deck the Halls,' and all that. I could tell that something was off—everyone was getting agitated, that much was obvious—so I went to take a look. A naked, high Santa Claus. Even as a college professor, I don't see stuff like that very often."

"And the gun?"

"What gun?"

Somers paused; for a moment, everything contracted to that question. "Did he have a gun?"

"I don't know. He might have. He must have, right, because he did all that shooting. But at the time—" A slight crease appeared in Jeremiah's forehead. "He had on a red Santa cap and he had a red bag over his shoulder. I think it was supposed to look like Santa's traditional bag, but it didn't."

"Why not?" Somers pressed the questioning, ignoring Hazard's look. "What was different?"

"The color, for one thing. It was red but too light. And the fur trim is usually white, at least, in most of the paintings I've seen, but this one was pink. Glittery."

No gun, Somers was thinking, his mind racing back to that night. His father had—no. No, it hadn't been his father who had said that Stillwell had a gun. It had been Sheriff Bingham. And he had said— what? Something else. Something strange.

Before Somers could recall the sheriff's remark, though, Jeremiah continued speaking. "He might have had the gun in the bag."

"What makes you say that?" Hazard said.

"He must have had a gun. Haven't we gone over this? You're the ones who said he had a gun."

"No, we asked if he had a gun. You assumed—"

Somers broke in. "Go on, Mr. Walker. Tell us the rest of what happened."

Jeremiah pulled at his Scotch. "Everyone rushed him. No, not everyone. Most everyone wanted away from him. No screaming, but you could tell the people were about a hair away from it. Nerves, you know, like the air could pop from all the tension. But people did go for him. They grabbed him. Your father," he nodded at Somers, "and the sheriff and his son. They were going to throw him out of the house, I think—they were shoving him that way, and you know how your father gets, John-Henry, like he'd shove Jesus off the cross if he wanted a little more room—" Jeremiah paused. "Yes, they were going to throw him out of the house. But then someone yelled, 'Gun,' and that stopped your father cold. They talked for a moment, so soft I couldn't hear what they were saying, and then they dragged him to the back of the house."

"But you didn't see a gun?" The sick feeling had returned, clouding Somers's thoughts. He knew that what Jeremiah was saying was important. He knew that it might be critical for the case. But his thoughts were slushy, granular, and why'd he have to drink that damn tequila?

"No."

"Who said that he had a gun?"

Jeremiah paused in the act of lifting the glass to his mouth. "I don't know. Why?"

"You can't remember? Or you don't know?"

"Is there a material difference?"

"In this case," Hazard said, "yes, there very well might be. Which is it: you don't remember, or you don't know?"

"I'm not sure." Jeremiah sounded petulant, put out by the harshness of Hazard's response. "I'd had a drink. Everyone had. And the action with that lunatic, it all happened fast. A few moments, that's all it took. And then it was over. They rushed him out of there, and the rest of us were so ashamed of being cowards, and still so frightened by what had happened, that we tried our hardest to convince ourselves we were happy and gay. Oh. Apologies. It just feels like a holiday phrase."

Hazard didn't say anything. Hazard didn't shift in his seat. To most people, it might have looked like Hazard hadn't heard Jeremiah's jab. But Somers wasn't anybody. He could read the anger in the clenched cords of Hazard's jaw. Even as a boy—skinny Emery Hazard, who probably weighed a hundred pounds when he was sopping wet—he'd always had that same way of being angry: silent, but filled with rage like gasoline and a match just rasping the striker strip.

"Mr. Walker," Somers said, "was it one of those three men who said that Stillwell had a gun?"

"Stillwell? Was that his name? Yes, I suppose it had to be one of them."

A thought struck Somers. "Where was the mayor?"

"Mayor Newton?"

"Yes. Where was he during all of this?"

"Right there. I mean, he wasn't helping with—what was his name? Stillwell?—he wasn't helping with Stillwell, but he was right there."

"He might have been the one who said that Stillwell had a gun?"

"It's possible."

"You're sure he was right there?"

"Yes, I'm sure. Sheriff Bingham took that red bag and passed it to the mayor. I remember that very clearly."

"And then?"

"The mayor carried it with him to the back of the house. That was the end of it. As I said, we all hurried back to being drunks and cowards. Until," a smile quirked the corners of his mouth, "the two of you made your dramatic entrance. That gave everyone quite a scare. Marita Baker just about jumped out of her garters, and she's on the shady side of seventy."

Somers rubbed his forehead. Another mistake, storming into the house like that. Another idiot mistake. They'd seen the front door, heard the shouting, and instinct and training had taken over. Another embarrassment for his parents to live down. Through the booze, though, something was calling to him about that moment.

And then Hazard was speaking. "How did Stillwell get into the house?"

"He walked through the front door. I already told you, remember? He was singing."

"He walked through the door?"

"Yes. Detective, I'm not trying to be rude, but aren't we talking in circles now? This is right where we started."

"He walked in," Somers said, and his gaze slowly drifted to Hazard. Their eyes met. Hazard's eyes, like straw at the end of a perfect summer, eyes that caught the light, eyes you could stare into for a day, a month, a hundred years, and you'd never get tired of them. "He walked into the house."

Hazard nodded.

"Mr. Walker," Somers said, reeling in his thoughts, trying to burn off the haze on his brain. "What—you and my—"

"What is the nature of your relationship with Mrs. Somerset?" Hazard said.

"Now we've reached the uncomfortable portion of our conversation. It's been coming. This is a talk that's been coming for a long time. Your mother hoped it wouldn't come to this; she never wanted you to know, John-Henry. She wouldn't want to hurt you. But I knew you'd find out. It's a small town. Nobody has any secrets."

Someone does, Somers thought. Someone has plenty of secrets. Someone tried to kill my father, and there's a secret lying under that.

"Your mother and I have been seeing each other for about five years. In fact, we'll be celebrating our anniversary at the end of January." Jeremiah laughed; neither Somers nor Hazard joined him. "It feels strange talking about this, I have to admit. Talking about it openly, I mean."

"Why should it feel strange?" Somers said. "You've been committing adultery with my mother for five years. I think it'd be normal by now."

The words landed like a slap, eroding the last of the good humor etched into Jeremiah's face. He took a sour sip of the Scotch. "You'll understand when you're older. Not now; you're too young now. You see the world, and you still see sharp lines and bright colors. You see everything as a choice, you chalk life up to free will, you make decisions the hinge on which destiny swings. When you're older, though, you'll see." He set down the empty glass and rubbed his fingers together, as though he had something sticky on them. "Homo economicus. You know that term?"

"The economic man," Hazard said. "The perfectly rational, perfectly self-interested agent. One of the underlying assumption of traditional economics."

"A lie. A fallacy. A myth. A waste of reams of paper and gallons of ink and a lot of lives. I, at least, have wasted plenty of ink on it. And too much of my life."

"What the hell are you talking about?" Somers said.

"Free will. Agency. Self-determination. Choice. I've studied them. I know them. I've held them under a microscope, so to speak, and seen how they wriggle, seen how they breed. We build our lives on them. Nations build their lives on them. And you know what? It's all bullshit. Nobody chooses. Not really. Oh, we think we choose. But all the choices we made, they were made for us, ten years ago, fifty, a hundred, a million. We're just riding mine cars down the rail. If the rail turns, we turn. Otherwise, we just hold on for our lives."

"Railroad tracks have switching stations," Hazard said. "Your analogy is flawed."

Irritation flickered on Jeremiah's face, and he dismissed Hazard's comment with a twitch of his fingers. "There's proof, you know. Einstein. God doesn't play dice. Economists, well, we've played our games and built our sandcastles, but it's all based on that ridiculous assumption that men are rational, that they make rational choices. It's not true, though. And the research is starting to show it. We make choices based on product placement, based on attractiveness, based on our 'guts,' based on anything except reason. We make a consistent stream of bad decisions, and we rationalize away our decision-making so that we feel like we're in charge. I bought it because I wanted it. I punched him because he deserved it. I kissed her . . ."

"I'm feeling like I made a few bad decisions myself," Somers said. The sullen, amber sloshing of the Scotch in him was crystallizing into a headache. "This is all really interesting, Mr. Walker—"

"Riveting," Hazard said. "Your students must be pounding down the doors to get to your class."

"But we're not here for a crash-course into new economics."

"You should be," Jeremiah said. "You should be listening more carefully."

"I think we've listened long enough," Hazard said. "Where did you and Mrs. Somerset go during the party? Towards the end of the party, more specifically. Before the shooting."

"You think I chose this," Jeremiah said, his eyes fixed on Somers. "You think I wanted this."

"Please answer the question, Mr. Walker," Hazard said. "Without another faulty analogy, without another long-winded pity party."

"You think I killed Glenn Somerset because I had a reason. But like most crimes, reason had nothing to do with this. You're looking for sane thinking, but whoever did this was not sane. You're looking for homo economicus, but this killer was not rational. The killing wasn't rational."

"So that means you didn't shoot my father," Somers said. "Is that what you're trying to say?"

"I didn't. I wouldn't. I respected your father. We were friends. We are friends. But your mother—" Jeremiah paused, helplessness flooding his face. "Homo economicus. When I was younger, when I still believed all that crap, I had a woman who loved me. She was younger. She was—" He paused. Something complex, a mixture of craft and cunning and terror, blended in his features. "She was not who I needed to be with. It would have been foolish to be with her, to stay with her. My career, my prospects, and then there was the boy." He swallowed. "And I told myself that I was being rational, that I had made the correct, self-interested choice. Now, though, do you know what I think?"

"I think," Hazard said, "you're a self-indulgent bastard who left Hollace shirtless in the cold. That's what I think of you."

The color drained from Jeremiah in one, sudden rush, leaving him looking more jaundiced than ever. He didn't respond to Hazard, though. He said, "Now, though, I know that it was because I wasn't in love. Love is a golden collar. Love takes you prisoner. Love drags you through the mud, skins your hands and knees, and throws you naked, helpless, to the wolves. And you can't run from it, you can't deny it, any more than you can run from yourself, deny yourself. Any more than you can tell the earth to stop spinning. You think I'm a bastard. Maybe I am. But I didn't choose it. Call it fate if you want. Collision. Catastrophe. Unstoppable forces rushing against each other. Call it whatever you want, but I didn't choose it."

Through the headache, Somers felt something shift inside him. Unstoppable forces rushing against each other, and in his mind he saw—

—the locker room—

—waves slapping white cliffs, collision, catastrophe, fate. That shift inside him, the fractional movement of the vast, supporting pillars of his identity, was dangerous. Something crucial to himself, to who he was, had just inched towards collapse. Somers shivered, and he turned away from the thought, away from the danger—aware of it, but not willing to face it. Not yet.

Collision. Unstoppable forces rushing towards catastrophe.

Then he shook off the words, realizing that Hazard was speaking.

"That's very poetic, Mr. Walker. Very eloquently put. Could you say a little bit more about these uncontrolled forces? What else have they caused you to do? Besides, that is, conducting an affair with a married woman."

"You don't understand," Jeremiah said, his long hands folding and unfolding around each other. "But one day, you will."

That structural prolapse, Somers thought with another wave of—what? Panic? He could feel it inside himself. The danger of everything toppling in a rush of dust and stone like a building imploding.

"What did you feel compelled to do?" Hazard said, leaning forward in his seat, his size suddenly magnified. "You said that you were friends with Glenn Somerset. Why did you say that you were friends, in the past?"

"It was a mistake. We were still friends. Are still friends. I didn't do anything to Glenn. I'd never hurt him."

"Aside from sleeping with his wife," Somers heard himself say. "My mother."

"He—" Jeremiah paused. "They had grown apart. They aren't in love. I don't know if they ever were, not really, not the way love takes hold of some people. Your father would have been hurt if he found out, and I never wanted that. And your mother didn't want that either. We were just—we were lonely. Both of us. And loneliness grows by the ounce, day by day, until you can't carry it anymore."

Collision, Somers heard inside himself, and the word came with the grating of massive forces stirring. Catastrophe.

"Drop it." The crack in Somers's voice surprised even him. "Enough of the shit about love. Enough of all your shit. Answer our questions. That's it. That's all. Then we're done here."

"Yes," Jeremiah said, rubbing the fingers of one hand together, as though testing for the same stickiness he had noticed earlier. "Go on."

"Where did you and Grace Elaine Somerset go during the party?" Hazard asked.

"We stayed in the house the whole time."

"Where did you go inside the house?"

"Several places. As you know, the party took up most of the main floor. We weren't together the whole time, but I stayed in the family room for most of the evening."

"And towards the end, shortly before the shooting?"

"Yes, we were together then. Talking in the family room, that's all."

"That's a lie," Somers said.

"No, it's true. We were in the family room, right by the big Christmas tree. Your father—he was trying to make your mother angry. There was a girl—"

"I know what my father was doing. I don't need you to tell me. You're lying. Where did you go? And don't tell me you were in the family room the whole time. I saw you leave."

"We went into the kitchen. And then into the garage."

"Why?"

"John-Henry," Jeremiah said, pausing, awkwardness contorting his voice.

"It doesn't matter," Hazard said into the strained quiet. "What did you see in the kitchen? Was there anyone else there? What did you see in the TV room?"

"In the kitchen? Nothing. No, wait—"

Somers interrupted him. "Of course it matters. What were you doing in the garage?"

This time, a flush infused Jeremiah's golden skin. "It's not really appropriate conversation, John-Henry. Your mother and I—we were—it's not—"

"Go back to the kitchen," Hazard said. "What were you going to say?"

The rational part of Somers knew to let it drop. The rational part of Somers wanted to pull back on the reins, turn the buggy around, and get out of this storm. But the rational part of his brain had dropped the reins, and the rest of him was running wild. His words cut into the silence. "You were going to fuck her? Is that what you were going to say? You were going to fuck my mother in the garage during the family Christmas party?"

Jeremiah looked down at his hands, which wrapped and folded and tangled themselves.

"That's enough," Hazard said. "Go get some air."

"I'm fine."

"You're not fine. Go outside. Cool down."

Somers couldn't though. He'd lost control of himself. All the chaos that had been brewing inside him, it had finally overflowed. Those tectonic shifts had upset whatever tenuous balance remained, and now the rational part of him could only sit back, shake its head, and hope it survived long enough to pick up the pieces. It felt like watching the world through a stranger's eyes, it felt like hearing a stranger's voice, his hands were a stranger's hands, running over the textured fabric of the sofa. He didn't even remember moving to stand there.

"No, I'm fine." Somers said. "All right. You were going to fuck my mother in the garage. Fuck her on top of one of those fancy cars my dad loves. You saw something in the kitchen? What'd you see? A box of condoms you forgot the last time you were there?"

"Jesus Christ," Hazard hissed.

"The bag. That fuzzy pink bag, the one that man, the shooter, had been carrying like a Santa Claus bag. It was on the floor at the far end of the kitchen, near the TV room. I remember because it looked so out of place."

"A bag," Somers said. "You saw a goddamn bag."

"What about inside the TV room?" Hazard asked.

Jeremiah stopped wringing his hands long enough to spread them. "Nothing. I mean, the man was sitting there. He was naked."

"That's all he was doing?" Hazard pressed. "Sitting?"

Jeremiah spread his hands again. His eyes crinkled at the corners as though he were seeing something far off, and he shrugged. "I wasn't really paying attention. No. Wait. I remember—" Another pause infused his posture with awkward discomfort. "I thought he was, well, pleasuring himself."

"You thought he was jacking off?" Somers heard that stranger say with his voice. "You really had your mind on one thing."

"But he wasn't. I realized that almost immediately. He was rocking back and forth, hands between his legs—you can see why I thought what I did—but then he sat upright. He was holding something between his hands."

"What?" Hazard said.

"Well—nothing. I mean, nothing I could see. And I didn't really try to see. To be honest, I was still a little afraid of him, and he was just sitting there in that chair, all alone. I thought he might—God, who knows? Come after us. Talk to us. Look at us. I told you, I'm a coward. We all were."

Through the insane, drunken cloud of his thoughts, a lightning bolt struck, illuminating Somers's mind for a moment. For that moment, just for that moment, rational thinking returned. His hands. He might come after us. Stillwell with his hands between his legs. And Jeremiah's words: *Then he sat upright. He was holding something between his hands.*

Whoever had uncuffed Stillwell, he had done it before Jeremiah and Grace Elaine passed through the kitchen. So why had Stillwell waited so long to start shooting?

CHAPTER TWENTY-THREE

**DECEMBER 23
SATURDAY
2:30 PM**

HAZARD DROVE SLOWLY. The VW chugged and whined as the tires sought purchase in the snow, but the car's rattling eased as they crested the hill and began the slippery slide towards Market Street. A few blocks ahead, the road flattened out alongside the river. It was the last Saturday before Christmas, and everyone in Wahredua had turned out to do last-minute shopping. And while Market Street couldn't exactly compare to the shopping mall past Wroxall College, it still had gift shops, specialty stores, and a few trendier clothing boutiques that had popped up along the revitalized waterfront. Cars clogged the road; the Crofter's Mark building, where Hazard and Somerset had their apartment, looked farther away than ever.

Since leaving Jeremiah's apartment, Somers had said nothing. He leaned against the glass. His breath fogged crystal rosettes on the window, and he shaded his eyes. He was sick, Hazard guessed—and not just from the drinking. Sick from having to find his mother in another man's bed. Sick from having to face truths about his family, about his parents, that he had managed to hide from himself for a long time. Sick mostly, Hazard guessed, from running face first into reality like a brick shithouse.

"Stop it."

"Stop what?"

"Stop looking at me out of the corner of your eyes like I'm going to turn green or explode or, Jesus, I don't know." Somers shifted his hand, as though a particularly tricky particle of sunlight had managed to reach his eyes.

"Are you going to barf?"

"For hell's sake."

"You're pale. You're sweating. You keep squirming around, and you've pasted your face to the glass."

"Can we talk about something else?"

"If you're going to throw up, you'd better open the damn door."

"Anything else?"

"You get sick in the car, you're cleaning it up."

"I'm not going to barf, Hazard. Jesus Christ. Like it would matter anyway."

"What's that supposed to mean?"

"Look, we've got to talk about what Jeremiah said."

"You don't like my car."

"If Jeremiah's telling the truth—and I'm not convinced he is—then it changes things. Someone uncuffed Stillwell earlier than I thought. Maybe as soon as I left him alone."

"I've had this car since college. It's paid off. It runs." Hazard fiddled with the climate control. "The heat works."

"Will you forget about the damn car? I don't care about the car. I'm talking about our case. This case. Somebody shooting my father."

"I heard what you said. I'm not deaf. Someone uncuffed Stillwell early. Then he waited."

"Yeah. Why the hell did he wait?"

"Because whoever hired him told him to wait. That's obvious, isn't it?"

"Why? Why not turn him loose?"

"Because the killer was waiting for something."

"What?"

"I don't know, Somers. If I did, we'd be finished. I'm more interested in the gun."

For a moment, Somers raised his hand and peered out at Hazard. "Huh? What gun? Stillwell's"

"Exactly."

"Exactly what?"

"What gun."

Somers let out a slow, controlled breath, like a man trying to blow out a burning fuse. "How about for us idiots? Could you start at the beginning?"

"Where did Stillwell get the gun?"

"I don't know. You saw where he lived. I'm sure there are plenty of guys in Smithfield who can sell you a hot piece, no questions asked. Or the killer might have provided it. We still don't even know why Stillwell brought the gun. Those emails, the ones we read on his computer, they didn't say anything about a gun or about killing."

"Yep."

"For the love of—" Somers lifted his hand again. His eyes looked a few degrees below murder. "What are you talking about?"

"I don't think Stillwell took a gun to the party. I don't even think he was hired to kill. Or, I should say, I don't think he knew what he was being hired to do."

"So where did he get a gun? My parents don't keep them in the kitchen cabinet, you know."

Hazard ignored the jibe. The old, familiar rush was taking over. He turned into the Crofter's Mark's underground parking, easing the VW out of the slush and cold and into the ventilated structure. This was how it always felt, the quickening thump in his chest, the nervous energy like he could get up and dance—yeah, he thought as a picture flashed in his mind, dance, and he saw himself grinding up on Somers—and the feeling that he had the edges of the puzzle. That was how it always started: edges first, moving in. This was why he became a cop. This was why he was a good detective. Not the physical conditioning. Not the weapons training. Not even—or at least, not only—the desire to do something good and meaningful. This: putting together the pieces. Finding order and pattern in chaos. Assembling truth.

"That's the other question," Hazard said, guiding the VW into a parking spot. "Once we know that, we'll have our killer."

"So you're saying—what?" Somers had dropped his hand. He was still pale, his brow still slick and shiny with sweat, and he was obviously trying to think through what Hazard had been driving at. "Someone said that Stillwell had a gun, but he didn't?"

"That's what I think."

"Why?" Somers shook his head, wincing. "No, I see it. That way, everyone believed he already had a gun. Everyone would believe that Stillwell had come to the party armed. Just like we did. Even after we read the emails, we assumed that he had brought a gun. If you're right, though, then it's more complicated than that."

"Too bad Jeremiah doesn't remember who shouted gun."

"Doesn't remember. Or doesn't want to remember."

Hazard grunted; those words came close to his own thoughts.

Somers spoke again, his voice thoughtful. "Jeremiah told us that the sheriff, his son, and my father were the ones who grappled with Stillwell. And Mayor Newton was right there. In fact, Mayor Newton was the one who took the bag that Stillwell was carrying."

"You've still got a hard-on for Newton?" Hazard shrugged. "It could have been any of them. Just because Newton had the bag doesn't mean anything."

"Unless Newton took the opportunity to put something in the bag. Remember, Jeremiah said that he saw the bag near the TV room. It was on the floor, as though someone had discarded it."

Hazard shrugged.

"It still could have been Newton," Somers said.

With another roll of his shoulders, Hazard opened the door and got out of the car. "I'm not saying it wasn't him. But why force us to look into it? No, don't answer. We've already gone round and round on that. I'm willing to keep an open mind."

As they rode the elevator to the top, Somers leaned against the mirrored wall. He looked wrecked. The mirrors threw back hundreds of John-Henry Somersets, stretching off into every direction, and all of them looked like they'd spent a couple of hours being dragged behind a garbage truck.

"You know what I'm thinking about?" Somers said, breaking the silence between them.

"No."

"You know what I'm still thinking about?"

A warning prickle ran up Hazard's spine. He wasn't normally attuned to the subtle clues that people gave off—at least, not the way Somers was. But he was attuned to Somers, attuned like a goddamn lightning rod in a thunderstorm, and something in Somers's voice, something in the thousands of cues of his chest, his hands, his jaw, something told Hazard that whatever was coming next was going to hit like a mother.

"Homo economicus," Somers said. He looked up. His eyes looked deeper than ever, bottomless blue, so deep that Hazard felt dizzy. "We don't do anything because it makes sense, do we?"

"Some of us do."

"You?" Somers laughed, and the sound was so genuine, so warm, that it was almost worse than if Somers had sounded cruel. "Yeah, I guess so, Ree. You're all brains. It's all analysis with you, calculus, planning. It'd be adorable if it weren't so goddamn annoying." He softened the final words with a smile. That smile could have softened steel. It could have softened the Himalayas. "The rest of us, though—hell, I'm not even talking about the rest of us. Me. I just keep fucking things up."

"You're drunk."

"Thanks."

"No, I mean—" Why was this so hard? "You're not thinking clearly. Get some rest. We'll pick up again in a few hours."

"Is that why we came home? So you can sober me up?" Somers played with the buttons of his shirt, undoing first one, then another, exposing the hollow of his throat, the firm line of his chest. Another button. And then another. The curve of his undershirt came into view. His fingers tugged at the thin white fabric, drawing it down, revealing the first swirl of the dark ink that marked his chest and arms. Hazard could follow that ink with his eyes. He wanted to follow it with his mouth. With his tongue. He wanted to trace the lines of muscle underneath. He remembered how Somers's skin tightened at his touch, and he wanted to feel it again.

The elevator dinged. The doors opened.

Neither man moved.

Somers had drawn the collar of his undershirt down further, exposing the trench that ran between his pectorals, his fingers moving lazily over smooth skin. He drew his lower lip between his teeth. His pupils were blown, his eyes lazy, and Hazard suddenly knew that this was what Somers would look like during sex, that this staggering beauty would be complemented by touch, by breath, by heat. Hazard wanted to take a step forward. That's all he would need: one step, and then momentum, momentum that had been building for twenty years would take over. His knees flexed. His weight shifted.

And then the moment had passed. Somers dropped his hand, and he smirked and said, "You know what, though? You're not as rational as you think."

Hazard flushed. He knew what Somers would say next: a mocking comment about how easy it was, child's play, really, to seduce Hazard. Rationality. Analysis. Calculus. Fuck all that, the rest of Hazard's hormone-drunk brain was saying. Fuck everything but this moment.

Instead, though, Somers said, "Nico."

Shaking his head, mute, Hazard waited.

"You and Nico. There's nothing rational. That's what Jeremiah made me realize. I keep looking for something rational, some reason the two of you are together. That's not it, though. It's not rational. Maybe it's not supposed to be. You and—" His smirk hooked at the edges. "You and that baby."

"Screw you."

"He's a toddler. I'm surprised he doesn't still have a curfew."

"You're an asshole."

Together, they made their way to the apartment. Inside, the afternoon sun brightened the wood, gave it a gleam. The air still smelled like Somers's cologne from the night before, and Hazard's heart thudded like it was falling downhill—like it wouldn't stop until it hit bottom.

"No," Hazard said when Somers opened the fridge.

With the door open, Somers hesitated, his hand inches from a bottle of Bud Lite. Something dark—something furious, Hazard thought, like Somers wanted to hit him—darted across Somers's face, but then he cocked his head and smiled. He snagged a water bottle instead and shut the fridge.

"Not all of us can be rational all the time," Somers said, popping the cap. He drank deeply. His throat bobbed in time with the swallows. Hazard felt himself starting to sweat. It was a water bottle. Just a water bottle. Lord, what could this man do if he really tried to turn up the heat? "Some of us," Somers said, lurching towards his bedroom. "Some of us just have to shit on everything now and then."

"Try not to shit on this case."

Somers raised the water in mock-salute.

"Two hours," Hazard said. "Then we're going back out."

"Aye-aye."

"Get some sleep."

Rolling his eyes, Somers shut the door to his bedroom, leaving Hazard alone.

Hazard thought about going to his room, but instead he stretched out on the couch. Not because of the refrigerator. Not because of the beer. Not because Somers might try to sneak back out. Not for any of those reasons, he told himself.

Kicking off his shoes, he squirmed on the sofa; he was a big man, and the cushions flattened under him. Something dug into his hip. Hazard fished out his mobile phone, tossed it on the coffee table, and flopped onto his side. Damn. There it was again, a block pressed against his hip. He fumbled through his pockets again, and again he retrieved a phone, but not his.

Turning Hadley Bingham's phone over in his hands, Hazard found himself suddenly overcome. Not by grief, not exactly. He hadn't known Hadley. He'd seen her only once, the night she died. But the feeling persisted. It resonated inside him. It seemed to start with the glass and plastic that he held, and it reverberated through him like some sort of exotic poison, African tree frogs, something like that. A poison that entered through the skin.

Hadley Bingham had died, and the thought tumbled inside Hazard. He wasn't sure what he was feeling. Not grief, no, definitely not grief. He had to remind himself of that. For Emery Hazard, who mistrusted—

—poison—

—emotions, this sudden surge of feeling was uncomfortable. It was worse than uncomfortable. He tossed on the couch, as though trying to rouse himself from a bad dream. He had the sinking feeling that he might be sick.

But he'd felt this way before, hadn't he? He'd felt it a long time ago. There was a blank space in his memories, a spot carefully effaced. But Hazard was afraid that if he looked too closely, he'd see what had once been there. Those weeks after Jeff's death. The weeks when he'd been close to dying himself. Not because of grief. Jesus, it sounded so archaic. Grief. Like he was some melancholy Renaissance poet. No, not grief. But he remembered, in those weeks after Jeff had put the shotgun in his mouth, Hazard remembered something like this feeling. Like looking into the stars and seeing only the empty spaces between, feeling that emptiness inside, letting it grow.

Hazard punched at the phone's screen. It flickered to life, displaying a photograph of a teenage girl, an arm around her shoulders. It was Hadley Bingham, and the arm around her belonged to a man. Or an older boy. Who could it be? Hazard focused on the question, trying to hedge out the memories. He wasn't going to think about those days after Jeff had killed himself. He wasn't going to think about—

—the black space—

—the stars, or anything stupid like that. He'd learned, hadn't he? He'd learned the hard way what it meant, leaving yourself—

—vulnerable—

—open like that, yes, open, that was the right word, like leaving the door to the apartment open, and anybody could just walk right inside? Anybody could go through the papers on his desk, anybody could nab a beer from the fridge, anybody could rifle his dirty laundry. And that was stupid; nobody did that, not anymore. What did you do? You locked things. You locked the door tight. That wasn't just safe; it was smart.

But Hazard's eyes had drifted away from the phone and the picture of Hadley Bingham and the arm across her shoulders, and he was looking at Somers's door now, and he was thinking, Yeah, a lock, a lock on the damn door, and it didn't help because the only person that Hazard really needed to keep outside, the only one who went through Hazard's life rummaging and poking and upsetting everything, he lived here too. He had a key. Somers had always had a key, even back in the worst times, even back when Mikey Grames had held a knife and cut three shiny lines into Hazard's stomach. Even then, Somers could have opened the door and walked right on in whenever he goddamn wanted. Why? Because Emery Hazard was an idiot. And Somers would do what he always did: he'd walk in, stay just long enough to turn things upside down, and then he'd leave. Like he had at Windsor last month. Like he had at Halloween. Like he had all those years ago in the locker room, nothing but one kiss between them, and here Hazard was, a grown man, and he couldn't forget it. Most days didn't want to forget it.

And worst of all, here Hazard was, mooning over Somers like—like—like that same damn Renaissance poet. Gripping the phone more tightly, Hazard swiped at the screen again. That arm. Who did that belong to? One of the boys at the party, he guessed. He wasn't sure why—the boys had been kissing each other, and the kisses hadn't been brotherly—but it had been in the way the bigger boy had been looking at Hadley. He'd been kissing his buddy, but his eyes, his eyes had been only for Hadley. And he'd been angry. Angry enough to plan a murder? Maybe. Hazard would need to talk to the boys and see.

A knock interrupted his thoughts. Slowly, Hazard swung his legs off the couch and made his way to the door. He hesitated, stood to the side, and reached for the .38 that he'd hung by the door. This was his home. It was the middle of the afternoon. It was a nice building in a nice part of town. But something about this case, the way it wormed through the department, through the mayor's office, through the richest families in town, made Hazard's skin bugger.

"Yeah?" he called through the closed door.

"Emery?"

With a grunt, Hazard undid the deadbolt and opened the door. Nico stood there, shivering in spite of his boots and parka. Doubtless, Hazard thought, he was shivering because underneath the parka, Nico was probably wearing the same ratty jeans and t-shirt that he always wore.

"Everything ok?" Nico asked.

Hazard realized he was holding the gun. He holstered it, leaving it by the door, and locked the door behind Nico. "Fine. What's up?"

"Nothing. Just wanted to see what you were doing." Nico moved deeper into the apartment, shedding the parka, scarf, gloves, trailing winter apparel across the apartment until he stood in—yes, Hazard had predicted it—jeans and a t-shirt, both of them with so many rips and tears that they'd be better suited for the rag pile. Pulling his dark, wavy hair from its bun, Nico shook it loose. He studied the apartment as though he hadn't been there a hundred times before.

"You wanted to see if I was screwing Somers."

Heat showed under Nico's coppery skin. No answer, just a shrug. But the blush was an answer. The shrug was an answer.

Somers would have known what to do next. Somers would have known why Nico was feeling this way. Somers would have known how to explain. Somers would have known all of it, beginning to end. He probably would have capped the whole thing with fantastic sex. Emery Hazard, on the other hand, wasn't likely to cap anything— from the looks of it, not for a very long time. His brain moved too quickly. His brain snapped up all the details, chewed them, and spat out an answer.

"Your buddy at The Real Beef texted you. He said something. You stopped answering my texts, so I knew you were angry. I also knew it had something to do with Somers. Then you show up here, unannounced, and say that you wanted to see what I was up to. No phone call. No text. Last I told you, I was out working."

"But I was right," Nico said. Dark eyes, very dark, the darkness—

—between those stars—

—that edged butterfly wings. "You're here. He's here."

"He's in his room. Asleep."

"Because he got wasted at lunch. I know."

"Your buddy told you that too?"

Nico's nostrils flared. "His name's Marcus. You know that."

"What do I care what his name is?"

"You've met him, geez, I don't know. A lot. Ten times."

"What do I care about him?"

"He's my friend."

Hazard shook his head. Moving past Nico, he collected his phone and Hadley's from the coffee table and shoved them into his pocket. "We're still working this case."

"Yeah, I can tell. You're working it really hard. This is just, what, a siesta?"

Without an answer, Hazard settled for giving Nico a cold stare.

Nico met the stare for a moment and then dropped his eyes. He paced back and forth, his boots squeaking, one hand toying with a hole in his shirt. As his fingers twisted the threadbare cotton, he exposed hints of satin skin and muscle. Hazard dropped onto the couch and waited. Ten seconds passed. The boots squeaked louder and faster. Twenty seconds. Nico twisted harder at the t-shirt. The cotton stuttered a long, ripping noise.

"Let's go to New York," Nico said, planting himself in front of Hazard. "Let's get out of here for the break. No, hold on. Just listen. I'm on break until the fifteenth. You've got vacation. You haven't used any of it, so I know you've got it. I'll buy the tickets. I've got some money left over from those summer jobs. Maybe I'll pick up a photo shoot while I'm in the city. There's this Fruit of the Loom job that my agent keeps floating." Nico smiled, and it trembled like a drop of water about to fall. So full of hope, that damn smile. And so full of fear. "You've never seen me on a shoot. You've never seen any of my pictures. You've never asked."

Hazard laced his fingers together. Best thing to do was wait. Wait and let him get it all out. That's what Hazard had done with Alec. That's what Hazard had done with Billy. Yeah, a traitorous voice said. Yeah, and look how that turned out.

"Well?" Nico said.

"What?"

"New York. A vacation."

"I'm working a case."

"No. You're—you're doing something, and I don't know what you're doing, but it's not a case."

"You know I'm working a case."

"Don't lie to me." The words emerged as a shout, deeper and louder than any tone that Nico had used with Hazard before. "Jesus, just don't lie, ok? Don't make me feel like even more of an idiot."

Hazard had gone still. The hairs on his arms, the hairs on his chest, the hairs on the back of his neck were standing up, like something out of a bad horror film. Alec had yelled this way. Billy had—no, Billy hadn't yelled. Billy had other ways. Mikey Grimes had yelled this way. Somers had yelled this way, the day he shoved Hazard down a flight of stairs. That's what faggots get.

Something of Hazard's feelings must have shown in his face because Nico bit his lip and said, "Damn," and then, of all things, he went down on his knees and grabbed Hazard's hands, ignoring Hazard's initial effort to pull away. "I'm sorry. I feel like—I don't know what I feel like. I've never done this before. This has never happened before. I shouldn't have yelled, but I don't understand."

"What?"

"Huh?"

"What don't you understand?"

"This. You. John-Henry. The sneaking around. The—" He had been about to say lying. Hazard could read it from a mile off. Instead, though, he said, "The times you just disappear."

"I'm working a case. I have a job, remember? Not all of us get to spend the summer trying on jockstraps and cash those big checks all year round." Hazard twisted his hands free. "And Somers is my partner. I know you don't like him. For all I care, you can hate him. I have a job, he's my partner, and that's the end of it."

Nico grimaced, and he latched onto Hazard's hands again. Looking up at Hazard, looking up through thick lashes, he shook his head. "All right. You tell me you're working a case. You tell me I'm,

I don't know, crazy. Jealous. Whatever you want, you call me that, and I'll nod and I'll own up to it. I'll wear a fucking sign in the middle of the street that says I'm a jealous bitch if that's what you want. But you've got to tell me why, when I ran into Albert at the grocery store today, he told me there's no case. What am I supposed to think when you're having lunch with John-Henry, when Marcus sees the two of you laughing and drinking tequila and—"

"Lender said what?" Shock forced Hazard into motion. He stood up, pushing Nico away, and strode towards the kitchen.

Nico scrambled to his feet, flushing, and followed. "There's no case. The shooter was killed last night while trying to escape."

"That piece of shit."

"Is he telling the truth?"

"That fucking piece of shit."

With surprising strength, Nico grabbed Hazard's shoulder and spun him. "Is he telling the truth?"

A growl was building inside Hazard. He wanted to knock aside Nico's hand. He wanted to shove—

—this child, this baby, this infant—

—Nico out of the way. He wanted to drive to Albert Lender's house and punch him so hard that the thick-framed glasses were permanently embedded in Lender's skull.

Instead, though, he managed to draw a breath. "That's not how it is."

"So the shooter wasn't killed last night?"

Hazard hesitated. He wasn't smooth enough. He wasn't fast enough. He was too used to delivering brutal truths; he had always preferred the brutality of truth, even from a young age. Keen analysis, insight, and effective delivery were a far more powerful combination than slick talking, he had found. And now, when he needed a bit of smooth, it failed him.

"Mother of God," Nico said. "He was. He was killed last night. And you're trying to lie about it."

"I haven't even said a damn word. Yes, he was shot last night. And Lender is the one who shot him."

"So he was telling the truth."

"No."

"You just told me: the shooter is dead. The man who killed that girl, he's dead. So what have you been doing?"

"Just because he's dead doesn't mean there's no case."

"That's exactly what it means. No, Emery, I get to finish what I'm saying. This is exactly what Lender told me was happening. You're—I don't know, you're obsessed with him. With John-Henry. And now you're using this, the shooting, all of it, as a way to spend more time with him. As a way to make him need you."

Shaking his head, Hazard flung open the refrigerator. He grabbed a beer, twisted off the top, and spun the cap into the sink. After a long drink, he wiped his mouth and let out a defeated laugh. "This is a joke. Yeah. It's a fucking joke. You think you have any idea what you're talking about? You think because a crooked cop comes up to you in the grocery store and plants this shit in your head, you think you know what's going on? You're the one paying sixty thousand dollars a year for a master's degree in theology. Why don't you put those critical thinking skills to work? Did you ever think that Lender might be lying? Did you think that maybe I know something you don't? Did you ever think to trust me?"

Nico swallowed. Under the burnt gold of his skin, he had gone pale, and he swallowed now, but he didn't break eye contact.

"You know what the worst part of this is?" Hazard said, taking another drink of the beer, wanting to spit it out because everything tasted like something he'd sicked up, everything: the air, his tongue, the beer. "It's not that you believed Lender over me. It's not that you don't trust me. It's that you're jealous. It's that you made him right. You're jealous of Somers, and all those times I defended you, all those times I told him he was crazy for thinking you were jealous, I was wrong. You made him right. You made him fucking right." Hazard shook his head in disgust.

"I'm jealous," Nico said. "I'm the one who's jealous. That's what he said. Me. I'm the one."

"You don't know anything about me," Hazard said. "Not if you think something could happen between me and him."

"Maybe I am. Maybe I am jealous. I don't—I can't think straight. Not when I'm feeling like this. Maybe I really am. Because you look at him, and you actually see him. You talk to him, and you're really talking to him. You go out with him. You—"

"That's what this is about? You want to go out more?"

"No. Yes, it's part of it, but no. That's not what I'm saying."

"Then what are you saying?"

"I'm saying I have no idea why you're dating me when you're obviously in love with him."

The silence that followed roared like radio static. Somewhere outside, somewhere on Market Street, a horn was blaring, and the sound was faded and small and flat. The beer curdled on Hazard's tongue. He'd throw it up; he needed to throw it up, all of it, and it was going to come up. But mostly, his brain felt stretched towards the closed bedroom door, towards the man behind it, and Hazard was waiting, listening, hoping.

But Somers didn't open the door. Just more of that staticky silence, like someone had snapped the tuner.

"That's what I'm saying." Nico was breathing raggedly. Those dark eyes, like the dark of butterfly wings, were full of tears. "That's what I want to know. Why? Why are we doing this?"

"We were fine," Hazard said. He set the beer down—sloppy, sloppy—and it tumbled into the sink. Glass cracked. "Last night, for hell's sake, we were fine. We were having a nice time."

"We weren't fine. Maybe we haven't ever been fine. I don't know if you're deluded. I don't know if you don't even know the truth yourself. I don't know if you're just lonely. But you know what? You still haven't told me. You still can't tell me why."

"Fine. I'll tell you why. I'm dating you because—"

Hazard's phone buzzed. He slapped his hand on his pocket, drew out the phone, and stared at the screen. Swinney's name flashed. He looked up at Nico. There wasn't any right way to say this, and once again, Hazard searched for something smooth and came up with all the harsh, broken things he was used to saying.

"You know what?" Nico brushed at his eyes, and he was trying his hardest to sound normal, he was trying so hard that it hurt

Hazard, hurt at some fundamental level that he wasn't even aware of. "You should take that."

"It's work."

"I know it's work."

Nico grabbed his parka and headed for the door. The hurt inside Hazard, the pain, had grown so huge that his hands felt like balloons. He gripped the edge of the sink, and he felt a flash of pain. Not from the broken beer glass. It was the old cut on his hand, the still-healing cut. It hurt like hell as he clutched at the sink, and the shock was enough for Hazard to draw a breath and thumb at the call.

"What is it?" Hazard asked. Nico didn't look back. Nico didn't slow down. Nico pulled the door shut. Not like a baby. Not like a child. No tantrums. Not like a kid at all. Just pulled it shut, and then he was gone.

Swinney's voice sounded like a bald tire, and it took Hazard a moment to realize she'd been crying.

"I need to talk about what happened last night."

CHAPTER TWENTY-FOUR

DECEMBER 23
SATURDAY
3:42 PM

SOMERS PUT HIMSELF at about sixty percent. He'd slept some, maybe three-quarters of an hour, until the yelling had started. The sleep had helped. The worst of the booze was running out of him, and in its place had come a throbbing headache, like his skull had turned to glass and was trying to shiver itself apart. He needed water. No. He needed another drink. And then another. And then another, until someone or something came along and put him to bed.

That was the easy way out. That was an old, well-trodden road for John-Henry Somerset. When things started hurting too bad, when things got hard, when the coin didn't flip heads-up, just walk away. Leave. Or get so drunk you were all the way out of your head.

But the yelling, this time, the yelling made him stop and listen and lie on his bed, his skin prickling like a draft was running over him. Hazard sounded raw. Furious. And wounded. All the years Somers had known him, all the torment he had inflicted on Hazard in school, and he'd never heard that kind of vulnerability in Hazard's voice. It was Nico, of course. It was that selfish, spoiled, primping drama queen. It was just like Nico, just like that immature piece of ass to do this to Hazard, to completely take the man apart.

But it wasn't just Nico's fault. That was too easy. That was too simple. Because it was Hazard's fault too. It was the big man's fault for—

—daring to love someone else—

—hooking up with an infant. With a baby. With a child who had no sense of the world, no sense of who Emery Hazard was, the kind of man he was, no sense of how lucky he was to be with Hazard.

And a very small part of Somers, a part of himself that he hated and buried under half-vocalized justifications and explanations, that small part of him hated the fact that Nico had managed to hurt Hazard in a way that Somers never could. Even as the thought stirred in its dark hole, Somers heaped more dirt on it. But it was there: the root of what had driven him to bully the skinny boy when they had been teenagers, the mixture of fear and desire that Somers couldn't control, couldn't escape, couldn't face in the daylight.

And then the shouting stopped. Five minutes passed. The prickling on Somers's skin dried up, and he felt mostly the headache and the sick guiltiness of eavesdropping—and, too, of the dark hope that maybe now, maybe this time, Hazard would end things with Nico. Maybe it would be over.

Fuck that, Somers told himself. And fuck you for being such a miserable, selfish fuck. You're not going to date Hazard. He's not interested in you—no matter what that baby he's dating thinks—and he's made that clear plenty of times. He made it clear at Windsor, didn't he? You practically threw yourself at him, and he didn't want you. So let him go. Let him have someone, at least. Someone who will make him happy. And a dark voice added, let him have someone who's not Nico.

The knock jolted Somers out of his recriminations. A moment later, Hazard's gruff, "Get up," followed.

Since Hazard had moved into the apartment, Somers had found himself acquiring furniture—not buying it, but just having it appear. Hazard's doing, he was sure, although, his partner never said anything about it. Somers's bedroom had transformed over the last two months. Instead of the mattress on the floor, there was an actual bed. Instead of the black garbage bags full of clothes, there were hangers in the closet. Instead of—well, instead of the emptiness, there was a dresser, a chair, a mirror.

In front of the mirror, Somers paused, forking two fingers through his hair, mussed but not too mussed. He adjusted his undershirt, sliding the scoop neck lower to expose the ink on his collarbone. Hazard liked that ink, Somers knew. Somers didn't care, of course. Somers wasn't telling himself, be normal, be casual. He wasn't telling himself that. He was a grown man. He didn't care, didn't give a shit about what Hazard liked or thought or did. But he still couldn't get the thought out of his head. Be normal.

When he opened the door, Hazard stood near the entryway, arms crossed over his chest, the muscles in his jaw tight, practically rippling with force.

"We've got to go. Get dressed."

"What's going on?" Act normal. A little sleepy because you just got up. No yawn, that's too obvious. But maybe—he scratched under one arm. Maybe something like that. "Was someone here?"

"Get your clothes on. Swinney called. She wants to talk about what happened to Stillwell."

Somers nodded, collecting a fresh shirt and clean pants from the closet and tugging them on. Through the open door, he called, "I thought I heard Nico."

No response.

Somers dragged on socks, shoved his feet into loafers, and joined his partner near the door. The headache had really gotten its teeth, and Somers swiped Tylenol from the cabinet and chugged a bottle of water. Hazard stood where he'd been standing five minutes before. He didn't look like he'd moved. He didn't look like he'd so much as breathed.

"Well?" Somers said.

"What?"

"Was Nico here?"

"If you want to say something, just say it, Somers. Don't piss all over the place." Hazard stormed into the hallway.

Following, Somers shrugged into his jacket. "It's just a question."

They met Swinney in, of all places, Smithfield. Hazard drove, and the VW's whine burrowed into Somers's head, taking up residence with the headache. Hazard was all stiff, angry silence.

Somers didn't bother trying to get anything out of his partner; he settled for keeping himself from tossing up everything in his stomach.

Driving them west, Hazard passed through most of Smithfield. The houses decayed steadily: neat, new buildings giving way to older, skinny brick structures, brick giving way to timber and scrap, windows giving way to broken, gaping sickles of glass. They passed the Haverford, where Wayne Stillwell had lived, and the broken beer bottles still poked out of the snow like the fangs of some beast from a very tacky ice age.

The next block was composed of a single building subdivided into storefronts. Many were closed—the glass broken or simply gone, and plywood that bled spray paint in a dozen different places. A wings-and-seafood joint occupied one of the remaining storefronts, though, its neon sign flashing something that Somers hoped was a shrimp. And a dollar store occupied another. There was a payday loan office, a Church of the Three-Day Nazarene, a beauty salon named Mystique with a smaller sign advertising wigs made from human hair, and a real estate agent: Berta Gutierrez, Into Your Home, Into Your Heart. What there was not, though, was any sign of Swinney.

"What the hell was she thinking?" Hazard muttered as he shifted the VW into park.

"She was thinking nobody from the department would be out here." Somers massaged his head, but he needed more force behind the movement. Hazard had big hands. Strong hands. If Somers asked him, if he asked him nicely, Hazard might—

"This is stupid." Hazard grabbed the keys. "Let's get out of here."

"Swinney chose this place for a reason. She wants to talk about Lender, and she's not going to do it where Murray or Carmichael or Orear are going to walk in on us."

"She chose a spot where she can hollow out our heads with a 9mm and nobody will ask her to sweep up afterward."

Somers, nodding, studied the street. "Maybe."

"What do you mean maybe?"

"I mean, you saw how she acted last night."

Hazard grunted. He still had his hand wrapped around the keys, like he was ready to fire the VW up and peel away.

"She was messed up," Somers said. "She was scared. She knew something was wrong, but she wasn't ready to say it."

"She barely said two words."

"You saw her. Tell me I'm wrong."

For a moment, Hazard's frustration was palpable. His fingers knotted in the keychain. "I don't know."

"I know. Swinney isn't the kind to shoot first. She wants to talk to us."

"What about the Haverford?"

"What?"

"That story your dad told you. The dirty cop, the one who shot his partner. What about that? I mean, here we are in Smithfield. Perfect place to get rid of a cop who's asking too many questions."

"Then you should be worried about me, not about Swinney."

Hazard snorted.

"We talk to Swinney and see where it goes," Somers said. "She's got something on Lender, and Lender's got something on Newton. It's the oldest trick in the book, Ree. We just keep squeezing until we get our guy."

For another moment, Hazard's fingers whitened around the keys. Then, with a gruff burst of breath, he kicked open the door.

"Somebody's going to steal my car. We're going to have to walk home."

That might not be the worst thing, Somers thought as he peeled himself from the VW's upholstery. Not even close to the worst thing.

Already the sun had dipped towards the horizon. Another hour of daylight. An hour tops. Somers shivered, although the air was still. The last of the sunlight was curling back from the ground in tired ribbons, and the temperature had dropped steadily. This cold, the air brought tears to Somers's eyes. It froze the inside of his nose. It did, however, blunt his headache, and that made the rest of it worth it. Well, almost.

"Where?" Somers asked, glancing up and down the block.

221

Hazard shook his head and moved down the row of storefronts. He passed the wings and seafood place—immune, apparently, to the flashing neon shrimp—passed Berta Gutierrez's office, passed the dollar market, its storefront tinseled and chromatic with mass-produced holiday decorations. The next storefront was vacant; the sign out front said, Goyo Sucks Ass, and at least a dozen other citizens had contributed their agreement that Goyo did, indeed, suck ass. The door was heavy, metal and yellowed glass backed by thick kraft paper. The lights inside were out.

Hand on the door, Hazard glanced back.

Somers gave the street one last glance. Was he sure? Hell no. But he'd worked Smithfield. He'd worked it for years, and he'd worked it well. A part of him, at least, was sure. He nodded. But he also eased the Glock from its holster at the small of his back.

The door swung open easily. Inside, only darkness. Then the air shifted, and on the frozen currents came a mustiness, like wet carpet and a dog that's been in the river and old socks all rolled together. Hazard's face registered his disgust, but he said nothing. He had his .38 in his hand, and he eased into the store, keeping his back to the wall.

Somers followed. What could go wrong: just about everything. Swinney with night-vision. Pop-pop. Two shots, that's all, and they'd bleed out here. Nobody would find them until—summer, maybe? That was optimistic. When the smell got bad enough, yes, that might do it. But Somers breathed in another mouthful of river-dog and thought, no, no, the smell won't be enough. Or maybe it would be Swinney and Lender both. Or maybe the place was rigged with explosives. C4. He eased sweaty fingers along the Glock. If it were just Swinney and a gun, he could go down shooting. If it were Swinney and a gun, he could throw himself in front of Hazard. Jesus Christ, where had that come from? But if it were a bomb—

"Easy." The voice was Swinney's. "Follow the wall straight back. No lights out here." Then her shoes clicked in the darkness. As Somers's eyes adjusted to the gloom and the weak, wintery afternoon that seeped in around the boards, he saw Swinney disappear into a back room.

Hazard still hadn't breathed. He might as well have been carved out of marble. Pale, translucent, hard. He moved forward, following Swinney's instructions, but he kept the .38 low at his side. Somers flipped the deadbolt on the door. Swinney hadn't told him to, but she hadn't told him not to, and he wasn't sure which one bothered him more.

When Somers reached the back room, Swinney spoke again. "Go ahead and close the door. Light's right by you."

Somers nudged the door shut and flicked on the lights. Blinking against the sudden brightness, he tried to take in his surroundings. A single panel of fluorescent tubes hung overhead, wires exposed, like something after the apocalypse. A shelving unit took up one wall, loaded with toasters and blenders and waffle irons and enough dust to keep everything from flying away. The rest of the room was empty, stripped down to the studs and the blue-flowered linoleum. Swinney stood near the edge of the fluorescent light.

It didn't look good on her, fluorescents. The tremulous light hollowed out her cheeks, gouged dark rings around her eyes. It washed color from her and left her looking sallow, like something that had been kept out of the sun, like old newspaper cracking at the edges. She was older than Somers and Hazard, and she'd stayed clear of the worst of it this far, but Somers could tell that when it did catch up, middle age was going to hit like a real bitch. Her hair, buzzed down to fuzz except for a few long strands in the front, was normally reddish blond, but the lights stole the color and left it looking rusty.

"You boys are jumpy," she said. She didn't have a gun in her hand, but she stood with hands on hips, her jacket pushed back far enough to show the holster under her arm.

"Jesus, Swinney," Somers said. "What is this?" He glanced around the room once more and holstered his Glock. "Are you playing some kind of spy game?"

Instead of answering, Swinney cocked her head towards the street. "Anybody else?"

"What?"

"Did anyone follow you? Did you bring anyone? It's pretty simple."

"No, just us."

"You tell anyone?"

"Come on, Swinney. You know me better than that."

She nodded, but her eyes speared Hazard. "You?"

Hazard shook his head.

"You should know him better than that too," Somers said. "After everything—"

"After what? After three months?" She balled up her fists and pressed them under her eyes—not like she was crying, but like she was holding her face together, like it might all come to pieces if she pulled her hands away. "I've known Al for, what? Ten years? Twelve?" She laughed, and Somers knew that sound, had heard plenty of guys make it after a hit in football, the breath knocked out of them and no way in the world they'd get it back right away. "Yeah, him, this guy, him I can trust. Sure. And Al—" She broke off with that same asphyxiated noise again.

Hazard cleared his throat, but Somers shook his head. He took a step forward, waited, and then another step. Swinney was tensed like she was about to run the hurdles, and at Somers's next step, she scurried back. He didn't press closer; he paused at the rim of the fluorescent light. Its buzz sounded like an old propeller plane. The river-dog smell had faded, and now Somers could smell booze: not yeasty, hoppy beer, but something hard, like whatever Swinney had been drinking was one step up from rubbing alcohol.

"He's cuckoo." The words seemed torn from Swinney. She gestured now with one hand, drawing circles at her temple. "Cracked up, I guess. That's the only thing. He won't talk to me about it. Won't look at me, not in the eyes."

"He's dirty, Swinney."

"No." Her hand moved reflexively to the holstered pistol. "No. He's not."

Behind Somers, Hazard shifted, but Somers waved a hand for Hazard to stay back.

"All right. So tell us: what's going on? Why call us out here?"

Outside, a car horn blared, followed by men's voices exchanging curses, followed by laughter, followed by silence. The fluorescent panel shivered. Swinney's face, in that light, was dead. Her hand hung in the air, inches from her sidearm, and then it dropped like gravity had finally caught up with it.

"He's got to be sick. He's got to be so sick he doesn't know what he's doing, you know? People get like that. For a long time, nobody knows. They get up. They go to work. My uncle. He was weird. Hard to get along with, I could tell that even as a kid. My aunt left him, and my mom and dad talked about it a lot at night when they thought I couldn't hear them, and they were glad. Glad that she'd left him. And he'd get up and go to work. Every day. He sold, shit, I don't know. Paperclips. That kind of stuff."

Hazard's cold voice cut through the break in her story. "What does your uncle—"

"Let her finish," Somers said.

Swinney blinked, as though startled to realize that they were still there, as though she'd become lost in her own story.

"Go on," Somers said.

"He got up and went to work." Swinney shrugged. Again, in the distance, horns hammered the air. "Until one day he didn't. One day, he didn't show up. And then another day. It must have been a while before someone called the police. My parents didn't even know he was missing. They'd stopped talking to him after my aunt left, and most of this I learned a lot later, as an adult." She hesitated, on the cusp of whatever she wanted to say, not quite able to bring herself to say it.

Somers waited. And, thank God, Hazard kept his trap shut.

"He was in his house. He'd covered everything with tin foil. The walls. The windows. The sofa. There was a picture in the paper, and I found it a long time after, and you can see the TV, one of those old models with the round legs, and the whole thing wrapped in tinfoil like a Christmas present. He was in the bedroom. He'd built a—it sounds like I've watched too many movies. A pod, I guess. He started with cardboard, but he'd been wrapping it in Saran wrap, tighter and tighter, and he covered that with foil, and one day he got inside and he wrapped plastic around the door, and that's how they found him. Sitting on a lawn chair he'd dragged into that pod. Asphyxiated; he'd wrapped the whole thing so damn tight he couldn't breathe. Just sitting there like it was summer and he could take another lemonade if you had one." She delivered the last words with wonder in her voice, seeing something Somers couldn't see, and then she was silent.

"You think Lender's crazy," Somers said.

"He's got to be. What he's doing, the way he's acting."

"Can you tell us anything specific?"

"You know what I'm going to say. You goddamn well know it. But yes. I can give you something specific. Thanksgiving, when the two of you got your asses frozen at that old house on the edge of town. Lender got weird. Real weird about all of it."

"You weren't even here," Hazard said. "Not at the beginning."

"I didn't need to be here. I talked to you on the phone. And I talked to Lender too, remember? You wanted to know if there was a way off that damn piece of land, so we called him up. He said there wasn't."

"Except there was," Somers said.

"Yeah. There was. And I asked Lender about that. I didn't think anything of it, really. I was just—it was ribbing, you know. He acts like he knows every square inch of this place, and then the one time it matters, he fouls up. So I said something about it, and he tried to play it off like a joke, but I could tell it wasn't a joke. Not to him. I could tell it spooked him a little."

"That's when you realized something was wrong."

"No. No, not really. I didn't think much about it at all. But it was here." She tapped the back of her head. "Just itching a little. And then other things started to happen. Little things. Phone calls that he wouldn't answer. Or calls he'd get off real sudden. Text messages. A lot of texts that he'd never explain, or he'd say something half-assed about his wife or about dinner or whatever. And he'd be gone sometimes."

"Spaced out?"

"No, gone. We'd be working, and I turn around to say something to him, and he'd be gone. He always had an explanation. He had to run to the pharmacy. He thought he'd pick up lunch. He wanted to fill up the car before rush hour. Any one of those things, I wouldn't have thought about it. Lender, well, it's like partnering with a goddamn efficiency checklist. But I had that bug biting at the back of my brain, and that's the hell of it, you know, suspicion. Once you think something might be wrong, all the signs of it are there. Could be everything's fine. Could be everything's in your head. But that's the problem: you can't tell."

"Until last night."

"Until last night." Full stop, like she never meant to say another word about the subject.

"Swinney, what happened?"

"I lied. I'm a fucking liar, and if that means you want to take this to Cravens and get my badge, that's fine. I'll go with you." She fetched a deep breath. "Honest, it'll be a relief."

"What did you lie about?" Somers asked. The river-dog smell had almost faded—no, not faded, his brain said, you're just used to it—but the booze smell on Swinney seemed stronger than ever. Her eyes were glassy with it. And glassy with grief and with pain and with the wall she was trying to throw up.

"Stillwell never went for my gun."

Somers struggled to control his breathing. Even breaths. You've got her now, but even breaths. Slow. Steady. Look her in the eyes, normal, everything's normal.

"What happened?"

"I don't know. Swear by my nieces and nephews, swear on their snotty little hands, I don't."

"But," Hazard rumbled, "you can guess."

"Yeah. Fuck me. I can."

"Go on," Somers said.

"We parked. Way back from the hospital doors, and that seemed funny, so I asked Lender what he was thinking. I mean, we had a naked man we had to march into the hospital, and there wasn't any reason to make it harder than it needed to be. Lender told me it was what Stillwell deserved. He said something like, 'You saw what he did. The bastard can stand for a cold walk.' Something like that."

"Doesn't sound like Lender."

"That's what I thought. But you know how it is after a call. Especially after a shooting. Your blood's going. And we'd caught the bastard. We had him right there. No messy detective work. No hunting him down. We had him. It felt good. I was pissed about what had happened to your father and that girl, but it was a righteous pissed off. So I went along with Lender. Let the bastard walk, I thought. If he's uncomfortable, so what. If he cuts his feet a little, so what." She paused. "If I'd said something, if I'd been a decent human being, he'd be alive."

"You said it yourself," Hazard said. "Nobody's thinking clearly after a shooting. Even cops aren't thinking clearly after one of their family member gets shot."

"What happened next?" Somers asked.

"We got out of the car. Lender was getting Stillwell out of the back. I was coming around the front of the car. I waited there, and Lender marched Stillwell towards me. I shuffled off to one side, and I started walking towards the hospital. That's when it happened. I heard the gunshots. So many of them. He just kept firing. I grabbed my gun. I turned around. Stillwell had staggered back against the car. He was already dead. Oh, yeah, his eyes were open, and he was moving, but he was dead. He had two holes in his chest, and nobody comes back from that, not unless Jesus himself decides to step in. But Lender kept shooting. Plugged him three more times, all center mass, all in a row, until he'd emptied the goddamn gun. Lender was sitting there in the snow like he'd fallen. And then Stillwell dropped, and I ran for the hospital. They couldn't do anything. I knew that. But— but I had to tell someone. It was like I was a kid again. I had to tell someone. I had to—" Her voice shook. "I had to tell someone it wasn't my fault. And then I lied."

"You told us Stillwell had his hand on your gun," Hazard said. For the first time since the conversation began, the big man moved into the cone of fluorescent light. In its glow, he became two-toned: the ghastly sheen of skin and the blue-black bruising of his hair and eyes. "You told us he was trying to get it."

"Lie. A big fucking one."

"You were trying to protect Lender." Hazard's voice had become brutal. "You were trying to cover for your partner."

"No. No, honest to God."

"Then what?" Hazard took a step towards her, and Swinney seemed to shrivel, paper folding in the heat of a fire, the instant before the flame catches. Swinney didn't answer, though; she only shook her head, frozen in the fluorescents' grimy light.

Somers's mind raced. Why had she lied? Not to cover for Lender, so what had she been trying to do? Something so horrible that she wouldn't even say it. Something about that instant—

Catching Hazard's arm, Somers gave his partner a shove and met Swinney's eyes. "Us."

The terror in her eyes made Somers sick.

"You did it because you were afraid Lender was going to shoot us."

After another frozen moment, she nodded.

There it was: the thing so horrible that Swinney couldn't even bring herself to say it, couldn't bring herself to speak out loud what had driven her to lie. It was one thing for a cop to shoot a suspect, especially a murderer like Stillwell. It was another thing entirely for a cop to kill another cop. And for what felt like the hundredth time that day, Somers found himself thinking of the Haverford, and of his father, and of the story of the dirty cop who had shot his partner in a crack-den. Was it the worst thing in the world, that special kind of betrayal? Somers didn't know. He thought, though, that it was one of the worst.

"I didn't know. I couldn't believe what I was seeing. And so I said what I did. As soon as I said it, I knew I'd made a mistake. And then Lender dropped the gun, and my brain started telling me I'd been seeing things, and it was easier to believe that I'd been hopped up on adrenaline, that I'd imagined all of it."

"What changed your mind?" Somers said, but his mind was still in the Haverford. It could have happened in a room like this. It could have happened with the same moldering carpet, the same linoleum with its tacks ripping free, the same smell of a dog marinating in the river. A place like this. Could Hazard put a gun to his head and pull the trigger? Could he do something like that to Hazard?

Why not, a horrible voice—horrible because it was his voice, because he recognized it, because he knew the truth of it. Why not? You've done it before.

He realized he'd missed something. "Say that again."

"Lender. I went to see him, and he wasn't in the house. So I started looking for him. I found him sitting in his car on Jefferson Street. He had a pair of binoculars. He was watching someone."

Hazard swore.

"Us," Somers said.

"You were sitting in front of the window at the Real Beef. And so I asked him what he was doing. He freaked out. He wouldn't talk to me. He wouldn't look at me. I started pressing him. I got real close. I was angry, in his face. I wanted some damn answers after all the shit he'd put me threw. Nothing. He got in his car and drove out of there as fast as he could."

Somers echoed Hazard's swear and shook his head.

"But," Swinney said, and with that single word, her voice grew hard and strong and hot. "The bastard didn't get away before I filched this."

She held up a small black rectangle. Lender's mobile phone.

"No passcode," Swinney said, flipping open the outdated model. "It's too old, too simple. But it does have call history. And I thought I wanted to see who called Lender last night."

"Who?"

Shaking her head, Swinney held out the phone. "I said I thought I wanted to see who called him. Turns out, though, I'm a coward. I ran the number."

"Who was it?" Somers said. "What happened?"

"This is as far as I go," Swinney said. "You want my badge, you can have it. You want to drag me in front of Cravens, I'll go like a lamb. But the rest of it, hunting down Lender, dealing with this. I just—look, I can't. He was my partner. Is my partner, I guess." She shook her head again, as though that explained everything and nothing, and then dropped the phone into Somers's hand. "Go ahead and call the number."

"Who—"

"Just call it."

The number showed on the screen—local, that much Somers could tell from the area code. He punched the call button.

A phone began to ring. The sound was disjointed. Doubled.

Hazard pulled out the mobile phone they had retrieved from the ME's office earlier that day. On its screen, where earlier there had been a picture of Hadley Bingham, now flashed Lender's number as an incoming call.

"How," Hazard asked in his deep, icy voice, "did a dead girl call in a hit on Wayne Stillwell?"

CHAPTER TWENTY-FIVE

**DECEMBER 23
SATURDAY
4:30 PM**

SWINNEY LEFT THEM. She left without further explanation, without further justification, without anything remotely close to hope. It wasn't just the fluorescents that had robbed her of her color; as she passed Somers, her eyes were soft and pliable, like dead things after rigor.

When she had gone, Hazard and Somers stood in the dark room, with the smell of moldy carpeting and rotting wood filtered through every breath they took. Hazard held Hadley Bingham's phone in one hand. He wasn't studying it. He was just holding it, looking at it, as though he could see inside the glass and steel. For all Somers knew, Hazard probably could. Just one more superpower that his partner possessed, like his uncanny ability to piece together the cases they worked.

"Well?" Somers said.

"Well, what?"

"Did you figure it out?"

Twenty or thirty seconds passed with Hazard still staring at the phone. Then he shrugged and extended it to Somers. Somer, taking it, gave it a cursory examination and tapped the screen.

"She's got it locked."

"Of course she's got it locked. If she hadn't, I would have already looked through it."

Handing back the phone, Somers sighed. "Yeah, I know. I was just saying it."

"Why?"

"Because people just say things sometimes, Ree. It's called communicating."

Hazard's big shoulders went up, and he snatched the phone and shoved it in his pocket.

"What now?" Somers said.

"Who would know the passcode for Hadley's phone? Assuming she didn't choose something obvious, something stupid, like her birthday."

That didn't sting, not really, but Somers knew Hazard had meant it to. "Have you tried her birthday?"

Hazard didn't answer, which meant that he hadn't.

"You think we need to talk to her parents?"

"They were at the party. Her father is one of our suspects."

"You didn't answer my question. Do you think we need to talk to them?"

"I didn't realize you were asking a question. I thought you were just saying something. I thought you were communicating."

"Jesus, Ree. I just—that's not what I meant."

"Let's go," Hazard said.

"To see Bing?"

Hazard didn't answer, and Somers finally had to follow his partner to the car.

"First thing that's gone right all day," Hazard muttered as he brushed snow from the windshield. Flakes drifted across the street in silent spirals. Above them, the sun had finished setting, and darkness had moved in. With darkness had come clouds, and Somers wondered what this storm would bring. A dusting? Or would it dump another three or four inches? He didn't know if he could stand any more snow. Ever since Windsor, ever since those endless days of snow and ice and clouds, he just didn't know if he could stand it.

"Great," Somers said, eying the cherry-red VW. "Yeah, finally."

The drive back into town was quiet. Hazard was still bristling like a porcupine, and Somers was dealing with the ache in his head.

It had come back now with a vengeance. His mind turned over and over, but just the same old questions, the same lack of answers. Who would hire Stillwell to shoot Somers's father? Why? Motives were plentiful. The old three standbys presented themselves for consideration: money, sex, and drugs.

There had been no hint of drugs, no whiff of anything like that in the investigation. Wahredua and Dore County had their problems with meth production, like the rest of Missouri, but those were small-time operations.

Money, however, was a powerful motivator, and Glenn Somerset was a rich man. Aside from his personal wealth, his influence and his investments in various financial organizations made him a force to be reckoned with, especially in the surrounding counties. Again, Mayor Newton seemed the most likely culprit. Newton had large investments in Dore County. His development firm, InnovateMidwest, had purchased up swaths of Wahredua and surrounding areas. Just the month before, Newton had tried to have a half dozen people killed in order to protect his investment on a valuable piece of land—never mind that Somers couldn't actually prove it. Did Glenn Somerset have something that Newton wanted? A piece of land? Stock in a local company? Had Somers's father refused to sell?

Or had it gone the other way? Had Somers's father been trying to get something out of Newton? Had Glenn Somerset pressed a little too hard to wring a concession out of Newton? Maybe with the aid of the recording that he had kept? From what Somers knew of Mayor Newton, any of those would be sufficient reason for a murder.

"I can hear you grinding your teeth," Hazard said. "Stop it."

"I thought you weren't talking to me."

"I wasn't communicating with you."

"Yeah. You're always so good about communicating."

Hazard's big hands wrapped more tightly around the steering wheel. After a moment, he said, "You still think it's Newton."

"I don't know what I think."

"No. You don't know what the motive is. But you still think it was Newton."

"You still think it was my mother."

"No. I don't."

"What? Why not?" Somers felt his mouth tighten into a grin, even though he didn't particularly feel like grinning. "Don't tell me you're trusting your gut."

Hazard scoffed.

"What then?"

For a few seconds, Hazard didn't answer. Then he shrugged. "Jeremiah doesn't have a motive. He already has what he wants."

"That's what he said. You believe him?"

"I do."

"Why? Because he's educated? Because he talks like a college man?"

"Because of your mother."

"What?"

Hazard shifted in his seat. "Why does it matter? I told you I don't think it was either of them. That's enough."

"No, go on. Tell me about my mother."

"This is stupid."

"You think you're so good at communicating, well, communicate. Open your fucking mouth. Tell me about my mother."

Hazard slowed the VW. They had eased past the edge of Smithfield, past the gray zone between the toxic neighborhood and its surroundings. Now, in front of a darkened elementary school, Hazard stopped the VW. Snowflakes kissed the windshield and melted.

"She's happy."

Somers undid his seatbelt, battered the VW's door open, and got out into the snow. It licked his eyelashes, clinging in fat drops as he came around to the driver's side and opened the door.

"Get out of the car. Get out here and say that again."

"I know you're upset—"

"Get out of the car."

Hazard didn't sigh. He didn't frown or grimace. He didn't show any sign of it, but Somers could feel the weary patience rolling off his partner, and it only made him angrier. The anger had come out of nowhere, like lightning. In 1997, lightning had struck a mostly dry wheatfield, and it had gone up in flames. The fire had spread across half the county before the storm got heavy enough to put it out. Somers remembered that, remembered not the heat—he hadn't been close to the fire itself—but he remembered the ground afterward, the blackened, split earth, and the stumps of plants, the char. This anger was that. It was hot. It ate up the ground quickly inside him. A part of him knew that it was leaving burnt, fissured ground behind, but he didn't care.

"You're emotional because of everything that's happened. Your father being shot, the confrontation with your mother—"

Somers hit him before he even realized he was moving. It wasn't a full-on punch, but it was a jab, and Hazard's head rocked back. Blood showed where his lip had split, black against Hazard's ivory skin.

"Say it again. Say that about my mother again."

Hand pressed to his bleeding lip, Hazard said nothing. No fear in those eyes. Those scarecrow eyes. They caught the ambient glow from the headlights and sparked. He'd always looked like that. In high school, when Somers and Mikey Grames and Hugo Perry would corner him, when they'd take turns slapping him around, kicking his ass, it had always been like that. This lack of fear. The cold fury. If he'd been afraid, they might have stopped. If he'd cowered, cried out, whimpered, they might have gotten bored. But this, the way those scarecrow eyes sparked like they were motherfucking meteors, this made a man want to do insane things.

"Say it again," Somers said.

"This one time. Just this one time." Hazard didn't look troubled, but the way he spoke—like he had a mountain on his chest. The sound of it made Somers hesitate. "Because of what you've gone through. But never again."

"Say what you said about my mother. Say it to me."

"She's happy—" Hazard didn't quite finish the word. The punch landed, cracking his head to the side, and then Somers barreled into him, hammering low on Hazard's ribs, driving the bigger man backward. They tumbled onto the ground, and the fight turned into a brawl—ugly, brutal, consisting of huffing breaths and wild, short-range punches. They rolled in the snow. They rolled in the yellow light of the VW. Somers had only bits and pieces of it in his head: a swath of light cutting across Hazard's face, the deadly calm that he saw there, the feeling of Hazard's belly caving under a punch.

Then they came to a stop. Hazard was on top of Somers, his weight pinning the smaller man's arms. For a moment, Somers struggled. It was like trying to uproot a tree. Then, as suddenly as the rage had come upon him, it was gone. He slumped into the cold of the snow. The pebbled texture of the road pressed against his neck. Hazard got to his feet and lurched away, and Somers lay there, staring up into the sky. Eyes wet. Just snow. Just snow in my lashes, he thought, as though that were the most important thing in the world, and he blinked rapidly.

When Somers got to his feet, Hazard stood in the middle of the road, hunched slightly. He tried to straighten when he saw Somers, and pain flashed in his face, pulling him back into his hunched pose. His lip had split in a second place, and blood stained his chin like the aftermath of a grisly feast.

"Ree—"

"She's happy, Somers. I know that's hard to hear, but it's the truth. There's no reason for her to want to kill your father. She has everything she wants right now. But it's not that. That's not why I think she didn't do this."

"I fucked up, Ree." Somers took a step towards the car, and then, shaking his head, he took a step away. "I really fucked up."

"It's me."

The words made Somers stop. His shoes had scraped snow clear of the yellow line down the center of the road, and Somers focused on the double yellow, trying not to be sick.

"I made a mistake at the party. I thought she was angry at your father. But she wasn't. She was angry at me. She hates me. They both do."

Somers wanted to beg him to drop it. He would have dropped to his knees. He would have kissed Hazard's shoes. He would have done anything to keep the rest of it from happening, but none of it would help. What was coming for him was an avalanche, and prayers couldn't stop avalanches, tears couldn't stop avalanches, pleading couldn't stop a goddamn avalanche. He'd started this avalanche fifteen years ago when he had lied because it was easier than facing the truth. And now here it was. It had taken all these years, but the avalanche was finally here. It was going to bury him.

But it didn't.

Hazard's shoes crunched the snow, and then the VW groaned as the big man's weight settled into the car. "Get in," Hazard said. "We've got to interview Bing and his wife."

"Ree, after what I just did—"

"You don't get a pass on this, Somers. Get in the car."

Somehow, the avalanche had missed him. Miracle of miracles, it had roared past him, furious, hungry, but it had missed him. It was gone, all of it shunted away. Somers's throat tightened. He tried to vomit, and his throat contracted and bobbed, but nothing came up. He spat, the saliva staining the slush red.

That avalanche had been rushing right for him. Right goddamn for him. And it had missed. Somers wiped sweat from his brow, no longer feeling the cold, and made his way on tottering legs to the car. So why didn't he feel any better?

CHAPTER TWENTY-SIX

**DECEMBER 23
SATURDAY
4:57 PM**

HAZARD'S LIP THROBBED as he pulled the VW into Bing's driveway. Somers had hit hard—not, perhaps, his full strength, but still plenty of it. It didn't matter that Somers had telegraphed the punches. A blind man could have read them from a mile off, but it didn't take away any of the sting. If anything, it only made the ache in Hazard's head worse. Why had he let Somers hit him? Why had he stood there and taken it? He could have stepped out of the way. He could have shut his fat mouth. He knew how Somers moved and how Somers fought, and with a little luck, he could have broken Somers's arm. But he hadn't. He let the blond man crack him in the teeth. Twice.

"He's doing all right," Somers said, glancing out the window.

The house was past the realm of doing all right and somewhere, in Hazard's evaluation, well into the realm of gross consumption. Bing's house was obviously new. Everything was perfect: the lanterns along the driveway, the white clapboard, the shutters the color of holly berries. There was even a Christmas wreath on the door. It might have weighed ten pounds—the wreath, not the door. It might have weighed more. It was a hell of a lot of wreath.

"You want me to talk to him?"

"That's what you usually do." Snow crunched under Hazard's feet as he left the car and started up the driveway.

Somers trotted to catch up, and for a few moments, the only sound was their footsteps shattering the crust of ice on old snow. Above them, the clouds had thickened, blotting out the night sky, and the snow continued at a trickle.

But Hazard's mind wasn't on the snow. It wasn't on the crisp, crystalline snaps of ice underfoot. It wasn't on the stinging cold. For the second time in two days, Hazard was going to be face to face with Bing. It had been—what? Fifteen years? Sixteen? No, fifteen. Fifteen years. You can look him in the eye, Hazard told himself, ignoring his heart as it thumped. You've got nothing to be ashamed of. You can look him right in the motherfucking eye.

But part of him was eighteen again, gangly, awkward, and filled with that mixture of private shame and public indifference that had cut him off from the world that surrounded him. Part of him was eighteen again, sitting on the sandy strip of beach of Lake Palmerston. He had gone with his parents; after Jeff had died, he had done almost everything with his parents. Hazard's mother, as usual, had packed crustless ham sandwiches on Wonder Bread, Orange Crush soda, two cans of fruit cocktail, and an ancient transistor radio. His father had brought two six-packs of Budweiser. Hazard remembered his father's hands, the blunt, thick fingers nestling the beer into the ice, twisting the bottles neck-deep.

At eighteen, though, there was only so much time he could spend with his parents. His mother worked a book of word jumbles, and every time she discovered something she made the same noise— Ah—and clicked her tongue and then the pencil scratched along the cheap paper. Ah. Click. Scratch. Ah. Click. Scratch. Frank Hazard had eaten fruit cocktail out of the can with a plastic spoon, and when the spoon snapped, he drank down the remainder of the can, syrup and all. Frank Hazard, who had never understood his strange son—who still didn't understand his son. He had sat under the beach umbrella, a cold beer resting on his chest, and he had talked in bursts, a staccato repeat that reminded Hazard of gunfire. It hadn't been directed at anyone, and at the same time, it had been directed at Emery. "Look at the ass on her. Those tits didn't come off a factory line. Cardinals are playing a doubleheader tomorrow. Pass me another."

On and on like that. Ah. Click. Scratch. Bet you most guys would kill to get in her pants. Ah. Click. Scratch.

And so he had left. Hazard had wandered down the beach, shooting past the crowds of teenagers he recognized from school, past the college boys playing volleyball with their shirts off—dangerous, keep walking, you might as well stare at the sun—following the curve of the shoreline. It had been afternoon by then. Late afternoon. The sun dropped like a wrecking ball, striking the edge of the lake, throwing long, golden light that looked like it would last forever. He had kept walking. The line of sand thinned, and the scrub grew denser until Hazard found himself no longer walking on the beach but walking behind it, screened from the last of the sand and water by knotted bushes.

It had been the laughter that had stopped him. Laughter like people having fun, nothing mean about it, just honest fun. He had laughed like that with Jeff. Not often, but it had happened. Not since, though. Since Jeff's death, well, a part of him had dried up. He was still carrying that around inside himself, something dead and dried up. But he liked the sound of the laughter, so he stopped and squatted on a rock. In just his swimsuit, he faced the low golden heat and listened. Just for a minute, that was all.

And then the tone of the laughter changed. It had gone from easy, open, and honest to tense. Not unhappy. Not yet. But there was worry in it.

Hazard looked.

Through the tangled bushes, he saw a rocky stretch of beach. No sand here. Four people were in the water: two boys and two girls. College age. He recognized Bing, of course. Bing was always at the high school. For shop class. For football practice. For the girls. Bing was always everywhere: at the park, at the Royale 8 Theaters, at Sully's Drive-thru. Even if you didn't see him, he was there because people were talking about him or thinking about him. That was just who he was. And as Hazard watched, Bing stripped off his t-shirt and swung it, lasso-style, before tossing it onto the beach.

He was beautiful. And right then, Hazard knew to look away, to walk away. But Bing was just so beautiful. Still trim, but with adult muscle that even the brawniest high school boy lacked. Every inch of him corded, rippled, straining. A short black stubble across his chest and under his arms, and the shocking realization in Hazard's mind that Bing shaved his chest, shaved his pits, the dark stubble just above the low-slung curve of his swimsuit, maybe he even shaved his junk, and then, because he was eighteen and because delicious thoughts hovered at the edge of his brain, Hazard had a titanium boner.

"Come on," Bing was saying, hooking his thumbs into the swimsuit. "It'll be fun."

And the girls were laughing, blushing, splashing backward, shaking their heads. Bing's buddy was laughing, hiking up his shoulders to wriggle out of his shirt, laughing but blushing too, nervous, wanting to impress Bing as much as he wanted to impress the girls, and Hazard didn't know anything could get harder than titanium, but Jesus fuck was he hard. And lonely. That thought was distant, clear, and the voice of an older, sadder part of himself immune to the rushing hormones.

"Aw, just do it already," Bing had said, laughing again, pulling on the suit, stretching it obscenely to reveal the dark stubble—thank you God, yes, it was stubble—under the red-and-blue polyester. And Hazard was drooling, his mouth thick with his own spit, choking him. "Come on," Bing said again, "just—"

Hazard never knew what called Bing's attention. He hadn't moved. He hadn't made a sound unless getting so hard your dick might pop, unless that was enough movement and sound to call attention. But at that moment, Bing's head swiveled. The girls turned, drawn by Bing's movement, and they spotted Hazard too.

Now, older, Hazard knew that if it had ended there—if nothing more had happened—he might have escaped with just getting his ass kicked. He might have even gotten clean away. But it hadn't ended there.

The girls had laughed. They had burst into hysterical peals of laughter, convulsing, sagging against each other, dragging themselves down into the shallow blue-brown of the lake.

Humiliation had flickered across Bing's face. And then, in its place, rage.

Hazard had tried to run, but Bing was bigger and faster, and he caught Hazard before he had reached the beach proper. He had dragged Hazard back, dragged him through the bushes, heedless of the bushes—scratching Hazard to hell, but scratching himself up even worse.

By now the girls had stopped laughing. They leaned against each other, their weight shifted away from Bing and Hazard, their faces a mixture of embarrassment and worry. The boy had dragged on his shirt, and now he stood on the rocky strip of beach, shifting from one foot to the other, inspecting his soles, looking anywhere but at Bing and Hazard.

"You know what we've got here?" Bing said.

Nobody answered. His buddy hunkered down, eyes fixed on the gravel.

"We've got ourselves a real live faggot. The only one in town." Bing's open-handed slap caught Hazard and knocked him sideways, but Bing caught him by the hair and hauled him upright. "On your knees faggot. Stay right there on your knees. Where a faggot ought to be."

"Bing, ease up," his buddy said.

"C'mon," one of the girls said, but when Bing looked at her, she splashed backward so fast that she slipped and fell.

"Right. There." Bing spoke each word with a full stop, and he punctuated them with slaps. "That's. Where. A. Fag. Should. Be." He hesitated. Hazard's ears were ringing. The world had gone white at the edges, and he would have fallen if Bing hadn't still held him by the hair. "Right?"

The white at the edges of the world intensified.

"I said, right?"

Hazard wasn't sure if he said something. Even now, years later, he wasn't sure.

"This is what you wanted?" And the next thing Hazard knew, his face was pressed into the red-and-blue polyester, against Bing's compressed junk. It smelled like dick, like the lake, like Banana Boat sunblock. It was both hard and soft, and the realization sent a cord of fear through Hazard, realizing that Bing was getting off on this. "Well?" Bing dragged Hazard in again, mauling his junk with Hazard's face, grinding against Hazard's mouth and burning Hazard's lips with the sand that clung to the red-and-blue polyester. "This is what all you fags want, right? What? It's not how you like it?"

"Jesus, Bing, get off him," one of the girls cried. Bing hesitated, and Hazard was dimly aware of the second girl marching off, her flip-flops dangling from one hand.

"Yeah, man. Leave him alone." Bing's buddy heaved himself to his feet, but he didn't move, as though still waiting for Bing's approval.

"He's bleeding," the girl said.

And that broke the spell. Bing pushed Hazard away, and Hazard went down, rocks biting into his back. His knees, sliced from the beach, bled in thin, pink trickles where the lake water still clung to him.

And then Bing had left, and his buddy had hopped along after him, and the last girl had stayed there, the lake sloshing against her calves, and she had called out, "Are you ok?" And after another minute, she had left.

Now, in hindsight, Hazard could lay it all out in facts, in statistics, in black-and-white—the way he liked it, the way he liked everything. Bullying was about power. Bullying was about control. And bullying was about an audience. Sometimes, Hazard knew, it was only an audience of one, but most bullies played to bigger crowds. Most bullies wanted a full house every night of the week. And when Bing's audience had turned on him, the game had lost its fun. Hazard had seen Bing again, plenty of times that summer, and Bing had never looked at him, never acknowledged him. He had seen Bing with Somers. He had seen them laughing together. And he wondered if they had been laughing at him, if Somers had become part of the audience. Back then, Somers had still been seeking out opportunities to torment Hazard. Maybe Bing had noticed. Maybe

Bing had decided to share some ideas. Not that it mattered. That was what he had told himself for a long time.

In hindsight, it was all black and white. But at the time, his knees bloody, his eyes burning with tears, it had been a huge, hideous knot inside him. It had been a nightmare, a horror. The pain, the humiliation, those had been bad enough. But worse had been the feel of Bing hardening against his mouth. Hazard had told himself, as he lay on the pebbled beach, that would be the last time anyone hurt him for pleasure. But then there had been Alec and the belt. Then there had been Billy. And then—

"Hey," Somers said, with the tone of someone repeating himself. "You in there?"

They stood at the front door, and from within the house came the sound of footsteps.

"Hey," Somers said again. "How hard did I hit you?"

Before Hazard had to answer, the door swung open. Framed by the jambs, Bing looked like something that had hit the highway at seventy miles an hour. His dark curls were in disarray, heavy and greasy. His clothes—jeans and a Shake Shack t-shirt—showed spilled coffee. But it was his face that shook Hazard out of the last of the memory.

This wasn't the face of the bully he had known in high school. Sure, the tight line of the jaw was the same. Sure, he had the same aristocratic features, like he'd been born to spend his life hitting golf balls off a yacht. But those features, all of them, had been flattened, as though something had scraped away a layer of Bing and left this paler, shallower version behind. Hazard found himself confronting a surprising—and disturbing—realization.

He felt sorry for Bing.

"John-Henry," Bing said, blinking into the darkness. "What—did something happen? Your dad—"

"No, nothing like that. We just came by to see how you're doing."

Bing blinked again. Backlit by the house, for a moment, he seemed not to understand what they were saying, as if the darkness beyond his threshold had cut all lines of communication. Then he nodded. "It's not a good time. We're—" He didn't sob or choke or cough. He just paused, and his throat rippled, like he might like a sip of water. "Can you come back another time?"

"Bing, we really need to talk."

"Yeah. Sure." He shuffled into the house, the door hanging open behind him, and it gave Hazard the momentary image of a submarine hatch let open, and all the air bubbling out while the water and darkness rushed in.

They followed him into the living room, and Bing motioned for them to sit. Everything in the place was expensive: real wood furniture—none of that particle board—and leather sofas like swimming pools. Hazard sank into the leather, trying to stifle a satisfied groan. His back hurt. His feet hurt. And now his head hurt, thanks to Somers.

"What happened to you?" Bing said. "You look like you got into a fight."

"Opened the car door too fast."

Somers rolled his eyes, as if to say that Hazard was a terrible liar, but Bing didn't seem to care. "What's going on?"

"Is your wife here?" Somers asked.

"John-Henry, what is this? Is this about—Jesus. Is this about Hadley?"

"We just want to talk to you."

"That's what you keep saying. I don't understand. Is this about Hadley, or isn't it? I talked to Chief Cravens. She said that son of a bitch got shot. He was trying to escape. You know, the guy that—the guy that—" He cut off again with that parched little swallow. "And my dad, he told me the same thing."

"That's true. Wayne Stillwell is dead."

"Then—what? Is this a follow-up?"

"Not exactly."

"Well, will you tell me what it is? You show up at my door, you tell me you have to talk to me—right now, you won't take no for an answer—and then you won't say what you want. I lost my daughter—"

"Bing?"

From a darkened hallway that stood off the living room, a woman's voice reached them. Then her shape appeared, nothing more than a glossy outline against the darkness: dark hair cascading down to dark shoulders, and the rest just a suggestion of a body.

"Go back to bed," Bing said. "Whatever this is, I'll take care of it." He flashed a furious look at Somers and Hazard.

"They're here to talk about Hadley?"

"I don't know what they're here to talk about." Bing rose and took a step towards the hall. "Daisy, you're upset. You should be in bed."

Hazard waited for a sob, or outright weeping, or even for anguished silence. Instead, though, what followed was a hard laugh. Hard, but brittle, like storm glass after too many seasons. Daisy Bingham took a step forward, and light picked out her features now. She was beautiful. Even Hazard noted that much. And her beauty, he realized, was a magnification of Hadley's. What he saw in front of him—chestnut hair with flecks of fire, delicate, doll eyes, even the mouth—they were Hadley's features given maturity and refinement. That mouth, though, compressed into a red slash as the laugh died away. Daisy took another step, and then another until the full light of the living room fell on her, and Hazard found himself studying her.

No signs of grief. That was the first thought, branded across the front of the brain. She wore a black negligee, and she seemed undisturbed by standing in front of two strange men. Somers, Hazard noticed, was staring at her too. Somers was staring so hard he'd be lucky if his tongue didn't drop right out of his mouth. Hazard kicked his ankle. Hard.

"Ow—Mrs. Bingham," Somers managed to turn his wince into a rising motion, and he held out a hand. "We haven't met—"

"No." She ignored his hand, and her gaze moved from Somers to Hazard. "But Bing has told me all about you. About both of you, in fact. You're here to talk about Hadley."

"We're here to talk about what happened last night," Somers said.

"Why?" Bing stood next to his wife, slipping an arm around her. "If that guy, whatever his name was, if he's dead, why are you here? My dad told me it's over." A bitter bark escaped him. "That's my dad for you. Doesn't ask me if I'm ok. Doesn't ask me what he can do. Just tells me it's over. As if any of this—" His gesture took in a circle—maybe the house, maybe his life, maybe the universe. "As if it could be over just like that, just because he says so."

"We're not convinced it's over," Somers said. "I didn't think you were either. At the mayor's office—"

"Oh fuck that," Bing said. "All he cares about is proving he wasn't up to his elbows in this shit."

"Do you believe he was?" Somers kept his voice even, but Hazard could sense the nervous, coiled energy in the man.

Neither Bing nor his wife spoke for a moment. "What kind of question is that?" Daisy asked. "What do you mean, saying something like that?"

"It means we think someone hired Stillwell," Hazard said. "I'd be interested to hear what you think about that."

Somers had enough self-control not to shoot Hazard a glance, but Hazard could guess at his partner's irritation. Bing and Daisy stood still, shocked—for the moment—beyond words.

"And you—" Bing spoke slowly like he was trying to find his way from one word to the next. "You think someone wanted to kill Hadley? On purpose? Who?"

"Does someone come to mind?" Somers asked.

"No," Bing said.

"Me," Daisy said. Fiddling with the strap of her negligee, she sat in a wingback chair facing them, her legs tucked to the side demurely. "Bing, don't look at me like that. They would have found out anyway. Someone would have said something."

"She's upset," Bing said. He took a step towards his wife, his big hands—quarterback hands, wide receiver hands, football hands—splayed open, as though unable to catch what was coming at him now. "She doesn't know what she's saying."

"I know exactly what I'm saying. Most days, I wouldn't have minded killing Hadley myself." Her lips curved, but Hazard couldn't call the expression a smile. "She was a special kind of hell." The cold grimace quirked at her lips again. "Brought out the mother in me, as you can see."

"What do you mean?" Somers said.

"Nothing." Bing was wiping at his forehead now. "They fought. Just mother-daughter stuff—"

"Please, Bing. You're embarrassing yourself. Our guests—" Daisy paused. "Do you want something to drink?"

Somers shook his head. Hazard didn't bother to answer.

"Bing will have something to drink, won't you, Bing?" Daisy flipped her head, and her chestnut hair glowed in the lamplight, looking more red than brown for an instant. Bing didn't answer, but he took an unsteady step towards the sideboard, and from within the heavy, paneled furniture he produced a bottle.

Daisy, ignoring him, continued, "You wanted to know what I mean? You saw her at the party, I assume. You saw her with—excuse me, Detective, but I'll be blunt—you saw her with Glenn Somerset."

"What was she doing with my father?" Somers asked.

"Flirting. Teasing. Taunting." Daisy shrugged, and the lacy strap of her negligee slipped down one creamy shoulder. "Who knows what she was doing with him in her free time? At the party, she practically pulled her skirt over her head and asked him to—"

"That's enough," Bing shouted. His drink—something coppery in a tumbler—sloshed over his hand, and he wavered, clutching at the sideboard for support. "Let it the fuck alone."

"You think she was sleeping with my father," Somers said, and now Hazard could hear those seismic shiftings in Somers's voice again.

Daisy gave him a pitying look and didn't answer.

"Do you have any proof?" Hazard asked. "Why didn't you bring this to the police? Statutory rape—"

"Isn't exactly the sort of thing that the Somersets get dragged into," Daisy finished. "Or the Binghams, for that matter. It never would have gone anywhere."

"Because she wasn't doing anything wrong," Bing said.

Daisy gave a helpless shrug, the kind of shrug that said, What can I do? "It doesn't matter anyway. To answer your question, no I don't have any proof. Although—"

"She doesn't have any proof because there isn't any." Bing was trying to steady himself, trying to take a drink, but more of the coppery booze sloshed down his chin and shirt than made it into his mouth. "Look, Hadley had her problems. She needed help. But what she didn't need—"

"She needed help." Daisy's mouth curved into that cold, icy smirk. "That's rich. When I wanted to—"

"You wanted to send her to a—a prison. Not a shrink. Not anyone who could help her. You wanted to send her to one of those places where they lock them up and throw away the key. We wouldn't have seen her again until she was eighteen, and you—"

"She burned down our house," Daisy shrieked. Her sultry composure had gone up like a sulfur strip. "My house, she burned it down, and the little cunt laughed about it. And you wouldn't do anything, all you'd do was cover up for her, make excuses." Daisy got to her feet, suddenly as unsteady as her husband, looking like she was fighting against a strong wind or a strong sea—something elemental throwing her world out of balance. "You wanted to pretend it was something else. You wanted to pretend we could come back here and it would all be all right because your daddy would—"

She never finished saying what Sheriff Bingham would do because Bing threw his glass so hard that it exploded against the wall. Hazard half-rose, hand on the .38 holstered under his arm, but Somers drew him back into his seat. Neither Bing nor Daisy moved again, both locked in a tableau. There was no sense of shock, Hazard realized, and that realization shocked him in turn. The whole scene had a feel to it. Not practiced. Not studied. Not rehearsed. But— familiar? Like they'd played this out so many times that they could do it blindfolded. He wished, again, that he had a better grasp of the social subtleties he usually missed. Was this a trick? A performance? Or was it something more? He glanced at Somers, but Somers's normally cheerful expression had vanished.

Another minute had passed. No one had moved.

"Sit down," Hazard said. "Both of you. You can sit on opposite sides of the room if you have to, but sit down and shut up."

"You can't—" Bing began.

"Shut up." That was all Hazard said, but he knew how to say it. The fight that was stirring in Bing's face suddenly liquefied, and he slumped onto an ottoman and stared at them blankly. Daisy, for her part, curled up into the wingback chair, pale fingers toying with the negligee again.

Hazard studied them for a moment. Ever since Daisy had entered the room, the conversation had gone wild, bucking away from Somers's attempts to control it. Now, for the first time since they had entered the house, Hazard had a moment to reflect. And one thought was the loudest and clearest: they assumed that someone had intended to kill Hadley. Not Glenn. Hadley. Why?

More importantly, could they be right?

Somers, for his part, looked like he had regained control of himself. He let out a slow breath, and in his best Somers manner, he said, "We wanted to talk to you about the party. Anything you noticed. What you might have seen. We're trying to put together a full picture of what happened that night."

Shaking amber drops from his fingers, Bing spoke without looking at them. "What do you want to know?"

"Can you walk us through what happened that night?"

"It was a party," Daisy said. "People like the Somersets, they only know how to throw one kind. If you've been once, you've been to them all." Flashing teeth at Somers, she added, "Apologies."

"Where were you when Wayne Stillwell—the man dressed as Santa Claus—arrived?"

"In the front room," Bing said. "Both of us."

"And what happened?"

"He was naked except for that stupid hat," Daisy said. "And he was singing. The sheriff and Bing—"

"That's all," Hazard broke in. "Just the hat?"

"What?"

"He didn't have anything else? He wasn't carrying anything else?"

"A bag," Bing said, glancing up. "He had one of those Santa Claus bags, you know, for presents."

"No," Daisy said. "He didn't."

"Yes, he did."

Daisy shook his head. "I've got an excellent memory. He was naked except for that hat. Then you and—"

Laughing, Bing spread his hands. "Wait. Wait a minute. So, what? I'm making this up? He didn't have a bag, and I just imagined it?"

"I didn't say you imagined it. I said he didn't have a bag."

"Are you sure?" Somers asked, and Hazard resisted the urge to kick his partner again. "Not doubting you, Mrs. Bingham, but are you positive? Think carefully."

"I don't need to think carefully," she said coldly, her hands dropping from the negligee to knot tightly at her waist. "I know what I saw."

"So do I," Bing said. He waved a hand at Hazard and laughed again. "He had that bag."

A frown creased Somers's mouth, and after a moment, he shrugged. "What happened next?"

"What color was the bag?" Hazard asked.

"Red. I mean, white trim, but red. You know, like in all the pictures of Santa."

"He didn't have a bag," Daisy said, examining her nails.

"Let's move on," Somers said, with a stern glance at Hazard. "Tell me what happened after Mr. Stillwell came into the house."

Hazard wanted to growl, but he quieted himself. Jeremiah Walker had claimed to see a pink bag. Bing saw a red bag. And Daisy had seen no bag. Were those simply the inconsistencies of eyewitnesses? Eyewitnesses, contrary to common belief, were notoriously unreliable. The brain simply filled in things. Was that what had happened here? Jeremiah Walker had also claimed to see that bag outside the TV room, just before Stillwell had come out shooting. There was something happening here, and Hazard didn't know what it was.

"Bing rushed him."

"Not alone," Bing said.

"But you did rush him. It was very brave, sweetheart. Bing is always brave. Very manly. Wouldn't you agree, Detective Somerset?"

The question was so odd that it pulled Hazard from his thoughts in time to see the red rising in Somers's cheeks. Somers, however, simply continued in the same tone of voice and said, "Not alone? Who else helped?"

"My father," Bing said, casting a dirty glance at Daisy. "And yours."

"You grabbed him? You punched him? What exactly happened?"

"They were going to throw him out of the house," Daisy said. "He was still singing. He didn't even seem to notice them."

Bing agreed with a shrug and a nod.

"And then?"

"And then someone shouted that he had a gun," Bing said. "It was absolute chaos. Everyone was screaming and trying to get away."

"Who said that he had a gun?"

"I don't know," Bing said with another shrug. "It happened so fast."

"Don't be silly," Daisy said. "It was your father."

"It wasn't my father."

"Of course it was."

"You were running just like the rest of the rats, Daze. You don't have any idea who said it."

"I know what I heard. That was definitely your father."

Bing spread his hands helplessly and shrugged.

"All right," Somers said. "After that?"

"We took him to the back room," Bing said.

"Did he have a gun?"

"No."

"Did he have a bag?"

"Jesus, it's like a rodeo. Yes. I already told you."

Daisy opened her mouth, obviously eager to pick a fight, but Somers forestalled her with a hand.

"What then?" Somers asked.

"Your dad called you. We decided to wait it out."

"Why didn't your father handle it? He's the sheriff."

"He said it's city jurisdiction. City means police."

Hazard held back a snort. That might technically have been true, but it didn't hold any real water. The sheriff covered the entire county; he still had jurisdiction within the city. What Sheriff Bingham had likely meant was that he'd had a couple of eggnogs and didn't want to leave a warm, pleasant evening to drag a naked Santa to the county jail.

"Anything else before we got there?"

Daisy rolled one shoulder. "I was having a wonderful time."

"She was so drunk she could have put a boy on fleet week to shame," Bing said. "But no, nothing happened. We just stood around with our dicks in our hands." He smirked at Hazard. "Sorry to get your hopes up. Just a figure of speech."

Hazard didn't respond. To his surprise, though, Somers didn't rise to the bait either. Normally, a comment like Bing's would have gotten Somers fired up. Anybody else would have been lucky to walk away with their nose intact.

Instead, Somers just said, "What about the rest of the evening? I made sure that Mr. Stillwell was handcuffed to a chair. Did you see anyone go near the room?"

Bing hesitated, as though about to speak, and then his mouth snapped shut.

For a moment, Daisy studied her negligee's strap. Then she said, "Hadley."

"What?"

"Hadley went back there. With those two horrible boys."

Yes, Hazard remembered that. The boys had practically ripped her away from Glenn Somerset and dragged her into the kitchen. But why would Daisy bring it up? In a stream of cold analysis, Hazard noted that for the second time Daisy had assumed—and suggested—Hadley's involvement: first, as the intended victim; and now as the culprit. That suggested either an inconsistency or a much more complicated explanation than Hazard expected.

Somers must have noticed the strangeness too because he leaned forward, his taut frame bent intensely, and said, "It sounds like there's a lot we don't know. You think Hadley was involved?"

"We know she was involved. She finally got caught up in one of her own games." For a moment, anger glimmered under Daisy's frosty surface. "She never thought about anyone. She never even really thought about herself. She was—she was just wild. All she wanted to do was ruin everything she could touch."

"Stop it," Bing snapped.

"No. No, they need to hear this. They need to know who she really was—not Daddy's little girl."

"You're loving this," Bing said. He twisted his fingers around each other, his dark complexion mottled with red. "Finally you're getting exactly what you want: Daisy the victim, Daisy the long-suffering mother, Daisy who didn't deserve any of this."

"They'd find out anyway, Bing. And they can judge for themselves."

"Why don't you start from the beginning?" Somers said.

"From the beginning?" Daisy flicked the strap free from her creamy shoulder. "Eighteen years ago. That's when everything went wrong."

"That's what you always do," Bing said, exploding out of his seat. "Always. You pin it on her. You act like you never did a thing wrong. Like you're some kind of goddamn martyr. But you were against her from the very beginning. You didn't want a daughter. You wanted a boy, and you didn't know what to do with a girl."

"I wanted a child. I didn't care if it was a girl."

"You wouldn't breastfeed her. You wouldn't even look at her."

"I was sick. You know I was sick. And she didn't want anything to do with me." Daisy spoke slowly, evenly, as though Bing were a particularly stupid child, but red mottled her throat and the expanse of chest exposed by the negligee. "She only wanted you. Eight days old or eighteen years old, she was always your little girl."

"That's because you—"

"This isn't productive," Somers said, his smooth voice slicing through the anger. "Did Hadley have a history of behavioral problems?"

"History?" Daisy smirked. "Enough history to fill a textbook."

"She—" Bing began, and then he broke off. "She had oppositional defiant disorder."

Hazard recognized the term, and Somers must have as well because he nodded. "How did that manifest? Hostile behavior? Arguing? Resentment?"

"Check, check, check," Daisy droned, ticking off invisible boxes in the air. "Check every box on the list. She couldn't take responsibility for anything. She was hurtful. Hateful. She wanted to make everybody else as miserable as she was. Everything I said was an argument."

"Everything you said?"

"Oh yes. Daddy never made his precious little girl do anything."

"That's not fair. She was sick. I made accommodations."

"Yes, accommodations. She kills the neighbors' cat, and we pay them off. Accommodations. She cuts up every piece of clothing she owns, and we buy her more clothes. Nicer clothes. Accommodations. She hires a lunatic to beat up a boy at school, and we have to be happy that we're not all in jail. Accommodations. She—"

"What?" Somers said, leaning forward in his seat. "That last part. What did she do?"

"That wasn't her," Bing said. "There was never any proof."

"He had an email from her. What more do you want?"

"I think you should tell us the whole story," Somers said.

Daisy flipped a hand, as though the effort exhausted her. "There was a boy at school she was seeing. Very polite. Very attentive. From the look of his swim trunks, very well endowed. But as soon as he got to know the real Hadley—the one who slashed the tires on his car, the one who punched out every window in the house with a shovel—he decided he wasn't interested in staying around. Of course, Daddy's princess couldn't stand that. She hired some madman from Craigslist to—"

"That's enough," Bing said. "That's enough, goddamn it."

"We need to hear the rest of this," Somers said, holding up a hand to forestall Bing's objections. "What did she hire him to do?"

"To beat that boy to a pulp. Too bad, really. Those swim trunks." A smoky smile lurked on Daisy's face, and she flipped the negligee's straps again. "Of course, the guy she hired was coked out of his mind, and he only got in a few punches before he lost interest and wandered away. Good thing, too. He had a gun. He could have killed the boy."

"What happened then?"

"Hadley had to get help," Daisy said. "The police had the emails from her account. They could have dragged her to court, but instead, they let her work out a deal. Daddy's money helped with that, of course. Part of the deal was that she had to get therapy."

"What did you want me to do?" Bing said. "Let her go to prison? Have her life ruined? You would have let her." He turned his gaze towards Hazard and Somers, as though proving his point. "I honest to God believe that. She would have let her own daughter go to prison."

Daisy didn't even seem to hear him. "You know, I think that's why Hadley burned down the house. I think she couldn't stand that she'd lost. She couldn't stand having to go to a shrink, take the pills he prescribed, and toe the line for once in her life. She lost, and she wanted to punish me."

Hazard had his own thoughts about who was being punished in that situation; Daisy Bingham didn't sound like she had much of the milk of mother's kindness in her ample, creamy breasts. But he kept that to himself.

"This guy, what happened to him?" Somers asked.

"God, who knows?"

"He went away. Locked up." Bing's face was dark with shame, and when he spoke next, the words had false hope. "Maybe he'll get cleaned up. This might be a good thing for him."

"He's still locked up?" Somers said.

"What? I don't know. Why? What's this about, John-Henry?"

"Is there anything else you can think of? The boyfriend, the one she paid to have beaten up, what was his name?"

Bing shook his head.

"Peter," Daisy offered. "Something with a J. Jennings? Peter Jenkins? And she didn't pay to have him beaten up."

"What?" Hazard said, surprise forcing him to break his silence.

"She didn't pay that lunatic."

"How do you know that?"

"It all came out. Every excruciating detail."

"Hadley told you that she didn't pay?"

"No," Daisy said, adopting the same slow, simple tone she had used earlier with Bing. "Hadley denied everything, right up to the end. But that crazy man went on and on about how he was just doing her a favor."

Inside Hazard, something clicked into place. He couldn't put his finger on it, not yet, but he knew it was important. Wayne Stillwell hadn't been paid either, as far as Hazard knew. There had been no mention of payment in the emails. And no mention of—

"Did she ask that guy to beat up Peter?"

Somers glanced at Hazard, the faintest surprise registering in his brow.

"I told you: Hadley kept insisting she didn't do it. She never admitted—"

"That's not what I'm asking." Daisy flinched at the brusque tone. "In the email, did she ask him to beat up that boy, Peter?"

"Yes, of course. Haven't you been listening?" Daisy glanced at Somers, as though he might make more sense.

Somers, shifting on the seat, picked up the line of questioning. "What my partner is asking is, did she use those exact words?"

"How the hell should we remember?" Bing said. "All we want to do is forget it, and now that Hadley's dead, you're dragging us through that shit—"

"No." Daisy had a slightly curious look on her face. "No, she didn't. I remember every word of that damn email. She said she needed help. She said she needed a real man to take care of her."

"You're sure?"

"I read that email a hundred times, Detective. A thousand."

"And it was sent from her email?"

"For the love of God," Bing said. "What is this? Are we chasing our tails in here?"

"Yes," Daisy said. "From her email."

Hazard spoke sharply, leaning into the words. "What is her email address?"

"It's her first and last name. What is this about?" For the first time, Daisy Bingham looked genuinely curious. "What's going on?"

A small but violent disappointment flared in Hazard. For a moment, he hoped he had caught a thread in this maze. But the email that had been used to contact Wayne Stillwell was different from Hadley's personal email account. That didn't necessarily rule her out; email accounts were easy to create. But for a moment, the similarities had been dizzying: contact with a strange man, no promise of payment, and the specific language about needing a man—not a boy, a man. Even without matching emails, it was clear that the messages were related. But had Hadley sent both of them? Or had someone modeled the second message on her first? And if so, who?

"Is there anything else from Chicago that we should know?" Somers said. "That boy, Peter. Has he tried to contact her? Made any threats?"

Bing shook his head vigorously. Daisy gave a languid shrug.

"Anything else?"

"Having our home burned down pretty much ended our time in Chicago, Detective. We lived a few weeks in an apartment—God, it was awful, carpet like you wouldn't believe—and then Bing dragged us all to the quietest shithole in the whole world." A smile dimpled her cheek. "Pardon my French."

Hazard barely heard her. He had the itch now, the maddening itch of being able to see—almost, almost—the shape of the puzzle. He was close, and his thoughts bent towards it completely, turning over everything they had uncovered in the past few days: the emails at Stillwell's, the blackmail recording that Glenn Somerset held, Mayor Newton's insistence that they abandon the case, and Swinney's revelations about Lender and the phone call that had ended Stillwell's life—a phone call that had originated from Hadley Bingham's mobile phone after the girl had died.

Somers was asking something—more questions about Chicago, but Hazard already knew, in the bluish-cold mixture of logic and intuition, that nothing else mattered about Chicago. He heard himself speaking almost before he knew what he was going to say.

Balancing Hadley's phone on his palm, he said, "Do you recognize this?"

Daisy began to shake her head.

"That's Hadley's." Bing glanced at the phone and then at his wife.

Her head frozen in mid-shake, Daisy's face became a mask.

She didn't know, Hazard realized. She hadn't recognized the phone. Now that was very interesting.

Bing was still talking. "How did you—"

"This was recovered with her belongings at the crime scene."

"Shouldn't it—" Bing made an enveloping gesture with his hands. "Doesn't it need a plastic bag or something?"

Ignoring the question, Hazard said, "Do either of you know her passcode?"

"Hadley wouldn't tell me what she ate for breakfast," Daisy said. Her voice aimed at something light, mocking, but her eyes had latched onto the phone. "She definitely never told me her passcode."

"You?"

Bing shook his head. "No. I mean, I can call the phone company. I pay the bill; they'll—"

"Yes, that'll be fine," Hazard said. "The sooner the better, in fact."

"I don't understand," Bing said. "Aren't you going to return—"

"Right now," Hazard said.

"What?"

"Call the phone company right now. See if they can unlock the phone."

For a moment, Bing seemed speechless. One big hand came up and wiped at his forehead, dragging sweat through the thick black curls. Then he sprang out of the seat and marched deeper into the house. Daisy watched him go, and then her eyes returned to the phone.

Would she admit that she didn't recognize it? Or would she keep up the charade? Whatever else she was, Daisy Bingham was a cool customer. The mask hadn't slipped an inch, except around those doll eyes. Those eyes had come terribly, vibrantly alive.

"Parental controls," Somers said. His voice shattered the silence, and it was all Hazard could do not to jump.

"What?" Daisy said.

"On smartphones. Almost all of them, they have these parental controls. Some of them are built into the phones. Some of them are apps you download. It's a way for parents to make sure they have some way of keeping track of their kids' digital lives."

Cocking her head, sending sparks through the chestnut cascade, Daisy said, "What are you saying?"

"Didn't you and your husband have something like that on Hadley's phone? It looks like an expensive model. I'm sure you would have wanted to keep track of it—and of your daughter, of course."

For a moment, Daisy didn't answer. Then she said, "My husband told me about you. When we moved back here, he started talking about the old days. I wanted to know all about this little shithole. I wanted to know about the movers and shakers. And he told me about you."

The words were hooked, each one sharper than the last, and Hazard watched as the color drained from Somers's face until his normally golden skin was splotched with red. "Did you have those parental controls installed on Hadley's phone?"

"Is it true? What he told me, I mean." And then her eyes drifted to Hazard. She waited, as though expecting a reaction from him, and Hazard stared back at her. After a moment, Daisy laughed—tittered, Hazard's mind said, she's fucking tittering, her fingertips pressed to her mouth—and said, "He doesn't even know, does he?"

"Please answer the question," Somers said, his voice cracking with undercurrents of emotion.

Daisy stared at Hazard for a moment longer, the tittering fading into a smile, as though still waiting for him to join in.

"Is there a reason you're not willing to answer my question?" Somers said. "You looked surprised earlier. Did you recognize the phone?"

An ugly scree of fury scraped the smile from Daisy's face. "Will you let up about that already? Bing takes care of all that."

"All what?"

"All of it. The money. The bills. Hadley. All the shit, he shovels it. If he had something installed on the phone, you'll have to ask him about it. It's something he would do. He had me followed once. Did you know that?" She straightened, her back slightly arched, offering a view down the plunge of her negligee. "We had been dating for a few years. Bing got this crazy idea into his head that I was cheating on him. I told him: I don't cheat. If I want somebody in my bed, you'll know. But he had me followed just to make sure. There's not a lot of guys who will do that. Not a lot of guys who care."

She was bragging, Hazard realized, and the realization brought the cold-steel gearwork of his analysis to a halt. This woman was bragging that her now-husband had hired a man to stalk her. And for a moment, Hazard was back in that shitty apartment he'd shared with Alec, and Alec had the belt, and he'd said—Jesus, what had he said? This is because I care? That didn't sound right; those memories were hazy. Hazard had done his best to block them out.

But not Daisy Bingham. Daisy was proud. Proud, especially, of the attention and desire her husband had shown. And now, in a different light, Hazard remembered the ways she had described Hadley: Daddy's girl, Daddy's princess, Daddy's favorite, all spoken with the twisted bitterness that underlay everything she said.

"Has your husband had anyone else followed?" Some of the color had returned to Somers's face. "Does he have a habit of hiring private investigators?"

"Do you think that's how he found out about you?"

Somers flushed again, but this time, Hazard spoke. "You're baiting a sworn officer of the law, Mrs. Bingham. Why?"

Those doll eyes batted and flitted. They looked like glass from a distance. Dark, dead glass. She didn't speak; she didn't have to speak.

That smile reappeared on her face and it just kept growing like she had a secret that might just make her explode.

"I'm very sorry," she finally managed to say, but that smile didn't budge, not an inch. "Please. Ask whatever you need to ask."

"How did Hadley handle the move to Wahredua?"

Daisy made a thoughtful noise, her finger mockingly perched on her lips as she pretended to consider the question. "Hmm. How did a teenage girl deal with moving from one of the best cities in the world to this shithole that smells like something stuck in the toe of a boot? Do you want to guess, officers?"

"Are you saying she was unhappy?"

"Hadley hasn't been happy since puberty. No, longer. Since she started school, really. But she was particularly unhappy about coming here. She had to leave behind everything. Bing and I agreed that was for the best, but Hadley hasn't changed."

"What do you mean?"

"That sofa, for example."

Hazard brushed the back of his hand over the leather, so smooth it glided under his touch.

"What about it?" Somers said.

"I asked her to vacuum the sofa cushions."

"And?"

"See for yourself."

Hazard rocked sideways and felt under the cushion. He found the ragged edges of leather spilling out batting.

"Cut the cushions like she was going to serve them for dinner. I guess I'm just lucky she didn't come after me with the knife."

"You were in the room?"

"Do you think I would have stood here and watched? No, Detective. I came home and found the place like this." For a moment, something genuine peered out from behind Daisy's mask—a weary, helpless look. "We'd gotten to the point that I didn't think we could leave her at home alone anymore."

"Did she have any friends? Bing said you've lived here for a few months. Someone from school—"

"Her grandfather," Daisy said immediately. "You couldn't pry those two apart. Both of them just as stubborn and just as awful as the other."

"Anyone outside the family?"

"Christ, you probably mean those faggots." Daisy's mouth curled into an expression of mock horror as she glanced at Hazard. "Oh, Detective. I'm so sorry."

Hazard didn't bother to respond. He was struggling inside himself, struggling to recapture the liquid-crystal clarity of thought that he had experienced earlier. What had he seen? What had caught his attention in this conglomeration of strange events?

"Who are you talking about?" Somers said.

"Those boys. The ones from high school. The ones she was dating."

"These boys are gay, but she was dating them?"

Daisy flapped a hand. "It never made any sense to me. One time, just once, I said something to her about it. I said if she wanted a boyfriend, fine. If she wanted to be on the pill, if she wanted condoms, if she wanted the HPV vaccine, fine. But I said, what good is any of that if those two are too busy screwing each other?"

"You were very frank with your daughter."

"No need to sound so judgmental, Detective. Hadley gave it back ten times over. She said their relationship was purer than that. She said—here's Daddy's sweet little girl for you—she said she didn't plan to grow up like her whore mother. Those were her words, to my face, in my house. Like her whore mother."

"What did she mean by that?"

"Fuck you."

Somers didn't press the point, but Hazard could feel his partner's sudden pulse of satisfaction.

Daisy had collapsed into moody silence, picking at the negligee's strap again, when suddenly she burst into speech again. "They're not even really faggots, though. I mean, they can't be. I don't know what kids call it now. Maybe they're bi. Maybe they don't even use labels anymore. But I saw the way the one, the big one, looked at Hadley, and he wasn't thinking anything pure. And—" She paused, as though her words had almost carried her too far.

"And what?"

She shrugged and took the plunge. "And they stole her underwear."

"What?"

"They were always over here, and one day I heard Hadley get in a huge fight with them. The next day, someone came into the house. We don't lock the doors—Bing promises we don't need to. Shows what he knows, I guess. Those boys walked right into the house while we were gone, and they tore Hadley's room to pieces. The weekend before, we'd driven into Saint Louis, and I'd bought Hadley all new things at Victoria's Secret. A bagful. And that's what they took—they couldn't steal old panties, I guess."

"I'd like to hear a little more about those boys," Somers said. "Their names. Anything else you remember about fights with Hadley."

Daisy opened her mouth, but before she could speak, Hazard got to his feet. "Can I use your bathroom?"

Jabbing a finger towards the hallway, Daisy said, "I know those boys weren't gay. Not all the way, at least. One time Bing walked in on them when they were here, and he swears they weren't doing anything wrong, but I know something happened. Hadley couldn't even look her father in the face. Not for a week. Back in Chicago—"

As Hazard moved down the darkened hall, he missed the rest of Daisy's story. His mind was still turning over the similarities between what had happened to Peter in Chicago and what had happened here. And the dynamic in the Bingham home, toxic and claustrophobic, mixed with his other observations. The doting father. The jealous mother obsessed with attention, sexuality, and control. And what about the sheriff? Where did grandfather fit into this horrible menagerie?

What was clear now—clear, at least, to Hazard—was that someone either wanted Hadley Bingham to appear involved in the shooting, or she actually had been involved. If it had been Hadley, then perhaps last night's events had simply spiraled out of control.

This time, the lunatic she asked for help had been too dangerous, too unpredictable.

But if it had been someone else, then it had to have been someone who knew enough about Hadley's past to make her involvement seem probable. Who? Her mother? Her father? Her grandfather? All three of them seemed likely suspects. But who else had found out? Her boyfriends—the faggots, as Daisy had called them? Mayor Newton? How hard would it have been to dig up a few pertinent facts from Hadley's background and use them to stage last evening's performance?

The problem, of course, was that Hazard had too many unknowns in his equation. It was impossible to advance his theories any farther without more evidence. Concrete evidence. Something that would either cement Hadley as the victim of her own twisted plan or vindicate her. That was what Hazard needed, and so he hurried down the darkened hall, checking doors, searching for her bedroom.

One door along the hall stood open, and weak light showed through the crack. Hazard, hidden in the shadows, examined the scene in front of him. Seated at an expansive glass-and-steel desk, Bing had his head in his hands, studying the phone that lay on the desk's glass top. He wasn't talking to the phone company; that much was obvious. But he also hadn't returned to their conversation. Why? Grief? The need to escape, for however short a time, his wife's caustic company? Guilt? Any of the three were possible. All three were possible. Hazard waited a moment longer, and then, just as he was about to skirt the doorway and continue his search, Bing's phone rang

Hazard froze, pressing himself against the wall, his heart stuttering wildly. The phone continued to ring, and not until the fifth ring did Bing scoop up the phone and swipe a big finger across its glass. He spoke dully, head still dropping forward, as though it were too heavy to lift. Then, all of the sudden, he snapped upright, every inch of him locking taut.

"What?"

For a moment, Bing was silent as the voice on the phone answered. Then, jerking the phone closer to his mouth, Bing shouted, "I heard what you said. I heard damn well. One fucking bullet. There? Is that enough for you? One. I heard the report—no, no, no, you shut up. Just shut your fucking mouth. This has nothing to do with you." Then he dropped the phone onto the desk. His chest was heaving as though he'd run straight up a mountain, and he ran heavy hands through thick curls, clutching so tightly that the skin around his eyes pulled tight.

One bullet. Hazard hesitated a moment longer, and then he shifted past the door, suddenly embarrassed to be observing Bing in a moment of hidden pain. As he crept down the hallway, Hazard heard weeping coming from the study behind him.

One bullet. The thought came again, clear, echoing in his head. What did that mean? One bullet had killed Hadley? That's what it sounded like, but who would call Bing with that kind of information? And why?

Hazard found Hadley's bedroom on the second floor and used the flashlight on his mobile phone to examine the space. It was a large room with an en-suite bath, and in no way had the descriptions of Hadley prepared him for what he saw. Hazard had anticipated huge posters of goth and metal bands. He had expected a spartan, utilitarian organization. This was a girl, after all, who had gone out of her way to defy her parents, to become everything they didn't want her to be. This was a girl, he had reasoned, who would seek out and embrace a counter-culture—maybe several of them.

Instead, he found princesses. Paintings of them. Figurines. Dolls. Embroidered pillows. Even the bedspread had a Disney princess stretched across its cotton. Hazard played the mobile phone's light across the room again and then once more. The shadows swept and loomed, and in the fluttering light, the dolls' eyes were luminous.

They surrounded Hazard on every side, those doll eyes: watching him, as though waiting for the moment the light failed. Too many of those stupid movies Nico likes, he told himself. Too much time with Somers. And maybe it was true because Emery Hazard had never had room in his life for imaginary monsters—there had been too many real ones. But now, even with his hand controlling the light's striations, something childlike and primitive stirred inside him. Just those damn movies. Just Nico's movies. Just Somers, with all his stupid intuitions and emotions, getting inside Hazard's head and screwing everything up, like a grain of sand in Swiss clockwork. But Hazard could feel—no, Hazard knew, he knew in his gut—that this might have been a room where a girl had slept, but she hadn't slept without nightmares.

He went through the drawers in her vanity, uncovering a hundred different shades of gray and blue and smoke-colored eyeshadow, dark lipsticks, mascara, foundation, and God only knew what else. Nothing incriminating, though. No secret diary. No hidden archive of photographs. Hazard searched her bed, too, even going so far as to lift the mattress. His hand ached, the old cut throbbing across his palm, but he found nothing. He lifted the lace ruffle, but he found nothing under the box spring. Nothing behind the headboard. Nothing rolled into the curtains or the valance. Nothing buried in the sweaters and skirts and panties. Nothing.

And that was strange. Hazard's own room was clean and sparse, but he was a rarity. Somers's room—or Nico's, for that matter—told a different story. Most people collected things, not really meaning to, but it happened nevertheless. Old movie tickets, cough drop wrappers, loose change, house keys, lint, receipts, school work. Christ, there wasn't so much as a tube of lip balm. Hadley Bingham, Hazard guessed, hadn't been this clean in life. So why had her room been cleaned the day after her death?

Without answers, Hazard moved into the bathroom. The light from his phone glanced off the enameled tub, sparkled on chrome fixtures, and painted porcelain the color of old bone. Nothing here either. No crusted toothpaste in the sink. No half-used bars of soap. No dust. Even the toilet paper roll was fresh and untouched. Hazard toed the trash can. Empty. If he wanted answers, he'd have to get a search warrant. He already knew, from what he had seen downstairs, that Bing and his wife wouldn't give up answers easily. Perhaps the cleaning had been compulsive, a way of avoiding the crushing grief of their daughter's death. But perhaps—Hazard hesitated, casting one last glance around the bathroom. Perhaps it had been more than grief.

As he turned to go, the light from his phone shone on something small and white behind the toilet. Hazard leaned forward, settling his weight on the sink so that he could stretch behind the porcelain fixture. Something long and white. Hard plastic. A toothbrush, maybe. Something that had missed on the way to the trash can, maybe. Or something that had been knocked—

Hazard's elbow caught the soap dish, and it shattered against the tile. Damn it. From downstairs, footsteps moved, and then Bing called out, "Who's up there?"

He knew he had only seconds before Bing found him. Hazard stretched, the cut on his hand burning, and his fingers closed around the plastic. He plucked it from behind the toilet, glanced at it, and then made a decision.

It wasn't an easy decision, but it wasn't hard either. It happened in the same way that all of Hazard's crucial decisions happened: with a kind of ghostly clarity, luminous without any sort of true light behind it. Someone else, someone not Hazard, would have called it acting on his gut, acting on intuition, and Hazard would have laughed at that. But he also knew that this decision, like others before it, would slip away from his best efforts at analysis. When the moment had passed, when he had time to think clearly, the trappings of reason would fall away, and the inescapable logic that Hazard felt so keenly would grow fuzzy and indistinct, and he would be left uneasy, the way he felt after drinking himself into oblivion, not quite sure what he had done—or what some unknown, unknowable part of himself had done.

This is how it happened, he thought, with Jonas Cassidy and the foil-wrapped bricks of heroin and that stupid, stupid, stupid kiss. This was how mistakes happened, he was thinking even as he made the decision. You screwed up then. You're screwing up now. And strangely, he thought of what Somers would do. Somers wouldn't do this. Somers would have found another way. That, maybe, was the real difference between them. The essential difference. Not logic. Not intuition. Not charm and snub-nosed practicality. This decision, and the dark place inside Emery Hazard where it came from.

As the footsteps reached the doorway, Hazard spun the pregnancy test and slid it up his sleeve like a magician prepping for a show. That image of the magician, too, felt like something that had seeped into Hazard's life through exposure to Somers and Nico. But the foreign image persisted. A magician doing a magic trick. And it would have been a hell of a show. Here's the big reveal, kids. Ta-da. Fireworks and everything. Because the pregnancy test, that little tube of white plastic that Hazard had found—forgotten, ignored—behind Hadley's toilet, that test had been positive.

CHAPTER TWENTY-SEVEN

DECEMBER 23
SATURDAY
5:39 PM

BING THREW THEM OUT of the house. Somers wasn't quite sure how it happened. One minute, he was sitting in the living room, jotting down names and descriptions of acquaintances from Chicago. Daisy Bingham was watching him like she wouldn't mind taking a knife and fork to him, and Somers was starting to wonder where the hell Hazard had gotten off to. The next minute, Hazard staggered into the room, barely catching himself from falling, and Bing surged in behind him. Before anyone could say a word, Bing shoved Hazard again, propelling him towards the door. Hazard was big. He was more than big; he was like a tank, like one of those goddamn Bradleys, muscle on top of muscle on top of muscle. But Bing was big too. And Bing was furious.

And that's how Somers found himself stumbling down the front steps as Bing shouted, "Get the fuck out of my house." He just kept shouting it, variations on the same theme, while Daisy clung to the doorframe, staring at them, oblivious to the cold, her glassy eyes wide with interest.

Hazard had retreated to the VW, his hands braced on the cherry-red roof like he was trying to hold the car in place against the force of Bing's fury. Somers stared up at Bing, who was transformed by rage: his dark curls whipped by the wind, his cheeks scrubbed red, but mostly the eyes. Jesus, those eyes. Somers remembered those eyes. When he'd thrown like shit, when he'd forgotten a play, when he'd fumbled. Those eyes, every damn time.

Those eyes, all that anger, and just like that, Somers fell back twenty years to that night in the car. In Somers's car. In the Camaro. The tap at the window. Bing staring down at him through the glass. And that picture, that fucking picture tumbling out of Somers's hand like someone had spring-loaded it.

Somers hauled himself back from the memory, back from the old, boyhood terror that accompanied it. He clutched at the present: at the cold stinging his ears, at the slush under his feet, at the tingle in his belly like he had to piss a river.

"Bing, what the hell?"

"Your queer-ass partner was sneaking around my house." Bing turned and marched into the house. "I see either of you around here again without a warrant, I'll shoot you myself."

When Bing was gone, Daisy lingered in the doorway, one leg drawn up, her weight supported by the frame, as though she were posing for some obscure winter photoshoot. She dipped towards Somers, a smirk teasing her features, and jiggled her shoulders. Hard nipples, the color of frozen molasses, twitched free of the negligee, and her smirk exploded into laughter. Still laughing, she twisted around and disappeared into the house.

"Insane," Somers said, stamping his feet against the cold. "Everybody in this whole town is fucking insane. You. You're insane. Fucking lunatic."

Hazard just got into the car.

Dropping into the passenger seat, Somers continued, "What the hell were you thinking?"

"Pretty standard," Hazard said, shifting the car into gear, snow squelching under the tires as they rolled forward. "Don't tell me you've never done it before."

Somers grimaced. He had done it before, but he sure as hell wasn't going to admit that to Hazard. It was an old trick: no warrant, not enough to justify a warrant, so you got someone to invite you inside. Once you were inside, you could look around as much as you wanted. With one important proviso.

Stretching to slap Hazard across the back of his head, Somers paused. In the pale glow from the dash, the crusted cuts on Hazard's lip looked like thicker patches of shadow. A surge of guilt washed up into Somers, and he pulled his hand back.

Hazard grunted. "Good choice."

"Screw you. You're not supposed to get caught, Ree."

"Don't call me that."

"Especially not when I'm in the middle of an interview."

"She didn't have anything left to tell us."

"She was giving me names. People that might have—"

"She didn't have anything valuable to tell us. So while you were enjoying the view, I decided to do some real police work." Hazard jimmied his arm in a funny motion, and something slid out of his sleeve and fell into Somers's lap.

A pregnancy test. The cheap kind—Somers knew because the year before they'd had Evie, he'd spent about half his salary on these things for Cora. Two red lines.

"She was pregnant?"

"You figure that out by yourself?"

"This is why people don't like you." Somers turned the pregnancy test over, not because he expected to find a name or some other relevant detail but because he needed something to do with his hands. "Where'd you find it?"

"Hadley's bathroom. Private. Only accessible through her bedroom."

"Maybe a friend?"

"You heard her mom. Hadley didn't have any friends."

"Not unless one of her gay boyfriends got pregnant."

Hazard didn't respond.

"That was a joke."

"Her room had been cleaned. The bathroom had been cleaned."

"The whole house was clean."

"I'm talking clean like a motel room. Like nobody ever lives there, but they want you to feel like someone does."

"So it was clean." Somers spun the pregnancy test again. Vaguely he thought that someone had peed on this piece of plastic, but it was too late to worry about that. "So they were grieving. In a frenzy. You know people get like that."

"You think they looked like they were in a frenzy? They keep a clean house, but only like any other normal people. They're not neat freaks; they didn't care so much about the sofa she ripped up."

Somers spun the white plastic tube again. "So that's it, huh?"

"What the hell does that mean?"

"Nothing."

"Don't do that."

"It's nothing."

Hazard's silence was deep. Deep enough to drop a rocketship into. Deep enough you'd never see that damn rocket ship again. And after a few minutes of that silence, Somers cracked.

"I just think it's funny that you've already switched sides."

"And what the hell does that mean?"

"You think Hadley Bingham was the intended victim."

"Her parents think that."

"You think that. That's why you were snooping around her room. That's what you think this is." Somers displayed the pregnancy test. "Motive. Right? That's what you think, isn't it?"

"You already know what I think. Must be fucking wonderful being you."

"If Hadley really was the intended vic, who wanted to kill her?"

Hazard didn't answer, didn't shift position, but his breathing changed. It was harder, heavier breathing now.

"You've got to be fucking kidding me," Somers said. "You really are insane."

"It looked like your father was pretty friendly with Hadley. If she was pregnant—"

"No. You don't even get to finish that sentence. We don't know who this pregnancy test belonged to. We don't know that my father had anything to do with her. We saw them for, what, five minutes? That's all. And she was on top of him, wasn't she? Don't laugh. Don't—don't fucking snicker at me."

"I coughed."

"So that's your theory now, is it? My father knocked her up. He hired Stillwell to come kill her. He arranged for Stillwell to shoot him five times just so it would look like he wasn't behind it."

"You're the one with all the theories. You're the one with all the big ideas."

"Yeah, you want another big idea? How about this? Say you're right. Say my father knocked her up. I don't believe that, all right, but just say. It could go the other way. You heard Hadley's parents. You heard what she did back in Chicago. That's her M.O. That's her track record. She probably was pissed that my father wouldn't marry her, and so she planned the whole thing."

"I thought Mayor Newton was behind all of this."

"Jesus fucking Christ. You really do. You really do think she was the vic."

"She was a vic. One of them, Somers. And your dad was a victim too. I don't think anything else. I'm waiting for evidence. Conclusive evidence, not hearsay, not speculation, not anecdotes summoned up by grieving and emotionally-distraught witnesses."

"So what? I'm just imagining all this?"

"Honestly, Somers? I don't know what the hell is going on with you. You're high as a fucking kite one minute. The next, you might as well be facedown in an alley, trying to find a quarter for booze. I've cut you slack. A hell of a lot of it, to be honest. Your dad got shot, and I don't know what that's like. But—"

"Go on. What?"

In the ashen light from the dash, Somers thought he saw red staining Hazard's fair skin. "But I don't get it."

"What?"

"Bing. You act different around him."

"How?"

The next breath Hazard took was deeper, like a man readying himself for a plunge. "Like you're afraid of him. And look, before you rip my throat out, I know I'm shit for this kind of thing. Most of the time, I don't get what's going on in people's heads. I don't want to get it. But when Redgie Moseby wanted to start something with me, you about broke his nose. And I've heard about other times too.

People talk. People even talk to me sometimes. I heard about that asshat at the supermarket. You chucked him in a dairy case or something. But Bing shows up, Bing calls me queer, Bing—I don't know. I'm not saying you have to handle any of that stuff for me. I don't need that. But I don't get this, what's happening."

It was, in a strange way, one of the most intimate things Emery Hazard had ever said to Somers. His acknowledgment of what Somers had done, driven by guilt and a desire to amend the past, struck deep at Somers. Hazard's tone, outside its normal range of icy dismissal or icy anger, had drifted somewhere warmer, somewhere that sounded dangerously like concern.

The shooting, the lack of sleep, the rollercoaster case, all of it had cracked Somers's foundations in a way he hadn't known possible. Those fissures sent waves of emotions through him, and now he found himself blinking back tears, his breath hot and moist, almost choking him. He had to say something. He had to say the right thing, the perfect thing, because this was so close to the perfect moment. Fifteen years he'd spent ashamed of what he'd done to Hazard, and here it was, the opportunity he'd never hoped would arrive. The perfect thing, that's what he had to say before the moment slipped away.

"Meat locker."

Hazard rarely looked surprised, but right then, his eyes were wide enough for boxcars to pass through. "What?"

"It wasn't a dairy case. It was a meat locker. A case, I guess, really."

"Uh—"

"He said he heard you liked sausage. That guy, Jimmy Redondo, at the supermarket. So I shoved him inside the frozen meat case with all the sausages. Ripped one open. Shoved as much of it as I could in his mouth. I took a picture and said it looked like he liked sausage too."

The air fizzed like the moment before a lightning strike. This was it, Somers realized. He'd screwed up. This was his last transgression, the perfect example of his failure to live up to anything like Hazard's own rigid control and discipline. What would Hazard do next? Pull over, kick Somers out, and tell him to walk home? Serve me right, Somers thought. It would serve me damn right.

Hazard started to laugh. It was a basso noise, and it rumbled through Hazard's chest, practically shaking the air. He laughed so hard he eased off the gas and let the car drift up against the curb. He laughed so hard he gripped the wheel with both hands and laid his head down on it. And then, from deep inside himself, Somers felt laughter bubble up.

The laughter went on longer than it should have. It spilled out of Somers, cresting over the wall he had built to hold back pain and fear and worry, and when it ended, Somers felt drained, relieved, but also energized. The pressure inside him, the pressure that had threatened to shear through his foundations and wreck him totally, had eased. It was still there, but hell, now Somers could handle it.

With silence falling between them, Somers found that he could think more clearly.

"All right."

"What?"

"All right, I see what you mean. About Hadley and my dad. About the different ways things could have played out."

Hazard, silent as a stone, showed no reaction.

"I'm not saying I agree with you. I'm not even close to saying that. But I'm saying I see it. I'm not blind."

"And?"

"And it could have been somebody else that got her pregnant, you know. It could have been one of the boyfriends."

Hazard was already shaking his head.

"What?" Somers said.

"The faggots? One of them got her pregnant."

"That was Daisy's word. For all the attitude and the act she put on, I don't think she actually knows a whole hell of a lot."

"Oh?" Hazard's tone was dry enough to crack skin.

"Why don't we at least talk to them? See what they can tell us about Hadley. No, hold on. You saw them at the party. You're the one that noticed they were upset."

"One of them definitely was."

"I don't think Bing or Daisy had a very clear idea of what their daughter was like."

"And you think these boys do?"

"I think we have a better chance of learning the truth if we talk to her friends."

"Even though you think this is all my bullshit. Even though you think she's not really involved."

"Will you not be an asshole about this?"

Hazard didn't answer, but he let the VW limp away from the curb, and when they were rolling down the street he asked, "Address?"

Somers consulted his notepad, where he'd recorded the last of his conversation with Daisy. He rattled off the address, leaned back into the seat, and stared into the snow strafing the darkness. He knew, in his gut, that Mayor Newton was involved. He knew his father had been targeted for a reason. But he also knew that Emery Hazard was the smartest person he'd ever met, and he'd be a fool to ignore Hazard's opinion. So for now, for the moment, he'd do this. He'd take a look. A part of him wondered what he'd do if push came to shove, if he and Hazard reached an impasse. No answer came to him; beyond that point in his thoughts there was only darkness like that darkness outside the VW.

As they drove into the slow spill of snow, Somers heard Hazard mutter something.

"What?"

"Nothing."

"No, what'd you say?"

"Shut up and let me drive."

But Somers knew what he'd heard. And he smiled. He smiled so hard his cheeks came close to cracking because Emery Hazard had said to himself, in that dark, smoky voice like the best Scotch, two words: *Meat case.*

CHAPTER TWENTY-EIGHT

DECEMBER 23
SATURDAY
6:00 PM

ONE OF THE BOYS lived in a small house on the northeast side of Wahredua. Here, all the old rail services had once lived and died: hotels, motels, diners, warehouses, train yards, and the Missouri Pacific station. Even in the dark, Somers thought he could trace where the MP lines ran, like an invisible brace that kept the city from spilling out into the rest of the world. Here, that ferrous presence manifested in electric signage that hadn't been updated since the 1950s, in rust-stains that dripped from old rivets, in brick that looked too soft and that sagged now, and, most interestingly, in a revival of urban chic stores, a chance at a second life for this portion of the city.

It was here that the Pretty Pretty stood, Wahredua's only gay bar. The only times Somers had been inside, he had been with Hazard. The men—and boys—inside had been nice. Friendly. Hell, they'd been plenty friendly. They'd bought Somers a few beers. They'd wanted to talk. About Hazard, sure, because everybody wanted to know about the local boy come back, about the city's only gay cop. But they'd talked, too, about Somers. He wasn't stupid. He knew why. He liked the attention. But that wasn't the reason he thought about it, not deep down, not if he were honest.

No, deep down, when memories flashed of the strobing lights, of the yeasty beer, of the press of hard, muscled bodies against his own, of the smell of a dozen different colognes and sweat, all that carried with it one other thing, like a spotlight shining on it, and then it didn't matter what else Somers remembered because that spotlight was just so damn bright. He remembered Hazard looking at him. He remembered the look—

—of jealousy—

—on Hazard's face. Like one of the searchlights that car dealerships used, that's how bright it was. Like he couldn't look at it too long, not without a hell of a lot of danger.

Hazard said something.

"Yeah, this is it," Somers said, flipping through the pages of his notepad again.

"I said what's his name."

"Frank. Hold on—yeah. Frank."

"I asked you two times."

"Sorry. My head." He left it vague, hoping that would be enough.

It wasn't. "What about it?"

"Just a headache."

"So why'd I have to repeat myself?"

"Jesus Christ. It's like the inquisition. How about we go in there and do our job?"

Hazard's face revealed nothing; as always, it was set in the cold indifference that he wore so well. But worry fluttered in Somers's gut. Could he possibly have guessed? Could he—

No. No, Hazard had no interest. None at all. He'd made that perfectly clear. And what the hell did it matter, anyway? What the hell did it matter with Cora and Evie and—

"Are you coming?" Hazard stamped his feet. "What the hell is up with you?"

"Nothing."

"I'm the one that got hit in the head. Twice. But you're the one acting like you've got a concussion."

"I said nothing. I'm fine."

Still no expression in that pale, brutishly beautiful face.

Somers sighed and followed his partner to the door. The house, a standard tract house that had most likely gone up in the forties, maybe the fifties, showed its age: the metal window frames had rusted and peeled, while the ancient green plastic canopy above the door looked ready to collapse under the snow's weight. The lights in those windows were dark, but Hazard hammered again on the door, and then again.

And the door opened. The boy standing inside was dark-complexioned, his hair messily tousled, his eyes bruised and hollow. Dressed in a t-shirt and shorts, he folded thin arms over a thin chest, and suddenly Somers thought of Hazard as a teenager, his slender frame, his defensiveness. There was some of that in this boy. Maybe a lot of that. It was in the way he cocked his jaw like he'd rather take a punch than open his mouth.

"Frank?" Hazard said.

Nothing.

"Is that you? Is your name Frank?"

"Who are you?"

"Detectives Hazard and Somerset. We need to talk to you about Hadley Bingham."

"My parents aren't home," the boy said, and he slammed the door hard enough that snow cascaded off the plastic canopy.

Hazard glanced at Somers, and Somers shrugged. "I'd say we found him."

With a grunt in response, Hazard leaned back, studying the house. "So we come back tomorrow when the parents are here?"

"Unless you want to force your way into this house without a warrant," Somers said, massaging one temple, "and interrogate a minor without a guardian present—"

Before Somers could finish, the door swung open again. The boy who stood there, though, was not the one who had answered the door. This boy had dark hair too, although in a cleaner cut than the first one, and dark eyes with even deeper hollows dug around them. Where the first boy had been thin, this boy packed plenty of muscle. He stood with a kind of casual arrogance that Somers remembered. It was teen jock arrogance. Somers had been pretty damn good at it himself.

"You're here to talk about Hadley?" His voice was deeper. From the bottom of those dark hollows, his eyes looked feverish.

"Are you—"

"If you're here to talk about Hadley, come inside. If it's anything else, get lost."

The boy disappeared into the house's darkness. Hazard glanced at Somers.

"We do our job, right?" Somers said. Hoping he wasn't making a mistake, Somers opened the storm door and stepped inside.

Within, the house seemed to hold only more darkness and cold. Somers walked deeper into the building. It wasn't a big house. It wasn't even an average size, not anymore, but the darkness and his unfamiliarity made every step seem longer. When Somers reached a short hallway, he saw light from under a door, and the bigger boy's silhouette against the light.

"Down here," the boy said before stepping into the room. Light swelled for a moment before the door shut again, leaving Somers blinking spots from his vision.

It was just nerves, Somers told himself, but his fingers were tingling. A dark house. Very dark. And this strange reception. Both of the boys looked like they might be on something. Drugs. Maybe just their dads' beer. Inside that room, they could have a knife. Or a gun. In the darkness next to him, Hazard's breathing was steady but harsh.

"This was your goddamn idea," Hazard whispered.

Somers strode down the hallway. He barely felt the splintered paneling on the door as he pushed it open. Keeping to one side of the doorway, he let his eyes adjust to the sudden brightness. His blood roared in his ears.

And when he could see, pity washed over him. The room was barren: a twin bed without sheets, a black and white TV the size of a cereal box, and a pile of tangled clothing near one wall. Overhead, a bare bulb gave the only light, and that same light made a flat glare against a naked window, blocking out the night. In one corner of the room, something silver glittered in the corner as though thrown there. Somers focused on it. A surge of excitement ran through him. Yes, he'd seen something like that before.

On the twin bed, the two boys nestled together, the smaller one sitting inside the vee of the bigger boy's legs, the two of them cocooned in blankets. Here, in full light, the differences were even more striking. But so, too, were the similarities. The grief in their faces. Or was it something else? Fear? Shame? Guilt? Again, Somers found himself facing the ghost of the teenage Hazard as he looked at the slender boy with the windswept hair.

"You can sit on the bed if you want," the bigger boy said. "We'll move."

Somers shook his head. Behind him, Hazard's presence was like a fire. What was Hazard thinking? Did he feel the same mixture of sympathy and concern as Somers? Or was it envy? Or was it distaste? It was hard to know; Hazard was close-mouthed about almost everything personal, but he was particularly close-mouthed when it came to other men, other gay men. But he could feel Hazard behind him, feel the heat of him like a goddamn inferno, and Somers couldn't push away the question: what was he thinking? Did he even see the similarities? Did he see what his own life might have been if he'd been born twenty years later? Without the hate, without the persecution, without the loneliness?

"We'll stand," Somers said. "Thanks."

"Why the fuck," the thin boy said, "did you invite them in?"

"They want to talk about Hadley."

"Yeah. I know. That's my point."

The bigger boy lifted a hand to smooth the other boy's hair, and the slender boy jerked away from his touch. Unseen by the smaller boy, the bigger boy's face contorted in a look of pain. No, worse than pain. Torment. His hand hovered in the air a moment longer before dropping to his side.

"Frank?" Somers said.

For a moment, neither boy spoke. Then the bigger one nudged the thin one. "He's talking to you."

"I heard him. I don't have to say a motherfucking word to him."

"Then that makes you Dustin," Somers said.

"Yeah," the bigger boy said. "Dusty. Or Dust. Could you come in and close the door? It's cold."

And it was cold, even in the stripped-down bedroom. Maybe the house didn't have heat. Was that even possible? Somers imagined the pipes bursting in February. He shuffled into the room, careful to avoid the piled clothes, and made room for Hazard, who shut the door behind them. Then the room seemed too small, and Hazard seemed too big. The elephant in the room, Somers thought. Jesus, what an elephant. And Hazard still hadn't said anything.

"We wanted to talk to you about Hadley," Somers said into the silence. Each word was like somebody throwing rocks at a frozen lake: the snap of the stillness, the plunge, the total disappearance of the source of the noise. Frank was staring off at the black-and-white TV like it had the cure for cancer, and Hazard was staring through the two boys at some point a few miles below ground. Dusty was the only one who seemed to have heard Somers; he nodded his head.

Scrubbing at his clean-cut hair, Dusty said, "You guys were there."

"Excuse me?"

"At the party. When she—" Suddenly, tears overflowed his eyes, and he swung a big hand around to press against his face. His whole body jerked, and the movement rocked Frank. For a heartbeat, the slender boy's eyes snapped down to the arms that held him. Then his cheeks colored and his attention went back to the TV.

"Yes," Somers said. "We were there."

"Sorry. I'm just—I can't even think right now. I'm really sorry. I am. It's like my brain is all mush."

"It's called trauma," Somers said, softening his voice.

Dusty swiped at his eyes, and then he buried his face in Frank's wild hair. Again, a moment of tenderness flashed in Frank's face, and then it was gone as he schooled his features to emptiness.

"She didn't deserve that," Dusty said. "Nobody deserves that."

And that, for the first time, brought out a lasting change in Frank's face. The boy's pale features twisted, and his knuckles whitened where he clutched at the blanket.

"Can you tell us about Hadley?" Somers said.

"Yeah, sure. What about her?"

"Well, just to get started, can you tell me how you knew her?"

"School," Dusty said. He had a kind of simple earnestness to him, Somers was starting to realize. The cockiness was there too, the standard dose of teenage over-confidence that accompanied good looks, athletics, and a few successful sexual encounters, but underneath it, the boy seemed eager to please. "She moved in a few months ago, right after school started. She's—" He paused as pain wrenched at his features, and then he forced himself to continue. "She was in our chem class."

"What was your relationship like with Hadley?"

"Fuck off," Frank burst out.

Dusty stroked his shoulder, pulling the thin boy against his chest. "C'mon—"

"No. Fuck off both of you, why don't you? Stop, Dust. I'm just—no, I'm not going to calm down. What the fuck do they want?"

"We just want to know about Hadley," Somers said, locking eyes with the furious boy.

Frank tossed his head, his long hair dancing in front of his eyes. "What do you need to know? She was an arrogant, selfish, psychotic bitch. There. Is that all? Can you get real busy and go fuck yourselves somewhere else?"

Throughout this rant, Dusty had been whispering warnings in Frank's ears, rubbing the slender boy's back and shoulders as though trying to gentle a startled horse. Now, though, his hands tightened on Frank, and genuine pain sparked in Frank's face. He didn't make a sound. He didn't try to pull away. But the pain was there, and Somers was starting to think the skinny boy was tougher than he'd realized.

"That's enough. That's just enough, all right? Cut it out." Red suffused Dusty's face, and he gave Frank one hard, furious shake.

Frank fought furiously, struggling against Dusty's grip, his legs whipping free of the blanket, his nails raking the lean, taut muscles in Dusty's arms, his head cracking backward against Dusty's shoulder loud enough to make Somers wince.

"She's a bitch," Frank shouted, writhing in Dusty's grip. "She's a stupid, selfish cunt. She's—get off me. Get off me you fucking pussy, get off, get the fuck off, get off!" The last words erupted in a scream, and then Frank dissolved into sobs. Shaking, Frank tried to free himself one last time. Dusty whispered something in his ear, drew him back against his chest, and this time Frank turned inwards, his cheek pressed against Dusty's smooth, muscled chest as he wept.

Somers tried to keep his eyes on the moment before him. He tried to think, tried to process what he saw. And part of his brain was successful. Part of his brain noticed the red lines of blood on Dusty's arms, part of his brain noticed the mixture of fury and—what? despair?—in Dusty's face. Part of his brain noticed the strength and gentleness in Dusty's embrace.

But another part of his brain had gotten tangled in memory, and again he found himself back in Windsor, in that attic room, where he had pressed himself against a naked Emery Hazard, only to be rejected. A fight. It had all started with the phone call to Cora, and she'd been angry that he was missing Thanksgiving, angry that after all the hard work to reconcile, the same old problem cropped up again: work interfering with his family life. And then Somers had found hooch. And then he had drunk himself stupid. Too stupid. Stupid enough to think about Emery Hazard, upstairs, naked, in the bed they shared, and stupid enough to think maybe—

—that kiss in the locker room, the stripped-down desire in Hazard's eyes—

—there was a chance, maybe he wouldn't feel so shitty if there was just a chance between them.

That had been stupid, of course. Hazard had made it perfectly clear that there was nothing, no interest, no reason for Somers to think otherwise. But now, watching the tenderness between these two boys, Somers felt a knot in his belly: self-pity, arousal, and a furious jealousy. Because it should have been like this, that night in Windsor. It should have been this, and it should have been more: to finally touch Hazard, really touch him, to finally feel those stiff, sparse hairs across his chest, to feel the ripple of corded muscle, to smell his skin and his hair and his sweat. And with an effort that was physical, that tore at his gut, Somers pushed the thoughts away because he had Cora, because he had Evie, because Hazard didn't want a goddamn thing to do with him, not after—well, Jesus, just look at today. Not after today when Somers had gotten plastered and punched him in the face. Twice.

"You want to explain all that?"

It was Hazard's voice, icily cold, and for a terrible moment, Somers had the dizzying impression that Hazard knew, that he had spoken his thoughts out loud and that now Hazard was demanding justification. Then, clarity returned, and he realized Hazard was addressing Dusty and Frank.

Jesus, Somers thought, wishing his heart weren't trying to crack his ribs. Just Jesus Christ, I've gotta get this under control.

"He's upset," Dusty said, still pressing Frank's head to his chest and stroking the loose, wild hair as the boy sobbed.

"I can tell he's upset. Why don't you say something I don't know?"

"All right," Somers said, throwing a warning look to Hazard. Then, to Dusty, he said, "What's going on?"

"Nothing," Frank croaked, trying to push himself away from Dusty. When Dusty wouldn't let go, though, Frank collapsed back against him and settled for giving Somers the finger.

"Hadley," Dusty said, his voice almost as creaky as Frank's. "Look, it's a mess, it's such a mess. He's just upset. Frank, hey. Baby." Brushing aside the long, dark hair, Dusty bent closer to the slender boy. "I'm going to go talk to them. Outside, all right? This was stupid. I was stupid. Can you just say something so I know it's all right?"

Whatever Frank said, it was muffled by Dusty's chest and too low for Somers to make out. Dusty skimmed fingers through Frank's hair and, pitching his voice low and obviously hoping Somers and Hazard wouldn't hear, he said, "You're not going to do anything stupid. I'm going to leave the TV on, I'm going to be just down the hall. You're not going to do anything, get it? I'll be right back."

This time, if Frank responded, there was no sign that Somers could discern. Slowly, Dusty disentangled himself from the other boy. He shrugged a hoodie over broad shoulders, tugged on track pants, and shuffled out into the hall. Hazard followed, and when Somers had joined him, Hazard pressed a hand against Somers's chest, stopping him.

"Something felt off in there."

Somers fought the urge to roll his eyes. "Really?"

"Yeah. Didn't you get that? Neither of them seems quite right."

"You're like a psychic."

Hazard's eyes narrowed.

"No, honest. Like, you could do a TV show. Read the audience, you know, that kind of stuff."

"Screw you."

"Ree," Somers said, snagging at Hazard's sleeve as the bigger man turned down the hallway. "What about me? What am I feeling?"

"I don't know," Hazard whispered, snatching his sleeve free. "Whatever a gaping asshole normally feels."

Light bloomed ahead of them—a warm, yellow light at odds with the cold and darkness penetrating the rest of the house. Somers and Hazard followed that light and found Dusty in the kitchen. It was a small, cramped room almost as bare as Frank's bedroom: a kitten-pattern border was the only sign of decoration, and it hung from the wall in tatters. Dusty perched on a stool at the battered table, his big shoulders folded inwards, his hands wrapped between his legs.

Somers sat in one of the rickety chairs, and it groaned under his weight.

"He better not," Dusty said, nodding at Hazard as the big man pulled out another chair. "I tried, and one of these split apart right under me. Frank's mom skinned me for that. I'm only allowed to use the stool now."

Nodding, Hazard stood back, folding his arms over his enormous chest.

Somers suddenly felt precipitously aware of the chair under him, of its every creak and protest, of the flimsy, splintered legs. As he leaned forward, a joint in the chair popped, and Somers froze.

Dusty, with a smile the color of old snow, just nodded.

"This seems like a rough setup," Somers said.

"Yeah," Dusty said, and all of the sudden emotion welled up in him, screwing his eyes shut, red flooding into his cheeks as he choked back a cry. He was a kid, Somers realized. He was just a kid, even if he was a lot bigger and ropier than the boy in the bedroom. Just a kid who looked like he'd spent the last twenty-four hours balancing the world on his shoulders. Just a kid who looked like he might drop all that weight right now if he could.

Dusty made a visible effort to take control of himself, and he repeated, "Yeah," but the word was gelled in his throat. "It's Frank's. I mean, it's his mom's place, but she's never here. Well, she was the night I broke that chair." Dusty paused. He looked like he wanted to say more, and so Somers kept his peace and prayed that Hazard's newfound intuition would make him hold his tongue. After thirty seconds, Dusty broke into speech again. "I can't even do anything about it. I told him he could stay at my place. I asked my parents, and they said yes. He could live there. We're not rich or anything, but I mean, come on." Dusty shrugged, his hands emerging to make an all-encompassing gesture at the house. "He won't. He just—he said I was being stupid." He squeezed his eyes shut again. "It's not usually like this. I mean, it is. It's always like this, but usually the heat's on. Anyway, you want to talk about Hadley."

Somers nodded, but Hazard spoke first. "We have her phone."

"Oh. Yeah." But Dusty said nothing more.

"Can you open it?" Hazard produced the mobile and passed it to the boy.

"That's not her phone."

"What do you mean?"

"That's not her phone. She had a different one."

"Are you sure? It's not just a different case?"

"Yeah. This is a Samsung. She had an LG."

Hazar and Somers exchanged a glance. Then Hazard asked, "So you can't unlock it?"

"What? No. Why would I be able to?"

"Because you were dating. You never saw her punch in a passcode?"

"Uh." Dusty drew out the sound, and Somers felt like he had aged fifty years. This boy was staring at them like they were from the Stone Age.

"Is that a no?" Hazard asked.

"Yeah. I mean, no. I don't know her passcode or anything like that." Hazard held out his hand, but Dusty kept the phone, rotating it, as though studying it for a secret clue.

"She didn't write it on there," Hazard finally said.

"What?"

"Never mind. Just give me the phone."

"Oh, yeah. Right." But Dusty still didn't relinquish it. He paused, holding the phone closer, and then rubbed at it with his sleeve. With a shrug, he passed it back to Hazard. "Dirt under the case. That's definitely not hers. Hadley would never let her phone get dirty. She'd go crazy if she saw that."

Hazard rotated the case. A slight tightening around his eyes. The flexion in his jaw. Maybe nobody else would see it. Maybe nobody in the world would look that closely. But Somers saw it, and he knew it meant something had shocked his partner.

Wordlessly, Hazard held out the phone for Somers's inspection. It took him a moment in the kitchen's yellow glare to find the spot that had drawn Hazard's interest. There. On the edge of the phone, trapped by the side of the case was a brown smear. Hazard tilted the phone, and light filtered through the case, turning the brown smear rust-colored. It wasn't dirt. It was blood.

And that was very strange. It must have been Hadley's blood; Somers was almost sure of it. That part wasn't strange. The girl had been shot—one bullet, sure, but that had still been enough to kill her. She'd bled a lot. So her blood had covered her clothes, stained her possessions. The phone wasn't stained, though. It had a single drop of dried blood. And that was strange. And it was strange, too, that Somers didn't remember seeing her with the phone at the party. When they had found it among her possessions at the ME's office, Somers had assumed—well, he hadn't really thought about it. But where had it been? And why was there only a single spot of blood?

"All right," Hazard said, pocketing the phone. "What about Hadley?"

Dusty thought for a moment, his big shoulders rolling in and out. "She's—she was so cool. And tough. You've been to her house?"

Another nod.

"She's—she had a lot of money, right? I mean, you saw that place. But she didn't act like it. She never acted like it. She came over here. A lot, actually. She never said anything. She never made Frank feel bad."

In spite of himself, Somers felt surprise on his features.

"Yeah," Dusty said, catching the look. "I know, Frank's pissed. But he's not really mad at her."

"Who's he mad at?"

"Me. Hadley. Everyone." Dusty laughed and ran the sleeve of his hoodie under his nose. "I mean, Frank's generally pissed at the whole world. It's kind of his thing. His mom—" Worry tightened his expression.

"We're not here about Frank's mom," Somers said.

"What happens if I tell you something?"

"About his mom?"

A tight, worried nod.

"If she's hurting him, or if it's something really bad, we have to do something. If it's something else, well, we're not here about her."

"She is. Hurting him. I mean, she never touches him. She just— she's gone. He's got nobody. I mean, he has me, but Frank doesn't, that doesn't mean anything to him. She's a prostitute. I mean, she's a waitress at Deb's, but she's always bringing guys back here. I've seen a couple of them. I've seen the cash they leave behind. You're not going to do anything, right? Frank would kill me. You're not, are you?"

"We're not here about that," Somers said, but the lie twisted in his gut because he knew he'd have to say something, because he couldn't leave a child in a life like this.

Dusty must have sensed the half-truth because worry still furrowed his brow. When he spoke again, the words were halting. "Hadley could make Frank laugh. He never laughs. I mean, he laughs at me. When I do something stupid, he laughs like he's going to pee his pants. But he doesn't laugh, not like a belly laugh. But Hadley could do it. And she was nice. She'd invite us over for dinner. She'd pack up leftovers. For both of us, but I knew she was just doing it for Frank because he wouldn't take any if I didn't. Sometimes the two of them, they'd come to one of my games, and I'd see them up in the stands, and Frank would look—" Dusty passed. Something close to fear sparked in his eyes. "He would look happy."

"I don't understand," Somers said, gesturing back at the bedroom. "I thought . . ."

"Oh. Yeah. We're dating. On and off for almost three years. More off than on, to be honest, but that's just how Frank is."

"Mrs. Bingham said that you and Hadley were dating."

"Yeah."

Somers waited, but Dusty seemed perfectly content with the explanation. It was Hazard's voice that broke the stillness, the words spoken in his usual calm lack of interest. "You're bi. And poly."

"Well, yeah. I thought—isn't that why you're here?"

A tremor ran deep down inside Somers. Bi. And poly. It was dangerously close to an echo of something already inside him. He forced the thought away.

"So you were dating Hadley and Frank," Somers said, hoping nobody—especially Hazard—could hear the raw edge in his voice. "Could you explain how that worked?"

"Well, I mean." Dusty's explanation faltered, and his cheeks turned bright red. Those big shoulders rolled even further inwards.

"I'm not trying to pry," Somers said, "but we need to know."

"Yeah." Dusty ran his sleeve over his forehead. The vee of chest exposed by his hoodie was flushed and dimpled with sweat. "Fuck. I'm sorry, I didn't mean to say that. It's just. It's kind of—I don't talk about this kind of stuff."

"Were you sexually active with both of them?" Somers asked.

Dusty's face could have started a fire. Several fires. Maybe a few acres of solid inferno. "No. I mean, with Frank, yes. And with Hadley once, but—Jesus, do I really have to—it didn't go well, ok? That's all I'm going to say about it."

"So your relationship with Hadley wasn't physical?"

"I mean, we kissed. She liked to cuddle with both of us. But she didn't want it to go any farther than that, and I had Frank, so that was fine with me."

"Was she jealous that you and Frank were having sex?"

"No."

"Was Frank jealous that you and Hadley had sex?"

"What? God. God, no." The look on his face betrayed something deeper, something unsettled that Somers's question had unearthed. Dusty rambled on, not seeming to know what he was saying. "It was just so awful, so awkward, but he just wouldn't let up about it, and she wouldn't say no. If she would have just said no, we wouldn't be in this mess."

"He?"

Dusty seemed to snap out of his reverie.

"Who wouldn't let up about it?" Somers pressed. "Frank?"

"He—he kept saying it would be hot. He wanted to see me—" Dusty's face could have reduced a few continents to ash. "He wanted to see me with her. He wanted to be, you know, part of it."

It took Somers a moment to process what he'd just heard. "And Hadley was ok with that?"

"She wouldn't say no. She didn't want to. I mean, I could tell that much. And I didn't want to. But Frank just wouldn't let up about it. It was just so fucking awful."

"Can you tell me what happened? Not in that way," Somers hurried to add when he saw Dusty's horrified expression. "But between the three of you after. Did that change your relationship?"

"Yeah. Completely. Hadley didn't want anything to do with us. She—she went wild."

"What do you mean?"

"Just crazy."

"She destroyed your car? She knocked out a window at your house? She trashed your locker at school?" Somers threw out possibilities, trying to conjure up his best guesses of what the highly unstable girl might have done to this oversized puppy. "Did she attack you? Ask someone else to hurt you? Did she go after Frank?"

295

"No, God. Nothing like that. Hadley wasn't violent. She never would have hurt anyone."

This boy, Somers guessed, hadn't known the real Hadley. He hadn't known the girl that had slashed the sofa cushions, that had burned down her Chicago home, that had hired a lunatic to assault her ex-boyfriend.

"What did she do? You say she went crazy; how?"

"She cut us off. Wouldn't pick up the phone, wouldn't talk to us at school, wouldn't even look at us. I tried apologizing. I mean, it wasn't even my fault, but I tried. Frank even tried apologizing. It was like—I don't know, I've never seen that before, not ever. Nothing, though. She just wouldn't have anything to do with us. And then this guy at school, Huang, he told us he'd seen her at a club. We didn't believe him. I didn't believe him, I mean. But Huang had pictures. There she was, dancing up on this old guy. I mean, not like you two." Somers fought to hide a smile, and he had to fight extra hard when he saw the flash of irritation on Hazard's face. "This guy was like, ancient."

"Do you have a picture of him?"

Dusty shook his head, but what came out of his mouth was, "Yeah." He dragged a phone out of the hoodie, pressed his thumb at the bottom of the screen, and when the screen unlocked, he began swiping through photos. "You just wanna see him?"

"What do you mean?" Somers said.

"Here he is." Dusty passed over the phone. Blown up on the screen was a photograph of Hadley in a black dress that barely reached the middle of her thighs and left most of her back bare. She was pressed up against an older man—no, Somers thought, beyond old, ancient really was a good word for him—clearly in the middle of grinding against him.

"That made you mad?"

"Yeah. I was furious. I mean, I was embarrassed. But I was worried too. And she still wouldn't talk to me. Or to Frank, and you know what? That really cut him up. He wouldn't show it, but I could tell. Walked past us like we were invisible, that's how she was. Then Frank cornered her, and he got, well, a little heated. He said some stuff he shouldn't have said. And it got worse. She started calling us the fags. The faggots, too, sometimes she'd say it that way. And somehow it—it kind of worked."

"What worked?"

"I don't know. People started seeing us that way, I guess. Guys I've known my whole life, guys who never cared that I played for the other team, they started freaking out that I was in the showers after practice. Nobody said anything to my face, but I heard them talking. And nobody did anything to me, not outright. But if I was walking down a crowded hall, you could bet somebody was going to find a way to crash into me."

"You said nobody did anything to you. Why did you emphasize that they didn't do it to you?"

"Frank always runs hot, you know? I'm not saying it's his fault, but he didn't make it any easier. He'd talk back. He'd give it right back to them. People really went after him. When I wasn't around, when I couldn't do anything, that's when they'd go. And Frank—" Dusty paused. He voice stayed even, but he dashed a sleeve over his eyes. "Frank just wouldn't tell me who was doing it."

"Doing what?"

"Shitting on him. Literally. I mean, throwing bags of shit at the house, that's how it started. That was a walk in the park, though, by the end. They'd throw it at him. Pelt him. He'd have these bruises all over and he wouldn't tell me why. I never would have known except one day I got out of practice early, and I got over here. Frank didn't know I was coming. He hadn't showered. He was just sitting outside. Dog shit. Dog shit all over him. He wasn't crying either. I'm the one who cries, the big, stupid jock, you know. But if I hadn't gotten out of practice early, I wouldn't have known. Even then, he wouldn't tell me who'd done it. He just took a shower. Wouldn't look me in the eyes. That's what did it. That's what set me off. I shouldn't have done what I did next."

"What'd you do?"

Dusty scrubbed at his hair, yanked up his hood, and generally tried to shrink into his broad shoulders, as though somehow he could make himself smaller, maybe even invisible.

"What'd you do?" Somers pressed.

"I went over there. To Hadley's, I mean. I just—I couldn't take it anymore. Frank says I'm just being a dumb macho jock. Maybe that's true. I don't care. She can do what she wants to me. She can't do that to him, though."

"She can't do anything to anyone," Somers said, his voice gentle as Dusty brushed at his eyes again. "How did Hadley react?"

"She wouldn't even see me. Her dad just about broke my shoulder when I tried to get in the house. Big guy, you know? He threw me on my ass. And the wife called the police, so I just scrammed." Staring at his feet, Dusty shrugged again. "Stupid jock shit, right?"

"No. Not at all. You were standing up for someone you care about. You were trying to protect someone. That's not stupid, it's not macho, and it has nothing to do with being a jock." Somers had to bite back the rest of his words: he wanted to tell Dusty that Frank was a little asshole, that Dusty deserved better, that there was someone else who would value him and appreciate the qualities that Frank mocked. But none of that was what a detective needed to say.

It was there, though. It was there, and that soundtrack played over vivid memories of Somers in high school: of the day he had held Hazard's arms and watched Mikey twist a knife through skin the color of Ivory soap; the day he had shoved Hazard down a flight of stairs—that's what fags get—even if he had done it to protect Hazard; that day in the locker room, his hair still damp from the shower, seeing true desire, real desire, for the first time in his life in Emery Hazard's eyes.

Hazard's voice bit into the silence. "How'd you end up at the Christmas party?"

"I don't know."

"You don't know? What does that mean?"

Somers waved Hazard back and said, "Why don't you explain how you ended up at the Christmas party?"

"Honestly, I don't know. She called me out of the blue. It wasn't even her number, so I didn't answer the first few times. Then I listened to one of the messages, and it was her, so I called her back—"

"Just a second. She called you from a different number?"

"Yeah."

"Where did she call you from?"

"No clue."

"Could she have called you from this phone?" Hazard's question interrupted the flow, and again he produced the mobile phone from his pocket.

"Yeah, I guess."

"Try calling her back. Let's see."

Dusty drew out his phone, thumbed the screen, and a moment later the phone in Hazard's hand buzzed. Wordlessly, Hazard stuffed it back into his pocket.

"So," Somers said. "She called you from this phone, not from the one she usually used. Is that strange? Did it seem strange at the time?"

"Yeah, of course. I tried to ask her about it, but she wouldn't tell me anything. She just—she kept talking about how good everything had been, how she was sorry, how she wanted to see us again before she moved."

"Before she moved?"

Dusty shoved his hands deeper between his legs, still trying to escape the cold. "Yeah, sure. Why are you looking at me like that? They're moving, right? I say back to Chicago, but Frank thinks they'll go somewhere new."

"Who told you they were moving?"

"I don't get this. Are they moving or aren't they?"

"Who told you?" Hazard barked.

"Hadley. What's going on? Why are you acting weird?"

"What did she say exactly?" Somers said.

Dusty's whole face screwed up in concentration. It was comical but somehow endearing—all that earnest energy spent in one single direction. It wasn't hard to see why Frank or Hadley or anybody else would have liked this boy. "She said something like, 'I just wanted to see you before we go.' And I asked where she was going, and she started talking about the Christmas party."

Before we go. Somers turned the phrase over in his head. It might have meant that Hadley and her family were moving. In some innocent context, absent any knowledge of Hadley's history of violence and psychosis, someone could have taken it for a statement about geography. Especially someone young and innocent and generous and perhaps slightly slow. Someone like Dusty.

"What? What I just told you, what about it? What are you thinking?"

"Hadley had been through a lot," Somers began slowly. "And she had a history. Do you think she might have meant—"

"She wasn't violent. She—she never would have hurt anyone."

"Except Frank," Hazard said with his typical brutality. "Except you. Except her parents. Except people back in Chicago."

Dusty was shaking his head. "You're wrong. She wasn't like that. She was—something changed, yeah, but she wasn't like that. That person, the one you're talking about, that wasn't Hadley."

"You didn't know Hadley," Hazard said, and there was so much pain in Dusty's face that for a moment, Somers wanted to sock his partner in the jaw. "The sooner you accept that, the easier this will be for you."

Still shaking his head, Dusty didn't answer, but the pain in his face only grew worse. He had been wounded in a way that he had never been hurt before, and this wound would leave a scar. "You think she—what? She was going to kill herself?"

Or did, Somers thought. Or she did kill herself. She hired that man just like she did in Chicago, and this time she got what she really wanted. The thought disturbed him, and not just because of the tragedy in the statement. It disturbed him because it meant that maybe there was no grand conspiracy behind his father's shooting. Maybe there was just a sad, sick girl who had engineered her own horrifying release.

"Tell us about the party," Somers said.

Dusty frowned; he looked lost, paddling to stay afloat in his own dark thoughts.

"Dusty. What happened at the party?"

"We got there late."

"You and Frank and Hadley?"

"No, just me and Frank. We—Frank didn't want to go. I did. We kind of had it out."

"But you went."

"Yeah, we went. And Hadley wouldn't have anything to do with us. She wouldn't talk to us. She'd barely look at us. Frank just wanted to leave, and I felt stupid. I mean, we didn't fit in. But I didn't want to leave either. Hadley had invited us. I knew—" He bit back what he'd been about to say, and the pain of it was visible in his face. "I thought she wanted to make things right. So I made Frank stay." The pain in his face intensified, pinching his features, and he burst out, "You think she did all that? You think she wanted to die? Jesus, I didn't know. I wouldn't have—I never would have let her do something like that."

"We don't know what happened, Dusty. That's what we're trying to figure out. Can you tell me about the rest of the night? What did you see? Were you there when Mr. Stillwell got there?"

"Is that his name, the guy who shot her?"

"That's his name."

Dusty considered that for a moment. His eyes looked dry, but he wiped at them again, and when he spoke, his voice was stronger. "We got there after him. People were still talking about it, and I knew he was in the back room, but I didn't really pay any attention. We were there for Hadley."

"You didn't see him?"

"No."

"You didn't see anyone go back there?"

"What? No. Just you guys. And then Hadley's dad came back, and then the sheriff and the mayor came back."

"Anything else? Anyone who went in the kitchen?"

"I don't know."

"What about you?"

"What?"

"You and Frank went back there. You pulled Hadley off Mr. Somerset and took her back there."

"No, we didn't—"

"Dusty, don't lie to me. We saw you go back, my partner and I."

"We just—I had to talk to Hadley. Frank told me I was being stupid, but I had to. I had to know if she'd been lying, if that phone call was a lie, if she just dragged us to that party to, I don't know, to rub it in our faces. But we didn't do anything. We just went into the kitchen."

"Not into the TV room?"

"Is that the big room? No."

"Not outside."

"No." That was a lie, though; it showed in Dusty's furtive glance away from Somers.

"You didn't go outside?"

"No, I told you."

"What did the three of you do?"

"Nothing. Hadley wouldn't talk. She wouldn't even stand still. She got away from us and went into the bathroom, and then Frank got pissed and left and I had to stand there like an idiot."

"Did you see a bag?" Hazard said.

"No."

"A pink bag with fake fur trim. White fur. Kind of like a Santa Claus bag."

Dusty's mouth dropped open. "How'd you know about that?"

"So you did see it?"

"Yeah."

"Where?" Somers asked.

"At her house."

"Whose house?"

"Hadley's. That's her bag, that's what you're talking about, right? Her Victoria's Secret bag?"

"Pink with white fur trim. Looks like Santa's bag, but the wrong color."

"Yeah, that's her bag. You found it?"

"Why don't you tell us about it first?" Somers said.

Again, Dusty flushed, and his eyes flitted to the darkened hallway. "This was back in November. Black Friday. She was doing some shopping, and I asked her to—aw, Jesus." He paused, buried his face in his hands, and in a muffled voice said, "Do I have to?"

"It's important," Hazard said, his voice a whip-crack.

"It was just for fun. I asked her to pick out some stuff. For—" He bit his lip. "For, um. Frank. Come on, do I really have to?"

"What happened?"

"She bought it. She showed it to me. Then she said she was going to play Santa this year, like she was going to keep it all in the bag and then give everything to Frank in person, just to see what he did. I couldn't talk her out of it. I didn't really want to talk her out of it. This was—this was before things had gotten bad, and I knew Frank would like that kind of game."

"Then you had a falling out."

"No. Well, yeah, but before that, somebody broke into her car and stole it. The bag and everything. I mean, I was bummed, but it was kind of a relief. I didn't know how I was going to look her in the eyes after I watched her give that stuff to Frank."

Somers fought to conceal a smile at the boy's discomfort. "And?"

"That's it. I mean, she never found it. I'd already given her the money for it, and that really sucked."

A trickle of the same worry ran through Somers. This was all so strange. It was obvious, now, that Hadley had somehow been involved in his father's shooting. But had she been an easy ruse, a way for the killer to try to hide his tracks by drawing attention to a disturbed girl with a violent history? Or had the shooting really been aimed at her, and Glenn Somerset was an innocent—at least, relatively—bystander?

"You didn't see the bag at the party?"

"What? No. Why?"

Somers didn't answer, but his thoughts turned to their other eyewitness statements. Jeremiah Walker had seen Wayne Stillwell carrying a pink bag. Bing had seen him carrying a red bag. And Daisy claimed that Stillwell hadn't been carrying a bag at all. Somers didn't have Hazard's ruthless logic, mapping out possibilities and then crossing them off. But he did have his gut, and he trusted his gut.

Right then, his gut was telling him something was wrong with all of this. Something that made him nervous.

"Anything else?" Somers asked. "Anything strange you noticed?"

Dusty shook his head.

"We're done here," Hazard said.

But as Hazard turned to go, another question bubbled up out of the depths of Somers's mind. He fished in his pocket and brought up the length of silver chain that he had found at his parents' house, dropped near the outdoor heaters. The heaters that had so conveniently been used to cause a blackout.

He already knew the answer to his question by the shadow of horror that passed across Dusty's face.

"Is this yours?"

"No."

"Dusty."

"No. It's not." A pause. "What? Why are you looking at me like that?"

"Dusty."

"It's not mine. It's fucking not mine."

"It's an interesting piece." Somers settled the length of chain, with its broken heart, across his palm. "This looks like it's meant to be one of a pair. I imagine boyfriend and girlfriend usually exchange them."

"Or boyfriend and boyfriend," Hazard said.

"Yeah, so what? I already told you, it's not mine." Dusty shifted in his seat and then sprang to his feet. "Look, can you go?"

"Sit down," Somers said.

"I want you to go."

"Sit down," Hazard said in that same whip-crack.

Color drained from Dusty's face, and he collapsed onto the stool. Hunched and shivering, his face washed white, he looked like he'd been dragged out of a frozen lake.

"This is yours," Somers said. "The clasp is worn out. See here. That's how it fell off; the clasp slipped, and it fell right off you, and you never knew."

Shaking his head, Dusty blew out his cheeks; he looked like a man desperately trying to hold his breath.

Somers spoke carefully. He wasn't sure of his theory, not entirely, and he knew he had to keep his outline vague or risk exposing himself to contradiction. "You're not telling me something, Dusty. You lied to me. You told me you didn't go outside, but here's the proof. Where did Frank go when he got upset? Where did you go while he and Hadley were gone?"

Dusty rocked silently on his stool.

"I guess there are a couple of possibilities. Maybe you went outside to the heaters. Maybe you knew what was going to happen because you'd set the whole thing up. Maybe you were tired of how Hadley had been treating you. Maybe you could have put up with that, but you couldn't stand what she was doing to Frank. For him, you would have done just about anything. Including getting rid of Hadley. You said it yourself. You couldn't stand it anymore."

"No," Dusty said, the word bursting out of him in terror.

"I saw the other piece of this necklace in Frank's room. It was just lying there. Did you have a fight? Did he throw it at you?"

"No," Dusty moaned.

Somers waited, considering the tortured boy. "All right. Here's another possibility: maybe it was Frank. Did he hate Hadley so much that he planned this out? Was he jealous that you slept with her? You say he wasn't, but a lot of guys don't know how bad jealousy stings until they feel it themselves. Maybe he didn't enjoy seeing you two together. Maybe that was eating away at him. And the way she treated him, the things she did to him—maybe you're right. Maybe it wasn't you out at the heaters. Maybe—"

"No," Dusty said, his voice thick, his eyes fever-bright and fixed on Somers. "It's mine. I did what you were saying. I went out to the heaters. I had to get out of that house. I just needed air, and it must have fallen off. But I didn't do anything else, I swear."

"You're a fucking terrible liar." The voice came from the hallway. Frank stood there. Wrapped in a blanket, his eyes red-rimmed and puffy, he looked like death—or maybe death after a round in the microwave. "It's not his. It's mine. I did it."

"What did you do?" Somers said.

"No," Dusty shouted. "Shut up, Frank." Somers tried to speak, but Dusty launched off the stool. "Just shut your mouth, all right? I'm handling this."

Even with the color of a day-old corpse, Frank still had a perfect sneer. "You? Handling this? Please. You don't even know what you're saying."

"What did you do, Frank?" Somers asked again.

"Nothing," Dusty said, interposing himself, his arms wide with incredulity. "He didn't do anything. He's just saying stuff. I don't know why, but he's just talking."

"I killed Hadley."

The words sucked the air from the room. Dusty grew smaller, shrinking into his hoodie, his broad shoulders drooping into a tired vee. "He didn't. He's just talking."

"How?" Again, Hazard's voice cut through the thick air.

Frank looked momentarily startled. "What?"

"How did you do it?" Hazard pronounced each word carefully, slowly, as though speaking to someone not too bright.

The words stained Frank's cheeks pink, and he tilted his head again, that look of a man ready to take a punch and then throw a mean hook. "Like you said. I went outside. I messed with the heaters. That's what made the lights go out."

Somers could read the lie in the boy's posture, in his belligerence, in the frantic light in his eyes as he scrambled to complete his story.

"And?" Hazard said.

"What do you mean?"

"She wasn't killed by the heaters. Or by the lights going out."

"All right. I gave that creep a gun."

"Where'd you get the gun?"

"What the fuck does it matter? It's my necklace. I was out there. I'm telling you I did it, all right? Jesus Christ, will you just arrest me already."

Somers shook his head and got up; the chair creaked in relief. "You're lying."

"I'm lying? I'm lying, you miserable piece of shit? I just told you I killed her. I did. I'd kill her again, a hundred times, just shoot that cunt right in the—" He had worked himself into hysterics, the words peaking into a shrill shriek before the boy threw himself at Somers. Dusty caught him, wrestled him back, and pinned him against the wall. Frank fought him for longer than Somers expected; it made the earlier struggle in the bedroom look tame, and when Frank finally collapsed, exhausted, he had torn the stitching in Dusty's hoodie and had left bloody scratches down the bigger boy's face.

"He didn't do it," Dusty said, breathing heavily. "If you want to take somebody in, you can take me."

"We don't want to take anybody in," Somers said in exasperation, "not yet. But we do want to know why this was outside near the heaters."

Dusty's eyes moved to Frank's face and then dropped to the kitchen floor. Neither boy spoke.

"I don't know," Dusty finally said, eyes still fixed on the ground. "It must be what you said: I went outside and dropped it. But that's all that happened. Neither of us wanted to hurt Hadley. Can you go? Can you just go now?"

"Did you see anyone else out there?"

"Half the party was out there at one point or another."

"Anything else you can tell us? Anything strange?"

"I don't know." Dusty's eyes flicked to Hazard and Somers and Frank and then back to the thick white cotton socks he wore.

"That's a lie."

"Look, can you just—hey."

Interrupting Dusty's answer, Frank wriggled free and started down the hall.

"Hold on," Hazard said, and without waiting for an answer, Hazard strode after Frank, his huge stride eating up the space between them. Frank barely had time for one panicked glance over his shoulder before Hazard had reached him. One of Hazard's big hands caught Frank's wild hair, and the other hand got his shoulders, and Hazard steered the slender boy to the end of the hall and spun him so that they faced each other.

"He's not going to—" Dusty said.

"No. He won't hurt him."

But what the hell was he doing, Somers wondered.

Hazard spoke to Frank in a low voice, so low that Somers couldn't make out the words. At first Frank shook his head. Then he tried to push past Hazard, with the result that Hazard slammed him back into the wall hard enough to shake dust from the light fixtures. Dusty took a nervous step, and Somers caught his sleeve. Still speaking, head bent low, Hazard was taut with some kind of internal force. This time Frank seemed to listen, and after almost a minute, he nodded.

When Hazard returned, Frank stayed right where he was, staring at the three of them like he'd sailed around the world in the last two minutes: a little wobbly, a little crazily, like he'd never see things the same way again.

"You finished?" Somers asked, hoping his tone sounded neutral.

Hazard grunted.

"You think of anything else you want to tell me," Somers said as he stuffed a card into Dusty's hand, "you call. Whatever you're worried about it, it can't be worse than letting a murderer go free." He slid the chain into his pocket. "Until then, I'm keeping this."

Together, Hazard and Somers left the two boys in the silent, freezing darkness of the house, with nothing for warmth but the yellowed light bulbs. The snow had settled. The wind had dropped. Their footsteps, as they followed the walk, raised the crackle of old, hard snow. There might have been nobody else in the world, and they were leaving those boys in a cold, black ocean. Somers felt his stomach flip over.

Once they were settled in the VW, as Hazard pulled away from the curb, Somers said, "They didn't do it."

Hazard grunted derisively.

"But they know something. They saw something. They're scared, maybe. But they're keeping something back."

No response from Hazard.

"What'd you say to him? Frank, I mean."

The silence felt as brittle as the crust on the old snow. A moment later, the VW's heaters kicked on, and the only noise was the whoosh of stale air.

"Ree."

Nothing.

"Ree."

"What?"

"Did you—the two of them, you know. Did it make you think?" Somers wanted to say more, but the rest of the words were stuck in his throat. Did it make you think about us, he wanted to say. About how things might have been. If I hadn't been afraid. If I hadn't been such a bastard.

"I thought we just agreed they didn't have anything to do with it."

"That's not—I mean, did they remind you of anything?"

Hazard shifted too hard and too fast, and the little VW lurched and croaked. The town blurred around them as they drove into the darkness.

CHAPTER TWENTY-NINE

**DECEMBER 23
SATURDAY
7:12 PM**

INSTEAD OF TAKING THE VW into the parking garage at the Crofter's Mark, Hazard pulled up to the curb. He turned too fast. The car clipped the cement and bounced. He hit the brake too hard. The VW snapped his head forward and then back. He was doing everything like shit tonight, everything, and he locked his hands on the wheel because they were still shaking.

Still. After fifteen minutes, he still felt like he was holding on to one of those electronic bucking broncos, one of those mechanical bulls that tried to throw you clean off.

It had been ok until the end when he had pressed that dark-haired twink into a corner and told him, just straight-out told him, that he was making a mistake. And then the shaking had started. Maybe he was sick. People got like this when they were sick, didn't they? He'd had the flu as a boy—not the stomach flu, the real flu, influenza—and he remembered lying in bed, covers tucked under his chin, shaking like he was going to work all his screws loose and fall apart.

"Are you sweating?" Somers said.

The engine rumbled. The heaters whooshed. Somers still hadn't gotten out of the car because he was Somers and couldn't make anything easier. When they'd walked out of the house, when they'd gotten into the VW, when they'd pulled away from the curb, they could have left it at that. But Somers had to ask. Somers had to put it into words. Did they remind you of anything?

Bad enough to have to see that, wasn't it? Bad enough to have to see those two kids. Hazard had never watched the *Twilight Zone*, but he knew the general idea, had picked it up from imitations, from pop culture references. The *Twilight Zone*. That's what he'd gone into. He just walked through a door, just like on that show, walked through a door and into a dark, freezing house, and he'd seen this other world. This whole other fucking world where he might have been happy. And that's what he'd told that shivering twink with the blanket wrapped around his shoulders. You're being stupid. What he really wanted to say was you're being a fucking moron, but he said you're being stupid.

"So," Somers said, drawing out the word. "Are you going to park?"

"No."

"Are you ok?"

No. Not even close. How could he be ok when he'd gone through that damn door and come out like this, with his head spinning, seeing that other life? If he and Somers had been born twenty years later, would they—

You're being stupid. That's what he'd said to the kid. Why couldn't the kid see it? He was lucky. He didn't have any goddamn idea how lucky he was.

"I'm going over to Nico's."

"We should probably talk about—"

"I'm going to Nico's."

"All right. Yeah, we can pick this up in the morning."

Then nothing.

"Get out of the car."

"Right," Somers said with an easy laugh. "I just thought . . ."

Again, that enormous silence.

"Ree," Somers said. "Do you want to talk?"

Hazard shook his head.

"All right, we'll hit this hard tomorrow morning."

"Hit what?"

Somers leaned back. "What do you mean? The case."

"Yeah? What's next?"

"I—"

"Who do we talk to? What do we do?"

"What are you talking about? We do what we always do: we keep looking, we go back over everything, we start at the beginning and work our way through it all over again."

"There's nothing left to look at. We've got no forensics—whatever they collected, we can't get to it because we're not working a real case. Our witnesses can't tell us shit about what happened. Nobody can agree on anything: did he have a gun, did he have a bag, who said what. It's all a mess."

"It's always a mess. And we always work through it. What's going on with you?"

"There's nothing logical about this. There's no rational explanation for why anyone would have tried to kill your father or Hadley. We had one lead, one solid lead with that recording, and then we turn around and the mayor asks us to stop investigating. Boom. There goes the only real motive we have, out the window. All we're left with are feelings, suggestions, innuendoes. It's a—it's a quagmire. It's like quicksand. There's nothing to hold on to."

"So, what? You want to give up?"

"Let's talk about this tomorrow."

"Forget that. We're talking about it right now."

Hazard kept silent.

"That's it?" Somers didn't sound angry so much as he did confused. And hurt. "You're not going to tell me anything?"

"Tomorrow."

"Yeah, Ree. Tomorrow. You're good at that. We can always push it off a little bit longer, right?"

Hazard locked his gaze on his hands.

With a disgusted noise, Somers got out of the car. Then Hazard drove to Nico's. He didn't remember the drive, only the sense of movement, rocketing through the dark until he stood outside Nico's door, his knuckles rapping an unsteady rhythm.

Nico opened the door an inch and leaned against the frame. This was it: a hundred percent Nico. Thick, dark hair spilling to the middle of his ears, coppery skin exposed by a ratty In-and-Out t-shirt, mesh gym shorts that barely came halfway down his long, muscled thighs. And those movie-star good looks that disguised intelligence and compassion and vulnerability. Everybody that had fucked this boy had also managed to fuck him up. Hazard understood that: Alec and Billy had done the same to him. Hazard's hands were still shaking, and he put one on the doorjamb.

"No," Nico said and started to shut the door.

Hazard slid his foot into the crack, wincing as the leather compressed. Planting his other hand on the door, he said, "I want to talk to you."

"I don't want to talk to you."

"You asked me a question."

For a moment, it looked like Nico might continue to fight him. Then, with a sigh, he stepped back and let the door swing open. He walked deeper into the apartment, past the kitchen, past a pile of dirty clothes, past a plate with a half-eaten grilled cheese, past a mountain of beer bottles. Those were new. Hazard took up his place near the brown glass. Nico kept moving until the sofa stood between them.

"I don't want to hear your shitty explanation," Nico said, folding his arms across his chest. His eyes, dark like the black edges of butterfly wings, glistened.

"You asked me a question."

Nico laughed, the sound broken and hitched. "All right, fine. I do want to hear your shitty explanation. You came over here. What? You want to break up with me? Fine, I'll save you the work. We're done. This is over. I'm going out of town anyway. I've got a job. Just a few days work for a shoot, but I'm going to stay in the city until classes pick up again." He kicked something, and a roller suitcase inched into view, already half-packed with Nico's normal messiness, the clothes looking like the aftermath of an explosion. "So you did it. You can go home. You don't have to worry about me. I'll—"

"Can I say one goddamn word?" It came out louder than Hazard had meant it to, and Nico jumped backward, bracing himself in the bedroom doorway like he expected Hazard to charge.

Nico nodded, but his fingers were white where he clutched the jamb.

"You think I'm in love with Somers." Hazard's eyes dropped to the sofa, to the tufted buttons pulling free, to the floorboards.

"You are in love with him. And if you say you aren't, if you even fucking try to deny it, I'll—Jesus, I don't know, Emery. I'll go crazy."

The worst part was making himself meet Nico's eyes. The worst, hardest part, but Hazard made himself, dragging his gaze up, across the sofa, across the holey t-shirt and the flat planes of Nico's chest, up until their eyes met. Those eyes were like bottomless wells, and Nico was really crying now, but his breathing was steady as though this, no matter how much it hurt, was better than what he'd been feeling before.

"I do." Those were the two hardest words Hazard had ever said. Twenty years of hiding, twenty years of lying—to himself, to the world, to everyone that had ever mattered to him—twenty years of fear, but now he'd said it. Now it was out there. "It's messed up. I can't explain it. I should hate him. For a long time, I did hate him. But I came back, and he was different, and what I felt for him when I was a kid—" He broke off, but he kept his gaze locked on Nico's face. Nico was crying harder now, but still silently. That was worse, somehow. Worse than screaming, worse than ragged sobs. "It doesn't make any sense, but I do. I love him. I wish I didn't. I wish I didn't feel any of this. I think about what he did to me, and I hate him. But— but it's like that was someone else. And the one here, the one with me, the one that's my partner, he's different. He's better."

"All right," Nico said in a muffled voice, slashing at his eyes with the heel of his hand. "I'm really happy for you. I wish you guys the very fucking best—"

"I'm not done. It doesn't matter how I feel about him. He's got a wife and a little girl. He's got a life. And I'm happy I fit into part of that life. I like being his partner. He's a good detective. We're a good team. But I don't want to ruin the rest of his life just because I have a crush on him."

"It's more than a crush."

"Maybe." Hazard shrugged. "But I care about you too. You're sweet. And you're funny. And you—you put up with me. Somers tells me that, and I'm not stupid. I know you don't want to watch documentaries on the weekend. I know you don't want to sit around the apartment and read. But you do it. And you're thoughtful. You bring dinner to the station when I'm working late. You throw in a load of laundry when I'm caught up in work. You remember things I like and buy them for me. Pomegranate juice. I said one time that I liked it, and you always have it in the fridge." This wasn't working, Hazard realized. He could make a list of all the things he liked about Nico. He could do it all day long. But it was missing something. It didn't get to the heart of it.

And what was the heart of it? What was the thing he couldn't put into words, the thing that he felt for this beautiful, intelligent, caring young man? "I like how I feel when you're around. I like that you make me want to be better. I like the way you feel under me, the way we fit together." Hazard's face felt hot, and he stumbled. "Fuck. I'm shit at this."

"No," Nico said. "You're doing all right."

And everything shifted. The tension in the air had changed, no longer a storm brewing, but something else. Something burning at the bottom of Hazard's belly. He knew that look in Nico's eyes. He knew what the boy needed. Hazard picked his way around the sofa, over the luggage, past the dirty clothes.

"We can't keep going the way we've been," Nico said.

Hazard kissed him. Hard. And Nico melted against the door jamb, his body wrapping around Hazard's. The hardness of his muscles. The hardness between his legs.

"All right," Hazard murmured, breaking the kisses.

"We aren't watching those dumb documentaries all weekend anymo—"

Hazard trailed kisses down the side of Nico's neck. Nico moaned and thrust against him.

"All right."

"We—we—"

Hazard's teeth had found Nico's collarbone, scraping over the skin, pulling it gently taut.

"We—we—we've got to go out sometimes."

Drawing both hands up Nico's chest, Hazard seized the In-and-Out t-shirt and ripped it in half. It fell away, exposing the planes of lean muscles.

"Oh fuck," Nico groaned as Hazard trailed kisses across his pecs. "Oh fuck. You've got to make time for me, you've got to talk to me, you've got to tell—" This time, he wailed as Hazard's teeth tightened over the stiff tip of a nipple. Hazard stayed there, his tongue massaging the bruised flesh, teeth flicking open and shut as Nico moaned and thrust against him. Hazard yanked the shorts down. No underwear. The boy was a fucking underwear model and he still went commando half the year. If that wasn't irony—

"You've got to be honest," Nico said, his voice a ragged echo of its normal confidence. "You've got to talk to me." They didn't sound like a list of demands anymore. Nico was begging. His long fingers tangled in Hazard's hair, pulling Hazard's mouth tight against his savaged nipple, while Hazard's hands stroked the inside of Nico's thighs. The boy puled, thrusting again, trying to achieve some form of contact while Hazard teased him, staying just out of range.

"I know," Hazard said, relenting to the sound of the boy's tortured cries, taking Nico's hardness in his hand as the boy collapsed into him. His breath was hot as he whispered in Nico's ear. "I will."

CHAPTER THIRTY

DECEMBER 23
SATURDAY
10:37 PM

NICO WAS ASLEEP, and his breathing was soft. Hazard lay next to him. For a long time, he lay thinking, and then he rose and carried his clothes into the kitchen and shut the bedroom door. He splashed water from the sink on his chest and cleaned up with a paper towel and then he dressed and went out into the cold.

Tonight, like all nights, was about emptiness. Emptiness between Hazard and the slushy streets. Between the streets and the city. Between the city and the wildness around it. Emptiness out to the stars. The only sounds were the granular crunch of Hazard's footsteps, and the VW's clunky turn-over, and the soft snow under the tires.

He drove back towards the old part of town, and his thoughts were divided: behind him, Wroxall College, the new developments of coffee shops and clothing boutiques and trendy bistros, and Nico; ahead of him, Market Street, and then Jefferson Street, and the Sheriff's Department, and—

—Somers—

—the case.

Instead of parking on Jefferson Street, though, Hazard wove through the back alleys until he found a stretch of curb to leave the VW. He trudged through the snow. Security lights splashed white cones across dumpsters and chipped brick. A convex mirror gave back Hazard's warped reflection, looming closer and closer and then shrinking back as he passed it. Even here there was a great deal of emptiness, even in these tight brick corridors, even with a tent of sodium lights blocking out the stars.

The Sheriff's Department, along with the county jail, was a long, low building. It buzzed with electric illumination. When Hazard passed through the automatic doors, the smell of burnt coffee whooshed out at him. At the desk, a tired-looking young woman wore a khaki deputy's uniform.

"Detective Emery Hazard. I need access to the evidence lock-up." He passed her his badge.

She nodded, barely seeming to see the badge, and produced a key with a large, plastic tag. "Don't lose it," she said. "Last guy from city PD lost it and we had hell to pay."

"Where do I go?"

"Down the hall. On your right before you hit the jail."

That was it. Hazard's bones were buzzing like fluorescent tubes. That was all it took. Just don't lose it. He'd had plans. He'd had stories. He'd had a whole explanation worked out, and that was it: don't lose it. Jesus, it was a small town, and somehow he kept forgetting that.

The lock-up was where the deputy had said, and the key opened the door, and Hazard found himself standing in a room that, on first glance, could have been mistaken for a janitor's supply closet. Bankers boxes sat on storage racks. Two light panels overhead thrummed; above them, darkness hung down. The linoleum stuck to Hazard's shoe as he took a step.

He moved between the racks, checking the dates, and moved towards the most recent cases. There, on the front of a single bankers box, were marked two investigations: Somerset, Glenn. And Stillwell, Wayne. Hazard slid the box from the shelf and opened it.

Inside, a cardboard divider separated the box. On one side, evidence bags held Wayne Stillwell's gun and the casings recovered from the Somerset home. Six brass casings. Five bullets had struck Glenn Somerset and he had lived. One had struck Hadley Bingham and she had died. Hazard withdrew from his pocket the casing that he and Somers had found in the garbage at the Somerset home. And that was seven. Seven casings. Because Wayne Stillwell had shot one of the ornaments. That had been his very first shot.

In addition to the casings, that side of the box held miscellaneous evidence collected at the Somerset home: a fragment of glass from a broken ornament; photographs of different rooms in the Somerset house, a hundred different angles showing the blood-stained floor under the Christmas tree; a scant handful of witness statements. Evidence, but surprisingly little of it. Or maybe not that surprising. The sheriff had made sure that the investigation ended as soon as Stillwell died. Hazard took his time flipping through the photographs, reading the statements, and thinking. He even lifted the glass shard in its plastic bag, turning it, studying. No revelations came. No handcuffs, either. The cuffs that Somers had used to secure Stillwell were missing, just as Cravens had said. Who had taken them?

On the other side of the divider, where a piece of Scotch tape read *Stillwell*, a revolver sat in an evidence bag. That was Lender's gun, which was still being held as part of the official investigation. Next to it were the five casings from the hospital parking lot. Five shots. That's what Lender had emptied into Stillwell's chest. That was a hell of a lot to kill a man who was handcuffed. And where was the rest of the evidence? At the police station?

There was something wrong here. Hazard knew it. He could feel it. His mind was turning the puzzle pieces, trying to make them fit. Something was wrong here, and at least in part, it went back to the casings. How had one of the casings ended up in the garbage at the Somerset house? Had it been an accident? Had one of the cops working the scene been careless or lazy? Or had it been more than that? Had someone intentionally removed the casing? And if so—this was what puzzled Hazard—why?

For a while, he stayed there, lost in the cool flow of proposition, evidence, analysis, conclusion, and then beginning all over again.

Nothing came to him, though. He was too tired. He smelled Nico on him, and his skin itched, and he wanted a shower and bed. Shoving the box back into its place, Hazard left the evidence lock-up and returned the key with its big plastic tag. The deputy didn't even glance at him. A pale glow from the monitor played over her face, and she was lost in the shuffle of another game of solitaire.

Then, instead of turning for home, Hazard went back to Nico's apartment.

CHAPTER THIRTY-ONE

DECEMBER 24
SUNDAY
10:00 AM

SOMERS HAD TRIED. He really had. He'd gone for a run. He'd taken a cold shower. He'd swallowed a couple of Benadryl and shoved his head under the pillows, determined to fall asleep by force of will.

It hadn't worked. He'd been angry at Hazard for suggesting that the case might not be solvable. And he'd been horny. Horny because fighting with Hazard often ended with him feeling horny. There was something about the way the big man shut down, about the brooding silence he wrapped himself in, that really cranked Somers's motor. He'd been horny, too, because of Dusty and Frank. Not because of them, the boys themselves, but because it had gotten him thinking about the past, and about what might have been, about—

—love—

—the mind-blowing, heart-pumping, nuclear-blast-furnace sex that he and Hazard could have been having. In high school. In college. And the thoughts and images had continued. He'd seen Hazard naked as a teenager. He'd seen him naked as a man. Somers had a good memory, and it wasn't hard for his imagination to fill in the gaps. And there were a lot of gaps he wanted to fill.

Finally he called Cora. It went to voicemail. He called again. Voicemail again, and this time he told her he wanted to talk. About finances. That had been a game, a code, something from early in their marriage when a fight about the water bill had turned into hot, steaming sex. And now, here he was, making a booty call to his estranged wife because right then Hazard and Nico were probably—

Jesus, he just couldn't finish that thought.

Cora had texted a simple reply: *Finances are all taken care of.*

And that had started the earthquakes again, those tremors so deep inside Somers that he thought he might be coming apart. Hazard had Nico, and that had been all right until now, until this moment. Finances are all taken care of. What did that mean? What the fuck did that mean?

And he'd started to drink, because it was either drink or drive over to the little house that he still paid a mortgage on and pick a fight, and it was easier to drink, and it was safer, and he could pack all those sharp-edged, dangerous thoughts about Hazard and Cora and about this case in alcohol's fluffy wool and not feel quite so shitty for a while.

When his phone rang the next morning, the sound hurt his head. But it was more than a sound. It had a whining, piercing vibration to it. Like somebody had put a drill bit to one of his teeth. Blindly, Somers groped for the phone.

"What?"

"Happy birthday." Cora didn't sound angry, but she rarely sounded angry. She got angry, sure. Often. But she usually didn't sound it. Unless you'd been married to her. Unless you could pick out those sharp slivers of silence.

"Oh shit."

"Are you going to make an appearance?"

"I'm sorry."

"Should I tell everyone to go home?"

"No, I'm—" Somers lurched upright. A white star of pain took up one side of his head, and for a moment, the room tilted and wobbled. "I'm sick, that's all."

"You're sick."

"I'm on my way."

"I'll just tell everyone—"

"No. You put a lot of work into this. It means—" He would have told her how much it meant to him, but the need to vomit overwhelmed him. For a moment, he fought the urge, and then he managed to control the bile rising in his throat. He struggled to speak, but all that came out was a short, sharp burp.

"Happy birthday, John-Henry." Cora ended the call.

He brushed his teeth, dragged on clothes, and grabbed a bottle of water and two Tylenol on the way out the door. Even as a walking disaster, Somers noticed that Hazard hadn't come home last night. Fuck him, Somers thought. His head hurt too much to even try to explain why his anger was justified.

When he got to the little house—his little house, technically, although he hadn't slept under the roof in almost a year—the cars lined the street on both sides, and he had to go to the end of the block and park in the cul-de-sac. Trudging through the snow, shivering in the cold, Somers tried not to count the cars, but good Lord, how many people had she invited?

The home that Somers had bought with Cora was, by any standard, small. Two bedrooms, one bath, an unfinished basement. The front of the house was a little more generously proportioned, with a substantial living room and a genuine, independent dining room (barely big enough for two grown men to play cards in). By Somerset standards, it had been the approximate size of a gardening shack.

But that hadn't mattered to Somers. At least, it hadn't mattered much. He'd put in the picket fence, and now he let his frozen hand slide between the slats as he walked. He'd rehung the front shutters. He'd painted the porch. Other things, too. Things you couldn't see. Some of the wiring had been bad, and Somers had ripped it out and redone it. He'd learned a lot in shop class. Learned plenty, even if he had, at the end, called in an electrician just to be safe. He'd put in extra supports for the basements stairs, and he'd chiseled out a crack in the foundation and filled it with hydraulic cement. He'd done a hell of lot to this house, but right then, with most of the world buried in pigeon-colored snow, the house looked worse than ever.

The thought put him in a foul mood. Maybe that was just the way of the world. Maybe that's how everything was. You put time and effort and energy and love into something. You work on it from the bones up. You make it yours—not because you did something silly like pay for it, but because you worked for it, because you put part of yourself into it, and so it became part of you. And at the end, what? You stand outside in the snow, and everything looks like shit. And he didn't know if he was thinking of the house or—

—Hazard—

—Cora or what. Maybe everything. Maybe that's just how everything was.

He stopped on the porch long enough to kick snow from his shoes, and the door swung open. Bing stood there. Inside the house. Inside Somers's house. And again Somers felt the old need to please, to impress, to win Bing's approval, and with it, he felt the old mixture of shame and fear. Because Bing knew. Bing just goddamn knew.

Bing had a pale grin, but it was a knowing grin, and that old fear spiked inside Somers. "Rough night?" He clapped Somers on the shoulder. "Jesus, man, what were you doing?"

"Just a couple of bad days." Somers realized what he'd said and added, "Sorry, I didn't—"

"No. It has. It's been a couple of really bad days."

They stood in silence there on the porch. Bing looked older than he ever had before. His cheeks sagged; the gray in his curls was more pronounced; his eyes were bloodshot.

"You didn't have to come," Somers said, tipping his head towards the house. "What you've been through—"

"You saw Daisy. What was I going to do? Stay home with that?"

Somers didn't have any idea how to answer.

"Come on," Bing said. "Cora sent me to find you." His pallid grin sharpened. "I was afraid I was going to have to drag you out of someone's bed."

"I was home," Somers said, trying to make the statement without sounding defensive.

"That's exactly what I meant."

Fear and humiliation spiked again inside Somers, but before he could respond, Bing surged back into the house, and Somers trailed him.

The house was packed, and cheers went up throughout the cramped space. Neighbors, friends, people from Cora's work with the arts. Birthday wishes rang out as men pumped Somers's hand and women planted kisses on his cheeks. Some of the kisses were boozy—Cora always served mimosas—and some of the kisses lasted a little longer than necessary. Some of the kisses, too, were followed by wandering hands, and Somers worked his way through the crowded space as fast as he dared. He knew he had a nice ass. He didn't even mind having it admired. But the crush of people, the sudden heat, and the barrage of sound and smell had combined with the hangover to put Somers on the verge of a migraine.

Bing cleared a path ahead of Somers, and eventually he completed the gauntlet of well-wishers. In the relative safety of the kitchen doorway, Somers finally had a chance to draw a breath and glance over the people assembled. This combination of birthday party and holiday celebration had become a tradition for Somers and Cora, and it was something that friends and neighbors had come to enjoy too—at least, Somers was fairly sure that they enjoyed it, based on how many mimosas they drank. Everything looked as it had every year: fir garlands, the Christmas tree moved back into one corner, a table laden with food—Somers noticed, his stomach flopping anxiously, that Miranda Carmichael had brought a variant of her onion-and-tomato salad. People were happy. People were singing. People were drinking. Wind back the clock 365 days, and John-Henry Somerset would have said that it was perfect.

So why didn't it feel perfect now? He was back in his home. He was with friends and family. Things with Cora were looking better than they had in months. In a little while, if things kept up, Somers would be back in this house. He'd be sleeping in his old bed. He'd be worrying his old worries: was the roof leaking? why had the water bill gone up? who was picking up Evie this Thursday?

"Back here," Bing said, interrupting Somers's thoughts. "Before she kills me."

They worked their way into the kitchen, into the domestic heart of the party. Cora stood next to the stove, stirring the potpourri, which filled the air with the smell of cinnamon and cloves and blood oranges. Beside her, a champagne flute in one hand, stood Grace Elaine. And on the floor between them was Evie.

She was bigger, and that hurt. But the hurt, even though it went straight to the core, wasn't enough to mask Somers's delight at seeing his daughter. She had Cora's dark coloring, but she had Somers's features—softened, of course, but very much the same. When she saw him, she screamed, "Daddy," and bowled into him.

Sweeping her up, Somers peppered her with kisses, laughing as she squirmed and tried to push him away. "Down," Evie insisted, wriggling. "Down!" The last was a half-amused, half-frustrated scream, and Somers was laughing even harder as he set her on the floor.

"What are you—" He started to ask, but Evie let out an animated shrieked and lit off towards her bedroom.

"Twenty-four seven," Cora said with a smile. "Like she's running off Duracell."

This was always the most awkward part, the moment that betrayed the fissure in their relationship: the initial contact after sleeping a night apart. Somers tried to ignore the pounding in his head. He tried, too, to ignore the way Bing was watching him, as though waiting for the moment Somers slipped up. Somers smiled, kissed Cora's cheek, and slid an arm around her waist.

"You're late," Cora said, angling her body to force him away.

"Lot going on."

She eyed him. The drinking had been a problem before their marriage had fallen apart, but not in the same way. Back then, drinking had been a way to escape—

—home—

—the monotony of it all. Drinking had been fun, not a black hole that he tried to crawl into. But Cora had known him since high school, and she knew what he looked like hungover. She didn't say anything. She just turned her body, sliding free of his embrace, and kept stirring the potpourri.

"Mother," Somers said.

"You didn't bring him, did you?"

"What?"

Grace Elaine sipped at her mimosa. "You know who I mean."

Painfully aware of Bing's attention, Somers fought to keep his voice steady. "You're talking about my partner. My roommate. My friend."

"You've always been like this, John-Henry," Grace Elaine said. "I really don't understand it. You have these inexplicable predilections." She paused. Grace Elaine was subtle. She'd been dishing out poison for longer than Somers had been alive, and she didn't do anything as crass as let her gaze slip towards Cora. But the message was clear: this woman, this one right here, she's another of those inexplicable predilections. And to judge from how hard Cora was now stirring the potpourri—it was going to be a slurry if she kept hitting it like that—Cora had heard the insult as clearly as Somers had. "In any case, after what that boy did to you, I really can't—"

"That's enough," Somers said. Bing hadn't moved, hadn't so much as goddamn breathed, but right then Bing felt like a magnet, and it took all of Somers's willpower not to look at the other man. "That was a long time ago, Mother. It's over."

"I still think your father should have gone after him. It was perverted, really, and to let something like that—"

"That's enough." Somers hadn't yelled. Not quite. A yell, an honest-to-God yell, that would have been louder.

"You're so touchy," Grace Elaine said. She peered through the doorway into the crowded living room. "There's Moody. I absolutely have to talk to her about the Pickens' Christmas lights. They look like they're putting on a vaudeville show." Without further explanation, she glided out of the kitchen.

Bing was still silent. Still staring. It raised prickles on Somers. Anything would have been better than that knowing silence. Anything. If only Somers hadn't yelled. If he'd kept his voice cool. If he'd pretended he had no idea what his mother was talking about, or if he'd just passed it off with a laugh—anything but letting her get under his skin like that. Especially with Bing here, watching. Just goddamn watching. Why didn't he say something?

The sound of a child's tears broke the stillness in the kitchen. With a sigh, Cora laid down the spoon and stepped away from the potpourri.

"I'll check on her," Somers said.

"No. She's been fighting with Sara Padaleski, and we've been working on sharing." As though that were enough explanation—What, Somers wanted to ask, I can't teach her about sharing?—Cora left the kitchen, and then Somers was alone with Bing, alone with that knowing stare, alone with that silence.

If he'd just say something. If he'd just say one goddamn thing. Just like that night. Just like that. If he'd just said something then instead of staring at me. If I'd—

—not been such a fucking coward—

—had five more minutes to think instead of—

"I'm going to check on them," Somers said, not even knowing what he was saying, and he hurried into the cramped living room to escape that stare and that silence.

But he didn't make it more than a step. He stopped just past the kitchen doorway, at the edge of the throng that had invaded his home. His heart dropped, and he felt it splat somewhere around his knees. His mind began the inevitable catalogue: two six-packs in the fridge, the mimosas that Cora was serving, a bottle of Prosecco his father had given them last Christmas—where had Cora put it? In the pantry, right? Mother of God, it had to be in the pantry. But just as quickly, he scratched out all those possibilities and went back into the kitchen. Bing was still watching him, but now Somers didn't care. He worked the toe of one shoe under the cabinets, found the loose board near the oven, and tipped it forward. The bottle of Jose Cuervo rolled into sight and sloshed to a stop against Somers's other foot. It was a quarter full. That would have to be enough.

Because in the other room, Grace Elaine was talking to Hazard and Nico. It had only taken one look, just one look at her powdered face for Somers to know she was telling him. And she was fucking loving it.

CHAPTER THIRTY-TWO

**DECEMBER 24
SUNDAY
10:27 AM**

SOME ANIMALS, HAZARD KNEW, chewed off their own legs when they were caught in a trap. Foxes? Wolves? Maybe something smaller, maybe some type of rodent? It had seemed like such a stupid trait. Yes, Hazard understood why they did it. Intellectually, yeah, he got it. But it had still seemed stupid. That was the human part of him. That was the part of him that wanted to use reason and logic and analysis to disassemble problems. But right then, at the edge of Somers's birthday party, Hazard understood with a flash of visceral insight. Yes, he understood perfectly, and right then Hazard would have willingly chewed off his leg. He would have chewed off about goddamn anything if it got him out of this hot room that smelled like CVS cosmetics and sweat and orange juice from concentrate.

Why had he let Nico talk him into this? That was the dominant question in Hazard's mind as he stood near the doorway, scanning the crowded front room of Somers's home. He recognized most of the crowd. Most of them, truth be told, he recognized from his childhood. Wahredua had changed, but not that much, and there were too many familiar faces in this crowd. And, exactly as they had twenty years before, these faces quickly turned away when they saw Hazard. If you couldn't see him, he might not exist.

"Are we just going to lurk near the door?" Nico asked. He was actually wearing clothes—real, adult clothes, which was a goddamn miracle. And he had been the one who wanted to come. Nico. Nico, who couldn't even hear Somers's name without spitting fire and venom and God only knew what else. And here they were, with Nico's hand like a vise around Hazard's, and Nico was wearing chinos and a sweater and somehow it made him look—

—like an infant—

—even younger than he normally did.

"We're not lurking."

"We're literally shrinking into a corner by the door. That's pretty much the definition of lurking."

"Where do you want to go? It's like a pigpen in there. Take one step and you're walking in shit."

Nico didn't answer, but he scanned the crowd. "Hey, it's Al. Look." He waved.

Hazard's stomach dropped because it was, indeed, Albert Lender. The crooked cop stood on the far side of the room. In this setting, with his bristly mustache supporting plastic-framed glasses that looked like something Hazard's great aunt would wear, Lender didn't look like much of a threat. He looked like the kind of fellow who might own a dozen different pocket protectors, who might get upset if his tuna casserole touched his canned green beans, the kind of guy who's not even a threat in a bowling league. But he'd murdered a suspect in custody. And the month before, he'd tried to help murder Somers and Hazard.

"Is something wrong with your teeth?" Nico asked.

"What?"

"You're grinding your teeth. Does something hurt? Jesus, your face—do you want me to call my dentist?"

"I don't need a fucking—" Hazard tried to draw breath. This was it all over again, the kind of stuff that had precipitated the blow-up fight last night. "I'm fine. I have a headache."

Uh huh," Nico said.

Hazard barely heard him. His eyes were back on Lender. More specifically, they were on Lender's new gun: oiled metal visible where Lender's jacket hung open. An automatic. Nine millimeter, most likely. Not a ton of stopping power, but Lender was just carrying it until they returned his revolver from the evidence lock-up.

But something didn't feel right. A grain of sand in the watchwork of Hazard's thoughts. Something about Lender shooting Stillwell—

"Grace Elaine?" Nico's cheery tone—like he was greeting an old friend—dragged Hazard out of his thoughts. His attention refocused on the room just in time to see Somers's mother cutting through the crowd like a shark. The tasteful gray of her hair, the fashionable dress that showed off her slim figure, even the artificially smooth skin around her cool blue eyes, they all bespoke money. She was smiling, too, and for all Hazard could tell, it was just a normal smile. But that didn't explain why he wanted to check the .38 under his arm.

"My God," Nico said. "I didn't even think about the fact that you'd be here."

"You," Grace Elaine said, kissing his cheek, "are absolutely wicked. This is the one you've been talking about non-stop." Those same cool eyes—

—a coyote, Hazard suddenly remembered, it was a goddamn coyote that chewed its leg off in a trap—

—locking onto Hazard. "Why didn't you just say his name, pet? All this mysterious talk about the new man, about how quiet he was, about his—" Her voice dropped into a mock-whisper. "—ass, you should have told me."

Nico was blushing, but it was a good-natured blush that only accented his impossibly attractive looks. "Emery and I like to keep things quiet. I never really thought—I mean, the last name, of course, but I never really put it together—"

Grace Elaine laughed. "That I'm John-Henry's mother? You're not the first. John-Henry insists on using that ridiculous nickname, and he's always been so sensitive about his legacy, about how people see him. I don't have to tell you two about that, of course." She laughed again. "Emery knows all about this, of course. He and John-Henry went to high school together. They weren't friends, not back then, but they knew each other. Is that right, Detective?" Her attention suddenly transfixed Hazard. "Have I put that correctly?"

Hazard shrugged.

"Dragging an answer out of him," Nico said, shaking his head. "You might as well get blood from a stone."

"I intend to," Grace Elaine said with a serrated smile. "Nico, my drink is gone. Would you be a dear and get me another?"

"What? Oh, yes. Emery, do you—"

"No."

"I'll be right back."

And then it was just Hazard and Grace Elaine. The room was still full of people. Maybe twenty. Maybe thirty. So full that the smell of sweat and countertop cosmetics made an almost visible haze. But it was really just Hazard and Grace Elaine. It was just the two of them as if they'd stood on the surface of the moon, just the two of them.

"You weren't friends," Grace Elaine said, "were you? Back in high school, I mean?"

"No."

"Are you sure?"

Hazard frowned. Had she somehow learned about—

—the locker room—

—all the shit that had gone down between Hazard and Somers? The bullying, the assault, the torture?

"I'm sure."

"That's so strange," Grace Elaine said, her tone puzzled as she tapped a finger against her lips. "Why were you always at the football games?"

"What?"

"His football games. John-Henry's? Why were you always there?"

"They weren't his. They were the high school games."

"Why were you at his football games? And don't tell me you weren't. You were at all of them. You were always at the top of the stands. You were always watching him."

"It was the only thing to do in the whole town. It was my school too."

"No. You went because of him. You watched him. You—you wanted him." Her words had dropped into a hiss. "You were obsessed with him." Her blue eyes had gone wide and electric, and now she latched onto Hazard, her nails biting the inside of his arm. "You, with your sick, degenerate obsession. With your perversion. Are you happy? Are you happy with how his life turned out?"

For a long moment, Hazard remembered the sight of Somers their last night at Windsor. Somers, naked, hard, aching for Hazard's touch, had crawled towards him on the bed. Because he'd had a massive fight with Cora, true. Because he was lonely and hurt and confused, true. But he'd wanted Hazard. He'd said, that night, that he chose Hazard. And Grace Elaine's question echoed in Hazard's mind: are you happy with how his life turned out?

"Trapped in this town," she hissed, oblivious to Hazard's thoughts. Her nails dug deeper. "With a whore wife. With a dead-end job. He deserves better than this. He is better than this. And you had to—you had to ruin him. Watching him. Following him." Her hand jerked spasmodically, her nails driving deeper, and Hazard felt warmth bloom under the sleeve: blood darkened the fabric where her grip had punctured skin. "Touching him."

The locker room, the steam wisping up from Somers's golden skin, his chest just starting to broaden but still boyishly thin, and the feel of Somers's hand on Hazard's collarbone, the sudden, aching erection between Hazard's legs, and the kiss like sandpaper—

But that was it. That was the only time. And Hazard hadn't touched him. Hadn't dared to touch him because it might have been a trap, the whole thing might have been a set-up. So what was Grace Elaine talking about? Touching him. What the hell did that mean? Did she know about that night in Somers's apartment, when Hazard had pushed his partner to the edge of reason, kissing him, mauling him with his hands? Did she know about Windsor, about the way Hazard's touch had raised gooseflesh on Somers's chest, about—

"Here you are," Nico said, the cheer in his voice fading as he sensed the tension in the air. "Is everything—"

"What are you talking about?" Hazard asked.

"You know exactly what I'm talking about. You finally got what you wanted. You watched him. You followed him. You—" A floodgate broke inside Grace Elaine, and words poured out. "You would sit outside our house with binoculars. You would trail after him when he was on dates. He told me about the time you pressed yourself up against the Camaro. He told me that you—that you pleasured yourself on the glass. You stole his underwear, he told me that too. And you wore it, you sick, perverted—" The string of insults choked her.

Nico's eyes were huge. "Grace Elaine, whatever—"

"You took away his life and left him with this—this travesty," Grace Elaine said, her voice hoarse as though she'd been shouting. "You broke him. He couldn't take it anymore, and he broke like a twig, and it wasn't his fault. It was your fault. And I'll never forgive you for that. All his hopes and dreams gone. He couldn't play anymore, not with you watching. He couldn't go out on that field. Couldn't even go near the team anymore. Glenn thought it would be enough, dealing with your father. But it wasn't enough. It won't be enough until you've got nothing left, until everything you wanted is ashes." She snatched the champagne flute from Nico, whirled, and plunged into the crowd.

Over her head, Hazard glimpsed Somers in the kitchen doorway. He held a bottle to his mouth, and he was sucking it back pretty hard. When he noticed Hazard's glance, he flushed and darted back into the kitchen.

"What was that all about?" Nico said.

Hazard shook his head. Grace Elaine's words echoed in his head: *He couldn't play anymore*. Play what? Football?

Holding out another flute, Nico asked, "What did you do?"

"No idea."

"She sounded—hey, what happened to you?" Nico set down his flute and rotated Hazard's arm. "Are you bleeding?"

"It's fine."

"What the hell? Did she do this?"

Hazard jerked his arm free. Or rather, he tried to. To his surprise, Nico held on tighter.

"I asked you a question." Nico's voice was low, low enough that somehow they still hadn't drawn any attention. But his tone was anything but low. It was hot and furious, and his grip was iron. "We talked about this. Last night, Emery, we—"

"All right. Jesus Christ, just—can we do this later?"

"No, we'll do this now. Let's find a bathroom and get this cleaned up."

"Great," Hazard grumbled, but he followed Nico as the younger man led him through the crowd. "We're going to find a bathroom together. The only two queers in the whole place and we're going to the bathroom together. Why don't we just tell everybody we're fucking and get it over with?" A doughy-faced matriarch—Hazard thought she was part of the Wiese clan—stared at them in shock. "Enjoying the fucking show?" Hazard growled at her, and she dropped her champagne flute with a squeak.

Somers's bathroom was cramped. Every available space had been filled with something: over-the-toilet shelves spilled towels and hand soap and a ceramic potpourri tray; cabinets mounted on the opposite wall held hairspray and styling gel and half-used bottles of cologne; a wire rack wedged between the shower and the far wall held bath bombs and body lotion and shampoo. It looked like someone had tried to shove an entire Bath and Body Works into this one room. And then, at some point, everything had exploded.

Nico found a first aid kit in the cabinets. "Roll up your sleeve."

"It's a few scratches." Four crescent moons punctured Hazard's forearm, and they bled more than he'd expected

With an antiseptic wipe, Nico cleaned the injuries. "I left you alone for five minutes."

Hazard grunted.

"No, not even five minutes. Two minutes."

He grunted again.

"Well?" Nico asked as he dug around in the first aid kit, eventually producing a box of Batman bandages.

"What?"

Pausing in the act of stripping the backing from the adhesive, Nico leveled a look at Hazard.

"I'm talking."

This time, it was Nico's turn to remain silent, but he slapped the bandage on so hard that he left red fingerprints on Hazard's arm.

"Yeow," Hazard said, shaking out the sting and trying to pull away. He was too slow, and Nico grabbed him. "Fine. You heard her. She's insane. She thinks I ruined Somers's life."

"Did you?"

"I don't know. It was pretty shitty already when I got here."

"That stuff she was saying. Did you do any of it?"

"No. I'm not a fucking lunatic."

"You didn't follow him?"

"Christ, no. He followed me. Him and Mikey and Hugo. Practically lived in my footsteps because they were always trying to knock the shit out of me."

"You didn't sit outside his house with binoculars?"

"You think I'd do that?"

"Maybe. You're downright bat-shit sometimes."

Hazard took a moment to control his voice before answering. "I didn't."

"You didn't steal his underwear and wear it?" Nico burst out laughing. "I'm kidding. So what's she talking about?"

"I already told you." As Nico applied the last bandage, Hazard withdrew his arm and flexed it. The shirtsleeve was still stained with blood, but he rolled it down to cover the wounds. "She's insane."

Nico considered this for a moment. He stood between Hazard and the door, his lanky frame blocking passage.

"Can we go back out there? Everybody's going to think I've got you bent over the sink or something?"

"Or that I've got you bent over the sink," Nico said with a smirk, but he spoke absently, and his eyes were looking at something Hazard couldn't see.

"C'mon, already," Hazard said, gripping a handful of Nico's shirt. "Let's go."

"Just a second. I want to talk about this."

Jesus, Hazard thought, barely biting back the word. Talk. Was that what they were going to do now? Talk? Talk about every goddamn thing like it was the Paris Peace Accords? If so, Hazard wanted a bullet right between the eyes. Right that fucking minute, if that's what they were going to do now.

"Did Somers stop playing football?"

"What?"

"You heard her: she said Somers stopped playing football because of you. She said he broke, or something like that. Did he?"

"I don't remember."

"Don't bullshit me. That's part of this deal. That's what this means." Nico gestured between them.

Hazard's face colored slowly. "He didn't play their last game. I don't know why. He got hurt, that's what everyone said."

"So something did happen."

"I don't know what happened. Frankly, I don't care. I didn't do any of that shit to Somers; he's the one that made my life a living hell. Maybe he finally started feeling guilty about all that. Maybe he got the yips, maybe he twisted his ankle banging some girl by the river, how the hell should I know?"

"This is important. You heard her. She said she's going to ruin your life."

"Good luck."

"This is serious."

"No, Nico. It's not. She's petty. She's self-involved. She's old. And she's got nothing left to worry about. But she's not dangerous. Except maybe to her husband."

Nico's eyebrows shot up. "You think she did that?"

"Jesus, I shouldn't have said anything."

"You think she hired that guy?"

"I'm not talking about an ongoing investigation with you."

"Oh my God. You do."

"No, I don't. I was shooting my mouth off. Which is one reason we should do less talking. So can we go now?"

But Nico still didn't move. One of his arms came up, his fingers mussing Hazard's long, carefully styled hair. Hazard shook his head and pulled away, but Nico didn't notice. His other hand hooked Hazard's belt.

"We're not—"

"Oh grow up," Nico said, his voice once again sounding like he was a few states away. "She's not that kind of wife."

"What?"

"Jealous. I mean, she might be jealous, but I don't think she's jealous of her husband."

"What the hell are you talking about?"

"Jocasta."

"What?"

"*Oedipus Rex*. It's a play."

"I know what the fucking play is. Look, we've been in here forever. People are going to start talking. Can we—"

"Jocasta is the mom."

"Nico, I swear to fuck that I'm going to—wait, you think she's in love with Somers."

"You heard her."

"That's sick."

"You heard what she was just saying. You heard how she was saying it. Insane, that was your word for it. Psychoanalysts call it the Jocasta complex, kind of like the inverse of the Oedipal complex."

Hazard paused, considering the statement. "How do you know all this stuff?"

"It's a theology degree. You wouldn't believe the kind of crap I have to read."

"Yeah, but—" Hazard couldn't finish his objection. Pieces began to fall into place. The bitter, twisted look of jealousy on Grace Elaine's face at the Christmas party. Hazard had assumed it was about Glenn and Hadley, but—but had she been looking at Glenn? Or had she glanced backward, looking at Hazard and Somers? Hazard couldn't remember. And he thought, too, of her predatory approach, as though she were in competition with Hazard. Cora's story filtered through Hazard's mind, the story about her engagement, and Grace Elaine's hidden rage that her son might marry. "Jesus, that's wrong."

Jeremiah Walker's words came back to Hazard, the echo eerily close to Nico's speech: *You're looking for sane thinking, but whoever did this was not sane. You're looking for homo economicus, but this killer was not rational. The killing wasn't rational.*

"That's life," Nico said. "Emery, you've got to be careful. Feelings like that, they make people do crazy stuff. Totally irrational, even when they seem like they're—hey, what are you—"

The killing wasn't rational. Hazard grabbed Nico and shifted the boy out of his way. Everything had fallen into place: the emails to Wayne Stillwell, the red Santa bag, the shooting that had claimed Hadley Bingham's life, and Lender's gun. Hell, why had he been so blind about Lender's gun? Charging into the party, he went in search of Somers.

CHAPTER THIRTY-THREE

**DECEMBER 24
SUNDAY
10:45 AM**

ALONE IN THE KITCHEN, Somers considered the empty bottle of Jose Cuervo and wondered if he could get away with a mimosa or two. Hell, maybe three. He'd had the kitchen to himself for a few minutes now. Ever since he'd peeked out the doorway and seen Hazard talking to Grace Elaine, seen Hazard glance up, seen the—
—pain—
—fury in Hazard's face. And then he'd retreated into the kitchen, suddenly, blessedly alone, and pounded the rest of the tequila. And he could grab a mimosa. He could grab two. He might even make it back to the kitchen before Cora came back or before another guest noticed him. It would only take—

"Somers, holy hell, here you are." Swinney stepped into his path, cutting Somers off before he could exit the kitchen and grab a drink or two. Or three. "It's your party, isn't it? I turned this place upside down looking for you, and you're in the kitchen. Happy birthday." She glanced over her shoulder and added, "I guess I'd be hiding out too if so many of those fucking Wiese rats showed up at my party."

For the first time, Somers noticed how she looked. Her reddish-blond hair lay dull and flat against her scalp. Dark pouches hung under her eyes. But her face had a jittery energy like she was running on a hundred and twenty volts of java. The corner of her mouth twitched when she wasn't talking, and what the fuck was that about?

"I got him," Swinney said, pressing into the kitchen and forcing Somers back. "I fucking got him, Somers. He's not going to get away with it." Her eyes blurred. The corner of her mouth twitched harder and faster than ever. "I'm not going to let him get away with it, not a chance, not a Christ-loving chance of it."

"Swinney, what are you—"

"Look." Producing a battered smartphone from inside her jacket, Swinney corralled Somers with an elbow, forcing him into a tight corner at the back of the kitchen. Her mouth twisted and twitched like she'd bit down on a jumper cable, and her hands shook as she punched at the screen. "Here. Just take a look at these stupid motherfuckers."

The first picture was so blurry that Somers, at first, thought he was looking at a piece of abstract art. Nice lines, he thought. Nice color. A certain dominance towards the horizontal. The kind of mouth-shit he'd spew when Cora dragged him to another gallery of another mediocre artist. But then he recognized, even in the jumbled photograph, the structure he was looking at.

"Big Biscuit?"

"Damn right Big Biscuit. And look at this." Swiping at the screen, she brought up the next photo.

It had been taken with steadier hands—or maybe Swinney had found a tripod or something—and the resolution was much better. This time, Big Biscuit's familiar walls and sign were perfectly visible, and slightly off-center in the photograph was one of the diner's plate glass windows. The picture had been taken from outside, Somers realized. From Swinney's car, he guessed. Silhouetted at the table closest to the window, three men were eating breakfast.

Swinney swiped again, and the next photograph was zoomed in. The resolution deteriorated, but some of the details were magnified, easier to pick out. One of the men had curly hair and an unmistakable nose, but in case Somers had any doubts, a big cattleman hat sat on the table next to the man, and a badge gleamed on his chest. The man next to him had a shock of snowy white hair. The photograph was too poor quality to expose the liver spots on his chin and jaw, but he was easily identifiable even in profile: the Right Honorable Mayor

Sherman Newton. The third man was thin, built more like an accountant than a cop, with a bristle-brush mustache and enormous glasses. Albert Lender.

Swinney swiped again. And again. And again. It was like watching a comic strip unfold. Newton and Bingham and Lender eating, eating, eating, eating, eating. Somers kept waiting for it: a wad of cash, a manila envelope, a roll of wrinkled bills. The payoff. Swinney swiped and swiped, and Somers waited and waited, and then the last picture jagged back and Somers realized they'd reached the end of Swinney's surveillance.

A ping went off inside Somers's chest, and then another ping, and then another. Hot, steady pulses of excitement. This was it. Not the smoking gun, not exactly, but this was almost as good. He'd suspected the three of them were working together. No, that wasn't right. He'd known. In his gut, he'd known it was the three of them, never mind what Hazard said. And here was the proof, picture perfect. They'd done it. Somers didn't know the details, not yet. He couldn't put this in front of Cravens or the county prosecutor. But that pulse in his chest, that steady pinging, it told him that he'd been right.

"This is it?"

"For now," Swinney said, dropping her phone into a pocket.

"It's not enough."

"You see it, though." Swinney had one hand on the countertop, and her index finger came down hard. "You know."

"I know—"

But before Somers could finish, Hazard burst into the kitchen. His color was high, staining his normally pale complexion, and Somers recognized the expression in his face. The tightly-controlled animation in Hazard's features, normally impassive, only arose when Hazard's mind was working at full speed—when he was cracking one of their cases.

"It's him," Hazard said in his low, gravelly voice, but even that voice trembled with excitement. "Bing. He did it."

"The sheriff, right. We've got the pictures—"

"No, not the sheriff. Bing."

Somers was already shaking his head. "Take a look at this." He jerked his head at Swinney, and Swinney produced the smartphone and thumbed through the pictures.

After perhaps a dozen of the grainy, distant shots, Hazard gave an irritated shake of his head and shoved the phone away. "That's nothing. That's bullshit. Listen, I'm telling you I figured it out. It was Bing."

"It was Bing."

"Yes."

Somers couldn't explain what happened next—not at the conscious level of his mind, anyway. But his shoulders tightened. His stomach dropped. A twisting tension began deep inside him, two powerful forces crashing against each other, the quaking that predicted massive, tectonic shifts.

"All right," he managed to say.

"It wasn't about your dad at all," Hazard said, that rare excitement controlling his face. "It was Hadley. Bing was going after her. I'm not sure why, not yet. She was going to tell someone, I think. We'll have to talk to her boyfriends again, but it sounded like she wanted to tell them, like maybe she'd even tried to tell them—"

"Tell them what?" Jesus, Somers thought, massaging his jaw. Everything was so tight. His shoulders, his neck, his jaw. How could his jaw be so goddamn tight?

"Tell them—" Hazard's eyes revealed his confusion at Somers's question. "What he was doing to her. Molesting her. Abusing her. Isn't it obvious—"

"No. No, Hazard. It isn't obvious." And damn, that sounded wrong. Hazard. Not Ree, that's not what he called him. Hazard. Since when had he gone back to that name? "Why don't you explain it to the rest of us? All the simpletons in the room, go on, you need to explain it."

"You're upset."

It made Somers laugh, and then it felt like his jaw would shatter like someone dropping a glass, just a crack and then a thousand pieces everywhere. "Go on. You've got some kind of proof? Tell me about Bing. Tell me about what you said he was doing. Do you have any proof of it? Those kids last night, did they even suggest something like that? Did they—"

"No. No, that's not what I meant. We'll have to ask them some more questions. We'll talk to Daisy again. We've got a new angle to work."

"A new angle?" Jesus. Just Jesus, how could anybody feel like this, like he was being pulled apart and shoved back together. Harder now. Like he might really go to pieces. "Buddy, we don't need a new angle. This case has a million shitty angles. And the one angle, the only angle that makes any sense, we've finally got proof on. Thanks to Swinney, Hazard. Not because of anything you and I did." The tremors had gotten worse, had really worked their way into his hands. "She's been doing the real police work on this while we've wasted our time chasing shit from the past. She's the one who's finally got something that can put us on the right track."

"Those pictures?" Hazard waved a hand, dismissing the phone, dismissing Swinney, dismissing everything Somers had been building up to. With one wave. With one casual, goddamn wave. "Those pictures," Hazard continued, "don't show a thing. Not one thing. Three guys eating breakfast, Somers. That's it. What do you think you've got there? Evidence of conspiracy to commit murder? Mary and motherfucking Joseph, Somers, open your eyes. You've got pictures of three guys at a goddamn diner. That's not a crime."

"We've got the recording. We've got proof that my father—"

"We've got proof that your father was into shit up to his neck just like he always is. That's what we've got proof of. We don't even know that anybody else knew about that recording. It was locked in his safe. I'm telling you, we've been looking at it all wrong—"

"Of course we have."

Hazard paused, thrown off by Somers's abrupt agreement. "What?"

"Of course we've been going about it wrong. Looking at it wrong. Whatever the hell you said. This is how it always is, right? I bumble along. I make an ass out of myself. And then you swoop in and all of the sudden you've got all the answers. Isn't that right? Isn't that how you like to play this? Go on. Explain."

Swinney, pocketing the phone, slipped towards the door. "You two hammer this out. I'll just—"

"No." Somers latched onto her. "Stay. You want to hear a genius at work? Here we go. Go on, Ree. Tell her why Bing wanted to kill my father. Or his daughter. Or whatever the fuck you think happened."

"I don't get this. I don't get what's going on. It's not me. It's not always me. At Windsor—"

And that was the worst part, the way he said those two words: *At Windsor*, like he was throwing Somers a bone, just a goddamn bone so Somers would stop bothering him. "Oh, you don't get what's going on? That's interesting. That must be the first fucking time in the history of the fucking world."

"Why are you angry?"

"I'm not angry. Swinney and I, we thought we had something. That was stupid, though, right? You don't even want to hear it. You've got it all figured out."

"Emery?" Nico poked his head into the kitchen and then came into the room, pausing, his gaze moving among them. "What's going—"

"Great," Somers said. "This is just perfect. Kindergarten. We're running a fucking daycare out of my house."

"Watch it," Hazard said.

"I am watching it. That's what a kindergarten is, right? I just watch. I watch kids, like this kid you're dragging around. It's all watching. That's all I do. I should just—no, Swinney, stay the fuck here, I want you to hear this—I should just watch kids, is that what I'm good for? Like this kid, the one you're dragging around town?"

"I said watch it."

"Yeah, watch it. Jesus, two syllables. That's all I can get out of you. Watch it. Watch it. You're some kind of fucking broken record right now, is that it? What should I watch? Him? I should watch this baby you've been stringing along until you get bored with him, even if he does have a nice ass and a pretty face—"

The punch happened so fast that Somers didn't even see it. His head cracked against the cabinets, and his legs went linguini, and just like that, just as fast as that goddamn punch, that massive, tectonic unsettling inside him stopped. Everything fell back into place, and suddenly Somers felt clear-headed and tired and ashamed.

Shaking his hand, Hazard grabbed Nico by the shirt and propelled him towards the door.

"Ree," Somers said, and he took a step, but his legs were still all noodles and his head was ringing like every Christmas bell west of the Mississippi. "Hey, wait, I'm sorry—"

Swinney caught him before he could fall, and then Hazard and Nico had disappeared out into the whitewashed winter. Somers stared out into the shocked faces of the closest guests. Then he turned and threw up into the sink.

CHAPTER THIRTY-FOUR

DECEMBER 24
SUNDAY
10:56 AM

HAZARD DROVE RECKLESSLY. The little VW slid across icy patches, skidded around corners, and, on their last turn, bumped up against a fire hydrant. Nico pressed a handkerchief to the still-healing cut in Hazard's hand. One of the stitches had popped, and the sucker was bleeding like hell.

When they hit a red light, Nico grabbed the steering wheel. "Either you pull over, or you let me drive."

"I'm fine."

"Like hell you're fine. You can't even breathe. And your hand—"

The light flipped to green, and Hazard punched the accelerator. He couldn't breathe? That was bullshit. He could breathe fine. He was taking a breath. A million breaths. The world spun, and Hazard forced himself to draw more air into his lungs. See? Fine. He could breathe like a champ.

"Emery."

"I said I'm fine."

"You're not fine. Will you pull over?"

Hazard didn't bother to reply.

"Pull over, or I'm getting out at the next light."

Hazard hesitated. "Maybe I won't stop at the next light."

To his surprise, Nico started to laugh. His slender fingers tightened, compressing the bandage against Hazard's palm, and

Nico laughed harder. In spite of himself, Hazard felt some of the rage seep away. He didn't laugh, not quite, but he suddenly knew he was acting like a fool, and that helped temper the insane anger that he felt.

When they rolled to a stop at the next light, Nico laughed even harder. A smile touched the corners of Hazard's lips. Not because he thought anything was funny but because there was something about Nico, about how open he was, how honest, how happy and easily amused he was, that touched a wounded, aching spot inside Hazard.

"That looks better on you," Nico said, his laughter subsiding into a grin as he touched the corner of Hazard's mouth.

Hazard turned his head and kissed the inside of Nico's hand.

"You're still shaking."

"I'm still angry."

"At what? John-Henry? Don't be. He was drunk. And he was—"

"He was a gaping asshole is what he was, Nico."

"He was upset."

"Because I was right."

Nico frowned, and then his eyes caught something outside the car and he nodded. The light had flipped to green. As Hazard eased forward, Nico said, "Are you sure?"

"What? Yes. I don't have the proof yet, but it's the only way all the pieces fit together. And if he weren't so hung up on—"

"His own father being shot?"

"It's blinding him. It's making him stupid."

"You didn't exactly take it easy on him, Emery."

Hazard paused, negotiating the next turn more carefully. Ahead of them, Nico's block had come into view: clean stucco, bright strands of Christmas lights on every storefront, the little brunch place on the corner swarming with college kids. "What does that mean?"

"It means this is personal for John-Henry. His dad was shot. He's a mess emotionally, and on top of that, he's got a personal interest in solving this case. You might be right, but that doesn't matter."

"It's the only thing that should matter," Hazard said. He drifted into an open parking spot outside Nico's building. "We've got a job, and our job is to find who did this thing and put him away."

"Yeah," Nico said with a droll smile, and he tapped the side of Hazard's head with one finger. "You got it, Emery. Logic. Analysis. Evidence. Proof. Problem solved. Maybe that works for some people. For the rest of us, though, there's a lot more happening. And it happens in here," his hand drifted down to rest on Hazard's chest, "and in here," his hand drifted down to Hazard's stomach.

"What happened today wasn't about Somers being hungry."

"Was that a joke?" Nico said, a smile tickling his lips.

"Don't start. You sound like him."

"He's pissed. And he's extra pissed because it sounds like he thought he'd just had his own crack in the case. Give him a day to cool off. And then work the case the way you always do. If you're right, you'll find what you need to prove it. Right?"

"What he said about you—"

"Come on, Emery. I'm not an idiot. I know I'm a lot younger than you. I know I'm attractive. I might even be out of your league," he added with a smirk. "If those are the worst things that John-Henry can say about me, even when he's mad as hell, then he's a pretty decent guy." The smile on Nico's lips took on a sharp edge. "I could think of a lot meaner things to say about him."

"I owe him a busted nose."

"Why don't you cut him some slack and settle for a black eye?"

Hazard leaned across the console and kissed Nico. And then he kissed him again. And Nico's hand wandered lower, and Hazard kissed him harder this time.

"That was hot," Nico breathed, his pupils blown as his hand groped between Hazard's leg. "I don't like violence, but that was hot." Another kiss, and Nico's attentions grew more confident, bolder as he worked Hazard's zipper. "Fucking hot the way you knocked his fucking lights out for me." His other hand tightened on the bandage, and Hazard winced.

That broke the spell. "Darn," Nico said, pulling back. "I, uh, I got a little carried away."

"It's fine."

"You're bleeding all over the place."

"It's fine." Hazard let heat leach into his voice. "Trust me."

"Let's get you to the hospital. They need to stitch this back up. And we can talk about—"

"Nico." Hazard said, yanking on Nico's shirt hard enough to pop every button. They pinged like pinballs as they struck the windshield. "No more talking."

They barely made it into the apartment before things really got serious.

CHAPTER THIRTY-FIVE

**DECEMBER 24
SUNDAY
12:17 PM**

LIKE THE NIGHT BEFORE, the sex had been rougher than usual. Nico had clawed furrows into Hazard's back, and Hazard winced as he shrugged into a shirt and did up the buttons. Rough, yes, but amazingly satisfying. Nico might be young, but he was definitely no baby. Especially not when he got that look in his eyes—

Hazard pulled his thoughts away from the memory, and he dragged his attention away from Nico's long-legged, sprawling nakedness. Nico had drifted into sleep; that hadn't been Hazard's plan, but it served his purposes nicely, and he took advantage of the opportunity to slip out of the bedroom. In the living area of Nico's apartment, Hazard laced up his wingtips and dragged on his coat. His hand still throbbed, and he'd need to see the doctor eventually. But not yet. Not quite yet.

Instead, he made his way down to the VW. Some of the shabby chalkiness was gone from the sky, and in the west, strips of robin's egg showed through the clouds, like paint underneath a layer of old paper. The light, where it escaped the cloud cover, turned the afternoon golden. It even smudged away the black crust of the snow. Things looked brighter. Newer. Well, not the VW. The faded cherry paint didn't look any newer. But the day—Hazard took a deep breath. It was hard to remember why he'd been so angry.

As he got into the car and drove, Hazard decided that Nico had been right. At least, he'd been right in part. Arguing with Somers about the case wasn't going to get them anywhere. Somers had already decided that this case was about his father. In some way that Hazard couldn't fully understand, Somers had made the case personal—not only in the sense that his father was the victim but in the sense that solving the case had become some form of personal atonement for Somers. It was easier to see that, now that Nico had drawn the outlines for Hazard. Somers wanted to solve this case, needed to solve it, and he needed it to be about his father. He needed to save his father. Hazard could follow the idea. He could grasp, in a mechanical way, the underlying psychology of Somers's obsession. But the emotional impact of it lay outside his reach. Somers was being an idiot. That was the short version.

The problem, of course, was that they were running out of time. It had already been more than twenty-four hours since the shooting. In that time, Bing might have destroyed any remaining evidence. Already this would be a difficult case to prove. As Jeremiah had pointed out, Bing's motive—as far as Hazard could tell—was utterly irrational. That was what had thrown Hazard off from the beginning. He had assumed—wrongly, it turned out—that this killing, because of the complicated planning behind it, had been driven by logic and reason—twisted, yes, evil, yes, but still rational.

The truth, though, was far from it. It had come to him in Nico's observation about Grace Elaine. The older woman's obsession with Somers had opened a new possibility for Hazard. What if the murder had been driven by a poisonous combination of desire and jealousy? Grace Elaine no longer made a likely suspect; her emotional energies were entirely focused on Somers, and Hazard felt a minor pang for his partner now that he understood more fully Somers's home life.

In that light, it left only four possible suspects: the sheriff, Bing, and Frank and Dusty. All four of them had access to Stillwell. All four of them might have unlocked Stillwell and provided him with a handgun. But it was Bing. Hazard knew it was Bing. And Frank and Dusty had provided the most important information, although it only made sense in the context of Daisy's long-winded complaints about Hadley's behavior. Dusty—blushing, embarrassed to the point of tears, sweetly stupid Dusty—had given Bing a reason to kill his own daughter. And Dusty hadn't realized it.

But proving any of it depended on getting a warrant for Hadley's phone, and getting that warrant required probable cause. In another place, Hazard might have been able to lay out the pieces of his case and get the support he needed. All the elements were there. The logic behind Hazard's assumptions was sound.

Wahredua, however, was a small town, and it still had a small-town mentality. It still had small-town royalty. The Binghams were among that royalty, and Hazard knew that the sheriff could bring to bear enough pressure to stall things indefinitely. No, Hazard knew that without solid proof, without physical proof, he wouldn't have the leverage he needed to take this case any farther. So the first step, the only step, was to get that proof.

Sitting in the VW, he dialed, and Dusty answered.

"Hello?"

"It's Detective Hazard."

"Oh, yeah. Hi. Is everything ok? This isn't about Frank's mom, is it? Because if it is, I was messed up the other night. I didn't know what I was saying. I got things all jumbled, you know?"

"It's not about Frank's mom. You lied to me."

"What?"

"About the necklace. You lied."

"Look, Frank was the one who was lying. He didn't do anything. It was just like you said: I threw it outside. I was mad because of Hadley, and I took off the necklace and I threw it outside. That's all, swear to God."

"You're lying."

"I'm not. I swear I'm not."

"He said he'd hurt Frank, didn't he?"

Outside the VW, laughter drew Hazard's attention. A young couple was walking down the sidewalk. The girl had stopped to fiddle with her boots. The boy was laughing, bending over to help her, and he turned his head and pressed a kiss to her cheek.

"Nobody said anything. I already told you. I got mad. It was just like you said, I swear to Christ, it was just—"

"Dusty, I'm not going to let him do anything. Not to you. Not to Frank."

The couple had finished whatever they were doing. They were walking again. As they drew even with the car, the girl laced her fingers through the boy's, and then they were past.

"Please. Please don't let him hurt Frank."

"I won't, but I need you to tell me what happened. What did Mr. Bingham do?"

"He followed us into the kitchen. Not right away. Hadley was already gone, and Frank went to the bathroom, and I was just standing there. And he grabbed me by the arm and shoved me outside. I should have done something, right? I should have yelled. Or pushed him. I'm a fucking jock, I mean, that's about the only thing I'm good for. That's what Frank always says. But I just, I don't know. He was scary."

"He took you outside."

"By the heaters."

"What did he say?"

"He said he knew what we'd been doing with Hadley. He said dads didn't have to put up with that, not under their own roof. He said she was his little girl. He kept saying that. And I said she was old enough to make her own decisions. It was stupid."

"And?"

"And he said if I ever came near his daughter again, he'd—he said he knew guys. Guys who'd been in prison. He said he knew where I lived. I said fuck off, and he said fine, he knew where Frank lived. And he said these guys, they didn't mess around, and the things they'd do to Frank, he said they'd rape him. Until he died. That's not how he said it, but that's what he meant. He said they'd split him open. He said they'd see how much he could take before they tore his ass in half. He said—"

"All right. All right, it's going to be all right."

Crying came over the line. "He grabbed me by the collar. His fingers got tangled in the chain. I didn't even realize it was gone until the next day, and by then I didn't care."

"And you didn't tell Frank."

"He'd just been through so much. He didn't need to know."

"Until we came around. And then he thought you'd done something stupid. You were covering for Bingham. And Frank was covering for you."

"Do we have to move now? Do we have to go into witness protection? Because it'd be all right, you know? It'd be good for Frank. Get away from all this. From his mom. I can't make him go, but it'd be good for him."

And nobody would have believed it, nobody, but Hazard's eyes started to sting, and he blinked rapidly. "It's going to be all right, Dusty. He's not going to hurt you. Either of you. I've got to go, but I'm going to need you to come down to the station and go over this again. You and Frank."

"And then maybe witness protection? I'm asking for Frank. His mom, it's not good here, you know?"

"We'll see."

"Detective Hazard?"

"Yeah?"

"What'd you say to him? To Frank, I mean. He cried about six hours straight last night. I thought it was a nervous breakdown. And when he fell asleep—" Something like wonder came into Dusty's voice. "He let me hold him. And today, today he's a lot better. He hasn't yelled at me. Not once."

"Sounds like he's finally got his head on straight. Come down to the station, Dusty. Today, if you can."

He drove to the Binghams' new house on its new road. In the crisp winter light, the house looked even more expensive, even more out of place in the quiet college town than it had before. Hazard parked. His stomach had become a hard knot. Walking up there, walking up to that door, knocking on it—it was going to be the lake all over again. He knew that in his gut. It was going to be the exact fucking same. Just like that summer day, Hazard was going to walk too far. He was going to walk out of reach of any safety or security. He was going to put himself within arm's length of Bing again.

Yanking on the door release, Hazard got out of the car. He set his phone to record and checked the .38 under his arm. Yes, he told himself. Yes, it would be the same in many ways. But he was different. Things would be different this time. He told himself that again as he shut the car door.

But it didn't change the knot in his stomach. It didn't change the slight feeling of dissociation, as though he'd lost contact with everything below the knees. It didn't make it any easier to climb the snow-covered drive. It didn't make his hand any less heavy as he reached for the door. Jesus, he thought wildly, he'd been stupid to think anything was different, he'd been stupid to think anything had changed. It was going to be the exact same: Bing's grip tight on his arm, the rocks slicing his knees, the total, utter helplessness.

Before he could knock, the door swung open. Bing stood there, as though he'd been waiting for this moment, as though the last fifteen years had been running towards this moment on railroad tracks. Again, Hazard was struck by the changes to the man: still possessed of formidable good looks, Bing now wore deep marks of grief. Hazard wondered if he had been wrong. Was Somers right? Had Hazard made a mistake somewhere? This was the face of a rich man—a proud man—brought low by fate. It wasn't the face of a man who had abused and then murdered his own daughter. It wasn't the face of a monster.

Except all the pieces fit, and Hazard trusted logic and reason and his own judgment. He did his best to firm up his voice and said, "Morning, Bing."

"Emery."

And that was the confirmation Hazard needed: the way Bing said his name. Not Detective. Not even Hazard. He had said Emery, and the way he had said it had been the same as fifteen years before. It had the same mixture of scorn, self-congratulation, and amusement that Hazard remembered from the rocky strip of beach on Lake Palmerston.

"You want to come in," Bing said, blocking the door with his body.

"We need to talk."

"No."

"Excuse me?"

"No, we don't need to talk. You know me, Emery. We go way back." Now listen. I've already played nice. I apologized, remember that? I looked you in the eyes like a man and I told you I was sorry. And when you came over here, when you wanted to swing your dick a little and show me I wasn't the big man anymore, what'd I do? I rolled over. I spread my cheeks and I asked how you liked it and I did it all with a smile. You were up in my daughter's room—my daughter's room, you remember?—and even then I played nice. I didn't go running to my daddy, and I could have done that. He would have given you your ass on a platter, but I didn't because I wanted to make things right between us."

"This isn't about us, Bing. This is about a murder. This is about your girl, and I need to talk to you. I'd like to come inside and do that."

"So that's how you want to play it now."

"It's just a conversation."

"So that's how it is. You really think you have the biggest swinging dick in town. That's how it is. I tried to be nice. I tried to put things right between us. I spread my fucking cheeks when you came over here to dick us around, and that still wasn't enough for you. And now you're back. What're you going to do now? You want to get into it, is that it? You looking for a reason to have a go at me?"

"You're upset. I can understand that. But you need to understand that this is my job, and I'm doing it even if that means upsetting you and your father."

"I get it," Bing said, his eyes narrowing as though in realization. "I get it. Jesus, now it's plain as day."

"We need to talk."

"No. You know what we need?"

Hazard fought the urge to lick his lips, to put his tail between his legs, to run. He ignored the question and said, "This is important,

Bing. I'd like to ask you some questions about Friday night. Can I come inside?"

"You know what we need?"

"I'll need to talk to—"

"You're not answering my question, faggot." The word popped like thin ice.

"I'll need to talk to Daisy, too." Hazard felt cool inside. Not cold, not frozen, but cool. He was still floating from the knees up, but he was cool. His hand wasn't itching. He wasn't even thinking about the .38, not at all. "We can either do this here, with some privacy, or we can do it down at the station."

"You're not going to answer. Is that it? You're going to keep talking. That's what you want, you want to keep talking, but you won't admit what this is: this is you long-dicking me, really giving it to me. This is payback, your mother-fucking payback. That's pathetic."

Hazard waited.

"All right," Bing said. "You won't answer? All right, I'll tell you. I'll tell you what we need. Maybe we need some decency around this town. Maybe we need some goddamn morals. Maybe the public figures—" Bing's hand came up, his finger jabbing towards Hazard's chest and stopping short by a bare inch. "Maybe the cops should be an example. Maybe we don't need them setting a bad example."

"I'm leaving. I'll talk to your father about this. And I'll talk to Chief Cravens. We'll have you down to the station for—"

"Come inside." Bing stepped away from the door, pantomiming a grotesque mockery of an invitation. "You want to talk so bad, come inside."

"We'll have you down to the station—"

"No." Bing was shaking his head, smiling now—that same smile, that same tone, so self-satisfied, so arrogantly entertained. "You get your ass in here. You wanted to talk. Get in here and talk. Right now, Detective."

"We'll have you down to the station for questioning, Bing. If we need to talk to your lawyer first, let me—"

"Let's talk about Somers."

Hazard opened his mouth to respond, but ice slipped between his lips and froze the words. He thought of Grace Elaine's accusations, her bewildering insistence that Hazard had somehow ruined Somers's life, that Hazard had harmed Somers in their last year of high school. And now, staring at Bing, Hazard suddenly knew that this was what Bing was talking about. Bing knew something. Bing, who taught shop, who had been Somers's coach, who had hung around the high school, who had been one of the guys—Bing knew.

About the locker room, Hazard thought, and the thought was filled with a sudden, irrational terror that reduced everything else to ashes. The logical part of Hazard's mind knew that didn't make any sense. Hazard's one and only encounter with Somers had happened in their junior year. But there was that look in Bing's eyes, that knowing look, that smug, scornful look. Like he'd seen Hazard naked, that's what it was like. Like he'd seen Hazard naked and it just made him want to laugh.

"Fuck," Bing said, and now he did laugh. "The two of you are just fucking made for each other." Without another word, he turned and sauntered deeper into the house. Snow blew through the open doorway. Beyond, the crisp winter light grew hazy and dim, and shadows swallowed Bing.

Just leave, Hazard told himself. Whatever it is, it isn't worth it. Whatever it is, that's not why you came here. You came here for proof. You came here for hard evidence, not for—not for whatever the hell is happening.

But—

A little voice in his brain kept insisting: but. But this is an invitation. This is your chance. Once you're inside, you just excuse yourself to the bathroom again. You take another look and see what you can find. And you want to know about Somers, that little voice insisted, the thought so dangerous that it lingered just at the surface of consciousness.

Hazard stepped inside. Shutting the door behind him, he glanced around, as though expecting to uncover a trap or a monster lurking in the house's gloom. Instead, though, he saw only a fanwork of snow that the wind had carried indoors, already melting against the floor. That was all. Big deal. Frozen water, expensive flooring, and a huge, silent house. So why was his heart hammering in his throat? Why did he feel like he was floating from the armpits now?

Bing was waiting in the living room where Hazard and Somers had conducted their last conversation. He stood at the sideboard again, pouring himself a drink, his face Roman in profile: the strong nose, the dark curls, the frenzied smile.

"He didn't tell you, did he?" Bing turned, swirling the drink as he waited for an answer.

Hazard refused to give him the satisfaction.

Breaking into a laugh, Bing shook his head. "Of course he didn't. You wouldn't have crawled in here like I've got a fish hook in your ass if he'd already told you. But you wondered, didn't you? You had to have thought about it at some point."

This time, Bing's silence matched Hazard's own, and finally Hazard heard himself say, "What?"

"He was a good quarterback. Not NFL, we're not talking anything like that. Not even Division I. But Division II, maybe. If he'd worked his ass off, just maybe."

"So?"

"So you never wondered why he didn't play?"

"He went to Mizzou. You just said it. He wasn't good enough."

"Come on."

"I'm telling you what you said."

Bing took a long drink. "You're stupid."

"I want to talk about Friday—"

"No. We're not done yet. When we're done, maybe I'll talk to you about those questions. Maybe. But I'm not finished." Bing took another drink, emptying his glass, and turned to refill it. "He had offers. Nothing on paper, but I'd talked to some scouts. Maryville. Truman. Drury. He could have played."

Floating. That's what it felt like to Hazard. Like he'd dropped into a swimming pool and the water forked around his armpits, suspending him over nothing.

"Jesus, at least tell me you wondered why he didn't play that last game."

Hazard was hearing Grace Elaine's words again: *You took away his life. You broke him.*

"The way you look at him," Bing said. "It's tragic. I mean, it's fucking hilarious, but it's tragic. It's like somebody got a Magic Marker and had to draw one fucking thing: a sad little queer. That's what it's like, just big black lines that tell the whole story. And you don't even know. You didn't even wonder."

"Shut up."

"You know we partied? I look back on it, and it's kind of sad. I mean, I was in college. I was the shit in this town. I stayed because I liked that feeling. I got off on it, to be totally honest. And coaching, I mean, Jesus, those kids worshipped the ground I walked on. So I'd buy them beer. I'd go to their parties and score with the hottest girls. Yeah, I know, it's pathetic. But at the time—" Bing shrugged. "A couple of times, the kids brought coke, and Jesus, they'd light up like firecrackers."

"You're a moron. You're telling a cop that you—"

"One night, we were at his house. Somers's. His parents were out of town—they were always out of town—and he had the place to himself. I bet we had fifty, sixty people there. And we had a back room going on. A kind of VIP lounge. Hollace Walker had coke. You ever done that stuff? No. Look at you: you might be queer, but you're about as boring as they come. Straight arrow. You know what coke does to you? I mean, it wires you, sure. You get all hopped up. But some people, holy shit, it makes them horny enough to drill through a concrete wall. Your boy, that's what it did to him."

"So what? Somers does a line and pops a boner. What do I care besides the fact that now I can haul your ass into jail?"

Bing burst out laughing, and then he pounded back his drink and slung the glass onto the sideboard. Advancing on Hazard, he continued speaking. "He went out to his car. I mean, I didn't know where he was, but this sophomore girl starting throwing up, didn't seem like she could stop, and I figured I'd better find Somers and start clearing everybody out. He wasn't anywhere in the house. I looked all over that place. I forgot about that girl because by then I was curious. I wanted to know where he was and why he'd snuck off like that. You remember that car?"

Hazard didn't answer.

Bing came closer, close enough now that the alcohol on his breath stung the air, close enough that Hazard wanted to take a step back—wanted to, but didn't. "The Camaro. You remember that?"

He was so close now that Hazard nodded, compelled by the intensity of Bing's gaze.

"You know what he was doing? He was jerking off. I mean, not just rubbing one out. This kid was about three seconds away from ripping off his pecker. And the noises he was making. Groaning. He could have been in a fucking porno, that's what it was like. I've never been into guys, but damn." Bing paused. Another wave of alcohol-soaked breath rushed across Hazard, and Bing reached down, adjusting himself, slowly, carefully, making sure that Hazard noticed. "That's right, Wahredua's next golden boy, the star quarterback, the town treasure, yanking himself so hard it was a capital crime, and he was doing it to your picture. Some dinky little thing he'd cut out of the yearbook, but it was you. Emery Hazard. Still had the little caption underneath." Bing was touching himself again, his hand running the length of the hardness outlined in his jeans, his breath on Hazard's face. "What do you think of that?"

"I think you were a pervert watching an underage teen. I think you supplied controlled substances—"

Bing moved so quickly that he took Hazard by surprise. One hand clutched at Hazard's hair, jerking his head sideways hard enough to bring tears to Hazard's eyes. When Bing spoke, his voice was low and dominant. "When I caught him, he freaked out. Literally. He drove away without saying a word. He never talked to me about it. Never talked to me again, not if he could help it. He quit the team. He'd cross the street to avoid me.

"His parents came to me, and they were the ones that told me. He'd spun a whole fable for them about this nasty little queer named Emery Hazard. Emery was following him. Stalking him. Emery was stealing clothes from his gym locker. Emery had given their precious boy a nervous breakdown. I told them I was sorry. I told them there wasn't anything I could do about it. I sure as hell wasn't going to get involved, not when Somers knew I'd been supplying coke and booze. But I didn't forget either."

"Get off me," Hazard said, trying to pull free.

Bing gave another shake, dragging Hazard half a step forward, and clicked his tongue. "You've wasted fifteen years on that kid, and you never knew he sold you out. You know what you need?" Bing's leg was between Hazard's now, forcing his thighs apart. "I think you need somebody to take care of you. Somebody who will be in charge of you." He gave another little shake of Hazard's head, his voice dropping even lower. "Somebody that can give you what you need. It sure as hell isn't the little bitch that betrayed you. I don't normally like guys, but what do you say? Ask nice. Ask really nice, and maybe I'll let you finish what we started at the lake."

Bing didn't wait for an answer. He twisted Hazard's head, forcing him down. For a moment, Hazard barely noticed. He was too busy processing what Bing had said. So many things made sense now. The hostility that Somers's parents showed. Grace Elaine's inexplicable claims. Somers's own mysterious behavior around his parents and Bing.

The pain from Bing wrenching Hazard's hair, though, pulled Hazard out of those dark thoughts. His eyes shot up and found Bing's. Just an instant, that's all the contact lasted. But it was long enough for Bing to realize his mistake. Hazard saw that realization dawn in Bing's eyes.

And instead of letting go, Bing doubled down: he clutched at Hazard's hair, shaking his head like he meant to break Hazard's neck. Hazard didn't bother trying to pull free. He struck once, his fist landing low on Bing's chest. Air exploded from Bing's lungs. The big man sank, his knees folding, as he wheezed for breath. But he hadn't let go. His hold only grew tighter, as though he were determined to drag Hazard down with him.

Hazard struck again. This time, the angle was off, and Hazard's punch glanced off. He had intended to take Bing in the throat, but instead, Hazard's fist scraped Bing's jaw. The blow rocked the man's head backward. Still gasping for air, Bing struggled to remain upright. His grip on Hazard's hair had become like that of a man clutching at a lifeline. Sharp pain ran through Hazard's scalp, and he felt skin and hair rip free, but Bing still held on.

Fighting back a shout, Hazard drove another punch, and this one went true. He slammed into the soft hollow of Bing's throat. Bing made a single, croaking noise. His hand came free, bloody strands of Hazard's hair sticking to his fingers, and he lurched backward. With both hands, Bing clutched at his throat. Another of those terrible croaking noises emerged, and his olive complexion darkened. Hazard straightened, shaking off the worst of the pain, and hammered at Bing with his fists: brutal, simple blows that were all power and no finesse. Blood spurted from Bing's nose as bone and cartilage crumpled under Hazard's assault. Bing's head whipped to one side and then the other as Hazard clobbered his ears. One blow, one really good blow, Hazard got in on Bing's jaw, and he felt something pop, and a vicious surge of satisfaction ran through Hazard. Good, he thought. Maybe his jaw was broken. Hazard would have been even happier if he'd knocked it clean off.

Bing hit the floor with two thuds: the first larger, louder, as his ass and back hit the wood; the second softer, like a melon falling off a produce stand, when his head struck. The big, curly-haired man rolled onto his side, a mask of gore darkening his face.

"You are one stupid motherfucker," Hazard said, planting a knee in Bing's back and forcing the man onto his stomach. Something hot—blood—ran down Hazard's neck. Jesus, how much hair had Bing ripped out? Forcing the pain to the back of his mind, Hazard drew out his cuffs and snapped them around Bing's wrists. "That's assault, Bing. Assault against a police officer. You're under arrest, you fucking idiot. That's a felony. That's prison time." Hazard checked to make sure the phone was still recording, and then he read Bing his rights.

Straightening, Hazard got to his feet. The side of his head hurt like hell, but he knew it was nothing compared to what he'd dished out to Bing. The bastard deserved it. It was fifteen years in the making. More than fifteen years. But—but Hazard knew he had screwed up too. He had let Bing get too close. He had lowered his defenses. He had—

—Somers had lied about him, Somers had blamed it all on him—

—been so caught up in worrying about Somers that he'd forgotten his real reason in coming here. Hazard wiped blood from his neck and flung the droplets from his fingers. He wouldn't make that mistake again.

"Where's your wife?" Hazard said, nudging Bing.

"I'm going to have your badge," Bing blubbered through the blood still pouring from his nose. "I'm going to have your ass ripped apart by—"

"Where's Daisy?" Hazard asked.

"You little cocksucker. You faggot asstoy. You don't have any—"

Hazard checked the handcuffs and moved deeper into the house, not bothering to wait for Bing to finish. He followed the same hallway he had taken before. He searched the study, where he had heard Bing's phone call—the phone call that had proven to be the man's undoing. He found nothing relevant to the case. He passed through the kitchen, gave the garage a cursory examination, and headed upstairs.

Hadley's bedroom was exactly as he had left it, and so he proceeded to the next room. It was a bedroom, most likely a guest room, and it showed no signs of recent use. He went to the next room. The master bedroom. He rummaged through the closets and the chest of drawers, and he gave the bathroom a cursory look. Nothing. There were expensive clothes in the closets, designer perfumes on the counter, and a bottle of Valium in the medicine cabinet, but nothing out of the ordinary. Nothing hard, nothing concrete, nothing he could take to Somers and Cravens and prove that Bing had been behind all of this.

Time was running out. There was still no sign of Daisy, but she'd likely be home soon. Even if she wasn't, Hazard knew he was taking a risk leaving Bing alone. Cuffed, yes, and beaten to shit, but alone. That was stupid. It was hardcore stupid. Hazard knew he should head downstairs, keep an eye on Bing, and call in the altercation. Have Cravens send officers out to the house. Hazard knew that

Cravens would do everything by the book, and Bing had made a crucial mistake by assaulting Hazard.

But Hazard didn't go downstairs. Even though he knew he was being stupid, he couldn't bring himself to give up this opportunity. His blood was up. Adrenaline burned like a gasoline fire along his veins. He wanted to hurt Bing, and he wanted to do it by finding the proof that Bing was behind everything that had happened. He needed to take advantage of this chance. Hazard's search of the house was legal because it followed the commission of a crime and an arrest. But although the search was technically legal, Hazard knew he needed to make the most of his dwindling time. Sheriff Bingham would doubtless use all his influence to discredit Hazard's story of the assault, and even though Hazard had an audio recording, he knew that it wasn't airtight proof of Bing's attack. Worse, Hazard had come here on his own, investigating a case that the sheriff's office had closed. And even if the story of the assault held up, Hazard knew that his fellow officers—perhaps at Cravens's direction—might not be nearly as thorough in their search of Bing's property. Cravens might not even insist on a search at all. Or Daisy might arrive first and destroy any potential evidence. The list of potential disasters went on and on.

No, Hazard knew that if he was going to find something that would lay the crime at Bing's feet, he had to do it himself, and he had to do it now. Abandoning the master bedroom, he retraced his steps to the kitchen and then headed downstairs.

To Hazard's surprise, the basement wasn't finished. Drywall had been hung, and can lights responded to the switch at the bottom of the stairs, but bare cement met Hazard's wingtips. There was no furniture, no finishings. The walls had been taped and mudded and sanded and were ready to paint. Hazard walked quickly through the open space, and at the far end his shoes scraped through thick, white dust, but he found nothing. A surge of frustration choked him. He had nothing. Yes, he had Bing on assault. If Hazard were truly lucky, he might even get Bing charged and convicted. But that would be a handful of years, maybe less, and then Bing would be back on the streets. And his daughter, the girl he had abused and then killed, would still be dead. Bing would still have everything, and Hadley would have nothing, and that made Hazard so angry that he punched the drywall. The board crumpled under the blow, and a painful shock ran up to Hazard's elbow. Blood from his split knuckles soaked the gypsum dust, caking it on his hand and turning it black.

Dust. The thought filtered through the pain, and Hazard found himself examining the basement again. Yes, the drywall had been hung and mudded and taped and sanded. The sanding would have thrown up a hell of a lot of dust, but for the most part, the cement was clean. So why did dust cover a length of ground near the far wall?

Hazard sprinted down the basement, his shoes slapping the cement and then scraping to a halt at the far wall. Yes. Yes, there was dust. A lot of dust, but only here. Hazard pranced back a step, and then another. A thrill ran up his spine as he tried to construct a mental map of the home. It was a very large structure. Bing had built it to show off; that was how Bing did everything. The house sprawled across the lot. But the basement was unfinished, and it seemed smaller than the floor plan should have allowed.

Running his hands along the closest seam in the drywall, Hazard searched for a gap, a fissure, something that would mark an opening in the wall. The blood-crusted gypsum on his fingers fell away like old scabs, and fresh blood welled up and ran down his wrist. Not here. He probed up and down the seam. Not here either. Not here. How could it not be right fucking here—

And there it was. A section of drywall popped loose, swinging on invisible hinges. A secret door. A goddamn secret door. Another thrill surged inside Hazard. What would Somers say—

He cut off the thought, but not fast enough. It didn't matter. It wouldn't ever matter, ever again.

As the panel swung open, Hazard slipped into the hidden room beyond. Immediately, a whiff of something like chlorine hit him. No, Hazard realized with a grimace, his stomach flipping. Not chlorine. Spunk. Fresh. His previous excitement faded, and his stomach dropped another inch as Hazard fumbled to find a light.

Finally his fingers brushed a string, and Hazard jerked the bulb to life. It was a cramped space, and Hazard imagined it had been easy to keep it hidden. Daisy had seemed preoccupied with other things, and the disposition of the basement hardly seemed like something she would spend any time on, especially with such a slight discrepancy in the layout.

Two small chairs stood nearby, painted white, and the pair was completed by a child-sized table set with a plastic tea service. Stuffed animals—unicorns, exclusively unicorns—were piled on the tiny seats. Hazard's stomach flipped again. Bing's little girl. That was the single, horrified thought that came to him: even at the end, Bing had wanted Hadley to be his little girl. And there, spilled onto the cement, lay a pink bag with white trim. A bag that could have easily been mistaken for something Santa Claus might carry if not for the coloring and the letters that said Victoria's Secret. From the open mouth, panties had fallen across the floor. The reek of Bing's spunk was thicker here, and some of the cotton was still dark and wet.

Someone else might have laughed at the sickening mistake of it all: they weren't even Hadley's, the panties. Someone else might have forced a laugh, trying to escape the horror of it. Not Hazard. The irony galvanized him. He wondered what Bing would say when he learned that he had been jerking off to lacy underwear that had been meant for a sixteen-year-old boy named Frank.

Hazard never knew what it was that alerted him. It might have been the scuff of bare feet on cement. It might have been breathing. It might have been something as subtle as a shift in air pressure or temperature. But in an instant, Hazard knew he was no longer alone, and a chain of realizations strung themselves out across his mind.

One: the killer had unhandcuffed Wayne Stillwell.

Two: the killer had keys for police handcuffs.

Three: the killer was Bing.

Four: Bing was free of the cuffs.

As Hazard turned, he brought up an arm, but he was too slow. The bat cracked along his forearm, barely slowing before the blunt tip thunked against his head, and then everything went dark.

CHAPTER THIRTY-SIX

**DECEMBER 24
SUNDAY
1:01 PM**

SOMERS WAS TIPSY BUT NOT DRUNK. He'd finished the last of the Jose Cuervo and gone looking for more, but by then the mimosas had already dried up, and Cora had found and pitched the rest of the drink he'd stashed. After the fight, after that goddamn explosion with Hazard, Somers wanted a drink. Needed a drink. And he needed air, needed away from those people, needed away from that house. So he left. Cora was screaming, but he left. Everybody was staring, everybody in the whole house, especially that gelatinous Wiese woman that Cora insisted on inviting, all of them staring at him. He left. And he climbed behind the wheel of the Interceptor, took a few breaths, and told himself he was good to drive. A few swigs of tequila? He could handle a lot more than that.

Driving aimlessly, Somers tried to relax. He felt like he was going to snap the steering wheel, that's how hard he was gripping it. He pictured calm waters. He breathed through his nose. He sang the chorus to a pop song, he couldn't even remember its name, and none of it helped. The fight, the memory of the fight, pressed its way to the front of his brain, taking up all his attention despite Somers's best efforts to avoid it.

It was the way Hazard looked at him, Somers finally decided. And immediately he shoved the thought away. He wasn't thinking about the fight. He wasn't going to spend one more ounce of emotional energy on that selfish, pompous asshole of a partner. He wasn't going to let Emery Hazard ruin his day—his birthday—by staying inside his head. Somers forced himself to concentrate on the street. Where was he? Jesus, how far had he driven? He'd just make his way over to Market, have a quick drink at the apartment, and head back to Cora's. He'd smooth things over. She'd forgive him once he explained about Hazard. Once he explained that his asshole partner wanted to turn the shooting into something else, once he explained that Hazard wanted to take this case away just when Somers finally had a lead, Cora would understand. She'd have to, Somers thought with a kind of stupefied tranquility that was only partly due to the drink. She'd have to because it was Christmas Eve.

But the thought kept coming back, kept jostling and shoving and elbowing its way to the center of his consciousness: it was the way Hazard had looked at him. That's what it was. That's what had made the whole fight go to shit. That's what had made Somers lose control and say every single thing he knew he shouldn't have said.

They'd argued before, but usually Hazard was the one who instigated it. Never before had Somers seen that damn look on Hazard's face. Hell, he'd never seen it in the past. He'd done every cruel thing he could imagine to Hazard when they'd been in high school. He'd shoved him. He'd spat on him. He'd thrown him in the mud. He'd kicked him when he was down, literally. He'd tossed him down a flight of stairs. For hell's sake, he'd held Hazard's arms while that psycho Mikey Grames tried to carve his initials in Hazard's chest.

And not once, not one of those times, had Hazard ever looked at Somers the way he had today. Sure, Hazard had been angry. People sometimes made the mistake of thinking that because Hazard was big and brooding that he had a long fuse, or a slow fuse, or that his temper took some monumental effort to get burning. But that wasn't true. Hazard got angry as fast as anybody. Faster than most, truth be told. And he'd been angry today. He'd been furious.

But he'd looked—Jesus, the thought made Somers's stomach drop, and he slammed on the brakes, and fuck for whoever was behind him and had to stop. Hazard had looked frustrated.

Voicing the thought, giving it shape and form, made it worse somehow. Somers groaned, nudged the Interceptor against the curb—Smithfield, he was definitely somewhere in Smithfield, and he'd driven here in some kind of blackout—and dropped his head onto the wheel.

Hazard had looked frustrated. Under all that fury, under all the rage, under Hazard's visible desire to break something, he had somehow looked frustrated. Not understanding. There hadn't been a raindrop's chance in hell of understanding in Hazard's face. The man was about as sensitive as a pile of bricks. But frustrated.

And that terrified Somers. It was, single-handedly, the goddamn scariest thing he'd ever seen in his life.

Because it meant that Hazard cared. In spite of a history marked by hatred, pain, fear, and desire, Hazard still cared about him. In spite of all the horrible things Somers had done, Hazard still cared. At the beginning, when they had first started as partners, Somers had hoped Hazard could forgive him. When things had grown between them, after Hazard's furious kisses, Somers had dared to hope that there might be something more. But after their nights together at Windsor, all that had vanished. Somers had screwed everything up, and then Cora had called, and it had been easier to try to work things out, easier to go back to what he knew, easier to choose something safe.

Then Glenn Somerset had been shot, and everything in Somers's life had gone to pieces. His usual calm had vanished. His underlying conviction that he led a charmed life had been shattered. Pressure had begun to build deep inside him, pressure that shifted the foundations, and nothing looked the same anymore: not his parents, not his job, not his wife, not his partner. And there were a million things Hazard did that were irritating: the way he clenched his jaw when he was angry, the way his hair fell over his forehead at the end of the day, the way he cleaned out the fridge and tossed Somers's leftovers, the way his knee popped when he rolled over on the sofa, the way he scrubbed the apartment, floor to ceiling, when Somers just wanted to watch a ball game. A million more annoying, exasperating, goddamn frustrating things Hazard did. His eyes were annoying, those eyes like wheat stubble at the end of autumn. His lips. His lips were fucking annoying, how firm they were, how full, how they bruised Somers's mouth against his teeth. His hands. Jesus, his hands were like catcher's mitts. And his ass—

Somers thought of Frank and Dusty, and he thought of all the things that could have been right between him and Hazard, all the things that could have been perfect. And he thought of Jeremiah's words. Love isn't a choice. Love is collision. Love is catastrophe. Somers had thought he'd understood. He thought he'd known how dangerous those words were, he thought he'd sensed how deeply Emery Hazard had upset his life.

But he'd had no idea. He'd had no idea that it could make him feel like this. Collision? Catastrophe? Damn it, this was like an asteroid smacking the dinosaurs off the face of the earth. That's what it was like: everything old gone, swept clean.

Somers took a breath, propped his head on his thumbs, and realized he was smiling. It was a tight, hard, painful smile. But it was a smile. He'd tried running. He'd tried hiding. He'd even tried, in his own cowardly way, to brush up against the truth. But now it hit him full on, and there wasn't anywhere left to run or hide. There was only the shattering impact of collision.

Somers loved Emery Hazard.

And what the hell was he supposed to do about it?

CHAPTER THIRTY-SEVEN

DECEMBER 24
SUNDAY
1:24 PM

Hello?" Nico's voice was thick.

"Were you sleeping?"

"What? Who is this?"

"It's the middle of the afternoon. Were you asleep?"

"Who is this?"

"Was it a nap, or were you and Hazard—" Somers hesitated. The old jokes that used to come so easily now stung.

"John-Henry? What are you—why are you calling?" Nico's voice sharpened. "Is Hazard ok?"

"What? He's not with you?"

"No. Well—hold on." From the other end of the line, there was silence. Then: "No. He went out. I thought he was going to talk to you."

"He's not answering his phone."

"Wait. He's not with you?"

"That's why I'm calling you. I wouldn't be calling you if I could get Hazard to pick up his damn phone. Did he leave it at your place?"

"No. He never leaves anything. What's going on? He's not with you?"

Somers didn't answer. His thoughts fired rapidly. When Hazard had failed to answer the phone, Somers had assumed that his partner was angry with him. When Hazard had failed to answer the third call, Somers had begun to suspect that Hazard and Nico were finding a creative way to spend the winter afternoon.

That hadn't stopped Somers. He wanted to talk to Hazard. Needed to talk to him, truth be told. It was as if all those years of waiting, all twenty of them, were suddenly pressing down on him. He felt jangling, like his nerves were piano keys and somebody was running a hand up and down the ivories. It was the kind of feeling that could make a man jump out of his skin if it went on too long. Twenty years. He'd wasted twenty years. What was another minute, another hour, another day? Somers didn't know, but it felt like a goddamn eternity.

But Hazard wasn't with Nico. And Hazard wasn't answering his phone. Maybe Hazard was still angry. God knew the man got angry like a burning junkyard. But—but there had been that look. That look in his eyes.

"Call him," Somers said.

"What?"

"Call him on your phone." And Somers disconnected.

A full minute passed. Eternity. That's what it was like. Twenty years he'd spent dicking around, hiding, denying, protesting, pretending. Twenty years, and now every fucking tick of the clock was an epoch.

As that minute ticked by, doubts filtered in. What the hell was Somers thinking? One argument. That's all it had been. And that look in Hazard's eyes—he'd imagined it. Hell, even if he hadn't imagined it, it was just a look. Just Hazard being frustrated. It didn't mean anything more than that. It didn't mean Somers needed to throw everything away. It didn't mean Somers needed to run after Hazard like—

—Dusty and Frank—

—a lovesick teenager. It sure as hell didn't mean that Hazard felt anything like what Somers felt. With rising dread, Somers knew what was going to happen: he was going to talk to Hazard. And Hazard was going to laugh. Hazard was going to think it was some joke. Or he'd get angry. Or he'd—

The phone buzzed, and Somers swiped the screen so hard his thumb slid off the edge.

"He's not answering."

"Did you have a fight?"

"No."

"Is he that pissed?"

"No. I mean, you saw him. But no. We talked. He calmed down. We came back here—" Something in Nico's voice, in the thick hitch, painted Somers's world red. So that's what they'd been doing. Sure, they were dating. Sure, Hazard was entitled to screw whatever he wanted to screw. But it didn't change the fact that Somers was seeing blood, didn't change the way his thoughts went, first, to what it might feel like to break Nico's teeth.

"You went back there?"

"I fell asleep. He left. I mean, I knew he left, but I thought he was going to work things out with you."

They'd reached the end of useful conversation, Somers realized. Nico was just repeating what he'd already said. Forcing himself to speak calmly—it wasn't Nico's fault, Somers reminded himself, that he was dating Hazard—Somers said, "He didn't say anything else?"

"We talked about the case. We agreed that you'd come around once Emery found something solid, something he could show you."

It was like someone pulled the plug on a drain at the bottom of Somers's stomach. Everything began to swirl, sliding down that invisible drain, leaving Somers shaken and cold and empty. "I'll call you in a few."

"John-Henry—"

Somers disconnected the call. He glanced around, blinking, as though suddenly waking up to the world around him. Smithfield. Yes. Ok. But where the hell in Smithfield was he? Flooring the gas, he launched the Interceptor out onto the street and swerved right at the next stop sign. Ballas. Ok, he recognized Ballas. And the next intersection was Jamieson—no, Landry. Another hard right, and then Somers knew where he was, and he punched the gas again. The Interceptor shot across icy roads. The sky had hardened into a perfect, crystalline blue. It looked like something that would shatter if you breathed on it. The whole day could shatter. Just like that, Somers realized, with fear and sickness still draining out of his stomach. A whole life could shatter if you so much as fucking blew your nose.

Bing's house. There were other places that Hazard might be, equally logical places, some perhaps even better choices: the sheriff's evidence lock-up, the station, the ME's office, the Somerset family home, Stillwell's apartment, on and on. But Somers didn't care about logic. He knew what his gut was telling him, and his gut was telling him that Hazard had gone back to Bing's house.

Why had Hazard been so insistent? The question turned with startling clarity in Somers's mind. It was hard to recall, though, what Hazard had explained. Somers had been so angry. Angry that Hazard had tried to take away his case. His case, the case about his father. And angry that Hazard had, once again, seen something that Somers hadn't. And angry—this was the most shameful, the one buried at the bottom of Somers's consciousness—that Hazard had contradicted Somers where Swinney could hear, where the other guests could hear, where Nico could hear. Nico. Somers's hands tightened on the wheel. That, that alone was enough to make him shove the pedal down harder.

Bing's house, when Somers reached it, looked pristine. A new house with new snow on a new street. It could have been something out of Midwest Living: the clean lines, the pristine windows, the glow that spoke of hearth and home—that was the only word for it, a glow, like this was the last warm spot before you hit an endless tundra, like you could put your feet up here and be happy. Wife, kids, Rover. The good life.

The hideous VW wasn't out front, and Somers took a shaky breath and eased up a little. That was something. Maybe Hazard had gone back to the sheriff's. Maybe he'd gone to the station. Maybe he was at the apartment, brooding. Maybe he was sitting there, waiting to talk to Somers. Somers let the Interceptor slow. He could roll past Bing's house. He could head back to the apartment. Hazard would be there, taking up the whole sofa by himself, bulky and brutish and brooding, and they would talk. For the first time in twenty years, they would really talk. Somers turned the Interceptor.

And then he saw the tire tracks in the fresh snow. Tire tracks on Bing's driveway. Again, the Interceptor slowed to a crawl. Maybe it was just coincidence. Maybe it was a friend, maybe it was out-of-town family, maybe it was a pizza delivery guy. It didn't have to be Hazard who had made those tracks.

But Somers knew it had been. He knew it in his gut, and he steered the Interceptor up Bing's drive and shifted into park. His legs had gone to lead. His feet too. His feet, his legs, his gut, all gone to lead, and he had to drag himself out of the Interceptor and up the stairs. By then, his hands had gone too. He could have lifted a mountain as easily as he lifted his hand. Because he was going to have to see Bing. And Bing knew.

Bing knew all of it. Bing had known for fifteen years, ever since he'd laid out a line of coke for Somers at that damn party, ever since he'd caught Somers red-handed. Jesus, wasn't that a great way of putting it. Ever since he'd caught Somers pounding his meat to a picture of Emery Hazard: scrawny, skinny Emery Hazard in a black-and-white yearbook photo. Fucking black-and-white. You couldn't even see the color of those eyes, and that was what had always gotten Somers going.

But back then a picture had to be enough. A black-and-white picture he'd cut out of the yearbook and stuffed in his glovebox, a picture that he moved from glovebox to locker to the desk in his bedroom, rotating it like it was the President's goddamn nuclear codes because no place was really safe, and Somers knew somebody would find it eventually. But back then, that's all he'd had. That's all he could risk. He couldn't even risk seeing Hazard, not after that afternoon in the locker room when—

—the desire in Hazard's eyes hot enough to buckle asphalt—

—Somers had come so close to throwing his whole life away. That's how he'd seen it back then. Throwing his life away. And now, when he thought of—

—Dusty and Frank—

—what the last fifteen years could have been, Somers realized he hadn't been close to throwing his life away. He'd been close to starting it. But instead, he'd put that part of himself on hold because it was easier to go with the flow, easier to do what everyone expected, easier to do what everyone wanted him to do.

It had been Bing who caught him. Bing who had stood there, staring through the Camaro's glass, his face almost comical with its shock. Somers still remembered the mixture of lingering arousal, so slow to respond to the threat before him, and shame. He had jammed the keys into the car and sped out of there, so coked up he was lucky he hadn't driven off the bluffs. Bing hadn't said anything. But he'd known. And just the fact that he'd known had been too much for Somers. The fact that anyone had known his—

—perversion—

—secret, it was almost enough to break him, to crack him like a glass tumbling from a high shelf. So he'd started lying. He'd lied and lied and lied until everything he touched was a lie.

Somers took a breath, startled to find himself still frozen in front of Bing's door, his breath wavering, drifting, vanishing like an exorcised spirit. He'd lied for all these years, and here he was, and the lies hadn't gone away. They'd only gotten thicker.

He knocked.

The footsteps from inside the house were uneven and heavy, and the door flew open so hard that it cracked against the inside wall. Bing, his nose bloody and puffed, his jaw and ear swollen, stood crooked against the doorframe. One big hand clutched at his jaw. The other gripped the jamb, the knuckles white—not from fear of collapse, Somers realized, but in anger. In fury. Bing was a man on the edge, and Somers felt a dark vertigo inside himself. On the edge of what? And what had carried him to that edge? Those were the important questions.

"What happened to you?"

"Did he send you here?"

"What are you talking about? You look like shit. What's going on?"

"Your partner happened." Bing's jaw barely moved beneath his hand. The words came out scrambled. "That's what happened." And without another word, Bing swung the door shut.

Somers intercepted it with his foot, and as he scrambled into the house, Bing turned away and walked towards the living room.

"Bing," Somers called after him. The cold air from outside swept between Somers's legs, drawing snow with it. Already water soaked the boards. Snowmelt. Lots of it. Somers felt a tightening in his gut without words to explain what it meant. "Bing," he shouted again, following the older man into the living room. "What do you mean Hazard did this?"

"What does it sound like I mean?" Bing had dropped onto the couch, his bruised and bloodied face gingerly suspended between the fingers of one hand, a tumbler with two shrunken ice cubes on the table in front of him. His other hand still clutched at his jaw. "My nose is broken. My jaw is broken. I'm going to have that son of a bitch in court. Police brutality. I tried to make things right with him. Somers, you know I tried. You heard me. But he's insane."

"What happened?"

For a moment, Bing didn't answer. When he spoke, the words still sounded like they were coming through a grain mill. "He's crazy. Insane. He's out of his damn mind. He came here to pick a fight. You know that? He came here saying I did—saying I did horrible things. Things you can't say to anybody. Sure as hell can't say them to a father."

"Yeah?" Somers kept his voice even. This was Bing. This was Bing, and Bing knew everything, he knew that deepest, darkest secret, and part of Somers wanted to haul ass. But he didn't. He had a job to do. But his voice still sounded like it was strapped into old ice skates. "What happened?"

"I'm telling you what happened. Aren't you listening? He said all that shit. He wanted me to take a swing at him." Bing let out a dark, pained laugh, and then he groaned and his fingers tightened on his jaw. "That's what happened, he wanted to do this." He jabbed a finger at his broken face. "And he got what he wanted."

"So you took a swing at him."

"Not a chance. Dad's a cop, Somers. I'm not stupid." Shifting on the couch, Bing rubbed at his chest, massaging his ribs, and then his lower back. "Motherfucker hits like dynamite in a tin can, you know that?"

"You gotta tell me what happened. Where's Hazard now?"

Bing grimaced and flipped the finger.

"Where is he?"

"Fuck should I know? Fuck do I care?"

"You going to tell me what happened? Or do I take you to the station and we start making things official?"

"Official? Official? The only thing official about this is going to be when your faggot partner gets that badge ripped out of his hands and goes to prison." Bing grunted, an amused noise. "Big guy, but I bet he bends over and plays the bitch faster than anybody else."

Somers forced himself to straighten his fingers. He forced himself to take a breath. This was Bing, and Somers's fear was so old, so deeply ingrained, that the thoughts were automatic. This was Bing. He knew the truth. So play it cool, that warning voice said. Don't do anything to get him mad. Let it roll right off. Count to ten. One. Two. Three—

"You know what really put his balls in a vise, though?" Bing's face was turned down, studying the ice slivers in his tumbler, but there was no mistaking the note of glee in his voice. Playground glee. The sound of a grade-school bully giving a purple nurple. "Fucker didn't know about you and that picture. Didn't even know why you'd quit the team. I didn't mean to tell him. I figured he knew, what with you two being so close now." And the glee deepened. Not just a purple nurple. This was all of it: titty twister, pink belly, wet willy, rugburn, every playground junkie's favorite games. And Somers's couldn't move, couldn't speak, like everything had gone solid from the neck down. "You like it? You like having that ass in the same room at night? Just get up and tap it when you hit a dry spell? Kind of your wet dream, right?"

The shock of finally hearing it, of finally hearing from Bing the words that Somers had feared for fifteen years, was so great, so terrible, that he was surprised he was still standing. The words had hit him physically. They had hit like a telephone pole cracking him across the shins. They should have knocked him up into the air. That's how he felt: like a hundred and sixty pounds of lead dropping fast.

"I don't know—" It was reflex. It wasn't even language. Just fifteen years of denial acting automatically.

"No, we're past that. What that motherfucker did to me," Bing jabbed another finger at his face, "we're past that. You're hot for him. You were hot for him back then. So hot you just about ripped your own dick off staring at that picture of him. And you're hot for him now. I mean, I knew you and Cora were together. I knew about your kid. But I knew that wasn't all of it. Not for you. When I came back, I wondered if I'd gotten it wrong, but then I saw you with him at the party. You're like a dog."

Somers couldn't find the words to reply.

Bing spoke in the same even, observational tone: a friend pointing out the next turn on a road trip, that kind of voice. "Like a damn dog in heat. That's what you're like. Panting along after him, your little prick hard enough to thread a needle. He doesn't give you the time of day, does he? I saw him at the party. He's got that pretty little piece of ass. You? He doesn't look twice at you. Oh Jesus. Your face. You think—oh Jesus Christ, you think he's into you? I've heard of some tough cases, Somers, but you, you take the cake. You're a piece of shit, remember? You made his life hell. And you think— what? This is some kind of fairy tale? That if you jerk out enough wads, somehow he'll forget that you held him down while Mikey Grames put a knife into him? Jesus, Somers. Open your eyes. Have a little self-respect. The whole town sees you sniffing his ass; you're embarrassing yourself. Embarrassing your folks. Embarrassing Cora, God bless her for sticking around this long."

"You don't know what you're talking about." The words were stiff; that made sense, a distant, logical part of Somers's brain rationalized: he'd gone to lead, solid lead, and he was surprised he could speak at all. He was just so heavy. Just so damn heavy. He didn't feel anything now, but that's how the worst wounds always were. When the pain caught up with him, Somers knew it was going to be bad. Worse than bad. Nuclear.

"You know what he said?"

"We've talked enough about Detective Hazard." It was a miracle. Anything at this point was a miracle, and Somers pressed forward, relying on momentum more than anything else to keep going. "We're going to talk about what happened between the two of you. And then we're going to go down to the station and—"

"You're not listening. You never listened. Not when you were one of my players. Not now. I'd say cut left, you'd cut right. I'd say drop back, you'd rush ahead. I'd scream at you, scream my head off from the sidelines, and you'd run whatever damn play you thought was best." Bing had gotten to his feet, now. He bumped the coffee table as he came around it, and the slivers of ice made tinny rattling noises in the tumbler. A finger stabbed into Somers's chest, and Somers retreated a step. "You're not listening now. I told you what happened." The finger drilled into Somers's chest again. "Your asshole partner." Again, stabbing into taut muscle and driving Somers backward. "Showed up." Again. "And broke." Again. Somers was in the entry hall now. On his next step, snowmelt slicked his foot, and Somers barely caught himself from falling. "My." This time, instead of a finger, Bing slapped his palm against Somers's chest. "Fucking." Again. "Face."

Somers slammed into the door, and he wrenched at the handle, fumbling the damn thing open. Winter met him, cold enough to bring tears to his eyes. Jesus, just let it be the cold, just let it be the cold that was stinging his eyes.

"You know what he said?" Bing, framed by the doorway, smirked through a broken jaw at Somers. "After he did this, after he'd gotten it all out of his system by knocking me around, you know what he said? He said maybe he'd fuck you after all. Maybe he'd go in raw, just rip your chute open. He said he'd like to see you spitted on his cock and screaming. He said he hoped he'd make you bleed. That's what he said. Make you bleed because you made him bleed."

Somers stopped. His brain stopped. The snow scuttling across the drive stopped. The world stopped.

Emery Hazard would never, not in a million years, have said something like that.

The realization was like the sun coming up—the summer sun coming up, hot and close and blazing—turning the snow to melt, the melt to steam, burning away winter in heartbeats. That's what it was like. It was like someone had set a blowtorch to Somers's belly.

He turned to face Bing.

"Ree wouldn't say that."

Bing's startled expression lasted only a moment, and then the smirk was back. "Ree? Is that what you call him? Is that what he wants you to—"

"Ree wouldn't say that. He wouldn't have said any of that."

"You haven't changed. You're still living that fairy tale. Your whole life has been one long fairy tale. Parents made you think everything you did was right. Kids at school worshipped the ground you walked on. College, a job, it all just fell right into your lap. And you think that, what? Because you're John-Henry Somerset, you can dip your wick wherever you want it and nobody will care? You think you're special? You think things are different? If I breathe one word of this, if I even hint at it, people in this town will tear you apart. They'll tear both of you apart. You want me to keep your secret? You want me to shut my mouth so that you and your faggot partner can bone each other? Get the fuck off my porch and get the fuck out of my life. That's the only way I'm keeping my mouth shut, Somers, because if I see you again, if I so much as see you crossing the street, I'll tell everybody I know about your itchy pecker and that picture of your buddy."

Somers surprised himself by laughing. He shook out his hands. He felt loose. In spite of the cold, he felt relaxed, limber, like he'd stretched out all the stiffness, all the kinks. Like he'd been packed in a box and now, just barely, now he could stand up. Yeah, something like that. Like he could breathe.

"It's the twenty-first fucking century, Bing. Nobody that matters gives a shit about any of that stuff anymore. If I love Ree, that's my business."

"If I love Ree," Bing repeated with a mocking simper. "You sound just like him, just like a perfect queen."

"Get out of the way."

"What?"

"Get out of my way, Bing."

"Nice fucking chance. This is my home, and I'm not—"

"You just admitted to an altercation with another police officer. That police officer isn't answering his phone, so I think I'm pretty well justified in looking around your house. Now get out of my way unless you want me to cuff you."

Red mottled Bing's face, visible even under the blood and bruises. One hand probed at his chest, massaging ribs, and then drifted to his lower back again. "You better not touch anything. Not one fucking thing, you hear me?"

Somers pushed through the door.

Bing brought around his hand, now holding a gun, and swung it towards Somers's chest. Somers was ready for him. He caught Bing's wrist and twisted. In half a moment, he had Bing's arm wrenched around, and the gun clattered onto the floor.

"And Bing," Somers said as he slammed Bing into the wall and snapped cuffs around his wrists. "I could hear you just fine during those football games. You called the same plays every time. Predictable. You were then. You still are now."

A raw nerve inside Somers urged him to hurry. Hazard could be hurt. Hazard could be—

—dead—

—in need of medical assistance. With Bing cuffed, Somers took a step towards the living room. He had to find him. There wasn't any time to lose. He had to—

No. Somers forced the compulsion down. Better to do things right. Better to do things step by step, the way Hazard would do them. So he took Bing out to the Interceptor, locked him into the back, and called in the incident. Then he waited for backup.

The black-and-white skidded into the driveway a few minutes later, spraying snow and slush across the yard. When the car screeched to a halt, Jonny Moraes—young, black, easy-going—

darted out of the passenger seat. He didn't look so easy-going as he trotted towards Somers. His partner, the big, red-headed Patrick Foley, followed a moment later.

"You sure put a bee up Cravens's ass," Moraes said, hand on his sidearm as he glanced through the window at Bing. Bing, for his part, rested his face on tented fingers, ignoring the cop's attention. "I bet the whole damn station will be here soon."

"One of you stay here with him," Somers said, jerking his head at the Interceptor. "I haven't cleared the house. We might have an officer down."

"You think—"

Please, no. That was what Somers was thinking, just those two words: please, no. But he managed to iron the worst of the fear out of his voice and said, "Nobody can get in touch with Ree. Shit. With Hazard."

Moraes pitched a sideways glance at Foley. Somers didn't care. He didn't have a damn to give about what they thought.

"Go," Foley said.

"Don't let anybody else near him," Somers said.

"I know what I'm doing, Somers."

"Don't let Swinney and Lender take him."

"What the fuck are you talking about? What do you mean Swinney and Lender?"

"Nobody. Not even Cravens."

Somers didn't wait to see what Foley thought about that. He headed towards the house, and Moraes followed Somers to the door. They went into the house with weapons drawn, clearing it room by room, floor by floor.

The main floor was empty. The second floor was abandoned. Somers returned to the kitchen, and this time, his eye caught the rust-colored smear along the basement door. Just a trace of it. Easy to miss from the wrong angle, in the wrong light. Dried blood. He nudged the door open.

Pitch black down there. Knocking the lights on with the back of his hand, Somers took the stairs carefully. Where was Daisy? Was she hiding in the dark with one of Bing's rifles? Was she watching Somers come down the steps, holding her breath, lining up the shot? Jesus, where was Hazard? And what was that smell?

"Gasoline," Moraes whispered, and he pointed to the next step. Gasoline still darkened the unpainted wood. "Gallons of it. Look."

Somers remembered the look in Daisy's eyes as she had talked about their home in Chicago. She had told them that Hadley burned it down. She had told them that it was proof of Hadley's oppositional defiant disorder. The truth, though, was clear in the spattered gasoline. Had Daisy lied to them, trying to cover up her daughter's murder? Or had Daisy not known the truth? Had she never known?

Somers's foot came down on cement. The fumes hung thick in the closed space, making him dizzy. Somers paced the length of the basement. Unfinished drywall and dust. That's all. Nothing else in the whole goddamn place. Where was Hazard? Somers's mind conjured up a litany of horrible possibilities: Hazard's mutilated body dragged out into the frozen emptiness; Hazard strapped into his car and driven into the Grand Rivere; Hazard dying, alone, where no one would find him. Somers's breathing quickened. His field of vision shimmered as the gasoline fumes poisoned him.

"No sign of him," Moraes said, covering his mouth and nose with his sleeve. "Let's get out of here before something sparks and we get toasted."

Somers nodded, following Moraes to the stairs. But something at the edge of his hearing stopped him.

"Come on," Moraes said. "This place could go up any minute."

Shaking his head, Somers held up a hand.

"Somers, we gotta—"

"Get upstairs then. Or stay. But you've got to be quiet."

Moraes, to his credit, stayed, but he glanced at the rectangle of light above them and sighed. Somers ignored him. The shimmering in front of his eyes had grown worse. A headache had started, a white-hot magnesium fire buried deep in his skull. He needed air, fresh air. But he stood still. He had heard something. He knew it.

A tap. The sound was so quiet that it barely even deserved the name, more of a brush of contact than anything else. But Somers had heard it. He took a few nervous paces deeper into the basement.

There it was again. He followed the noise. His heart jittered every time the soft rap sounded. Please, please, please. That was all Somers could think, and he knew it wasn't helping, but the headache was getting worse, and he felt like he was seeing everything from under six feet of water.

Then the sound was right next to him. Coming right out of the wall. Somers stared at the taped and mudded drywall; the headache pounded like a war drum. No, he realized, his thoughts sluggish. The sound wasn't coming out of the wall. It was coming from behind the wall.

He started hammering on the drywall. Then, realizing he needed more force, he backed up and rammed into the wall. Gypsum and paper crumpled inwards. Rubbing his aching shoulder, Somers bent to peer through the hole he had made. More darkness met him, but Somers could tell that the space was large—larger than he had expected. And someone was in there. Someone was breathing, and the breaths were ragged and pained.

"Ree?" Somers pounded on the drywall, and gypsum shifted loose and spun and dusted his trousers. "Jesus Christ, Ree? Are you in there?"

It felt like an eternity before a familiar deep voice croaked, "John-Henry?" Another pause intervened, and when Hazard spoke again, he sounded like a man getting off the Tilt-a-Whirl. "It's dark."

Somers fought back maniacal laughter. "We're coming. Just hold on. We're coming. Moraes, for fuck's sake, get over here. No. Go get Foley. Get whoever the hell you can find. Ree, we're coming. Hold on. Hold on, Ree. I'm coming."

CHAPTER THIRTY-EIGHT

**DECEMBER 25
MONDAY
9:13 AM**

HAZARD REMEMBERED THE AMBULANCE ride to the hospital, but only because the jarring movement had threatened to shake his head to pieces. He remembered, too, the sudden glare of fluorescent lights, the swish and rattle of curtains sliding along tracks, the occasional hiccup of the stretcher caused by an irregularity in one of the wheels. He remembered thinking that he needed to tell somebody because it was damned uncomfortable.

Pain chopped the rest of the night into fragments: the pinpoint prick of a light in his eyes, a doctor's voice asking questions and demanding answers, the thrum and blitz of the x-ray machine, murmured voices talking about an MRI, maybe a CT scan, and the feeling of long, slender fingers sliding into his hand, and Nico's voice, and then the starched coolness of a hospital gown, and the papery sheets pulled up to his chest, and darkness. Blessed, perfect darkness before he slipped away.

When he woke, day was already in full progress, beaming through the windows. The room looked familiar: the curry-colored walls, the fading border overhead. And then the headache kicked him like a mule on a bad day, and Hazard groaned and clapped hands over his eyes. The light stabbed right to the brain. How could there be so much light in the world?

Someone shifted, clothing rustled, and a cool hand touched his arm.

"Somers?"

The silence was answer enough, and even through the headache, Hazard knew he'd stepped into it again.

"No. It's Nico."

"Sorry."

"No, it's ok."

"I just—" Hazard expelled a breath. "My head. Could you close the blinds?"

Another long silence. "They are closed, Emery."

"Yeah. Ok."

The sound came of Nico settling back into the chair. His slender fingers ran up and down Hazard's arm. The bandage rustled under his touch, the bandage that Nico had applied to cover up the puncture wounds Grace Elaine had left. The headache didn't get any better, but it didn't get any worse either.

"I'll find a nurse."

"Yeah."

Nico's soles squeaked on the linoleum, and he came back with a woman as old as the railroad and built out of the same stuff. She made Hazard opened his eyes, ignored his explanation—a very rational, detailed explanation of why his head was hurting—and ran him through a battery of questions. Not until she had finished did she give him a paper cup with two blue pills, which Hazard swallowed. Then she left, and Hazard covered his eyes again, and Nico's hand feathered up and down Hazard's arm again.

After a while, Hazard managed to say, "Head's better."

"That's good."

"What happened?"

"Why don't you rest some more? We can talk about it when you're feeling better."

Hazard thought carefully about how to phrase the next question. "Is everyone ok?"

"Besides you?"

"I'm fine."

"You got hit in your head so hard you have a skull fracture. You're not fine."

"I'm all right."

"You're lucky you're not—I don't even know. You're lucky you're not in a coma. You're lucky you're not dead." Nico was shouting.

"My head, remember?"

When Nico spoke again, his voice had lowered, but the edges were still ragged. "Sorry."

"Everybody else was—"

"He's fine, Emery. Can't you just ask me what you want to ask me? John-Henry is fine."

Hazard subsided into silence. The drugs had taken off some of the headache's edge, but he still felt like his head might come apart at the next loud noise.

"He's not here," Nico finally said. "If that's what you're wondering, he's not sitting out in the hall or anything."

"I wasn't wondering."

"Bullshit."

"I wasn't."

"He rode with you in the ambulance, and when I got here, he left."

"All right."

"I've been here the whole time."

"Nico, for fuck's sake." Hazard paused to draw a breath and smother the flicker of rage. "Are you trying to pick a fight?"

Something like ten minutes must have gone by before Nico spoke again, and now his voice was soft, conciliatory. "They got Bing."

"That's good."

"Everybody's ok. Oh, God. That's not really true, I guess. They found his wife. He . . ." Nico didn't seem able to finish.

"He killed her."

Nico's fingers tightened on Hazard's arm. "Yes. Well, someone did. But it must have been him, right?"

"I guess so."

"She was out in her car. They didn't find her until this morning."

"Gunshot?"

Nico didn't answer, but by the way his fingers tightened again, Hazard knew he'd guessed correctly.

"Emery," Nico said, and from the sound of his voice, Hazard knew he was crying. "Your head. You could have—"

Hazard peeled his fingers away from his eyes. Nico had his head down, and he was rubbing his wrist across his face. Taking Nico by the arm, Hazard pulled him towards the bed.

"Come here."

"No, it's just—"

"Get up here."

Slowly, with his usual coltish grace, Nico clambered up beside Hazard and curled against his side. Burying his face in Hazard's chest, Nico drew a deep breath. A tremor shook him, and then another, and then another, until he was crying in earnest. Hazard ran his hand through Nico's thick black hair, ran his hand down the younger man's broad back, and waited until the worst of the crying had stopped.

When Nico had calmed down, Hazard pushed shaggy hair behind the younger man's ear and said, "You didn't sleep."

"I don't know. I dozed for a little."

"Go on, then."

"Are you—"

"My head's killing me. I'd like to close my eyes."

"If you're sure."

"I'm sure."

In moments, Nico had dropped into sleep, curling against Hazard possessively whenever Hazard shifted. For a while, Hazard dozed, but the pain in his head hovered at a knife's edge. When the door clicked open, Hazard glanced over.

Somers looked like he always did: so hot he could have started a grease fire just by turning his head. Dressed in his usual casual clothes—a t-shirt that looked like it had been wadded into a ball, jeans with a million different creases, battered sneakers, a fleece-lined denim jacket—Somers still looked like he could have stepped off a runway.

When Somers saw Nico, he cocked an eyebrow and whispered, "I'll come back."

"Like hell. Sit down."

With a grin, Somers dropped into the chair, kicking his legs up onto the bed.

"Were you raised in a barn?"

Somers's grin turned into a smirk. "Guess you finally got the medical diagnosis, right?"

"What? Oh. Sort of. Nico told me there's a fracture."

Somers snorted. "No, the real diagnosis."

"Huh?"

"You know how everybody always wondered why you were such an ass?"

"Jesus Christ."

"No, I'm just saying, it's been a mystery how you can consistently be the most stubborn, pig-headed, arrogant man to ever walk the earth."

"Is this why you came here?"

"But medical science finally has an answer."

Hazard waited. He felt a smile teasing at the corners of his mouth and he quashed it.

"Thick head," Somers pronounced, as though he were naming an incurable disease. "Like, three times thicker than any normal human's."

"You're a dick."

"It's not me saying this. It's science."

In spite of Hazard's best efforts, the smile slipped onto his lips. Somers's grin could have lit every Christmas tree for a hundred miles.

"Thanks," Hazard said.

"You fucked up."

Hazard didn't know how to answer.

"You really fucked up."

"I know."

"You shouldn't have gone by yourself."

"It was just an interview."

"You shouldn't have left him alone."

Shifting uncomfortably, Hazard nodded.

"You should have talked to me." Before Hazard could object, Somers held up a hand. "I know. I was an asshole. I deserved getting socked in the jaw, and I deserved more. But we're partners. You know I've got your back."

And for some reason, the next two words were the hardest Hazard had ever spoken because they came so close to the truth, so close to what he had buried inside himself for all those years. "I know."

Somers paused, as though making sure the words had settled, and then a smile crept onto his face. "Cravens is going to peel your hide with a butter knife."

"God. I'll be lucky if she doesn't—no, it's all right. You can go back to sleep."

Nico blinked up at him. His hand flexed across Hazard's chest, and he stretched.

"We're talking about the case."

"I know." Nico rolled up, rubbed a pillow crease along his cheek, and swung his legs off the bed.

"You can stay."

"I know."

But he loped out of the room, and when the door closed behind him, he still hadn't even looked at Somers.

Hazard glared at his partner. "Don't say anything."

Somers held up his hands. He was trying—and it looked like an honest effort—but he couldn't hide the satisfaction in his face. Hazard fought the urge to huck a pillow at him.

"So let's hear it," Somers said.

"What?"

"You're the brilliant detective. What was it that gave Bing away?" Somers hesitated, worry creasing his forehead. "You didn't guess, did you? If you went to his house on a guess, I'm going to rip your balls off."

"No. It was—" Hazard stopped himself before he could mention Somers's mother. "It was something Nico said. About parents who become infatuated with their children. Pathologically, I mean."

"Uh huh." Somers's tide-pool eyes flickered. He wasn't a dummy, and Hazard hurried on before either of them said more.

"So I tried that scenario out: I put Bing at the center of it all."

Somers ticked off his words on his fingers. "The boyfriend in Chicago, he arranged that. The house burning down, too. He must have decided that his plans worked so well the first time, it wouldn't hurt to try them again. He framed Hadley plenty of times before. And Daisy believed it."

"Or she wanted to believe it. Daisy seemed like a woman who only knew what she wanted to know, and I don't think she wanted to face the truth."

"That's harsh. You think she knew Hadley was being raped by Bing and didn't do anything to stop it?"

Hazard shrugged. "People do worse things all the time. She might not have known, but that's like I said: she didn't want to know. Not really. Easier to blame everything on Hadley's moodiness—as though the girl didn't have every right in the world to be angry. Bing used it to his advantage."

"He had access to her phone," Somers said. "We know that; they told us that. All he had to do was find a chance to get the phone, when she was asleep, maybe, and send those emails. Same thing with the fire. It was easy to pin everything on Hadley; easy when she was too frightened to tell anyone the truth." And then a thought pinged inside Somers. "Until she wasn't. Afraid, I mean. She was going to tell Dusty and Frank."

Hazard nodded. "Because she was pregnant. That's what started all this. That's when she couldn't take it anymore."

For a moment, Somers didn't respond. Emotions flickered across his face like heat lightning, and then, in a rough voice, he said, "Let's start from the beginning."

"He was abusing her. Sexually, obviously, and undoubtedly for years."

"It might have gone on that way for even longer," Somers said. "Bing must have thought he had her good and scared. He liked that feeling. He liked being in control of the situation. And he knew how to manipulate people, up to a point. He knew how to—" He stopped.

"He was good," Hazard admitted grudgingly. "He knew how to punch my buttons."

"Me too," Somers said, and again emotions stormed across his face. Pain, this time. Even Hazard could tell that much. Somers spoke again, "Could have gone on a hell of a lot longer. Until she went to college, maybe. But something went wrong. Something Bing thought he could prevent, but somehow it slipped past him."

Hazard nodded. "She got a boyfriend."

"And that raised all sorts of new dangers."

"Yes. Hadley now had somebody she could confide in. Somebody she might trust, somebody she might think could protect her. If they had sex—even if they didn't—he might come to suspect what was happening."

Nodding, Somers said slowly, "Yeah. You're right. But for Bing, I think it was more than that. Worse than that. She was his. That's how he saw people. Not just sexually either. I think he saw me as his—his player, his property as far as that was concerned. Hadley was his too. And somebody was touching something that was his. So he had to put a stop to it."

"As you pointed out earlier, Bing had parental access to Hadley's phone. It wouldn't have been difficult for him to get her phone, forge those emails and hire someone off Craigslist to assault the boyfriend."

"But the situation escalated," Somers said. "The police were involved. Hadley faced charges. Again, there was the chance that the truth might come out."

"It didn't, though." Hazard slapped the bed's railing, and the metal chimed. "That's what I don't get. She had a thousand opportunities to tell. But she didn't. And before you lecture me, I know the psychology behind it. I know that it's common for victims of abuse to conceal the crime, even to aid their abuser. But I still don't get it. It doesn't make sense."

A long moment passed. Somers's tropical blue eyes flitted around the room. Then, with a glance that lasted less than a breath, Somers looked at Hazard and then away again. "Sometimes people can't say what's inside them, Ree. Sometimes they just can't." And the hell of it was that Hazard could have sworn Somers was talking about something else entirely.

The thought unnerved Hazard, although he couldn't say why, and he forced himself to continue their conversation. "In any case, Bing must have been worried that things had become too dangerous in Chicago. He burned down the house. And no, I don't have any proof of that, but you have to admit it fits."

"He'd already done good work painting Hadley as unstable. Oppositional defiant disorder covers just about every bad behavior you can imagine. It was the best lie, the most effective lie. And we believed it. At least, I believed it. Frank and Dusty, they tried to tell us that wasn't what Hadley was really like, but—I don't know. I thought they were trying to speak kindly of her. I thought maybe they just didn't know."

"We both did."

"Bing, with a convenient scapegoat, burns down the house in Chicago. They have to move. They come here. Home. Where he's got a golden reputation. Where he knows people. Where his father's the sheriff."

"A fresh start," Hazard agreed, "and an added layer of protection."

"But the same problems started up again. Hadley had a boyfriend." Somers's mouth quirked into a grin. "Two of them, actually. They were close. They might have learned the truth. So the question is, why didn't he go through with his old plan? Why not just hire someone to scare them off? Hell, his dad's the sheriff—he could have scared them off without hiring anyone. What was different?"

"Daisy told us. She didn't know it, but she told us. Remember she said that Bing walked in on them. She was very clear about that. Bing said they weren't doing anything wrong, but she said he walked in on them. And Dusty told us what they were doing."

"Sweet Christ," Somers said. "Dusty kept saying how horrible it turned out, but I just imagined—I mean, I thought they just couldn't make it work. But Bing walking in on them, Jesus, they're lucky he didn't kill them."

"I think he wanted to. He certainly wouldn't have minded." Hazard paused. "I hadn't considered this before, but I think you're right: he saw Hadley as his. Finding out that someone else—anyone else—was having sex with her must have driven Bing crazy."

"He threatened her," Somers said. "He raped her. He beat her. And he put down a hard rule: no more boys. She had to cut it off with Frank and Dusty. That's why she went so cold on them. She was scared of her dad, and she had to prove she was toeing the line."

"I talked to Dusty. After I left your house, I called him. I knew I'd missed something, and I wanted to find out what it was. Dusty told me. At the party at your parents' house, Bing confronted Dusty while Frank was in the bathroom. It was a physical altercation; he ripped off the chain, and that's why we found it outside. Dusty told me that Bing threatened Frank. He said that he could make some very bad things happen to Frank. That's why Bing used the bag, I think. He took it to the party, made sure people saw it, made sure everyone thought Stillwell was carrying it and that there was a gun inside, and then he took it with him when he left. If anyone saw it, he was hoping it would lead us to Frank and Dusty. I think Bing must have made those same threats to Hadley. I think that's how he got Hadley to call it off with them. And I think that's why Hadley turned on them."

Somers arched a perfect blond eyebrow. "She was protecting them?"

"Trying to."

"Damn."

"So Bing walks in on them. He's insane with rage. He has to hurt somebody, and he hurts Hadley. He—" Somers hesitated. "He rapes her. He's not careful. And he gets her pregnant." Again, Somers hesitated. "But did he know?"

With a shrug, Hazard shook his head.

"She's pregnant," Somers said, speaking like a man stringing beads and finally seeing a pattern. "She's scared, but not just for herself. That changes things. She decides she needs help, and she contacts Dusty. She's going to tell him. She's going to ask for his help. Running away, I think, because she talked about leaving. But her parents control her phone. No. Wait." His eyes shot up to Hazard's. "That wasn't her phone. It was a new number, Dusty told us that."

"Yes. That part I haven't worked out yet. I assume she bought the phone on her own, but I'm not sure how she got the money. Bing lied, remember? He tried to claim the phone was hers. Daisy wasn't quite fast enough; she didn't recognize it."

"So Bing didn't know about the new phone. And that means he didn't know about the phone call to Dusty. Why does he decide to kill her?" Somers raised a hand, stopping Hazard from answering. Those blue eyes, the color of Cancun waters, so beautiful that they stopped Hazard's heart like Superman stopping a train—and God help anybody still riding that train—narrowed in concentration. They were darker when he concentrated. A darker blue, the deep blue of when you swam below the warm waters. He was so beautiful, Hazard thought, and he knew it was a crazy thought, knew he was crazy for still thinking things like that, but it was the truth: Somers was just so beautiful. And smart. And intuitive. And talented. And funny. And annoying as hell, but God, was it insane that Hazard even loved that, even loved that goddamn annoying streak that ran a mile wide through Somers?

Somers spoke, interrupting Hazard's thoughts. "Because she was pregnant. Somehow he found out, and he knew that he couldn't keep it hidden any longer. He had to get rid of her. And he—are you ok?"

"Fine."

"You're flushed."

"I said I'm fine."

"I'll get a nurse. Your face looks like it's on fire."

"Somers, sit down. We're not finished. And if you leave, Nico's going to come back in here, and I don't think I can—" Hazard broke off the speech. He wasn't sure what he'd been about to say, but he knew his face suddenly felt a hell of a lot hotter.

"Yeah," Somers said, sinking back into his chair, as smug as if he'd just gotten a hole in one and trying—honest-to-God trying, which only made it worse—not to show it. "If you're all right."

"Yes."

"Because your face—"

"Anyway," Hazard said gruffly, "you're right. At least, I think you're right. He knew she was pregnant and decided to eliminate her. Frank and Dusty were his backup plan."

"He was trying to frame Hadley. That's why it seemed so similar to what had happened in Chicago. But we never could figure out who sent those emails. His plan didn't work; we didn't lock onto Hadley as a suspect."

"Because of the phone. That was what Bing didn't count on. He didn't know she had a second phone. When she was killed, he expected us to find her phone. When we took it to him, he would have used his parental access to unlock it. We would have found emails from Hadley to Stillwell. We might have even found something more incriminating—a draft asking Stillwell to bring a gun, or a picture of your parents' house, something like that. But it all went to crap, and instead, we started looking at everyone."

For a long moment, Somers was silent. Emotion tightened his features. "So my father was—what? Collateral damage?"

"Probably."

"That's stupid."

"I said probably."

"No, that's not what I meant." Somers blew out a breath. "Am I pissed that I went at this from the wrong angle? Sure. I focused too much on my father. I get that now. Hell, I don't even know if I could do it differently even if I wanted to. It was too personal. But what I'm saying is that it was stupid to shoot him. He's too high profile. It drew too much attention."

"I don't know," Hazard said. "If it hadn't been you—if you hadn't pushed on this, if it hadn't been personal—he might have gotten away with it. The case would have looked closed. Stillwell was dead." Hazard frowned. "I still don't know how he managed that. Did you see Bing somewhere near the phone? Somehow he used

Hadley's phone to call Lender. That doesn't make sense, though." Hazard shifted in the bed. "Damn it. I thought I had all this."

Thought creased Somers's forehead, but he didn't speak.

"What?" Hazard asked.

Somers shook his head. "I don't know. Smartphones stay unlocked for a certain amount of time. Maybe he grabbed it while it was still unlocked."

"I guess so."

"Bing got lucky."

"In a lot of ways. But not lucky enough."

"No, I mean with the shooting."

"I don't think so," Hazard said. "He planned the whole thing carefully. He broke into your parents' house and rigged the breaker box; he taught shop, remember, and he knew that kind of stuff. Then, the night of the party, Stillwell showed up—naked and high and singing. Your dad and the others would have thrown him out, except Bing shouted that Stillwell had a gun. That was worrisome enough that they held onto him and called you. Bing had the gun in that Victoria's Secret bag. It looked a lot like a bag that Santa might carry. Nobody really doubted that Stillwell was carrying it because it matched his Santa Claus hat. Bing probably hadn't expected us to show up, but he was prepared anyway: he had a set of handcuff keys." Hazard touched fingertips to the bandage around his head, and even that faint vibration sent shockwaves through his skull. "Either from his dad, most likely, or that he bought online. When Bing was ready, he uncuffed Stillwell, gave him the gun, and hurried back to the party."

"That's exactly what I mean, though. Think about it: Bing made it back to the party. He must have told Stillwell to wait because Stillwell didn't come out immediately. But Stillwell was also high as a kite. His brain was fried. When he got to the party, he—he was slow. He didn't know what to do. His first shot was way too high, and then he fired at Hadley, but it was only luck that he actually hit her. Jesus, five of the bullets went into my father."

Hazard couldn't help it. In spite of the ache in his head, in spite of his usual reserve, a smirk stretched his mouth.

"What?" Somers said.

Hazard shrugged.

"You're going to play it coy all of the sudden? Bullshit. What am I missing?"

"You just said it. You said all the facts you need."

Somers thought, his brow tightening. After a moment, he added, "This coy business is really annoying."

"You'll get it."

"You're being an asshole."

"Stillwell had a revolver. A Ruger GP100."

For another moment, confusion clouded Somers's gaze. Then he said, "That's too many shots. That's seven rounds. One into the ornament. Five into my father. One into Hadley. I knew something was off."

"Bing was very careful: he made sure both guns were loaded with the same cartridges. Unless we ran a ballistics comparison, we never would have known they were fired from separate guns." Hazard paused, "Technically, we still need to do that comparison; everything I've got is theoretical. It was a brilliant switch, and it would have worked if things had gone as Bing hoped. Stillwell probably wasn't supposed to fire overhead. If he hadn't hit that ornament, and if glass hadn't gone everywhere, people might not have remembered the first shot. Hell, I might not have remembered it if we hadn't found the casing in the trash. Six casings in the evidence lockup, plus one that someone tried to hide. Seven shots fired."

Somers pursed his lips, still thinking. "So there were two guns. And that doesn't make any sense. The risk was enormous; why would Bing orchestrate such a complicated murder and then still end up being the one who shot Hadley?"

"He's insane. Totally irrational. And besides, nobody caught in a firefight is going to count the shots."

"Nobody except you," Somers said, but he softened the words with a smile. "I don't think that's it, though. At least, not entirely—I think it was more than that. Hadley was his, right? And Bing was all about ownership. About control. You heard Daisy: he had her followed just because he wanted to. This was part of the same way of thinking. He wanted Hadley dead. He didn't want to go to prison for it. But he had to do it himself."

Hazard thought back to his last encounter with Bing: to the force of the man's words, to the insistence in his voice, to the overwhelming sense of control that Bing had exerted. It hadn't worked. Hazard was past that part of his life. He'd done that shit with Alec already. But still—he repressed a shiver as he remembered the look on Bing's face.

"That's it, then," Somers said.

"You think there's more?"

"No. I wish we had some answers. Why did Bing call Lender, for example? And why did Lender do what he asked? Where'd the second phone come from?"

"Unless we can link Bing to Hadley's phone—unless someone actually saw him placing that call—we're out of luck. All we have right now is a strange call to Lender from a dead girl's phone. It's weird. It's weird enough that Cravens might even do something about it. But it's not enough to make Lender talk." Hazard let out a frustrated breath. "That's if Swinney will even take our side. You saw her: she's a mess."

Somers opened his mouth to speak, but before he could, the door swung open. Nico stepped inside. In one hand, an envelope dangled; in the other, he held a sheet of paper. Even through the paper, Hazard could see the letters that had been cut and pasted onto the page.

"What is that?" Hazard demanded.

"What? Oh. Some guy handed it to me."

"Some guy? Who?"

"I don't know."

"What did he look like?"

"I don't know."

"You don't know what he looked like?" Somers asked.

Nico, flushing, kept his gaze on Hazard. "He was just a guy. An older guy, I guess. He had a ballcap on. He didn't even stop. Shoved this into my hands as he walked past."

"And you opened it?" Hazard scooted towards the edge of the bed. "Let me see it. What does it say?"

"Stop," Somers said, directing a stern glance at Hazard—stern enough, anyway, to keep Hazard in bed. Then, snatching the letter from Nico, Somers read over it.

"Hey," Nico said, reaching for the letter. "Give that back. That's not yours. I had it. John-Henry—Emery, make him give it back."

Somers ignored him; the only concession he made to Nico's demands was to turn away when Nico reached for the paper, putting it slightly out of reach. As Somers read, his face colored, and he muttered a swear under his breath.

"What is it?" Hazard said.

"It's about you," Nico said, making another attempt to grab the letter. "It's—Jesus, John-Henry give it back."

"It's nothing," Somers said.

"Like hell," Hazard said.

"I'm telling you it's nothing." Somers folded it carefully and set it down on the chair next to him.

"Either you give it to me, or I'll get out of this bed and take it."

Blowing out a breath, Somers ran a hand through his hair. "You're recovering. We'll deal with it—"

"Like hell," Hazard repeated, holding out a hand.

Somers, a grimace plastered on his face, passed over the paper.

"It's about you," Nico repeated, but Hazard barely heard him. For a moment, Hazard didn't hear anything.

Pasted to the page, letters cut out of magazines and newspapers spelled out five simple words: *Leave before word gets around*. That was it. Five words. And below, two more: *Jonas Cassidy*.

"What is this?" Hazard said.

"Blackmail," Somers said. "Somebody wants you to keep your mouth shut."

"What the fuck is this?"

"This is the mayor. He threatened you once, remember? He was talking about you, back in St. Louis, and those were his words. Those were his mother-fucking words: word gets around. Remember?"

"Who gave this to you?"

"I said I don't know," Nico snapped. "And who's Jonas Cassidy? And what are you talking about, blackmail? What happened in St. Louis? What does it mean, leave?"

"You've got to remember something besides a ballcap. How old? Hair? Clothes? How did he walk?"

"I said I don't know. What do you want me to do? Make something up?"

"Was he breathing?" Somers asked with that bastard grin he kept sharp for moments like this. "That'd be nice to—"

"Get out," Nico said. "Just get the fuck out. Everything was going fine until you showed up."

"I didn't do anything."

"Yeah. You're damn right you didn't do anything. You let him," Nico gestured at Hazard, "do everything. You aren't there. You're never there. He gets shot. He gets beaten within an inch of his life. He gets his skull cracked. And where are you? Drinking mimosas with the good old boys from high school. That's where you are. Drunk off your ass because that's what you are, a worthless drunk. You think I don't know? You think people don't talk? You think everybody isn't laughing at you behind your back while your wife—"

"That's enough," Hazard said. He didn't even remember getting out of bed, but he was standing now—standing on legs like old sponges, but standing.

"He—" Nico began.

"Enough."

Hazard turned. Somers's face was white. He still had that bastard grin, and it still looked sharp enough to cut. Sharp enough, anyway, to cut through all the bullshit. And Somers's face, underneath the pallor, said it all: this is what you get. This, this kind of behavior, this is what you get when you date a child.

He didn't say it. He hadn't said a word. He didn't need to; it was all in that damn smirk.

"I'm sorry," Hazard began.

"No. No, at least he said it to my face. I'll just—I'll go." Somers moved towards the door, every motion languid and fluid, like he'd just gotten up from sunbathing. He stopped and looked back and spoke to Nico. "I'm sorry. About letting him get hurt, I'm really sorry."

And then he looked at Hazard. Just a glance really. And to anybody else, to the whole world, he would have looked wounded, like a whipped dog. But those eyes said differently. Those eyes were the eyes of a man who's called a coin in the air and won—not just once, but ten times running.

CHAPTER THIRTY-NINE

DECEMBER 25
MONDAY
11:58 PM

AFTER THE TALK WITH HAZARD, Somers drove. Nowhere in particular; he just needed to be out and moving. He found himself laughing from time to time, as fragments of the conversation worked their way into his memory. Laughing at Nico's anger, mostly. Sure, he was pretty. Beyond pretty, if Somers were honest—the kid was gorgeous, all that shaggy dark hair, his toasted skin, the whole package, pun only slightly intended.

But pretty didn't make up for petty, and the kid had shown himself petty as shit. So Somers laughed as he thought of the way Nico had screamed at him. He laughed as he thought of how easy it had been—candy from a baby—to poke the kid into a fit. He laughed as he thought of that bozo look on Hazard's face because Hazard knew, he knew this kid was on a whole different planet when it came to what mattered: being an adult, being a man. The laughter came in spurts, though—never hard and heavy, never a belly laugh. And then the spurts slowed like a motor that wouldn't quite turn over. And then Somers found himself on a dirt road a mile outside of Wahredua, head on the steering wheel, fighting back a sob that was trying to crack his breastbone.

And when he could breathe again, when that pain wasn't splitting him down the middle, he drove back to Wahredua Regional. He parked the Interceptor at the back of the lot, near a snow-dusted pickup, and walked through the flurries into the hospital. He found his father's room. Glenn Somerset looked bad. Not as bad as the day before, or the day before that, thank God, but bad. His skin was yellow in the hospital lighting, and his hair was listless and snarled, and everything sagged, his face worst of all, as though he were fighting twice the gravity as everyone else. He'd been shot five times in the chest, and that number meant something. Wayne Stillwell had been shot five times in the chest as well. Five times wasn't a coincidence.

Somers thumbed through the contacts on his phone and sent a text.

He waited hours in the darkness, with the smell of an old man and the muffled sounds of castors and voices and a TV somewhere running episodes of *Night Court*. Hazard wasn't far, and that thought was tempting. Not far at all: a hallway, two flights of stairs, an odd-number of doors. Just a few hundred yards, all told. A few hundred yards and one giant roadblock. That was ok, as far as tonight went. Somers needed to be here. He had a meeting.

Shadows had swallowed the room. They had swallowed the tan-colored walls. They had swallowed the chrome bed rails. They had swallowed the clock. It was only by his phone that Somers saw the minutes ticking down towards midnight.

The door opened. Light from the hallway sliced a wedge out of the darkness, and a figure moved through that light, and the door shut. There were three men breathing in that room, and the beep and rattle of the machines, and the old man smell and now something else: leather, sweat, brass.

"You might as well turn on the light," Somers said. "Unless you're planning on shooting me in the dark."

There wasn't an answer, but a moment later, the lights came on. Somers blinked against their brightness. As his eyes cleared, they settled on the gun held in front of him. It looked very small. Like a toy, like it might fire caps but nothing else. Sheriff Bingham, behind the gun, looked small too. He had shrunk over the past twenty-four hours. A few stray white hairs curled at the end of his chin; they were so small Somers might not have noticed, but they were surprisingly luminous in the fluorescents.

"You might as well sit down too."

Vinyl squeaked. The gun never wavered.

"If you shoot me in the hospital, they'll hear it." Somers smiled a hard, tight smile. "If you have your son's luck, they'll probably just patch me up while they drag you to jail."

"Shut up."

"I'm sorry."

"I said shut up." The gun jabbed forward. For a minute, maybe more, Somers was silent. Then the sheriff spoke again. "I didn't know. If that's what you're thinking, you don't understand jack."

Somers didn't bother answering. He knew the sheriff's reputation. He knew you'd need more than Ivory soap to get the stains out of this old man. And anyway Somers had learned how to wait. He'd watched Hazard, hadn't he?

"We called him Moe." The sheriff paused; the gun tilted towards him, and for one bizarre moment Somers thought the sheriff might be planning to kill himself. Then the sheriff seemed to realize his mistake, and he set down the gun and scratched the back of his neck. "Bing, that started in high school. Everybody needs a name, but Moe—he never liked that."

"I'd heard the stories," Somers said. "Your deputies talk. Not all of them, but some. When they get drunk, then they really talk. I'd heard about people who had an extra hand tying a noose in their cells."

One of the machines beeped steadily between them.

"Bing wasn't a bad boy. He wasn't a good boy, not by Jesus, but he was just a boy like you'd expect a man like me to have. I didn't think anything else. Sometimes—" The sheriff's hand came down from his neck, and he held it out in front of him, studying it, as though he hadn't seen it before. "There were girls. Nothing serious, not really, but they made a stink. Could have set him on a bad path. We had to clean things up. Once or twice, that's all. Any father would have done it, but I never . . ." He trailed off.

413

"I'd heard about women who couldn't pay their speeding tickets," Somers said, his voice getting hotter in spite of his best efforts. "I'd heard about that place you keep out off 23, your private work camp. I'd heard about heat stroke, and hypothermia, and dehydration. But I had my own shit to deal with."

Again, between the two of them, there was only the steady beeping of the machines.

"This, though." The sheriff turned his hand palm up, waiting for something—grace, intercession, spare change. "Nobody thinks about this. I've seen it all. I've seen the worst you can imagine, and I didn't think about this."

"Until she told you."

The sheriff flinched.

"She came to you," Somers said. "She told you. She told you everything."

"Not everything," Sheriff Bingham said, his voice loud and cracking at the end.

"You didn't know she was pregnant. Fine. Maybe that'll let you sleep at night. But you knew enough. You knew what he was doing to her. You knew, and what did you do?" Somers waited, and when Bingham didn't answer, he said, "You bought her a phone."

"She told me that was all she needed. She told me she could—she could leave." The sheriff's hand spasmed, and then he snatched up the gun jerkily. "I couldn't. Not my own son. This place, the town, I might as well cut my own throat. I said I'd send money. We had a plan. We were going to figure it out."

"You ought to put that to your head and blast out your brains. That's what you deserve."

A shaky laugh escaped the sheriff. New light came into his eyes, and his hand steadied, and the gun rested firm on Somers again. "Is that it? I kill myself, or I let you drag me into a cell? For what? Neglect? You've got nothing. Stories. Imagination."

Somers produced Hadley's phone from his pocket. "I've got this." He flipped over the phone, displaying the fingerprint sensor on the back. He tapped the case where a brown smudge marred the plastic. "I've got Hadley's blood on her phone. Under the case. Isn't that interesting? No blood anywhere on the outside. That makes sense since she had the phone in her clutch. But right here, near the fingerprint sensor, there's blood under the plastic. Her blood."

"You can't prove that."

"It's a pretty straightforward test."

"You planted it. You've got no chain of custody. You—"

"You bought her the phone. You agreed to help her—not a lot of help, but something. And then it all went to shit. You said it yourself: you didn't know. Bing had the whole thing planned out, and you couldn't do anything but watch. How soon did you know? Did you know when Stillwell got to the party? Did you remember what had happened in Chicago?"

No answer from Bingham. The gun might have been held by a statue.

"It doesn't matter, I suppose. When the shooting was over, when the lights came back on and Hadley was dead, you knew."

Bingham's mouth cracked. Breath rasped between his teeth.

"And you did what you'd always been doing: you covered up Bing's shit. You were hugging him. I remember that clear as day. Hugging him. Comforting him, I thought. The first human behavior I'd seen out of you in my whole life. I should have realized then. You weren't hugging him; you were getting the gun from him. Hiding it. Everyone's attention was fixed on Stillwell. I saw you with the gun. Can you believe that? I goddamn saw you, and I just thought it was your service weapon."

"This one?" Bingham said, the words barely more than a creak.

Somers ignored the threat. "And then you got Hadley's phone out of her purse. You used her fingerprint to unlock the phone. That was the mistake—the blood, remember. And then you called Lender and told him what he had to do."

"And what," the sheriff said, his voice growing stronger, "was Albert Lender going to do?"

"He killed Stillwell. Shot him with the same gun that Bing used to kill Hadley. It was the perfect way to get rid of the gun. The only way you could be sure we'd never find it. Even if we chanced onto the different ballistics, we could have spent a hundred years looking for that gun and never found it because it was already sitting in the sheriff's evidence lock-up. That was good. That's pretty damn close to genius, especially for something you cooked up on the spot. Of course, you've had a lot of practice."

"Plenty," Bingham said, his teeth suddenly shining huge, his voice as hard as those yellowed teeth. "That's it, then? What's it going to be? Conspiracy? Obstruction? Murder?"

"All of it. As much as I can."

"You want a confession? You've got this all on tape?" Bingham leaned forward, and again the gun jabbed the air. "I'm not as good a shot as I used to be. My eyes are still good. My aim, too. But speed, that's where age gets me. You'll move. I'll still get you, but it won't be clean. Lots of ways to make it look like a man shot himself, though. At my age, easiest just to make it look like an arrest went bad, and then the other fellow went for the gun, and that's the whole story."

"I keep my mouth shut," Somers said quickly. Uncertainty froze the sheriff, and Somers spoke again. "I don't say a word. And neither do you."

"What's that supposed to mean?"

"You sent that message to Hazard. You're threatening him. Us, I suppose, but you've got him in your sights." The figure of speech, as Somers stared down the barrel of the sheriff's gun, made his stomach flip. "I thought at first it was the mayor, but that was before I put the rest of it together. You want him to keep quiet. You want both of us to keep quiet. And don't bother denying it." Somers grinned. "I'm a dumb son of a bitch, but I'm not stupid."

Bingham didn't move. He didn't speak. The gun didn't look like it shot caps anymore.

"I don't say anything about your part in this. I've got my lines rehearsed: Stillwell died escaping arrest. Good riddance. He shot my father. We'll never know how Hadley got that second phone. That's it. That's all. You go on being sheriff." Somers paused. His mouth felt dry. His breath felt like a sandblaster. "Bing goes down for the rest of it, and you leave Hazard alone."

"That's it?"

"That's it."

"Glenn Somerset, he's a dirty bastard. Dirty every way you can imagine. Shit up to his armpits. But all the talk says you're clean. Guess that's just talk."

"Guess so."

"Your dad getting shot, that was an accident. You know that, right?"

"It might have been an accident, but I think Mayor Newton will still find a way to turn it to his advantage. That's my father's problem, though, and he can deal with it on his own."

"It's your problem too. Yours and that faggot partner. Mayor's got his teeth into this now. Even if I keep my mouth shut, he might still talk. He's got a hard-on for the faggot."

Somers displayed two fingers and then reached carefully into his pocket. He withdrew the digital recorder and tossed it to the sheriff. "Give him that. Tell him that's for staying quiet about Emery Hazard's past, but he'd better stay quiet for a real long time."

Sheriff Bingham turned over the recorder, studying it, and then pocketed it. "You queer for him? That what this is about?"

"As a three-dollar bill," Somers said. He got to his feet and pushed past the sheriff, ignoring the gun and the old man. "If you don't like it, go fuck yourself."

CHAPTER FORTY

**DECEMBER 31
SUNDAY
6:42 PM**

SINCE THAT DAY IN THE HOSPITAL, Somers hadn't seen Hazard. Not for lack of trying: Somers had driven to the hospital six times. Six. Hands locked on the wheel, he'd driven to the hospital and parked the Interceptor and stared up at Wahredua Regional. Then the sick feeling, like a lead balloon plummeting inside him, would grow worse, and then all he could think was the same old things: what will everyone say, what will my parents think, what will I tell Cora, what am I doing, and, loudest of all, what will Hazard say? He'd had fifteen years of those thoughts, fifteen years to perfect them in all their different versions, and now here he was, facing them again and finding them as sharp as they'd ever been. The clarity that he'd felt on Christmas when facing Sheriff Bingham had melted. And six times, every single time, he drove out of the parking lot and back into Wahredua.

Today, he'd waited until it was late, with the half-formed idea that maybe he could screw up his courage a little better in the dark. He'd sat in the Interceptor. He'd watched the sun go down. And in the darkness, staring up at the hospital's lighted windows, he'd still been a coward.

He drove home now in silence. No swearing. No ranting. No chewing himself another asshole. Just silence where those sharp questions could dart in and slash at him. And the worst of it was that none of the questions, not one, was all that bad on its own. Somers knew it didn't matter what anyone else said. He knew it didn't matter, in the long run, what his parents thought. Even Cora, he was fairly sure, could be handled in a way that would ultimately make them both happier. But the questions had been with him so long, and they had worked on him all those years, and it was like death by a million paper cuts. That's what it was: it was insane.

This is pathetic, he told himself. This whole thing, this whole act, driving around, keeping your head down, what's the word—skulking—yeah, skulking like you're a dog that's just got rapped on the nose with the newspaper. Pathetic. Kid stuff. High school stuff. And then he groaned, and his hands flexed on the Interceptor's wheel, and he thought maybe if he banged his head hard enough he'd finally have some quiet.

Pathetic, that's what it was. Pure and simple pathetic.

He'd go to the hospital tomorrow. Tomorrow, he'd tell Ree everything. For sure this time. No more excuses. Tomorrow.

From the underground garage, Somers rode the elevator to the fourth floor, and he let himself into the apartment. To his surprise, the lights were on. The dishes, which Somers had left piled in the sink, were washed and drying in the rack. A week's worth of dirty socks, which Somers had left like confetti tossed around the room, had vanished. The TV was on, and grainy black-and-white footage passed across the screen. Somers squinted, trying to decipher the images. Was that a snake? God, he hoped not. A DVD case on the table bore the title *Lesser-known Footpaths of the Italian Alps, Traveled 1929-1935*.

And then another groan escaped him before Somers could muffle it. He was home. Ree was home. He was here. Nobody else in the entire damn world would be watching something like that. Ree was here, in the apartment. The groan deepened; it found the bottom of Somers's stomach. Why hadn't he done the dishes? Why—Jesus—why hadn't he picked up those socks?

"Somers," Hazard said, poking his head out of his room. He was running a towel through his hair. Normally so tightly styled with comb and product, the long—too long, really, for a cop—locks curled across Hazard's forehead and around his ears. He studied Somers for a moment. "You going to come in?"

Somers tried to stifle the groan. He tried to swallow it. He tried to stomp it out. But as he shut the door, he was still groaning. Just a little. But still.

"Are you sick?"

"You did the dishes."

Hazard came out into the room. He was dressed in tight-fitting gray slacks—tight didn't really do them justice; they were painted on, every curve of that slab he called an ass perfectly defined—and he was shirtless. Again, Somers was struck by how big Hazard was: massive, really, with dense layers of muscle. So different from the boy that Somers remembered. But perfect, too. Brutishly perfect, with that dark scattering of hair across the definition of his chest and stomach. And with his hair curling in front of his eyes, Hazard looked wild. Like he could do anything. Like he might take hold of Somers's shirt and rip it off in one movement, the way he had months ago, popping every button—

"You're flushed," Hazard said, scrubbing the towel over his head one last time and then slinging it around his neck. "And you're making that noise again. Is it your stomach?"

"What? No. I'm fine. You did the dishes."

Hazard shrugged.

"You washed my socks."

"Somebody had to."

"You're hurt. You should be—I don't know. Lying down. Resting. Eating soup. Not washing my dirty socks."

"I had to throw in a load."

For a moment neither of them spoke. Hazard rolled his huge shoulders, and Somers felt giddy at the rush of desire that ran through him. How long had he hidden from those feelings? How long had he tamped them down? Since college, when he'd met Ricky Wade in the men's room and let Ricky slide his thumbs under the elastic waistband of Somers's briefs and slide them down to his knees, and that was the first time for Somers? Since senior year of high school, when he'd cut a picture of Emery Hazard out of the yearbook? Since—since before all of that? Since he'd touched Emery Hazard once, just once, in the locker room and seen raw need in the other boy's eyes? Somers wanted to laugh. If that's where it had started, the universe had one sick sense of humor, because everything had flipped, and Somers didn't know if he'd ever wanted anyone, anything, the way he wanted Hazard. Raw need. That's what it was. Somers would have laughed, would have busted a gut, except his mouth was a gravel pit.

Both men spoke at the same time.

"I want to talk to you—" Hazard said.

"I need to talk to you—" Somers said.

Somers laughed, scratching the back of his neck. Hazard didn't laugh. His big hands tightened on the ends of the towel around his neck.

"You first," Somers said.

"You're acting strange. I know why."

"I haven't been acting strange."

"Yes. You have."

"Nah."

"Somers, you have. I'm telling you. And I know why."

That lead balloon dropped again in Somers's stomach.

"You're mad at Nico," Hazard said.

"Huh?"

"You're angry at him. The way he talked to you. I know." Hazard paused, glancing at the door to his room, and suddenly Somers was aware of the sound of the shower.

"He's here."

"He wants to apologize. We had a long talk." Hazard fidgeted with the towel. "We've been talking a lot lately. About a lot of things."

"I'm not mad at Nico." Somers took a deep breath. This was it, this moment. Now or never. "Look, I need to—"

"Hold on. I know you're angry with him. You don't have to say it; I know you won't. He's going to apologize. But I want to apologize too. I shouldn't have done what I did, going off to Bing's alone. I shouldn't have done a lot of things. I shouldn't have kept secrets."

Hazard paused. Red deepened the hollows of his cheeks. "It means a lot to me. This."

"What?"

"You know what I mean."

"This as in, us?"

"I'm just saying—"

"No, no, no. You don't get off that easily. You've got to say it, big boy. You can't just beat around the bush."

Hazard, scowling, was silent for a moment.

"You'd better say it," Somers said, folding his arms across his chest and leaning against the door. "Go on. I know you can do it."

"You know what I—"

"Yeah, Ree. I know. I'm not an idiot. But sometimes—try to get this through your head—sometimes it's important to actually say things. Even if the other person knows it. Because maybe they want to hear it. Just maybe."

"I like being your partner," Hazard said, his voice firm, almost stiff, but the heat in his face betrayed him. "I like working with you. I think you're a good cop. Actually, I think you're a great cop. I trust you. You're the best partner I've ever had, and I think we make a great team. I don't want any of that to change, ever." He paused, and his face darkened. "Is that enough?"

"It was sounding pretty good."

"I'm being serious, Somers."

"You could have added something about the times I saved your life. You could have mentioned how interesting I am, how I'm a fascinating conversationalist, how I brighten your day, how I'm the perfect complement for all your foibles and weaknesses, how I'm the living embodiment—"

"Fuck you."

Somers's smile was about to split his face. "No, that's not really in the same spirit. Don't worry. You'll get better with practice."

"Fuck you. I'm serious. Fuck. You."

"Come on, Ree," Somers said, fighting a laugh now. "Don't go. I'm just joking."

Somers's laughter dried up, though, at the silence that followed. A nervous tingle spread through his chest. Maybe this was it. Maybe Hazard would take the first step. Maybe Hazard needed to say the same thing as Somers.

"I need to tell you something," Hazard said.

"All right."

"That blackmail letter, the one from the mayor. I need to—you deserve to know the truth."

"About St. Louis? I don't need to know. I don't care. What I care about is what I've seen here. That's all I care about."

"No. You need to know. I want you to know." Hazard's breathing had changed. It sounded labored now, and his voice had grown choppy. "I've been thinking about what you said earlier. A lot, actually."

"What did I say? What are you talking about?"

"Last week. When this all started, when we were on our way to Stillwell's place."

Somers racked his brains, trying to remember.

Hazard spoke again. "I had a partner. Jonas Cassidy. He was young."

"Stop. I don't care."

"He was the captain's son, too. He was pissed about being partnered with me at first, but he'd had trouble in the past. A string of bad partners, that's what the captain told me. Just hadn't found the right match. I thought the captain was just looking for a way to rattle the kid, match him up with me for a few weeks and then see if he didn't behave better. In the end, though, we worked it out. We got along. We even became friends. Like I said, he was young, and he was excited about being a detective. For him, the work came first, and we did good work together."

Somers didn't need Hazard to tell the rest of the story: he could picture Jonas Cassidy—darkly handsome, in Somers's imagination, and looking surprisingly similar to Nico. Straight boy, but a straight boy who was curious. What was it? A stake-out? A late night at their desks? Or had Cassidy stopped by Hazard's apartment one night, had he simply shown up and taken what he wanted? Someone had wrapped Somers's chest in baling wire, and he couldn't take a full breath.

"I don't. Care." He couldn't breathe, not anything close to a full breath.

"Just listen, all right? One of our cases, it was drugs. We had a source that gave up a safe house. It was a team, not just Cassidy and me. We took the safe house. Found plenty of drugs and money. Hiding places all over that damn house. And Cassidy and I, we were out in the garage, and we found one of them. Bricks of heroin. Kilos of it." Hazard stopped again. The choppiness in his voice had increased, as though anger mutilated all his words. "I didn't know. I didn't fucking know. But something just felt . . . off. Cassidy was different around me. For days, things were weird. I went to his apartment. I didn't know, Somers. Swear to God. That much, you have to believe."

"I believe you. You didn't know. But you suspected something."

"Yeah. I don't know what I thought. But I—I broke into his place. I found it in the kitchen cabinet. I mean, the little shit didn't even bother to hide it. Two kilos. He'd stuffed them under his vest, I think, when I wasn't looking. So I waited. Cassidy came home. He didn't shout. He didn't even seem surprised. He told me that he was sorry, that he'd wanted to tell me. He told me a story about a family member—a cousin, I think—who was sick and needed the money. He talked and talked and talked. And then he kissed me."

"Fucking piece of shit."

"He told me he'd been wanting to do that for weeks. He told me he loved me. He told me he'd never been brave enough to come out. He kissed me again. I let him, Somers. I just sat there and let him kiss me. And he kept talking. It was like—it was like he meant it. I believed him. I think I believed him, anyway. But I told him it didn't matter; we had to tell the captain everything." Hazard shook his head; his eyes, those scarecrow eyes, glittered with memory. "He screamed. He threw things—broke every damn plate in the house. He talked about love. I love you. If you loved me. That kind of stuff. Eventually I left. I couldn't do it anymore." Again, Hazard stopped. He licked his lips. "He ran straight to daddy."

"And he believed him?"

"The captain wasn't an idiot," Hazard said. "He knew his son. He knew Cassidy had gotten into trouble before—maybe even something similar. And he knew me. He didn't like me, but he knew me. But—" Hazard shrugged. "Blood is thick. The captain called me in. I told him my side, and the captain said I had a choice: either I left, and I kept silent, or he'd do everything he could to pin it on me. 'I may not win,' he said, 'but I'll sure as hell try.' Like we were playing chess. He promised he'd put in a good word with Cravens. He promised the whole thing would stop there."

"And you left? You let that shitbag do you like that? You weren't guilty of anything, Ree. You didn't do anything wrong."

"I could have stayed. I could have fought it. I would have won, I think. But it was over. I knew it was over. The one partner I'd trusted, the only one I'd thought of as a friend—that was over. And I knew that no matter what the captain promised, word was going to get around. The faggot cop forcing himself on his partner. Or that I'd been the one who took those bricks. And you know how this stuff can go: just a whisper that I was dirty, that'd be enough. Shit like that sticks no matter how you try to scrape it off. Things would get worse; I knew it. I could have stayed. I could have faced all that. But seeing Cassidy, seeing him for the rest of my career, that's why I left. Because I couldn't do that. Anyway, it's going to come out here. All that stuff I tried to leave behind. I wanted to be the one to tell you. If you need to ask Cravens for a new partner—"

"You've got to be kidding me."

"I'm serious. I'll understand. You shouldn't have to—"

"Have we worked well together? Don't just sit there. Answer the question, yes or no: have we done a good job together?"

"Yeah."

"Have we closed cases? Look at me. Have we?"

"Yes. That's not the point, the point is—"

"No. The point is, you said you trust me. That's great. You should. But at the same time, I'm some kind of idiot. Is that it?"

"Huh?"

"I'm stupid? I'm gullible? I'm some kind of wet-behind-the-ears that doesn't even know how to holster his gun? Is that it? Because if that's it, fuck you."

"What are you talking about?"

"I know you, Ree. I've known you for most of my life. You think—what? That the minute I hear something bad about you, my brain goes out the window? Jesus, man, you couldn't be crooked if you tried."

Neither man spoke for a moment. Then Hazard said, "I'm sure as hell not straight."

"Was that a joke?"

No response.

"Because if that was a joke, if that was Emery Hazard cracking wise, I might have a heart attack."

"You're an asshole."

"Next thing you're going to be on stage at open mic night."

"Shut up."

"Maybe add in a song and dance routine."

Hazard's eyes narrowed, and he gave Somers the finger. Somers smirked, but tension still tightened Hazard's posture. He shifted, knotting the towel around his hands, his eyes skating over the glass coffee table and the sleek, modern lines of the sofa.

"I just—I've been thinking about that stuff. What you said, I mean. That's why I had to tell you."

"What did I say? Did I accuse you of stealing dope? Did I say that I thought you were involved in drug trafficking? Did I tell somebody you were dirty? What the hell is this about?"

"At Stillwell's apartment. That story, the one your dad told you, the one about the cops who were partners."

"Jesus."

"They went into that place and they didn't come back out."

"Hazard, that's not us."

"I know. That's not why I—" Hazard broke off. For a moment, his mask shattered, and frustration etched lines in his face. "Somers, I'm telling you I don't want to be those guys. I'm not going to lie to you. I'm not going to hide things." He was trying. God, Somers thought, he was really trying to slap the mask back into place. All that pain in his eyes, all the years of being alone on the force, all the failed partnerships that had culminated in Jonas Cassidy—all of that was naked in Hazard's face, a wound that hadn't healed and might not ever heal. "I need a partner, Somers." His breath grew choppy. "John-Henry. That's what I need." With what looked like a great effort, Hazard pulled the pieces of his mask back into place, drawing up the cool reserve that he normally wore so easily. "Anyway," he said, and he cleared his throat. "I thought I should tell you that."

Now, Somers thought. He had to tell him now. It was one of those moments that balanced on the tip of a needle, and during this one, perfect moment, Somers knew he could say anything, he could say what he needed to say, and it would be perfect, the words would be perfect, and they would be perfect, the two of them, perfect, finally. It was now. It was this moment. And he opened his mouth.

The bathroom door swung back, and Nico stepped out, a towel low on his hips and revealing the deep notches at his groin. "Oh, damn," he said, pausing, adjusting. Water dripped from his shaggy hair. Sex dripped from the rest of him. He was making a damn mess of the place. "Sorry, I didn't know. I mean. Listen, John-Henry, about the other day—"

That was it. Somers saw it as clearly as he'd ever seen anything: the moment passed, tumbling off its needle-tip, and the world had gone back to normal.

"It's ok," Somers said.

"No, really—"

"Nico, it's ok. I was an asshole. Am an asshole. It's ok." He took a step backward. It's ok, he was saying inside himself. It's ok, it's really ok, Jesus, God, it's ok, you've been fine for twenty years, you've been happy, you've been perfectly fucking happy, so this is ok.

Nico, taking a firmer grip on the towel, crossed the room to stand next to Hazard. The younger man looped an arm around Hazard's broad shoulders: one bronze and leanly muscled, a dark trail leading from his belly button; the other pale, almost luminous, and built like a bulldozer. Beautiful. And as Somers fumbled for the door, Hazard planted a kiss on Nico's cheek, and Hazard smiled, and Hazard looked happy.

Hazard. Emery Hazard looked happy. It was like the sun coming up at midnight. It was like spring in the middle of winter. The realization twisted Somers's stomach, a hard, gripping pain like he might shit himself, and he knew it was only going to hurt worse later, that this kind of pain only got worse.

Emery Hazard was happy. He hadn't been happy as a teenager. He hadn't been happy as a man. He hadn't been happy, Somers thought, until now. And wasn't that a real kick in the balls? Somers felt shitty for even thinking it.

"Where are you going?" Nico asked. Then, to Hazard, "Did you invite him?"

"We're going to the Pretty Pretty. We've decided we need to get out more. You should come." Amusement softened the lines of Hazard's face. "There are plenty of boys that will buy you drinks."

"Most of those guys would buy you a bubble-bath of Dom Perignon," Nico said with a grin, "if they thought it would get them even half a chance."

"Another time," Somers said. His mouth felt stiff. His whole face was plastic. That was new. That, that was fucking new. Was he smiling? He was sure as hell trying. "Raincheck. You two need this. Tonight, together. Just the two of you."

"Somers," Hazard said, and there was a question, as though Hazard had sensed something. The question was painted on his face, and that twisting pain in Somers's gut grew worse, and he thought this is it, this is what it's like to really shit yourself.

"Have fun."

"Are you—" Hazard stopped whatever he'd been about to say, and then he asked, "I'll see you tomorrow?"

"Sure," Somers said, and he was positive, a hundred percent, that he was smiling. He just couldn't feel it. This was what Hazard had said he needed. That's what Somers told himself. Love wasn't a choice. It was collision. It was catastrophe. And for the first time in his life, Somers was going to do right by Emery Hazard. It didn't matter how Somers felt. He was going to give Hazard a chance at being happy. That was what Somers could give him, and if that was it, if that was as much as Somers ever had, it would be enough. It had to be.

"Sure," Somers repeated. "We're partners."

Guilt by Association

Keep reading for a sneak preview of *Guilt by Association*, the next Hazard and Somerset mystery.

CHAPTER ONE

**FEBRUARY 10
SATURDAY
9:47 PM**

EMERY HAZARD NEEDED TO BREAK UP with his boyfriend.

As soon as the thought surfaced, Hazard buried it in a landslide of sensation, turning his attention to the sights and sounds flooding his senses. The music in the Pretty Pretty seemed louder than usual to Hazard. Everything was worse tonight: the music was louder, the swiveling lights were brighter, Hazard's headache was angrier, and he was definitely more drunk than usual. Even his dancing—which mostly consisted of swaying in place while his boyfriend, Nico, moved around him—was off. He'd just about broken Nico's toes when he accidentally took a step.

Nico, aside from a yelp, had borne it all pretty well. He didn't seem to notice that the music was louder, that the lights were brighter, that Wahredua's only gay club was somehow worse than it normally was. Tall, slender, with skin the color of toasted grain and with his shaggy dark hair, Nico didn't need to notice anything—everybody noticed him, and that was enough. Nico could just dance up on Hazard, peppering the grinding with long kisses that tasted like appletinis, and enjoy life. For Nico, the Pretty Pretty was heaven.

Hazard needed to break up with him.

There it was again, that thought worming its way through the pounding in Hazard's head. The pounding, too, had gotten worse tonight. Ever since an unfortunate collision with a baseball bat—

wielded by the last killer Hazard had apprehended as part of his work for the Wahredua PD—he'd suffered from periods of severe headaches. Over the last six weeks, bruises and abrasions had healed; the gunshot wound to his shoulder and the deep slice across his palm had closed; but the headaches, although they had grown less frequent, persisted. And tonight, they were persisting like a bitch.

Nico, his shirt unbuttoned to the center of his chest, his skin gleaming with sweat, pressed his mouth against Hazard's, his tongue forcing a path between Hazard's lips. The kiss was hot, especially in time with the feel of Nico's muscled body thrusting against Hazard's. Everything about Nico was hot. He was an underwear model; well, to be fair, he was only a part-time model, and most of the time he was a graduate student in theology who didn't like to pick up his socks. But he was hot as hell. And kind, Hazard forced himself to remember. Nico was kind; he wasn't just a pretty boy. And smart. And funny. Not the kind of jokes that made Hazard laugh, not usually, but plenty of people thought he was funny. Plenty of people like—

—not Somers—

—well, plenty of people. And why the hell did it matter who thought he was funny, anyway?

As the kiss broke, Hazard took the opportunity to shout over a thunderous bass line, "I'm headed to the bar." He pointed at his head. "Need to sit down."

Something flickered across Nico's face, but it was gone almost as soon as it had appeared. He nodded, kissed Hazard again—more coolly, this time—and as soon as they parted, a crowd of eager, attractive young men surged towards Nico. A second crowd surged towards Hazard, but most of them veered off when they saw his face. The few who didn't, the few who tried to talk to him, the few who might have thought they had a chance at a dance, bounced off him— one of them, literally.

Propped on a stool at the bar, Hazard nursed a Guinness. He didn't want it, not really. He definitely didn't need it. And it sure as hell wasn't doing anything for his head. What he wanted was to be back home, the lights low, his eyes closed as he listened to a book on tape and waited for the pain pills to kick in. What did he have from the library right now? *Munitions of the Spanish Civil War, Small Caliber?* Had he finished that one? Large caliber? God, his head.

This was the price of a relationship, though. After his last blow-up fight with Nico, Hazard had been forced to make concessions. No more staying at home on the weekends. That had been the biggest one. Nico, almost a decade younger and far more social than Hazard, thrived at the Pretty Pretty. Yes, thrived was the right word. Nico seemed to come alive here.

From his post at the bar, Hazard watched his boyfriend, glimpsing him through the crowd. Nico danced well. He was sexy in just about every way imaginable. He was kind. He was funny—yes, goddamnit, even if Somers didn't think so. He was—

Hazard groaned and rubbed a big finger between his eyes, trying to massage away the headache. He was making a list. Jesus, he thought, shoot me now.

This was how it had been with Alec. This was how it had been with Billy. The lists. List after list after list. Pros and cons. Plus and minus. Some lists that went on and on and on, only the good things. And the other lists that he never dared put on paper where Alec might see, where Billy might come across it. But lists. So many goddamn lists. And here he was again; it all started with the lists.

It was all because of the Pretty Pretty. Hazard just needed one weekend of quiet. One night of calm. That's all—and then things would be all right again. Things would go back to normal.

But Hazard couldn't quite get free of his own thoughts. It always started with the lists. Every time—well, to be fair, there had only been two—both times his relationships had gone bad, he'd started the lists way in advance. With Alec, it had been early. Hazard had started the lists before Alec had ever begun using the belt, back when he just used his hands, when he'd still laugh and pretend it was a joke, when he'd land a slap, when he'd leave a handprint like a neon sign, when he'd growl and say how sexy it was. Even back then, the lists had started.

With Billy too. With Billy, the lists had started—God, what? Eight months ago? Ten? Before Hazard had lost his job. Before he'd left Saint Louis and come to Wahredua. Before, and this was the real bitch of it all, before Hazard had suspected, before he had let himself suspect, what was going on between Billy and Tom. Tom was just a friend. Tom was just a good friend. Sure, Billy and Tom were close, but Billy had lots of close friends. Sure—sure, sometimes Tom stood a little too close. Sure, sometimes, after parties, when Hazard had had too much to drink, sure, sometimes there were fights about Tom. But he hadn't known. God, he hadn't suspected, hadn't even let himself think those thoughts all the way to their conclusion. And before any of that, he'd started with the lists.

Hazard rocked his glass of Guinness, unsure if he could stomach any more of the dark liquid. Like chewing a sponge, that's what it felt like tonight. Normally Guinness was his drink of choice, but tonight—it had to be his head. The music had gotten louder if that were possible, and the pounding in his head was off-beat. Hazard didn't want to be here. There. He'd managed to think it to himself, which was one step closer to saying it out loud. Hazard never wanted to be here.

And Hazard wouldn't be here, he wouldn't have had to give up every weekend, if he hadn't fought so hard about the apartment. The fight had dragged on close to eighteen hours—not steady going, but on and off. Hazard hadn't wanted to move. He'd liked his place, the place he shared with another detective, John-Henry Somerset, his partner. Somers. He hadn't wanted to move.

Fast forward, and here Hazard was: he'd lost the fight about the apartment, and he'd lost his weekends too. He dug his finger deeper into his forehead, as though he could punch through the bone and massage away the worst of the ache. Just shoot me, he thought again. A list, a fucking list all over again, just shoot me.

Things were going to turn out the same, a dark voice told him. Things were going to get worse. It was a matter of time. It was only, always, exclusively a matter of time before they saw—

—the real Emery Hazard—

—whatever it was inside him that had made Alec reach for the belt, that had made Billy reach for Tom, that was going to make—

"Nico's looking good out there." The voice was familiar: catty, warbling, an exaggerated lisp on the only S. Marcus, dressed in a sleeveless t-shirt and cut-off jeans in spite of the February cold, slumped against the bar next to Hazard. "Better be careful."

"Go away, Marcus."

Marcus sniffed. "I'll tell Nico."

"Tell him whatever you want."

Marcus stayed right where he was, swishing his hips to the beat, and Hazard could feel the younger man's eyes on him. "He's got good taste," Marcus said. With a twirl of his wrist, Marcus traced a finger down Hazard's arm.

"Keep that up and you won't be able to use that hand for a month."

"You're always so mean to me." Marcus sidled closer. He had finally shaved his ridiculous mustache, and he wasn't a bad-looking guy, even if he wasn't Hazard's type. His hip bumped into Hazard, and then again, and then again as Marcus swayed to the music. "I could be really nice to you. Nico wouldn't mind. We've shared before."

"Get lost."

"Let me blow you."

"I'll say it a different way: fuck off."

"Only if you're doing the fucking," Marcus hissed, arching an eyebrow.

Hazard got to his feet, and Marcus must have finally caught a hint because he scuttled backward, his eyes wide.

"This isn't smart, Marcus."

He must have expected something else because fresh confidence rushed into his face. "If you think Nico will be mad, I promise, he won't. We've—"

"I don't care. I don't care if the two of you fucked your way through City Hall together. You think I don't know what this is about? You don't like me. Fine. No, don't try to deny it. You think I don't remember back at Christmas when you called Nico and tried to rat me out?"

"You were—I thought maybe the two of you—"

"Bull. Shit. You like stirring things up. And now you're doing it again. If I say yes, you run straight to Nico with a story about how

I'm cheating on him. If I say no, you run straight to Nico with a story about how mean I am, how I can't take a joke, how I'm boring, how he deserves so much better. How am I doing?"

The change in Marcus's expression was immediate and remarkable: his eyebrows knitted together, his mouth thinned into a line, and he bit his lower lip so hard that it turned white under his teeth. "You aren't good enough for him. You're—you're a phony. You're a joke, that's what you are. You're one of those butch gays who thinks he's better than everybody else. Repressed. You're trying to play it straight, but you moan like a bitch when Nico's inside you. Yeah. He told me. He told me how you screw up your face when he really sticks it to you, just like a good bitch—"

It wasn't really a punch, but Hazard's fist was closed, so maybe it technically counted as one. It was more like knocking on a door. He rapped the side of Marcus's head, that was all. Sure, maybe it was a hard knock. Harder than Hazard knocked on a normal door. But it was still just a knock.

Marcus staggered sideways. He clutched at the bar, but wood and metal slipped out of his grip, and he hit the ground. He scrambled to his feet again, and he didn't seem to know what to say or do. He just stood there, frozen, eyes wide. Hazard guessed nobody had ever hit him before.

"Run," Hazard said in his best cop voice.

Marcus ran.

When Marcus had disappeared into the dance-floor crowd— there would be hell to pay when Nico heard about it; Jesus, Mary, and Joseph, there'd be hell—Hazard dropped back onto the stool. Party boys watched him, their expressions a mixture of shock at the outburst of violence and persistent interest, but Hazard ignored them. In a matter of minutes, they went back to dancing and drinking and humping, although plenty of them still turned eyes toward Hazard now and then. He ignored them. His headache was worse than ever, and now his knuckles throbbed with heat. He slid the Guinness across the bar, but he couldn't bring himself to take a drink. Thick as a fucking sponge tonight. He was done drinking. Throwing up—throwing up a lot, in fact—was climbing his to-do list.

"Don't tell me," a voice said. "He bought you the wrong drink."

The man was tall, well-built, dressed in a sports coat and tie that made him look sexy instead of officious. He had the classical good looks of a politician—of a Kennedy, for that matter, the kind of good looks that run straight through the bloodlines at Yale and Harvard. Dark hair in a conservative cut, strong jaw with a cleft, muscular without being a meathead. He probably rowed. He probably played squash. He probably owned a polo horse. Outside of the Pretty Pretty, Hazard would have hated him. Inside—well, inside, Hazard suddenly found his head wasn't hurting quite as bad. It was hard to focus on a headache when a perfect smile flashed your way.

"He thought I wanted a Bud Lite," Hazard said, not quite sure why he said it.

That perfect smile glowed about ten degrees brighter. "That was stupid of him. You're obviously a—" The man paused. His dark eyes darted to the half-drunk Guinness and then to Hazard. "You're obviously an Old Fashioned man." He tipped a hand at the bartender and then moved into the empty seat next to Hazard.

Hazard raised an eyebrow. "You saw what happened to the last guy."

This man laughed, and even his laugh sounded like it had cost a couple of grand. "I like taking chances."

"There's no chance here, buddy. I've got a boyfriend."

"I don't mind talking. Half of the guys out there look like they're still in college, and about seventy-five percent look like they're trying to find a daddy." His eyes were almost smoking as he studied Hazard. "Boyfriend, huh? Not that guy you gave a concussion, I hope."

"No, he's—oh, you've got to be fucking kidding me."

Across the room, Hazard watched another guy shove his tongue down Nico's throat.

CHAPTER TWO

**FEBRUARY 10
SATURDAY
10:04 PM**

HAZARD DIDN'T REALLY THINK about clearing a path across the crowded dance floor. He was out of his seat, charging across the room, before he had a chance. He didn't think about a lot of things. He didn't think about his headache. He didn't think about the need to toss his cookies. He did think, briefly, of Billy. He did think, slightly longer, about Tom. In his head, in his fantasies, his fist connected with Tom's nose, cartilage crumpling, blood hot between his fingers. Then he only had room in his head for the snapshot he'd seen. It had lasted only a moment before the crowd closed again, but it had been clear: Nico pressed against another guy, making out like a horny teenager.

To Hazard's credit, even though he didn't think about clearing a path across the room, he still managed to do it well. Some of it came down to his hard, efficient shoves that sent gay boys sliding out of his way. Most of it, though, was what Somers would have called pure Hazard: a brooding, hulking thunderstorm of dark hair and muscle. Dancers hurried to get out of his way. They damn well scurried.

And then the crowd parted. Nico was fending off a guy who looked like he was trying his hardest to pry Nico's mouth open with his tongue. Hazard shoved the guy. He had an impression of the guy, just a flash, but the guy was clearly frat material: hair buzzed down on the sides, long on the top; a red tank top that showed just how much time this guy spent toning and flexing and grooming; and expensive sneakers that probably cost more than Hazard's car.

"What the hell is going on here?"

"Nothing," Nico said, drawing his hand across his mouth, the movement reflexive and furtive and guilty.

"Yo," the frat boy yelled. Yo. That's what he said, not ironically, not mockingly, but like he meant it, like that was the only word he knew. "Yo, what the fuck?"

Hazard ignored him and spoke to Nico. "It didn't look like nothing."

"It was a misunderstanding. It was—" Nico's shoulders curved inwards, and he dropped his hand. It looked like it took a lot of effort, prizing his hand away from his mouth, and he couldn't look Hazard in the eyes. "Let's get out of here. Let's go, all right?"

"Yo, motherfucker," the frat boy said. He walked like an ape. He walked like he was all shoulders, and Hazard saw the punch coming about five years before the frat boy threw it. When it came, Hazard moved, and the punch went past his chin.

Hazard caught hold of the frat boy and tossed him before the guy even knew what happened. Five yards. Six if you counted where he stopped sliding. Hazard rolled his shoulders, conscious of a new ache; he was getting old.

Frat boy was picking himself up.

"Stay down," Hazard said. He turned back to Nico. "Why should we leave? We're having a nice time."

"Emery, come on, we've got to go, he's—look out!"

This time, the punch was wild. Frat boy, red-faced and swearing, swung his hands like he was trying to catch flies. Hazard ducked one punch, bobbed out of the way of another, and planted his fist in frat boy's solar plexus. With a wheeze, frat boy collapsed.

"He wasn't doing anything wrong," Nico said. "He didn't know, goddamn it."

The music continued to pound, but around them, the dancing had stopped. In spite of the throbbing beat, the space seemed dead. The Pretty Pretty's patrons stood and watched. Two of the bouncers were working their way through the crowd, and Hazard knew they only had moments before they were dragged out of the place—and, if he were really, really lucky, banned for life.

Frat boy had gotten to his knees. A long strand of saliva hung from his mouth. He was still wheezing, but it sounded like more of the air was reaching his lungs now. He looked like he didn't know what time zone he was in. Hazard walked towards him.

"What the fuck are you doing?" Nico shouted, and it took Hazard a moment to realize Nico was talking to him.

"Getting that guy off your ass."

Nico glanced around. It was hard to tell in the darkness and with his complexion, but he might have been flushed. "He's just some drunk jerk-off. I don't need you to do that. He can't even stand— Jesus Christ, Emery, I'm talking to you. Stop. You can't do that."

Inside, Hazard was thinking, he isn't Billy, and that isn't Tom, and whatever the hell is going on you'd better get a hold of yourself fast, but it didn't matter what he told himself. He was thinking of Billy. He was thinking of Tom. He could practically see Tom, see his face overlaying the frat boy in front of him, the two faces swimming together in his vision. And he heard himself say, "Yes. I can."

The frat boy was trying to pick himself up. Hazard looked at Nico. Then he looked at the frat boy and planted his heel in the center of frat boy's back. He shoved down hard enough that he heard frat boy's jaw click against the floor even over the music.

"Stay down," Hazard said.

Nico, shaking his head, said, "You're unbelievable." He pushed his way into the crowd.

Over the heads and shoulders of the crowd, Hazard saw Marcus emerge, as though sliding out of nowhere, and enfold Nico in a hug. The bouncers came next, ignoring Marcus and Nico and beelining for Hazard. Hazard watched as Marcus urged Nico towards the door. He was holding Nico's hand and speaking into his ear. They were gone, vanishing out of the club before Hazard could take a second step.

"Let's get some shots out here," a familiar voice called from the bar. The guy in the suit and tie jerked a thumb at the bottles lining the wall. "On me until the first guy pukes."

The stillness broke. Many of the men surged towards the free drinks. A handful picked up frat boy, still limp and floppy, and dragged him away. Some of the boys—Hazard noticed that they were exclusively young, with the kind of gleaming skin that vanished around twenty-two or twenty-three—clustered around Hazard. They grabbed at his arms, his ass, his crotch, and they talked over each other, telling him how brave he was, how hot it had been to see him trash the frat boy, what they'd do to Hazard if he gave them half a chance.

At the bar, the guy in the suit and tie tipped a shot glass at Hazard—an invitation, or perhaps a salute. Or perhaps, Hazard thought when he glimpsed the man's smile, a kind of commiseration.

"Detective Hazard," one of the bouncers said, as the two big men finally worked their way through the last of the crowd.

"Are we going to have a problem?" the second one said. They looked like they came as a matching set: bald, tall, and built like cement trucks.

"I'm leaving. Anyway, he took the first swing. You tell Bradley that. Tell Will Pirk too." The Pretty Pretty's manager and owner weren't Hazard's friends by any means, but Hazard knew he had enough status as a local celebrity to buy him some wiggle room.

"Are you walking out of here?" the first bouncer said.

"I'm walking."

"Will might ban your ass," the second bouncer said. "Doesn't matter who you are."

"Tell him not to do me any favors."

Hazard worked his way free of the last of his clinging admirers, gave the man in the suit and tie a last glance—he was still watching Hazard, and his interest was obvious—and found his way out of the club. The February air was cold. Dead cold. It snapped into his lungs like a rubber band, and the shock doubled Hazard's headache. At least it was cold, though. At least it smelled clean. It didn't taste like sweat and vinyl and a hundred different colognes. It tasted sweet like car exhaust and sweet like upper-crust snow.

Nico and Marcus huddled at the end of the block, with Nico facing the length of the sidewalk, staring right at Hazard, and with

Marcus between them like a bodyguard. Hazard's steps sounded like explosions. It's the cement, he thought. It's frozen. That's why I'm hitting it so hard. I wouldn't walk like this. I never walk like this.

"Move."

"Fuck you," Marcus said.

"I'm not telling you again."

"Stop it," Nico said. His eyes were red, but he wasn't crying. The cold, maybe. And that must have been why he hunched his shoulders, why he was practically folded in on himself.

"I'm not going to stop it. Not until he gets lost."

"See?" Marcus said in a harsh whisper. "This is what I'm talking about."

"Emery," Nico said, "just stop. You're being a jerk."

"I'm being a jerk?" Hazard's head was pounding. Not a drum. Nothing like that. It was bigger. Much bigger. Like somebody standing inside an abandoned freighter with a jackhammer and giving it hell. That kind of huge. "Some guy's got his tongue down your throat—"

"You don't know what you're talking about."

"Some guy's got his tongue down your throat, and I get him off you—"

"You're an asshole."

"And I get him off you, and somehow I'm the jerk. That's it, huh?"

Nico didn't say anything; he was staring out of those red eyes like he'd gone to a week's worth of funerals, but he wasn't crying. Marcus didn't say anything either, but he looked pretty happy, pretty goddamn happy, like he was watching Hazard eat shit by the shovelful.

"I'm staying at Marcus's tonight."

"You're fucking kidding me."

"No. I'm not. We can talk about this tomorrow. Marcus, let's—"

"You're not going home with him." Hazard took a step forward, knocking Marcus aside, barely even feeling the impact. Seizing Nico's arm, he yanked him a step towards his old VW Jetta. "You're coming home, and we're going to talk about this like adults whether you—"

The blow to his head wasn't that hard, but combined with the headache, it felt like it had cracked Hazard's skull. He had the dizzied worry that somehow the punch had collided perfectly with the still-healing fracture and his brains were sliding out the back of his head. Hazard lost his grip on Nico and staggered.

By the time he'd pulled himself half-upright, Marcus had an arm around Nico and was hustling him down the block. Hazard watched them go, partly because his bell had just been rung like fucking New Year's and partly because he had absolutely no idea what to do. After fifteen yards, Nico stopped and looked back.

"We'll talk tomorrow," he said, his voice so thick that Hazard barely understood the words. Or maybe that was the headache again. Or maybe something was really wrong, something inside Hazard's head. Aphasia. That's what it was called. When words didn't make sense anymore. That's how it felt, tonight. Like they were talking nonsense at each other, and Jesus, how had it all gone sideways?

Emery Hazard thought he might have an answer, but before it could fully materialize, he dropped forward and sicked up all over his shoes.

CHAPTER THREE

**FEBRUARY 11
SUNDAY
11:15 AM**

THE PHONE'S RINGING went through Hazard's skull like a couple of inches of good steel. One minute he was asleep. The next, awake and feeling like someone had shoved a spear through the back of his head. It went on for a long time. Then it went quiet. Later, it rang again. A fragment of memory—*not for us, the flashing bronze*, was that Homer?—because the noise was like the blade of a fucking spear going into his brain. And then, again, blessed silence. The pillow, he thought drowsily as he tried to sink under the headache and into the gray stillness of sleep, smelled like Nico.

For a while he was there again, inside that grayness, while a part of his brain recycled the past night. The hammering music inside the Pretty Pretty. The smell of sweat and superheated lights and Guinness. Nico pressed against him—no, Nico across the room, far off, while Hazard talked to Marcus. No, to the hot guy in the jacket and tie. No, to the bouncers. And through it all, that mixture of headache and bass line, pounding, pounding, pounding—

Pounding on the door. Hazard jerked free of the tangled bedding. Immediately, he regretted it. The headache surged back to the front of his head, and he had to steady himself against the nightstand. The clock marked a bleary eleven. Whoever was knocking was really going to town.

"Just a minute," Hazard shouted.

Pants. And a shirt. But he had no memory of where anything had ended up last night, and he came up with a pair of shorts and a t-shirt. The shorts fit. The shirt didn't. It had to be Nico's, but it felt like a child's. A child's small. Jesus, maybe an infant's. It was choking the life out of Hazard.

And somebody was still trying to pound down the door.

Squeezed into the tiny shirt—had Nico bought it for a nephew? what the hell was it doing on the floor?—Hazard stumbled to the door and glanced through the peephole. Groaning, he turned back to the bedroom.

"I can hear you," Somers called from the other side of the door.

Hazard kept going.

"I'll keep knocking."

Hazard kicked aside Nico's empty laundry basket. His toes caught in the plastic mesh, and he swore as he ripped them free.

"I've got Big Biscuit."

At the bedroom door, Hazard stopped.

Somers had gone silent. Even without seeing Somers, even with a solid door between them, Hazard knew the bastard was smug. Probably grinning. Hazard knew he should go back to bed. He should take one of those pills for his head and pull the covers over his eyes and just go back to bed, and when he woke up, he'd call Nico, and he'd figure out what he'd done wrong last night, and he'd apologize the way he'd apologized to Billy, the way he'd apologized to Alec. He'd eat the same old shit out of this shiny new bowl. That was it. He'd just get into bed and ignore Somers. He'd—

By that point, he'd already unlocked the front door.

"Took you long enough—Jesus God, what are you wearing?"

"Shut up."

Somers, a plastic carryout bag hanging from one hand, appraised him. And it was exactly that: pure, fucking appraisal. Somers was hot. He was runway hot, swimsuit hot, blond and golden-skinned, even in the middle of winter, fuck him, and with eyes like Caribbean waters. Today, like every day, he managed to look like he'd just rolled out of bed—and like he hadn't been alone. His button-down was rumpled, his jacket was askew, his hair had that perfect messiness that made Hazard itch to run his hands through it. And he was still standing there, still appraising Hazard like he might buy him at auction. Now there was a thought. Hazard barely suppressed a second, very different kind of groan.

"What happened?"

"Give me the food."

"You look like shit."

Hazard tried to shut the door; he blamed his headache and hangover for the fact that Somers still managed to sneak inside. As Somers always did when he came to Nico's apartment—Nico and Hazard's apartment, Hazard amended—he made a show of considering the mess. Nico's clothes, Nico's books, Nico's shoes, Nico's latest shopping. There were about three square inches of space that weren't covered by something that Nico owned.

Somers went straight to the table and shoved a pile of unmatched socks onto the floor. Then, after a moment's consideration, he shoved a stack of textbooks.

"Hey."

"I'm messy."

"Please don't start."

"I know I'm messy."

"Somers, I've got the worst headache, and I'm hungover, and I—"

"I mean, I know I'm messy. I know that's why you moved out. One of the reasons."

Hazard gave up and waited for the rest of it.

"But this," Somers gestured at the chaos—he paused, Hazard noted, when he saw a stack of some of Nico's more provocative underwear. Hazard shoved them under one of the sofa cushions.

"Pervert."

Somers, smirking, continued, "But this is insane. It's like you're living in a dorm. Or a frat. And as much as you might have enjoyed close quarters with all those rich, athletic boys, sharing showers, dropping towels, a few playful wrestling moves turn into something not quite so playful—"

"Somers, I swear to Christ."

"—you've got to admit you don't like living like this."

"Are you done?"

"Finished."

"You're sure?"

"Perfectly."

"Because if you've got more jokes, get them out now."

Somers spread his hands innocently.

"Any more comments about my—" He had been about to say boyfriend, but the word stuck in his throat. For once, his hesitance to acknowledge his relationship with Nico had nothing to do with how he felt about Somers. "—about my apartment?"

"It's not yours."

"Jesus."

"I'm just saying, it's not. It's Nico's."

"You're a real piece of work."

"I mean, I get it. You're living here now. But it's not like that's going to last forever."

The last words struck home hard. Hazard dropped into a seat at the table, head in his hands.

"Hey, what's going on?"

"Nothing."

"Ree, I was just teasing. Well, mostly. I mean, this place is a mess, but I'm not trying to—come on. What's going on?"

The pounding in Hazard's head had gotten worse. He needed one of those pills, but he couldn't drag himself out of the chair. Not yet. Just a minute, he just needed a minute.

"All right," Somers said. "Your hair is all loose and wild and sexy barbarian, which means you either just finished banging one out with Nico or you haven't showered yet. You're wearing a shirt that's about eighteen sizes too small, and those gym shorts—well, you're going commando, buddy. So again: either you just nailed Nico the wall, or you're—" Somers whistled. "You're hungover."

"I'm not hungover."

"You are. You had a fight with Nico. You got plastered. You're wrecked."

"You don't have to sound so goddamn happy about it."

Neither man spoke for a moment. Then Somers touched the back of Hazard's neck, at the base, and Hazard flinched.

"He hit you? That motherfucking piece of shit put a hand on you?"

"What? God. No."

"You've got a bruise about a mile long back here. Doesn't he have any fucking brains? Didn't he even think about the fact that you're still healing, that you shouldn't even bump your head, let alone—and the little bitch hit you from behind, didn't he? Where is he?" Somers hadn't moved, hadn't raised his voice, hadn't so much as lifted his fingers from Hazard's neck. But it was like someone else had come into the room. It put a shiver down Hazard's back. And deep in his brain, at the surface of conscious thought, he realized he liked it. "Where is he?" Somers asked again. "That's all you have to say, just tell me where."

"You're acting crazy."

"All right. All right. You don't say anything. You don't have to say anything."

"You're out of your damn mind. Will you stop acting like this?"

"Don't worry about it. I'll find him myself."

"John-Henry, will you sit down and listen to me?"

Somers fell back into his seat. They sat that way for a moment, neither of them speaking, both watching the other as though seeing something new. Hazard had grown up in Wahredua. He had grown up hounded, persecuted, tormented by the man who sat in front of him. He had come back to this place, to this town he hated above all else, unwillingly, and he had found himself partnered with a man he had hated for most of his life—hated and, even worse, been attracted to. And instead of the bully, instead of the thug, instead of the cocky football star, he'd found an intelligent, funny, skilled detective who had wanted to make the past right. It hadn't hurt that Somers had grown up to be the kind of hot that, in a cartoon, would have made the mercury in a thermometer shoot up so fast the glass exploded. Somers's hand was still on the back of Hazard's neck. His fingers felt good there. They raised a strip of goosebumps down Hazard's chest.

"I'm listening."

So Hazard told him.

"He's just not that kind of guy," Somers said with a shrug.

"What kind? And don't say something asshole-ish. Don't say he's not the kind that's mature or something like that."

"Me? I meant he's not the kind that likes jealousy."

"I'm not jealous."

"You beat up a guy for kissing your boyfriend."

"I didn't beat him up. You make it sound like I'm in eighth grade."

"In eighth grade, you were so scrawny you could barely hold a pencil." Somers smirked. "Well, I guess you were definitely strong enough to hold your pencil, if you get what I—"

"I get it."

"I meant your dick. That's what I meant by pencil."

"Jesus Christ."

"Not everybody likes jealousy. Some people get off on it. Some don't mind—they might appreciate it, but they aren't looking for it. And some people don't like it. Hate it, even."

"I'm not jealous."

Somers fixed him with a look.

"All right, I shouldn't have hit that guy."

Somers waited.

"I definitely shouldn't have thrown him."

Somers shrugged.

"And I should have let Nico handle it."

"Yeah, well, you definitely shouldn't have done that."

"What's that supposed to mean?"

"Nothing."

"What did you mean?"

"I'm an idiot, all right? Stuff just comes out of my mouth sometimes."

"You meant something. You—" Before Hazard could finish, his phone buzzed. He pulled it out, and a message from Nico showed on the screen. *I'm staying at Marcus's place for a few more days. Can you tell me a time you'll be out of the apartment so I can pick up a few things?*

"What?" Somers said.

Hazard dropped the phone on the table. Picking it up, Somers read the message. His eyebrows shot up, but he didn't say anything.

"Don't."

Somers put the phone back on the table.

"Don't fucking say you're sorry. Don't act like you're not thrilled. Don't act like this isn't what you wanted."

It took a moment before Somers answered, and when he spoke, his voice was carefully neutral. "I didn't want you to get hurt."

"Well, I didn't."

And it sounded so pathetic, like such an absolute, flat-out lie, that Hazard was blushing as soon as it was out of his mouth, and he was grateful Somers didn't even acknowledge the words.

"Let's eat. You're hungover. Your head hurts. You need food." Somers unpacked the clamshell containers of takeout from Big Biscuit, and then he touched the back of Hazard's neck again. "You've got to eat something. And you need a drink. Water, I mean. Lots of it. And those pills for your head, have you taken any today? Christ, of course you haven't."

Hazard knew he should get up. He could grab plates and forks. He could pour a glass of water. He could clean the rest of this shit, Nico's shit, so there's was actually a decent space to eat. He didn't, though. He barely had the energy to turn the phone face-down so he didn't have to see that damn message any longer.

"Here."

Hazard swallowed the pills dry, and then a cool glass was pressed into his hand.

"Drink."

He drank, and when he'd finished, Somers opened the clamshells. Steam wafted off home fries, eggs over easy, and biscuits the size of dinner plates. Buttery, flakey, pillowy biscuits. Hazard waited for the smell to turn his stomach, but he was surprised that instead, he was hungry.

They ate, and as they ate and as the pills took effect, the worst of the pain—both emotional and physical—started to pass. It wasn't gone. It wasn't even close to gone. But it got better, and the world didn't seem like one big turd waiting for the flush. At least, not completely. Not—

—with Somers there—

—while the biscuits lasted.

It wasn't until Hazard had dragged the last home fry through a smear of ketchup that he noticed the third clamshell. Reaching over, he popped it open, and three delicate slices of strawberry french toast met his eyes.

"Are you shooting for three hundred?" Somers asked as Hazard speared the french toast and dragged it towards him.

"Screw you."

"You're not going to fit into your pants." A smile crinkled Somers's face, and it was so boyish, so genuine, that for a moment Hazard forgot about Nico and forgot about his cracked head and forgot, even, about the french toast dripping strawberries down his wrist. "You can barely fit into your shirt as it is."

"You're an idiot."

"An idiot who made you smile."

"I didn't smile."

Somers's grin got bigger, but he didn't say anything.

"All right," the blond man finally said, shoving away the rest of his food. "We've got to think strategically." Hazard barely heard him; a half-eaten biscuit was staring back at Hazard. Half. Half of one of those perfect, heavenly creations. Half just tossed aside, like Somers was going to throw it in the trash. "Oh for heaven's sake," Somers said, knocking the styrofoam container towards Hazard. "Just eat it before you choke on your own spit."

Hazard did.

"They'll have to order one of those shipping containers to bury you."

"I'm recovering. I need to build up my strength."

Rolling his eyes, Somers said, "Here's what we're going to do: you're going to take a shower. I'm going to make some phone calls. Then we're going to do it."

The biscuit went sideways in Hazard's throat, and he began to choke. When he'd managed to clear his windpipe, he said, "What?"

A rakish grin peeled back the corners of Somers's mouth.

"You did that on purpose," Hazard grumbled. "Going to do what?"

"Get Nico back."

It took a moment for the words to sink in. "No."

"Come on."

"No. Whatever this is," he gestured at the phone, "however it works out, it'll be fine. I don't need you—"

"Do you want him to break up with you?"

Hazard hesitated. Yesterday, at the Pretty Pretty, he would have said yes. But now—now things were different. Facing into the loneliness, facing into the abyss, Hazard found himself unsure. Things were good with Nico. Things had been really good. So they'd had a fight. So they'd had one little fight. All they had to do was work it out, figure where things went wrong, and things would be good again.

A little voice in his head, though, asked if that were true, then why hadn't he answered Somers yet?

"That's what I thought," Somers said. "So we'll take it from the top: flowers, a card, reservations at Moulin Vert. I bet if I ask, Cora will call him and get him to meet you there. She's good with people, she really is. And we'll have you dressed to the nines, and that poor boy won't know what hit him." Somers's grin tightened. "You're Emery fucking Hazard. He doesn't have any idea how lucky he is, but we're going to change that."

"Somers, this isn't—"

But Hazard never finished the objection. Somers's phone rang, and he glanced at the screen and answered it. His questions were short, sharp, and familiar.

When Somers ended the call, he shrugged and stood. "No time for a shower, I'm afraid, but you'll probably want to change out of the shirt. It's a little cold for that."

Hazard ignored the jab. "What is it?"

"Shooting."

"This isn't one of those fake shootings, is it? This isn't Batsy Ferrell calling because she's upset about the gun range at Windsor?"

"No. This is the real deal. Looks like a murder."

"Any ID on the victim?"

Somers blew out a breath. His eyes were very bright. They were bright like the sun flat on top of tropical water. But some of the color had left his face. "Oh yeah, plenty of ID. Just about everybody there ID'd him."

"Well?"

"The sheriff."

Acknowledgments

My deepest thanks go out to the following people:

Cheryl Oakley, for the corrections in this revised edition.

Monique Ferrell, for her enthusiasm, support, and invaluable advice about all things legal. Any mistakes in the book are mine; anything I got right is due to her diligent research and gentle corrections. I've learned so much from her expertise, and I'm very grateful, especially for her insight into the human dynamics that underlie the crimes I'm so quick to write about.

Austin Gwin, for his excellent suggestion regarding the book's ending and for his beautiful articulation of what I need to do in book four—I owe a major debt of gratitude for putting in words things that I'd been trying to articulate to myself for a long time!

And, as always, the weekenders group, for friendship, encouragement, and for (of all things) putting up with the Duchess when I couldn't think of anything else.

About the Author

Learn more about Gregory Ashe and forthcoming works at www.gregoryashe.com.

For advanced access, exclusive content, limited-time promotions, and insider information, please sign up for my mailing list at http://bit.ly/ashemailinglist.